AS WE WERE THEN

MARGARET McKAY

ΣΦinx Books

Printed by Spiegl Press, Stamford

2024

PART ONE: The End of An Era

CHAPTER 1

The Wheel of Fortune

For more than eight years Stanley Ruskin was the youngest of six, but before he had passed his ninth birthday he had become the youngest of only four, the two girls of the family having died in a flu epidemic when they were barely in their teens. And his father, his exuberant, roistering father who had roistered a little too exuberantly until he brought on an apoplexy in his forty fifth year, had now left his already grieving wife a widow. The family's once modestly prosperous shoe manufacturing business, built up from nothing by Charles' shrewd and hard-working father and grandfather, had been brought to the brink of bankruptcy by Charles' drinking; as a result of which he had gradually lost control of what was going on in the workshops. There is nothing better calculated to lower the morale of a workforce than the knowledge that the boss is in an almost permanent state of inebriation and doesn't know what is happening to the business and what orders are being fulfilled and paid for. For a shoemaker the old adage that a business could go "from clogs to clogs in three generations" was particularly apt and bitter.

    Thus it was that when Charles dropped down on the floor of the tanning room in a fatal apoplexy at the age of only forty five, his widow was left without a penny, soon to be without a roof over her head and with two children still in school and totally dependent on her. The two oldest, Jack and Fred, were still in their teens but they had already found work and could at least keep their own heads above water. Indeed Jack, at nineteen, had already started speaking about trying his fortune in one of the colonies. Two fellows he knew had gone just a couple of years before to Canada and Jack heard from the brother of one of them that the letters their mother had received painted a picture of a land of great opportunity, especially if you had a skill to offer. Jack was already a hard-worker: the mixture of shame and contempt that he had increasingly felt for his father as, growing into manhood, he saw him sinking more and more into drunkenness, had served only to strengthen his own determination to forge a better future for himself and to protect his mother. Now, almost at the conclusion of his engineering apprenticeship, (his overseer at the workshop already talked about Jack as being the best worker he had), Jack began seriously to think about Canada and the opportunities there were for good engineers.

The time for that move had not quite come but Charles' widow, Sarah, had to make a swift decision about herself and the two youngest boys. The funeral had been paid for and the business was sold for a more or less symbolic sum. Sarah knew she had been lucky to find someone to take it over at all - with all its outstanding debts; but it salved her conscience at least to know that the men, skilled workers all, would still have their jobs to go to, and if the new owner was serious and hard-working there was no reason why the business shouldn't prosper again. But for the moment Sarah herself was penniless. Jack and Fred had tried to help as much as they could but Sarah had a fierce kind of pride that wouldn't allow herself to become a permanent burden on her still young sons. Consequently, within three months of the death of Charles, Sarah moved back to her home town and arranged for her two youngest to be boarded, one with a brother, the other with a sister and herself as companion and maid of all work, living in with the rich widow of one of the town's foremost, now late, dignitaries. It was heartbreaking to have the family so dispersed and in the first weeks of the new dispensation there was scarcely a night when she did not shed some tears as soon as she got into bed. But of one thing at least she could take comfort: she and her two youngest were all in the same town; they could all be together on Sundays, usually indeed at her sister's house. And they had avoided the worst fate of all - to have to go to the Workhouse.

Sarah's sister, Annie, had no children of her own and her husband, a kindly man, would have liked to take both the boys, but their means, like the house, were small. Bert had suffered an accident at work which meant that he couldn't continue with the job he had and the one the firm offered him instead came with a significantly lower wage. The compensation awarded him by the firm was not large; it in no way compensated for the loss in income and so he and Annie had been compelled to look for a smaller house where the rent was lower. Bert knew that with his disability the chances of getting a job anywhere else would have been small. "We'll just have to grin and bear it," he said to his sorrowing wife, who amid all the worry and upheaval, had also just suffered a third miscarriage. Well there would be no children now. She couldn't go through all that again and anyway there was little money and no room. A tiny box room with one small window high up was the only one that could have been the baby's room and, of course, after the final miscarriage it became the lumber room instead.

Sarah was closer to Annie than any of her other sisters and so she was immensely relieved when she and Bert agreed to have young Charlie live with them, and Bert even emphasized to Sarah that, as far as he was concerned it was "for as long as you like". To Annie he said, "You know we must look on this as a gift from God. He taketh away with one hand and giveth with another." Bert had been brought up in a strict Methodist household. His command of the Bible was extensive and, since his accident, he had taken to reading it every night before bed. Annie had had little religious instruction, nothing from her parents and only scripture lessons in school and Sunday school on Sunday mornings before church; but she liked that Bert knew his Bible and tended to attribute his kindliness, which had first attracted her to him, as coming in some measure from it. Nevertheless she had her reservations about the goodness of God. "Why did he need to punish me first then," she said. "All those miscarriages and a stillbirth! What great sin did I ever commit to be so afflicted?" Bert, in his honest heart had no satisfactory answer to this so all he could do was put his arm around her and say gently, "well, I really don't know, but I do think we should consider this boy of Sarah's as a gift that has come to us unbidden. And if we take him to our hearts, for whatever time he's loaned to us, it can only be a God given blessing."

Charlie, one year older than Stanley, settled in quickly with his aunt and uncle and the tiny box room, cleared of its lumber, did become a child's bedroom. Charlie had never had a room to himself before, having always to share, in the old house, not only a room but also the bed, with at least one brother. The box room became his precious sanctuary; it remained his, and precious, for all the six years that Charlie was eventually 'loaned' to Annie and Bert.

It might have seemed strange to some that the older boy, Charlie, should have been granted the luxury of this home rather than his one year younger brother, Stanley. There was a reason, however, and it rested on Sarah's knowledge of her sons. From birth Charlie had been the frailest of her babies. He was small at birth; he grew slowly and suffered a succession of the childhood illnesses, which could easily prove fatal at the time. But the worst affliction of all perhaps was that the next and last baby of the family arrived when Charlie had only just emerged from one serious bout of illness and had but recently celebrated his first birthday. Apart from the scares and alarms caused by his many illnesses, and Sarah was always an attentive mother, there still never seemed to be much time for Charlie, at least when he was well. He was a timid child, easily upset or frightened and he was smaller than his younger brother. At this crossroads in the family's life some difficult choices had to be made and, of her two younger sons, Sarah knew that Charlie might not even survive in the harsher environment of her brother's house, but Stanley was made of much sterner stuff.

Sarah's older brother was the landlord of one of the town's biggest public houses which also provided accommodation. It was a three storey building, the most imposing in the market place. Replacing a much older and by then more dilapidated hostelry, the Blue Lion was built at the beginning of the nineteenth century, in yellow brick and Regency style. Despite its appearance there was not infrequently a degree of rowdiness emanating from the public bar - to which only men had access - on Friday and Saturday nights. The publican needed to be tough, to be commanding, and big. Sarah's brother was all of these things. Raised in the country doing heavy work on the family farm Alec, in his youth, had seen military service in India. He knew what men were like and he knew what harsh living conditions were. Now nearing sixty and beginning to feel, just a little, the weight of years, he was nevertheless still the perfect man for the job of controlling inebriated revellers on a Saturday night.

Alec Benson had seen a lot of life and he was tough, but he wasn't heartless. He was fond of his little sister, Sarah, and he had observed, with a degree of disgust and concern (the concern being for his sister and her children,) how Charles had let a good business go to ruin "for the demon drink". It was a sight he had seen in the public bar of the Blue Lion all too often. So yes, he was willing to give house room to one of her sons, but he wasn't in the business of charity. The boy would have to earn his keep and do as he was told. There were attic rooms to spare at the top of the house; they were mostly bare or used to house broken furniture, but there were one or two straw mattress beds, low like army cots, and even one or two kitchen chairs that had four legs, but wobbled if you tried to sit on them. Yes, Stanley could have one of those rooms under the eaves. Of course there was no lighting on the attic floor but the boy could take a candle in a jar to see his way to bed if it was dark, as long as he was careful to put it out when he got into bed, and didn't burn the house down. At nine years old Stanley had a great deal of respect for this towering, formidable uncle, but he was not cowed by him. (Alec was six feet two in his stockinged feet and he was broad chested too). Dealing with a rational and sober man, even if he was big, was a great deal easier Stanley found than trying to defend your mother from an irrational and inebriated one. On that score the change was a positive one. Also, he liked all the activity of the place and in particular the bustle of life in the kitchen.

His uncle spoke truly when he said that Stanley would have to earn his keep. On his first day, left early in the morning by his mother with the uncle whom he scarcely knew and who towered above everyone in sight, he was taken to the kitchen, presented to the cook and her assistants as the new errand boy and general help.

After the initial shock of suddenly finding himself bereft of everyone and everything he knew, within a week of arriving at the Blue Lion Stanley found that he liked being in the kitchen best of all. From early in the morning to late in the evening there was always someone there. There was warmth, and chatter and food! It was the most homelike place of all, and mostly the people were kind to him. Though he'd been introduced as the errand boy the staff knew he was Alec's nephew but, they also soon discovered the story behind his sudden appearance among them, and there was compassion for the plight that had left the widow and her child homeless. In addition they soon found out that Stanley was a good worker: he did what he was told to do, and soon learned to do it well; and he was reliable. He never tried to sneak off to escape a task and he was equal to all the errands that they gave him. For so small a boy he was amazingly strong and, strangest of all, he seemed to like being in the kitchen even when he wasn't needed. He had found a three legged stool in one of the outhouses and he managed to find a niche for it out of the way of the cook and close to one of the black cooking ranges. Here he would perch, observing everything that was going on, taking in all the stages of food preparation and listening to the chatter and gossip. He stayed very quiet and nobody seemed to mind him being there. In fact his unobtrusive presence was soon taken for granted, so much so that, if he wasn't there someone would be sure to ask "where's the boy today?" And when he was, someone would occasionally throw a remark in his direction. In this way Stanley came to regard the kitchen as his home. The initial wrench and sense of loss of a home, a mother and brothers thus slowly became transmuted.

Stanley hadn't been in his uncle's house six months before he started to be given tasks that were strictly speaking out of his range but, when the staff were under pressure, the hotel and bars busy, they would put Stanley to work. Thus it was that one day when one of the fowlers delivered two braces of pheasants and six chickens and there was no one available to pluck the chickens or take out the innards, Stanley was called into service and given an express course in plucking and disemboweling. He disliked the disemboweling for some time but he soon became a champion plucker and before he had been in his uncle's house one year he had also become an expert at skinning rabbits.

Sundays were Stanley's favourite day, however, and the one he looked forward to all week for, on Sundays his mother came. Sometimes they went to aunt Annie's house where he could see his brother and they all had lunch together. His mother always took something with her as a contribution to the meal for she knew her sister and Bert had little money. These Sunday visits were a highlight of the week; they were the best family gatherings since the death of Charles and the breakup of their home in Melcaster. On one or two occasions they were surprised at aunt Annie's by the unexpected arrival of Jack and Fred too. These were occasions of great celebration with the whole family gathered together for a few precious hours.

Life at the Blue Lion was not a bed of roses for Stanley, however. In fact his bed chamber was the worst part about it since the attic room without lighting proved to have other occupants besides Stanley and he first became aware of them just a few nights after arriving. The truth was that his fellow lodgers were - rats. In the middle of the night when he had been sleeping soundly for several hours, something moving over his legs and brushing against his arm, woke him up and he screamed. Confused, and thinking for a few seconds that he was having a bad dream, he heard then a scratching scuttling sound on the bare floorboards and a shrill squeaking sound that he recognised. Few old houses were without rats at some time or other and most householders kept rat traps handy. But they weren't quite so often found in the upstairs. Frightened and horrified Stanley shot up in bed and pulled the blanket around him. He dare not put his feet on the floor so he drew them up and sat Buddha like, but shivering, with the blanket wrapped tightly around him for the rest of the night. He had never felt so lonely and abandoned. Life "before" had not been easy as his father more and more often returned home drunk, even latterly, raising his fist to his wife, but there were always at least brothers there who could help to disperse or deflect the aggression. This was something different: it was dark, he could not see the enemy and there was no one to help him. He passed the most miserable night of his life and when at last it became light he pulled his clothes from the wobbly chair onto the bed, where he dressed, put his feet down, gingerly, on the floor and ran down the two flights of back stairs to the kitchen. It was so early that there was only one person there; this was Evey, the kitchen maid, who had the job of reviving the fire in the kitchen range, before which no bacon could be cooked nor water heated. She looked up surprised when Stanley burst into the kitchen. "My goodness, what's the matter with you? You look as if you'd seen a ghost?" Stanley stammered out something incoherent about a bad dream which evinced a murmur of sympathy from Evey who added, "You don't look as if you've slept at all. You're all white. Don't you feel well?" Stanley could never quite work out why he didn't want to say that there were rats in his room and that they had run over him in the night. Something stopped him, a vague feeling that his uncle would be angry if he heard that, and even might blame him for the presence of the rats, ridiculous as it was. Also, somewhere obscurely in his mind was a feeling that just this fact might cause trouble between his mother and his uncle. What if his uncle said well then he'd better not stay there if he couldn't stand the conditions, for there wasn't anywhere else for him to go. So he bit his lip and said no more.

Living, or rather sleeping, with rats did not get any easier however, and after three more almost sleepless nights Stanley was finding it more and more difficult to stay awake, both in school and when he was sitting on his stool in the kitchen. The cook and the serving maids had already noticed it, and his unusual pallor, and one afternoon Stanley fell asleep on his stool with his head leaning on the hot cooking range so that his hair began to singe. The cook cried out and a pair of strong arms suddenly lifted him into the air and deposited him on a chair. Bill, the ostler and outdoors man, had just entered the kitchen bearing an armful of logs for the fire when he heard the cook cry out and saw Stanley's hair about to smoke. He dropped the logs and swept Stanley up and away from the hot range. He may have saved Stanley's life, certainly he saved him from a terrible burning.

"What on earth is the matter, lad?" Bill and the cook were as much in shock as Stanley when he opened his eyes and felt and smelt his singed hair. Overwhelmed by what had just happened and by fatigue, for the first time since his arrival at his uncle's house Stanley burst into tears and when the cook asked again what was the matter he blurted it out. "It's the rats!" he said, "It's the rats.."

What Stanley had dreaded happening, had happened. His uncle was told and Stanley would have to face him. Certainly Alec Benson looked forbidding when he came into the kitchen where Stanley was recovering from his ordeal. "What's this I'm hearing," Alec began, looking down at the dischevilled boy. Through his tears Stanley told his uncle about the rats in his attic and how they ran over his bed at night. Alec frowned and asked the cook how many cats there were about the house. There were currently two, (the latest litter of kittens had recently been drowned shortly after birth). Right, one of the cats known to be the best hunter would be shut in the attic rooms for a couple of days together with two of the cage traps, baited, and for a week Stanley could sleep on a camp bed in the room of the live-in maid.

The cat caught one rat and the cage traps two and the lingering smell of the cat apparently discouraged any others from visiting Stanley's room for some months afterwards. When they started to reappear again, as with time they did, Stanley was allowed to take one of the cats to share his room at night and gradually a bond was forged between the boy and the half wild feline who, before being posted to control the rats in the attic, had not been much used to being inside the house at all. The upshot of the initially terrifying experience of having rats run over his bed at night was thus that he gained a night time companion in his dark attic room.

Stanley spent four years as a lodger in his uncle's house. Truly he earned his keep but he also incidentally learnt almost all there was to know about preparing food and running a hotel! The errands he was required to run, either before or after school, often involved fetching fruit and vegetables from market traders or farmers who came into the town with a cart load of produce. Alec, grown up on the family farm just three miles from the town, got some of his supplies from it, although it was his five year younger brother who had eventually taken over the farm from their father. In addition Alec himself had acquired a bit of land not far from the Blue Lion where, with the help of another younger brother, he grew and supplied his hotel with some of its basic necessities. In this way Stanley too was introduced to market gardening, and what began as just another chore became with time a passion. First of all he learnt to plant and sow. Being out in the open air and seeing, over the course of a few weeks, things he had pushed into the soil as seeds start to show above the ground and sprout, was a joy to him. And then, one early autumn he discovered mushrooming.

Alec came into the kitchen one evening in early September just as Stanley was about to climb the back stairs to his attic bedroom.
"Ever been mushrooming, Stanley?" he asked. By and large Alec was a man of as few words as were necessary, with the result that his utterances often sounded brusque and even threatening, but Stanley had learnt in the nine months

he had now been lodging under his uncle's roof, that this was a character trait that did not necessarily imply ill will.

"No," he said, wondering what was coming next.

"Well," said Alec, "there are some very good patches for mushrooms up by Brindley Wood and we have them on the menu at this time of year if we can get them. Old Jimmy Burns - you know Jimmy?" Stanley nodded. "He's a champion forager; he's been bringing in baskets of them for us for years. Thing is he's getting too old, he's gotta stop. But he's said he'll teach you what to pick and where to find them, so I want you to go with Jimmy for the next few weeks and see if you can pick up the know-how, all right?" Of all the tasks that Stanley had been given 'to earn his keep', this sounded like the most boring, and his heart sank. Nevertheless there being no prospect of his saying no to anything that Alec might ask him to do, he merely nodded glumly, before learning that this particular activity required the additional effort of getting up and out 'with old Jimmy' by six o'clock in the morning.

Old Jimmy was there in the kitchen before him when Stanley, still rubbing his eyes and pulling on his shirt came down from his attic room before six the next morning. Jimmy was nursing a mug of tea that he had made for himself and he eyed Stanley up and down as he tumbled into the kitchen and finished buttoning up his shirt. "All ready, lad?" he asked. Stanley, still not quite wholly awake, nodded dumbly. Then they set off.

The walk to Brindley Wood took less than ten minutes during which Jimmy said not a word but, in spite of his age, he kept up a steady pace and Stanley could just about keep up with him. The morning was fine and the sun not long risen but there was a dew on the ground and a light mist hovering above it. Suddenly, just entering the wood, and stepping away from the path Jimmy motioned to Stanley to follow him and within a couple of minutes he stopped at a clearing, bent down and, parting some grasses and low gorse he revealed to Stanley a carpet of white capped field mushrooms and a bit further on, under cover, growing out of a mossy bank a smaller patch of beautiful yellow trumpeted chanterelles. Jimmy showed Stanley how to cut them at the base so that the stalk came away as well as the cap and how to identify the true chanterelles from the false by cutting them down the middle to see if they had the white inside flesh that characterizes the true and edible kind. In quite a short time they had more than covered the bottom of the basket with a mixture of field mushrooms, yellow chanterelles and one or two giant puff balls. In spite of himself Stanley discovered that the search for likely spots and the examination of their finds to see that they were the right, edible, kinds was peculiarly satisfying. It seemed that his hunting instincts were aroused.

After accompanying Jimmy two mornings a week for the following month until the middle of October, Stanley had learnt and absorbed all that Jimmy had to teach him about edible fungi and where to find them. The result was that when, one bright Saturday morning, Jimmy did not appear when Stanley came into the kitchen ready to 'go hunting' - as he had come to think of it - and he learnt that Jimmy had been taken ill and couldn't go out with him, it turned out to be no great hardship for him to go by himself. Indeed that was the beginning of Stanley's career as chief forager of the Blue Lion. The fungi season petered out in November but it resumed in the following spring and Stanley found himself promoted to chief expert on edible fungi. For Stanley that was not the only thing, however. There was something else, and it was something that was entirely his own since he was the only one who knew about it: it was the fact that he was in possession of a secret, or rather a number of secrets; he had become the only one who knew where the treasure could be found.

Stanley had no place indoors that he could really call his own and feel 'at home' in. His attic room was cheerless; he only ever went there to sleep and it was never entirely safe, even with the cat for occasional company. The kitchen was the best room in the house for him since it was always warm and there were people there; but at any moment he could be called upon to carry out some chore or other or to run an errand, to fetch or carry. Out in the countryside however, in the wood and at any of the places where only he knew that the mushrooms could be found, he was his own master. It was quiet except for the sounds of nature: the sighing of wind, the rustling of leaves, the occasional sight and sound of a rabbit or fox crossing his field of vision. But no human voices to demand that he go here or there, or to ask what he was doing when he was doing nothing. He found an old tree stump, just the right height, where he could sit and soak up the silence, could look - or not look, could think his own thoughts without interruption. These secret woodland spots became his most precious places - his own places. This most unpromising sounding chore turned out to be a blessing in disguise.

………………………………………..

Mrs Tanner was used to commanding and was a stickler for having things done her way. But Sarah had learnt long ago to be adaptable and if her employer was ever displeased or finicky about something Sarah soon learnt how to mollify her. If Sarah at the beginning felt dependent on Mrs Tanner it became clear with time that Mrs Tanner had become dependent on her.

Sarah stayed with Mrs Tanner for nearly four years in which time her wages increased only once, by a modest amount. Mrs Tanner relied on Sarah to be living under her roof so of course there was no way in which she could keep her position there if she didn't 'live-in'. As it turned out, however, God, or at any rate some higher power, was about to intervene in such a way as to compel Sarah to look seriously for other work. In the winter of Sarah's fifth year at Mrs Tanner's, the same, taking a ride on a cold day in her carriage, to visit a cousin who lived outside of the town, became ill. What began as a head cold moved to the old lady's chest and all the embrocations and inhalants could not shift it. Within a fortnight it became clear that she was in a decline and the only outcome was likely to be death. On a cold bright February morning Mrs Tanner breathed her last - and Sarah was faced with once more being without work or having a roof over her head.

The lawyer was empowered to pay Sarah her wages to the end of the month, however, and the cousin who was Mrs Tanner's heir, needed her help to clear out and clear up and prepare the house to be sold. Still, at the end of the month Sarah would be once more homeless and, although she knew that her brother would be willing to give her shelter, she did not want to be even more beholden to him than she was already, and, what was more, she was tired of being a lodger in someone else's house. She wanted to have a place of her own, however small, where she could have at least one of her children living with her. She therefore summoned up all her energy and made a round of all the hotels, boarding houses and offices in the town to enquire if any had an opening for her. None had, however, and she was fast approaching despair when suddenly, a few days before the end of the month, a lifeline was thrown to her. As sometimes happens, it came from an unexpected quarter, and quite by chance.

As she was leaving Mrs Tanner's house, with a heavy heart and in the knowledge that she had only three more nights of guaranteed shelter there, the cook from one of the neighbouring houses, who Sarah had got to know in the time she had been working for Mrs Tanner, came running along to intercept her. Mrs Wilson had grown fond of Sarah in the four years of their acquaintance and she knew of course that Mrs Tanner had died and that Sarah was looking for a new position. In a state of some excitement she caught up with Sarah and put out a hand to catch her arm. "Oh my dear Mrs Ruskin," she cried, "have you found a new position yet?" Sarah had to admit she had not. "Well," said the other, "I don't know if this is any use to you but, ...you know my nephew is ostler at 'The Bull'. He came by last night with a message from my sister and he told me there was a great upset and kerfuffle at The Bull all the day, for the housekeeper, Mrs Chalmers - she's been there many years you know - had got into an argument with the landlord and suddenly she dropped down dead. What a thing to happen! But the thing is, Mr Grimes is desperate to find a replacement. He's been going up and down all day Jem says, wringing his hands and wailing 'what am I going to do without Mrs Chalmers?' He's a poor sod that Mr Grimes; his wife died suddenly like that just last year and Jem says he seems to think he was to blame for Mrs Chalmers going like that too. Anyway, the thing is they need somebody who can do the job, and as soon as maybe. Oh Mrs Ruskin, go round right away why don't you....." Mrs Wilson was out of breath. Astonished at what she had just heard and with a flutter of hope rising, in spite of herself, in her throat, Sarah thanked Mrs Wilson and, hardly knowing what she was saying, hurried away towards The Bull.

The Bull hotel was by way of being the main rival to Sarah's brother's Blue Lion, though The Bull was smaller. But the truth was that there was plenty of custom for both establishments, the reason being that Sprinton was happily located on the Great North Road that went from London to York and thereafter all the way to Scotland. In the days of the stage coaches, an era that had but recently passed, there had been eight coaches every day, in both directions, and several more travelling from east to west, which passed through Sprinton. For hundreds of years there had been a high demand for accommodation for both horses and men in the town. Now, at the dawn of the twentieth century, that demand had diminished only a little for, instead of horse drawn coaches there was now the railway, the main east coast line from south to north and the west east line from industrial towns of the midlands to the east coast. Both The Blue Lion and The Bull were thus still in business and indeed in good business.

When Sarah arrived at The Bull, just a little out of breath, she saw that in all the ground floor windows the curtains were drawn, and the outside door, which usually was fastened back early in the morning to reveal a porch and the inside door, was still closed. However, a sharp pull on the outside iron bell soon brought one of the servants to the door and Sarah, asking for Mr Grimes, was admitted into the front hall and someone went to find the landlord. And then, later Sarah recalled, the strangest thing happened. Mr Grimes appeared through a door leading to the kitchens and back of the house. He saw Sarah standing in the middle of the hall. Sarah said "I looked at him and I saw in his eyes that he saw me and that he knew why I was there and that I was like, well, a gift from heaven!" Almost before she had had time to explain why she had come, Mr Grimes had given her the job. She said it was just as if Mr Grimes knew instinctively not just why she was there but also that she was the right person for the job. The only thing 'personal' in it was that they worked together so well that you could say it turned out to be a kind of platonic marriage. In the event Sarah was to stay in her post, alongside Mr Grimes, for almost twenty years.

Of course running a household where there were paying guests (The Bull had three double rooms and two smaller single ones) was a different proposition from running a household for one; but many of the tasks to be done were similar in themselves: it was just that they were on a different scale. Apart from that Sarah had had experience in hotel work as a young woman, before her marriage. It did not take her long to learn what the job demanded and since she was not expected to live-in she would be able to look for a house to rent so that she could at last have a home of her own once more. The pay Mr Grimes was offering was from the start considerably more than she had been paid by Mrs Tanner, but of course now she would have rent to pay as well as other living costs.

When Sarah returned to Mrs Tanner's house she told the cousin that she had secured a new position and that she hoped to be able to find somewhere else to live very shortly. The cousin, who was there sorting out some things that she wanted to send to auction, was genuinely pleased that she had found a suitable position and she reassured Sarah that if her search for somewhere to live should take a little longer than the three days she had left on her contract then she was welcome to stay on in Mrs Tanner's house for one more week, since it was going to take that time before the house was completely cleared and ready to be put up for sale.

Two days later Sarah secured the tenancy of a little house but it would be another week before she could move in. The house she found was in a terrace of brick houses which had been hastily put up at the time the railway came to Sprinton and the railway engine workshops sprang up on the outskirts of the town. Sprinton had had engineering works which built steam engines, signals and railway lines, for more than half a century and the men and their families who were going to labour in the manufactories created a need for several hundreds of new houses. Now there was a generation shift in the manufacturing. Some of the men had died or retired or had moved on to other things. At any rate the railway company that owned some of the terraces had houses available for rent by people who were not necessarily employed by the railway company. They were 'basic' houses,'two up and two down' as the saying went, that is to say, two bedrooms upstairs, a living room and kitchen downstairs and a 'privy' in a separate little brick built hut at the end of the back yard. There was no bathroom but each house had a tin bathtub that was kept in a little shed next to the privy and which would be brought into the kitchen to be half filled with warm water for the family bath night.

Despite the meanness of the house and the inconvenience of having to go outside to go to the lavatory, Sarah was overjoyed at having been granted the tenancy of one of them. To be independent at last, to feel that she was in control of her own life, was what she had longed for. Her own life and her work were separate spheres once more and the feeling of liberation was tangible. Of course there were problems, of a financial kind mainly - the house was almost bare, for example, and she would need at least some sticks of furniture - but she knew 'they', and a surge of joy went through her when she thought about the fact that now she would be able to have at least one of her children living with her, yes 'they' would be quite happy to manage with a minimum of furnishings to begin with.

....

The death of Mrs Tanner and the consequent changes it brought about in Sarah's life also therefore affected Stanley and in a positive way. Stanley was about to leave school; he was nearly fourteen and he had the great good fortune to be taken on as an apprentice at the town's major engineering works. Sarah, having got the tenancy of one of the railway's terraced houses where there was a second bedroom, Stanley could, at long last, move out of the attic of the Blue Lion and go to live with his mother once more. This was the best part of all - to have their own home, even a room of his own, where there were no rats and Sarah had managed somehow to acquire a proper bed for him as well as a chest of drawers and a chair that could be sat on without collapsing. There were even some hooks in one wall and on the back of the door to hang clothes on. This seemed pure luxury to Stanley and the day he carried his small bundle of clothes and his few other possessions, from his uncle's house to his mother's newly acquired one, he all but wept with joy when he found himself in his very own, rat free room. He opened up his bundle of clothes, not many, and his treasures: there was a penknife (that he always used when he was out foraging), some clay marbles, most of which he had won off other boys at school, and a wooden box, six inches by four, which he had managed to make for himself out of some bits of wood that he found and nailed together. With the same penknife he had carved a little spray of leaves on the lid. He opened the top drawer of the chest of drawers and carefully deposited everything he had with him, there. To think that he had a proper set of drawers to keep things in, instead of the old orange box that he had found and used in his attic room at the Blue Lion. He could scarcely believe it. In all the houses that he lived in later in his life, Stanley never forgot the sensation of happiness that he had when he first stepped into this, his first own room, at his mother's house in number three, West Sidings, Sprinton, in the summer of his fourteenth year.

Horner's engineering works where Stanley got an apprenticeship was the oldest company in the town. It predated the railway works by thirty years, its first products having been iron parts for horse-drawn carriages and carts. With the advent of railways and the setting up of steam engine manufacture in the town, Horner's branched out and began to adapt its manufacturing to parts that were required for locomotive steam engines.

From childhood, and even though his opportunities had been few, Stanley loved making things. His treasured box was the first thing he had succeeded in making and it was 'old Jimmy' that same expert forager who had taught him all he knew about identifying fungi, who gave him the knife that he had used both in gathering mushrooms and in whittling and carving in the lid of his box. And Bill Blackwood, that same ostler who had saved him from burning, had taught Stanley how to saw a piece of wood without cutting off his own fingers. This happened after Stanley had found the orange box and taken it to his room to use to keep his clothes in; for he had soon discovered that his co-residents, not rats but the mice and the moths, had found his clothes and had introduced openings in his one and only woollen jersey and in his spare pair of socks. The box that he had found, had no lid and there were openings between the slats. Stanley saw that the only way to make it safe from predators was for the slats to be closed and a lid to be fitted to the top. Expert forager that he had now become, Stanley had gone to the hotel woodshed one day to see if he could find any pieces of wood that could be used to make a lid and close in the gaps between the slats.

While he was there Bill Blackwood came in and, surprised to find Stanley, asked him what he was doing. He didn't know, he said, that the fires needed more kindling; he'd filled all the log baskets just that morning. Feeling for one moment as guilty as if he'd been found with his fingers in the till Stanley managed to stammer out the reason why he was in the woodshed. He needn't have worried however, for ever since the hair singeing incident. Bill Blackwood had become his friend and as soon as he understood what Stanley was looking for he immediately set about trying to find some wood that would suit his purpose.

Stanley's predicament in the hair singeing incident had touched the ostler's heart. Although he knew that Stanley's mother was in the town and that Alec Benson was his uncle, yet it seemed to Bill that Stanley was in effect an orphan. He spent all his time, it seemed, in the hotel kitchen except for when he was at school or sleeping in the attic. Yes, Bill's heart went out to the boy who always did what he was asked to do and who watched with observant and intelligent eyes all that was going on around him.

"So, you want to make a lid for this box of yours do you?" he asked kindly.
"Yessir," said Stanley.
"Have you ever cut wood or used a saw?" Bill looked serious and he narrowed his eyes at Stanley. Stanley's voice fell, "No," he murmured as if sensing the imminent defeat of his project.
"Well then, you'd better learn how," said Bill.

That afternoon Stanley learnt how to measure and saw a piece of wood, how to use sandpaper and how to screw on hinges. He was sent to fetch his orange box, the sight of which evoked Bill's pity for the boy when he saw what a poor thing he had in which to keep all that he possessed. Bill took hold of the box, examined it from all sides, and then let Stanley join with him in looking for pieces of wood that could be used to complete its enclosure.

"Woodshed" was a bit of a misnomer for the place they were in. It was a woodshed in that it was there that all the wood for the fires was cut into logs and kindling; but half the space was used as a carpentry repair shop. In a hotel the size of the Blue Lion there was always some piece of furniture, chairs especially, that needed repairing. Anything that got broken but which could be mended, was mended - on the premises. Consequently, in the "woodshed" there was not only wood, of various kinds and sizes, but there was also a workbench and a collection of the basic tools needed for cutting, screwing and hammering. On that afternoon, under Bill's guidance, Stanley got his first real lessons in carpentry and ever after, if Bill was doing a job in the woodshed which could be done a bit easier or a bit quicker if there was somebody else around who could hold a tool or a piece of wood, then Stanley would be called out from the kitchen and his help enlisted. In this way he learnt a lot about the different qualities of different woods; he knew the names of many tools and gained confidence in handling them; and he learnt how to combine metal with wood.

In his last year in school - he turned fourteen in February so would finish school in July - Bill started to ask him what he was going to do when he left. Stanley shrugged and shifted uncomfortably. His mother had already broached the subject with him and he knew he would have to find something to go to as soon as school finished in the summer. But what?

"Fred thinks I should get a job on the railways." At nineteen Fred had got himself well embedded with the railway company in Melcaster and he was warm in his recommendations of the job. But the idea of becoming a wheel tapper, for example, did not appeal to him at all. Bill regarded Stanley thoughtfully.

"If you could choose, what would you do?" he asked. Stanley's eyes lit up, "Oh, I'd like to make things," he answered. The boy's spontaneous outburst of enthusiasm brought a smile to Bill's face.

"Well, what about Horner's?" The name of the town's chief engineering company made Stanley frown. "Oh I'd like that," he said, "but they say they're laying folks off right now and I wouldn't have a chance. You have to know somebody before you can get in," he ended sadly.

"Yes well, that depends" said Bill, a bit mysteriously. They returned to the job in hand - putting a new leg on a lounge bar chair that one extraordinarily overweight client had unwisely, and heavily, sat down on two days before. He might have been a relative of Daniel Lambert of Leicester, dead at thirty nine and weighing fifty two stone, someone had joked. Well, the chair was broken, but it could be repaired. Bill Blackwood, with the help of his faithful assistant, Stanley, returned the chair to life.

A few days later Stanley found himself trudging up the hill to meet with the foreman of the engine fitter's branch of Horner's. Bill Blackwood's influence apparently extended beyond the woodshed of the Blue Lion hotel. Looking back on his life many years later Stanley was not ashamed to say that the day he secured his apprenticeship at Horner's and moved into the little house in West Sidings, Sprinton, with his mother, was the second happiest day in all his life!

Stanley could hardly believe his luck when, after enduring almost an hour's interrogation by Reginald Brown, the Foreman of the engine workshop, he was offered an apprenticeship and told he could start at the beginning of the following month. His heart almost missed a beat when Reg Brown, who had worked at Horner's for more than twenty years, took a long pause, looked at Stanley quizzically, fixing him with a penetrating stare and then said, "All right lad, we'll give it a go, but remember what I've said, you have to pay attention at all times. There's a lot of big, heavy machinery here and we don't want any accidents. Nor do we want any faulty parts leaving this plant, so remember what you're taught and keep your eyes skinned at all times." Stanley could scarcely believe what he was hearing and, transfixed, he went pale and just about managed to nod his head in assent. Words were beyond him.

"Right, let's go and speak to Mr Lowndes, in the office and get you put on the books." Dumbly, but with a rising sense of elation in his chest, Stanley followed the foreman out of the workshop and up a short flight of stairs to the office.

When he walked out of the main gate of Horner's a short time later, Stanley's first impulse was to go and seek out Bill Blackwood at the Blue Lion and tell him the good news. He found him in the stables contemplating the rear hooves of the hotel's dray horse. He looked up when Stanley, breathless with excitement, burst into the stable and, without waiting for Bill to put down the horse's back leg, cried out, "I've got it Bill, I got the apprenticeship!" Bill looked at the boy's eager and glowing face and his own broke into a smile. "Well done Stanley, well done lad. You deserve it. When d'you start?"

Stanley related to Bill all that had happened at Horner's, the quizzing by Reg Brown, with his final words of caution and the signing of the papers with Mr Lowndes in the office. "Well then," he said, at the conclusion of Stanley's account. "Now you'd better go and tell your uncle." Alec Benson had always been a man of few words and he didn't wear his heart on his sleeve, but in the four years that Stanley had been living under his roof, Alec had come to appreciate his good qualities and, insofar as he was able to show affection for anyone, he had become fond of his nephew. He even realised, as Stanley told him of his success in getting into Horner's, that he was quite going to miss his presence around the place. He found himself doing something uncharacteristically demonstrative: he patted Stanley on the shoulder and said gruffly, "Good luck to you Stanley, you've done well. And you're a good worker. We've all seen that here, so stick in at Horner's, learn your trade and you'll go far."

Two weeks later Stanley bundled up his belongings in an old cloth donated by the dining room maid and went to say goodbye to Bill. His mother had just completed her first week as housekeeper at the Bull Hotel and had moved into the house in West Sidings the day before Stanley carried his bundle from the Blue Lion to join her there. It was a day of happiness and rejoicing for both of them when Stanley walked into his new home and found his mother there, her face wreathed in smiles and tears in her eyes. One brother, Charlie, was still missing from their little family group but they knew that Charlie was happy in the home he had found with his aunt and uncle. They had come to treat him as the son they could never have; they would be loath to part with him and he, in his little box room, but all his own, would be loath to leave it too. In the four years he had been in his aunt's house Charlie had blossomed. He had gained in confidence and in health as the years of anxiety and tension preceding their father's death faded from the boy's consciousness. And, apart from all that, the distance from West Sidings to Charlie's home with his aunt and uncle was no more than a ten minute walk. Why, it was almost as if they all shared the same household.

Now their precious family meetings, on Sundays, did not always have to take place at Annie and Bert's house. It was a joy to Sarah to be able to have Charlie and Annie and Bert over to her and Stanley's house for dinner on Sundays. What a treat that seemed and Stanley, who had now had a four year apprenticeship in the domestic arts, could take part, even sometimes a leading part, in preparing the Sunday lunch that they all shared. The pleasure and even novelty of this never really wore off. Both Stanley and Sarah were ever after mindful of what a precious thing it was to have their own place, their retreat, their home where they were their own boss. They both knew what it was like to be always living in others' houses, at someone else's beck and call and where the only things that were truly your own were the clothes you stood up in. Now Stanley could blossom too and his apprenticeship at Horner's, where he was learning new things every day and was finding his feet among the men and older apprentices, gave him new confidence.

One year into his apprenticeship and life in West Sidings, Stanley, not yet fifteen was no longer the fatherless, charity boy who must constantly do others' bidding. He was on the way to becoming his own man. The years in his uncle's house, unprotected by a parent, had taught him much about life and how, though vulnerable, it was possible to negotiate a way through the jungle of human intercourse, and not be crushed. Sarah breathed many a sigh of relief in that first year of their freedom and independence when she saw that Stanley was not just coping but was blooming.

CHAPTER 2: 1914

The Atkinsons

The harvest had been a good one and George Atkinson, now feeling the effects of a lifetime of hard physical work on the farm, was seriously considering handing over responsibility for it all to his son, William. Then, suddenly, everything changed. Until the middle of July, and harvesting just getting under way, they had never heard of Grand Duke Franz Ferdinand and could not have pinpointed Serbia on a map if anyone had asked them to. Now, it suddenly looked as if everything could be turned upside down in the blink of an eye - or the flash of a sabre as George said. It had been possible, by pulling in every member of the family over the age of eight and living within a ten mile radius, (fortunately that was most of them) to bring in the harvest in good time. But now there were already murmurs from the government suggesting - and how long would it be before it became a 'demand' - that the nation's farmers should abandon livestock and revert pasture to crops since cereal was what would be needed in ever larger amounts if it became difficult to import foodstuffs from abroad. And yet, at the same time, they were saying that the war would almost certainly be over by Christmas!

 The Atkinsons had been farming their two hundred acres for more than seventy years. George's father, also William, by hard work and good farming instincts, had secured the tenancy in 1859 and a year later George was the first child to be born there. For the most part, fortunately, it was good rich Limeshire soil, doubtless in millennia past largely submerged under water, but now since its draining some two hundred years before by Dutch engineers, some of the most fertile soil in the country. They'd had both arable and livestock since his father's time and George had no wish to see the animals disappear from their land, but he realised there would be pressure to get rid of them if the war did in fact drag on and it would be hard for his son to resist. And what would they do for harvest help if conscription was introduced? To be faced with a new swathe of problems was not how he had imagined his imminent retirement would be. In fact he couldn't see how he could now withdraw his labour and put everything onto the shoulders of his son. William was young and strong, as George had always been in earlier years, but there were limits to what one pair of hands could do, or shoulders could bear.

He leant on the gate which opened from the crew yard into the top meadow and found himself looking, not at the land but back over the last thirty years. A blessing at least that there were sons to take over and continue on the land, though it had been a blow when his oldest, Harry, had rebelled, said he wanted another kind of life, went to Canada, and stayed there. But perhaps it was just as well: Harry had always been reluctant about the farm, while William was keen, especially around the animals, and couldn't wait to leave school so he could be on the farm all the time. Philip, though much younger, was shaping up to be just the same. It was different with the girls, of course, though several of them George had had to admit, could do almost everything that the boys could do with the exception of handling some of the machinery and lifting or carrying the heaviest loads. Rose and Violet had always wanted to marry farmers if they got the chance. Rose got the chance, and took it. Violet did not and reluctantly took the only opening that came her way: she was taken on as maid by the local squire and inadvertently had her prospects changed, or in sister Kate's view, widened, when she found herself accompanying the family to their London house. Ivy, fourth daughter and seventh child, had declared that she didn't want to marry at all. She was the only one of the girls who was still at home on the farm.

But Kate, the third daughter and fourth child, was different, and always had been. She loved the countryside around the farm, the woods and wild flowers; and she had tended the chickens and orphaned lambs with care, but she nevertheless somehow had always kept a little aloof from the hustle and bustle of the everyday business of the farm. Strange therefore that, despite being markedly different from the others and less devoted to the land, she was the father's favourite; and although they all knew it, it was not resented but was simply accepted. More than that: if any of the girls wanted something from their father that they suspected he wouldn't be willing to allow, then they often got Kate to be their go-between and Kate with her instinctive understanding of their father's mind was more often than not successful in persuading him.

When Kate was just a girl and not at school, or doing her chores at home, then she had always liked to walk or read. Of the ten children born to George and Susan only one, the tenth, died at birth and one in early adolescence. All the rest, to the surprise of some, attained a strong and vigorous adulthood. The surprise was that while George was tall, sinewy and strong, Susan was a whole head shorter, and fine boned, but she was lively and had a quick intelligence, and her pregnancies, all but the last, went well. The children had inherited the parents' size, it seemed randomly: Kate and Ivy were tall, Violet and Rose were small; among the boys William and Philip were tall, Harry and Lionel were small – and Lionel was the one who died, in his early teens, kicked on the head by Florrie when she stumbled, pulling a cart full of hay up the farm's steepest meadow in summertime.

None of the children, except the youngest surviving son, Colin, had given George cause for great concern and none, not even Colin, had been reluctant scholars – except sometimes in winter when there was snow on the ground, for their school was a mile and a half away in the next village. But Kate was the one who positively revelled in learning and who soaked up all knowledge whether it was poetry, arithmetic or anything mechanical. Her biggest regret was always that the nearest library was ten miles away in Sprinton and it was only meagrely stocked with books about history or science. Nevertheless the town was her goal when the day came for finishing school. Like her oldest brother Harry, Kate wanted a different life from that of the farm but, unlike Harry, it was not in a spirit of rebellion but rather that her reading, however limited it had been, had nevertheless stirred her imagination and opened her mind to other prospects. She was aided by being a girl for, while it was generally assumed that the sons of farmers would themselves become farmers the daughters might be too many to become the wives of all the available younger farmers. It was less necessity than inclination in Kate's case, however, which made her set her mind on a move to the town and work of another kind.

The one who had caused George and Susan some stirrings of anxiety was Colin the baby of the family. It was common folklore that the baby of any family was liable to be more indulged, 'spoilt' even, people would say; but George truly did not believe that Colin had been more indulged than any of the other children. Nevertheless it became clear early on that he was more quixotic than any of the others had been when growing up. He was quick to take an interest and quick to tire of any new thing. The only thing he did not tire of, and he seemed to have a real talent for it, was horses – especially, riding them. When the era of horse drawn carriages, and riding for transport, appeared to be about to pass, though, what future would there be for a man whose only passion was for horses and anything to do with horses? The worry about Colin did not go away – until the day when he returned from a visit to Sprinton, whence he had gone early in the morning on the back of the bay, Foxglove, and announced that he had successfully been recruited into the Limeshire Yeomanry. The family was momentarily stunned and then, as the fact sank in they suddenly realised that "Yes, of course" this was just what Colin was meant to do. The caring for the horses, the moving about, even the discipline demanded in looking after gear and learning to handle weaponry, all of this would answer to his craving for activity and excitement. Yes, they agreed, by joining up Colin had answered to the call of his nature. And so, finally, his decision was not just accepted but was endorsed. He had just turned twenty, the time for the spreading of wings. Colin's wings needed spreading and they would not have been able to had he stayed on the farm. But Colin, George ruefully had to admit, as he turned from the gate and made his way back to the house, had always been what his old Irish auntie called 'a heart scald', and now with a war starting and his regiment on the alert, was he not about to be a 'heart scald' all over again?

    Like many times before when there were worries to be aired or arguments to be wrestled with, George just wished that Kate was still nearby to talk to. Susan was a good companion; she had shared all the struggles, all the setbacks, and the good times in making the farm pay - and bringing up the many children. She had a good head for figures had Susan; she was the family's accountant and George could not have done better for a wife. Life had moulded her into the supreme practitioner but had left her with neither time nor energy for the theoretical. Politics only interested her insofar as taxes and prices were the consequences of Government decisions, and philosophy of any more elevated kind she admitted to be beyond her. For this reason Susan also wished that her husband could talk to Kate more often, but Kate had fulfilled her dream and moved into the town soon after leaving school.

    Sprinton was a town of thirty thousand souls, and rising. Although always, since Roman times, on the main eastern route between London and York, it had, until the beginning of the nineteenth century, been an entirely agricultural community. The industrial revolution, however, from the beginning of the eighteen hundreds brought about changes; at first it was the need for new agricultural machines whether drills or threshers, and the first factories were set up; later in the century it was steam ploughs and steam engines for the new railways. The iron producing midland towns were not so far away either and Sprinton got its railway early on. All these developments meant that the town grew; red-brick terraced streets sprang up in what had been the adjoining countryside and the town centre boasted new shops and, regrettably for many of the women of the town, several new hostelries, some of which offered accommodation.

This was the town that Kate had set her heart on moving to, as soon as she should be finished with school. The plan was made easier by the fact that there were relatives living in Sprinton and Kate had been in the habit of going and staying with her favourite aunt, Aunt Daisy, Susan's youngest sister, from childhood. Ostensibly, by the time she was twelve, she went to help with a new baby, but in truth that was only half the excuse on Kate's part. When she first, with the enthusiasm of extreme youth, mentioned her ambition at home her father's heart missed a beat. Of course he couldn't reasonably oppose her; realistically it made good sense. There wasn't enough work on the farm for all the children, and it was clear early on who wanted to stay on the land, married or not, and who didn't. But George knew instinctively how much he would miss just this daughter. From early childhood Kate had been able to make him laugh and before long to talk to him, with a serious and enquiring face, about all kinds of both existential and mundane questions. She learned to tease him and to steer him away from a bad humour and, she got away with it. None of the others dared, or knew the way, to do it. Well, Sprinton was only ten miles away; she could come home at weekends and tell all that she had been doing, keep her parents up with all the town gossip and the latest ideas in fashion or factory. At least that was how George consoled himself for his loss.

For Kate the move into the town had felt like coming to adulthood. The first weeks in the town were exciting in a number of ways. With persistence and her school records in her hands Kate went round the town's chief retailers and before the second week was over she had got herself taken on by the one she most desired. It was the oldest established and most venerated firm in Sprinton. Binns' Emporium was a firm with historic roots in the town and had been founded at the beginning of the nineteenth century. It had started as a purveyor of textiles of all kinds from cottons and wools to silks and even satins. The textile manufacturing towns were not far away and they were in their glory days: there were cottons coming in through Liverpool and Bristol, silks from the near and far east, and wool from closer at hand. At first Binns had sold the cloths and provided a service of tailoring and making up gowns by their own seamstresses; then they expanded into all kinds of hosiery and ladies' accessories until finally they added, for which a whole new building was required, a department selling ready made ladies and gentlemen's outfits. Kate counted herself lucky to have been taken on at Binns'.

For the first month in Sprinton Kate had stayed with her aunt. Daisy was Susan's closest sister. They were also a farming family that for many generations had farmed the same hundred acres not ten miles distant from the Atkinsons. Daisy was one year younger than Susan and from early childhood they had formed a unit in the family that was recognised by the rest of them. If one of them was missing or wanted for something that sister would always be found with the other one. They grew up more like twins than just sisters. But this changed in their teens when Daisy, just seventeen, became attached to the lad who came each day from the dairy to fetch their churns of milk to be made into butter and cream cheese. Daisy's main task on the farm was to milk and look after the cows. She was a champion milker and seemed to have a natural ability to soothe and calm the beasts who always stood very quietly while Daisy milked and talked to them. Evan Williams was the son of the dairyman; he was tall with curly dark hair and had laughing blue eyes. He was nineteen to Daisy's seventeen and always teased her and made her laugh when he appeared in the doorway of the milking shed and started to haul the milk churns onto his cart before setting off to cover the last two miles to the dairy where his parents would be preparing to churn the creamy milk into butter.

It wasn't long before Daisy was 'walking out' with Evan on Sundays and it wasn't long after that before Daisy came to the realisation that she was, as the saying was then, 'in an interesting condition'. Evan's charm and laughing blue eyes had led to more than 'walking out'. As Daisy's older brother, Tom, put it less delicately, there had obviously been some lying down as well as the walking out. The parents of both parties, after some grumbling and head shaking, came round to acceptance of what had happened. Such turns of events were not exactly unusual among country folk. Evan was considered to be an honest lad, if maybe a little bit wild and the family dairy was a good business. It was the Williamses who were more put out by what had happened. Evan was the only son and they would have liked him to be more in the way of running the business before settling down and starting a family. Still, what was done was done and Daisy came from a good family; she wasn't known to be a flighty 'hojden', quite the reverse, so it was deemed wisest to make the best of things. Thus, Evan and Daisy were married, in church, and the young couple were given the little, somewhat run down cottage, next to the dairy, where their first infant was born just four months after the wedding.

In the following years Evan proved that he wasn't just a handsome face but he had ideas too about expanding the business and his initiative paid off; his parents supported his innovations and before the fourth child was born Evan and Daisy were able to move from the cramped and primitive cottage of their first years of marriage and three children, into a semi-detached house in Sprinton which had not just 'two up two down' but three up and three down and included a separate bathroom and an indoor toilet. Daisy's happiness at the sheer luxury of the new house she later claimed to be responsible for the sunny disposition of the child that was born shortly after they had moved in and which was the reason for Kate first coming to stay with them. When the fifth, and as it turned out the last, child arrived Kate came once again to help her aunt and then, two years later, after leaving school, Kate had come to stay with her aunt Daisy as she herself made her way into the adult world.

Like her mother, Kate proved to have a good head for business and within a few years of joining Binns', although still young, she became a valued employee. She took full advantage too, of the amenities that the town had to offer. In particular she became an assiduous frequenter of the library on Saturdays after work and she trained herself, with the help of the library, in bookkeeping. Thus it was that after just a few years Kate had gained enough knowledge and experience to be treated with respect by even the senior salesman, Mr Widdicombe. This meant that when there were celebrations to be organised, or special window displays then Kate was given responsibility for organising the event with the help of the other younger employees. The success of these special events served to catapult Kate into high esteem with the company.

Eventually too, the most senior assistant, and buyer, who had taken a shine to Kate, when about to go into retirement herself, helped her become proficient in textile know-how. Kate loved the feel and texture of many of the materials that they sold – some of which she could have no hope of possessing herself until she had advanced some degrees in the trade and, as she explained to Ivy, until she had more money in her purse. But, young as she was that hardly mattered as she was free to handle them, to admire colour and pattern, and even, she claimed, to breathe in their various fragrances. Her enthusiasm for the materials that she was dealing with meant that she wanted to know all about them and so her visits to the library soon involved searching out sometimes quite recondite information involving the history and cultures of far away countries which she had never visited nor, as far as she knew, was she ever likely to visit. That didn't matter; it was the journeys in her mind that she enjoyed.

It had taken some time, after Kate left home, for George to become accustomed to her not being there but time eventually softened the blow and in any case, as Susan pointed out to him, Kate had secured a good position for herself and she came home regularly and gave them all her news. Kate's visits home to the farm were always eagerly anticipated. The first year she was in Sprinton she went once a fortnight, travelling with the farmer's cart, back to the countryside on a Saturday afternoon after the carter had delivered farm produce to Sprinton's market and greengrocers shops in the morning. Her father was always near the gate of the house or in the woodshed at the side of the house when Kate arrived. He would be chopping wood or preparing feed for some of the animals when he heard the unmistakable creak of the cart or the snorting of the carter's horse as they approached the farm. Then he would down tools, call out to his wife, who was always in the kitchen at that time, and who would emerge from the front porch still drying her hands on her apron as the cart drew up at their gate and Kate jumped down from it as the horse came to a standstill with one final snort and toss of his head.

There was an atmosphere of celebration whenever she arrived, to be followed by questioning about what had been going on in the world outside the farm since the last time they had met. Saturday's tea, with them all gathered around the big old kitchen table was a joyous occasion. As well as Susan and George, who never stopped smiling when Kate was at home, there would be William and Philip, youngest sister Ivy and, until he joined the Limeshire Yeomanry, usually Colin too. Kate's youngest sister, Ivy, hung on her every word and thought her tales of what was going on in Sprinton and in particular at Binns' department store were the most thrilling and glamorous events that she could imagine. Kate's twenty four hours at home once a fortnight were the highlight of Ivy's life. Kate felt a pull at her heart-strings when it was time to leave them all on Sunday afternoons. Nevertheless, there was no doubt in her mind but that her life was now in a different world and that it had been right for her to move away.

For the first month of her new life in town Kate stayed with her aunt, who was pleased to have her, but Kate was aware that her presence made even the three bedroomed house crowded; and anyway she wanted to be independent. The lodgings she found, in the house of a widow of the town, were comfortable ones. As well as one quite large bed cum sitting room she also had a small extra room where she could prepare her own food. In this way she had the satisfaction of independence while at the same time knowing that there were other people close by. Her landlady, Mrs Roberts, was respectable and concerned that her tenant should be too. The rooms that she let to Kate were clean and well maintained and, beyond making it plain that she expected her tenant to keep them like that, Mrs Roberts was not intrusive.

Although living in another part of the town Kate kept in close touch with her aunt, and often on a Sunday she would visit Daisy, where there would always be at least two or three of her cousins. The oldest boy, Edward, just a few years younger than Kate, had an apprenticeship at the town's biggest and oldest steam engine manufacturing company. How significant that was to prove to be Kate could not have imagined.

CHAPTER 3

The Wheel Turns

Stanley put on his Sunday shirt, combed his dark hair back and surveyed himself in the mirror on his bedroom wall. Eyes brown and thoughtful looked back at him. His expression, in repose, was always serious, but tranquil, more the expression of one who was willing to wait to see what the outside world would throw at him before he took up an attitude towards it. And in the years he had been at Horner's and had had a home with his mother in Sprinton he had grown in confidence and changed. He considered himself fortunate and felt a surge of happiness as he got ready to go to the house of his friend, Ed Williams, where he was to have Sunday lunch.

It was late spring and the lilacs were in bloom. Although the town had grown in the previous decade it was still relatively small and from the terraces of West Sidings you could see quite clearly and quite close by the countryside outside the town where the flatter eastern farmland gave way to gently rolling hills to the west. On a sunny Sunday morning, with the trees in spring green bud the landscape presented a smiling face and Stanley unconsciously smiled back at it.

The walk to Ed's house took less than ten minutes in time, but it took him to a different part of the town. The terraced houses of West Sidings and Turntable Road opened straight onto the street; the houses in Ed Williams part of town were all detached; they had front gardens, back ones too, and the streets were tree lined. It was a part of the town that Stanley had rarely had occasion to visit and he noted with interest its difference from the streets of terraced houses close to the factories and workshops that he was used to. He slowed his pace as he passed the front gardens where some early summer shrubs and flowers were already in bloom or about to blossom. How his mother would love to have a garden like these, he thought. Well, not only his mother but he too.

For the previous three years Stanley had been cultivating an allotment. A workmate had told him that a new area of land, on the edge of the town, was to be given over to allotments and anyone over the age of twenty could go to the town hall and register their interest in acquiring one. Stanley's love of growing things, first awakened in the four childhood years he had spent living at the Blue Lion, had lain dormant for his first years in the adult world of work at Horner's, but he had never forgotten the world of nature and its outdoor freedom, and work of another kind. When Harry Tompkins told him of the plan for new allotments his heart raced, just a little; he told his mother of the plan and before another day was over he had 'engineered' half an hour off work to hasten down to the town hall and register his interest in getting one.

    His allotment was rectangular, seventy five square yards altogether, with a narrow grassy path all around it, as there was around each of the sixty or so allotments that the one acre given over to them had allowed. Stanley planted raspberry canes, one row across, also rhubarb, then a variety of vegetables and, because his mother loved flowers so much, he kept a strip across at one end for a variety of daisies and marigolds that he knew she liked. Sarah had visited Stanley's allotment a number of times and she took almost as much pleasure in it, at least in hearing about it, as he did. Certainly they both would have delighted in having a garden such as the Williamses had.

    Ed Williams' house was the third in the street, coming from the town end, and as he came up the path to the front door Stanley could hear laughter somewhere inside. Ed was a storyteller with a fund of tall and short stories that could make people laugh. That was one of the things about him that appealed to Stanley and had made the two become friends in the first place. Although Stanley's temperament, formed by childhood experiences, had made him more watchful and reflective than his friend, yet he responded to Ed's fun loving nature. Ed could tease and poke fun, but was not unkind. It never occurred to Stanley to analyse their friendship - it was simply a source of pleasure and companionship such as he had not had in his earlier childhood.

    The door was opened by Ed himself, smiling broadly even as the peals of laughter continued in the background.

Elsewhere in the town a cousin of Ed's was getting ready to join her cousins for lunch. Unusually, Kate was displeased with the reflection thrown back at her by the full length wardrobe mirror. She had always enjoyed dressing up for Sundays whether it was simply to go to church, to meet her closest friend Lucy Staines or to go to her Aunt Daisy's for lunch. But today, one of the first blossomy days of spring she suddenly became aware that she'd had nothing new to wear since two summers before and the cotton print dress that she had thought stylishly cut, for the last two years, suddenly displeased her; but she had nothing new to put on so it would simply have to do. Still, it was just her aunt and uncle and a couple of her cousins who would be there; it was only Daisy who ever remarked on her appearance and Daisy always seemed to approve of what Kate was wearing.

The truth was that there were deeper reasons for the feeling of dissatisfaction that was afflicting Kate just then. Something was missing in her life. In the years since she had left her childhood home on the farm and had been working at Binns, she had known great satisfaction in learning all she could about textiles, design and fashions. She had developed an interest in all the aspects of the trade and her dedication and intelligence were seen and rewarded by the company early on. In her own spare time she still read voraciously and she was one of the most frequent and regular visitors to the town library. Nevertheless the other side of her nature was fun-loving and she was incorrigibly gregarious. She had become friends with two of the other young assistants at Binns and, together with her childhood friend Lucy Staines, they had formed a little group who spent much of their free time together. Lucy had also decided to seek her fortune in the town after she finished school in the village where she and Kate had had their elementary education together, and the two country girls formed a natural twosome.

It was Kate who always wanted to know more, however; she was never satisfied with a first emersion in any subject and her interest could be as easily sparked by the headlines of an article in a newspaper as by the titles on the spines of the books in, especially, the nonfiction sections of the town library. It was in this regard that her friends from work were different. They were amiable girls, but their interests centred on their future prospects of marriage and to a lesser extent on the demands of their work and the gossip current in their workplace. Lucy was closest to Kate and had followed her and admired her since their infancy together in the village school. But she could not keep up with her intellectually. Lucy, like Kate, frequented the town library regularly, although she mainly borrowed works of fiction. At their village school they had both devoured the stories of Robert Louis Stevenson and of Dickens, with fervour. Lucy truly and copiously cried when their school mistress read aloud to them the account of the death of 'little Nell'.

Kate was more impressed by the story of Silas Marner and of Maggie Tulliver, but she felt mildly indignant about the fact that the author, George Eliot, in reality Marian Evans, had found it necessary to take a male pseudonym in order to increase her chances not only to get published but also to be taken seriously. Kate devoured stories too, but in everyday life she was always curious to know how things worked. What was electricity, and how did diseases come about? There seemed to be no one in her immediate circle who knew these things or could discuss them with her. She knew that the discoveries and inventions in science had been authored by men and that boys were always more interested in these kinds of questions than any girls she knew; but she had few male acquaintances in Sprinton and her thirst for this kind of knowledge remained largely unsatisfied.

Ironically it had been different at home on the farm. Apart from her father, who was interested but had little time to spare after the demands of animals and crops had been satisfied, there were her brothers. Of these it was William and even more, Colin, who were interested in any advances being made in science and technology. Quick and quixotic Colin always seemed to know somehow - and Kate rarely saw him reading - what was going on in the world of science. But Colin had joined the Limeshire Yeomanry and since that day he was rarely at home. Kate probably missed him more than anyone else in the family. Yes, there was a hole in her life; she had no intellectual companion.

Daisy's house was always bright and cheerful. From the day when she and Evan had moved in with their three young children and the fourth about to be born Daisy had been determined that this should be a house of light and sunshine. The old cottage that they moved from and where the first three children had been born, had been cramped and dark and primitive. This was going to be different. And it was. Evan had built up the dairy that his father and mother had started. He had shown foresight in the ways he expanded and developed the business so that by the time he and Daisy bought and moved into the new house there was even some money to spare for furnishing and decorating the rooms. It always lifted Kate's heart to enter that house and she was not surprised either on this bright Sunday morning to hear the voices of her cousins raised in welcome when she knocked and opened the front door. They were gathered in the dining cum sitting room at the back of the house. French windows opened onto a lawn at the back and they were open on this first really warm late spring day. Ed was teasing his youngest sister, Lizzie, and was asking Stan to agree with him as Kate entered the room.

"Ah, here comes Kate," Ed announced, "She can confirm that the state of the economy can be exactly correlated with how much the wealthy wives of Sprinton are spending each week at Binns' Emporium. Isn't that right Kate?" Ed looked at her quizzically, with a half smile on his face. "And" he added, "I have just been explaining to my innocent little sister that the situation is becoming dire and by the time she has any money to spend, in her dotage, there will be nothing left to buy, Binns' will be no more and she will have to join cousin Kate and go milk the cows on her grandpa's farm for a living!" Kate shook her head and pulled a face at Lizzie to let her know that she should not take anything her brother told her too seriously. Then she turned her gaze to the young man who was sitting quietly on the other side of her cousin.

"Oh yes, Kate," Ed continued, "and this is my good friend Stanley, of whom you have heard me speak: my companion in crime and engine fitting these many years, my wise senior at Horner's. Stan, meet my cousin, Kate, whose way with wool has kept Binns, for the time being at least, on the credit side of business!" Stanley gazed up at Kate, but for the moment words were beyond him. He scarcely heard anything else his friend said for he truly thought that this was the most beautiful creature he had ever seen. Kate's "Hello, Stanley" seemed to come from somewhere far away and for the life of him he could never remember whether he replied to her or not. Kate's impression of Stanley was of a serious, sallow faced young man with lustrous brown eyes whose warmth somehow belied the seriousness of his expression. Kate smiled at Stanley and his face relaxed in response. Ed laughed, "Here, Stan, she hasn't bewitched you has she? You know she used to babysit me and Peter and she'd beat us up when mother wasn't looking!"

"Obviously not enough, I should have cut out your tongue as well," Kate replied laughing. "Stan, you do know that you can't believe half of what Ed says, don't you?" With Stanley's eyes still glued to her face Kate turned to Ed, "I must say hello to your mother," and she disappeared towards the kitchen.

Daisy was basting the roast and the kitchen was filled with the aromas of rosemary and lamb. She looked up as Kate came in, "Hello love, I thought I heard you come in."

"I've just met Stanley," Kate said. "He seems nice, serious and nice."

"He is that, a really good lad," said Daisy as she struggled to get the hot roasting pan back into the oven. Daisy's milking days were twenty years behind her but her energy seemed undiminished in spite of the five children, of whom Lizzie, the youngest was eleven, and in spite of the work she had put in to helping Evan build up the business. Kate set to to help her, and Lizzie was sent to lay the table while Kate strained the vegetables and put out Daisy's mint sauce. Peter and Rosie, three and four years older than Lizzie, would be back from church at any minute and, although it was Sunday, Evan had still had to visit the dairy to check on some deliveries. He got back just as they were sitting down to eat.

Stanley fetched in more chairs that were needed and went to help Daisy bring in the food, without, Kate noticed, being asked. In the twenty years since Evan first set eyes on Daisy at the farm he had filled out and acquired, as his mother said, 'physical pondus', but he had not lost his charm nor sense of fun (qualities which his oldest son seemed to have inherited). So now at the Sunday dinner table he opened with a, not quite serious interrogation of Peter and Rosie about their morning's experience at the church and in particular about the sermon given by Sprinton's much respected Vicar. But the report given by the two was decidedly indifferent and it earned from their father a stern rebuke: "Well, either you weren't in church at all," he said, regarding them severely, "Or else you were sleeping, for I have it on the best authority that today's sermon, by the very excellent Reverend Winbush, whom we all much admire," turning towards Kate and Stanley, he added, "and whose family consumes more cream and butter than any other in the town - as I say, his sermon was scheduled to be on the subject of 'the indolence of youth and its evil consequences'. As we don't want any evil consequences hereabouts you two can be in charge of the washing up after this wonderful dinner that your mother has produced more or less single handedly!" Everyone laughed and Peter and Rosie groaned and giggled but accepted their fate with a good grace. This was how dinner at Daisy's house should be, Kate thought, as she glanced around the table where eight people with cheerful faces and much chatter were consuming Daisy's lamb and mint sauce. Even Stanley, she noticed, who before the meal had been a quiet observer of the scene, was taking part in the general conversation.

The young ones all helped to clear the table. In the kitchen water was heated for the washing up for which Peter and Rosie were 'aproned up' by their mother. Evan had retired to the little room behind the kitchen, which he called his office, to do, he said, some booking; Ed opined that he was actually going to have a nap in the comfortable wing chair that he had installed there. Daisy, coming into the room as Ed was saying this, reproved him,
"If your father has a nap he is more than entitled to it, young man. You know as well as I do how hard he works every day of the week, and some nights too."
"Yes, I know mother. I was joking you know," Ed was a warm hearted boy who actually admired his father for what he had done, so he looked somewhat sheepish at his mother's rebuke. The chance to make amends arose soon afterwards, however, when in the course of conversation it emerged that Daisy, who had recently acquired one of the new treadle sewing machines, was baffled by the needle threading mechanism. Mending and making new clothes had been

a major activity for Daisy while her children were growing up. She had made shirts by hand for her husband and sons and dresses for the girls, since, when no more than a girl herself, she had found herself married, with a baby, living in a run down cottage and, at the time, with slender means. She had become in time an accomplished seamstress and took pride in her handiwork. This machine could save her precious hours of toil.

"Oh, let me have a look at it," cried Ed, eager to show that he could fix things too even though he was still an apprentice; however, to his dismay, and humiliation, it foxed him. Stan, whose attention had been immediately aroused when he saw the machine, could not long suppress his curiosity and interest and when Ed confessed himself puzzled Stan jumped up and approached it. Kate watched with interest as Stanley, at first with a slight frown on his face put his fingers to work. He seemed, Kate thought, to have an intuitive understanding of it and indeed within minutes he solved the problem and could show Daisy what she had to do to get the machine working. "You see," Ed threw open his arm as if to introduce Stan to an audience, "my friend Stanley is the Brunel of Sprinton. He is the master engineer and has taught me all I know, though apparently not all there is to know about sewing machines!" His speech and grimace at Stanley raised general laughter. "Seriously though folks," Ed went on, " Stan is a genius with these things. You know he won the top award for apprentices at Horner's last year." Stanley, always embarrassed when pushed into the limelight, tried to silence Ed and, if he had been a girl he would have been thought at that moment to be blushing. Kate shot a question at Stanley, "What was the award, Stanley?" Stanley turned and allowed himself to look her full in the face. He smiled, "Oh, it was just a certificate and a book." Peter, who had been paying close attention to the conversation, interjected eagerly, "What was the book?"

"It's called The Romance of Engineering." Ed's response was a frown and a grunt,

"I don't know where the 'romance' comes in. All I seem to be doing is trying to fit pieces of heavy metal together and getting covered in oil!"

"Oh but it is romantic, just getting an idea how to solve a problem and then constructing something beautiful - like the Menai Straits bridge!" Kate couldn't resist bursting in. "And isn't Aunt Daisy's sewing machine also beautiful in a way, even" she added mischievously," though it's mechanism foxed second engineer Ed here!" General merriment accompanied Ed's comic glare at Kate, and Daisy, who was hoping for a little nap herself, used the break in conversation to remind them that they hadn't had any exercise that day and what about their customary Sunday afternoon walk? "Talking of engineering, Ed, have Kate and Stanley seen what they are doing to Gravity Park, just behind the grammar school? You should take a walk over there."

"Well that's hardly grand engineering, mother," Ed protested,

" Maybe not but even small changes can make a difference to people's lives. They've laid down new paths and constructed a pretty fountain where there wasn't one before."

"All right mother we'll take a walk that way," laughed Ed, "I guess you want a bit of peace yourself." Daisy nodded and a party of five prepared to set off from the house.

The way led to the end of Daisy's street, at which point they turned into a narrow path, for the street was a cul de sac. The path led to the northern end of the town centre and thence to the old grammar school beyond which was Gravity Park. Peter and Ed led the way and Stanley fell into step beside Kate and Rosie. Stanley, still the victim of conflicting emotions, chief among which was an overwhelming admiration for his friend's cousin, walked in silence. His suffering was only relieved when Kate broke the silence with a question.

"Is Brunel the greatest engineer we've ever had?" She asked.

"Ooh yes, I'd say so," Stanley was enthusiastic, "At least over the last hundred years. For boats, bridges and railways - well, he was unbeatable."

"The book you won, have you read it?" Kate queried. Stanley looked at her, "Yes, why?"

"Well," Kate laughed, "I've got a book in my bag here that's by the same author. I got it out of the library yesterday but haven't had time to look at it yet!"

Stanley turned to look at Kate again,

"I don't know many girls that would be interested in this sort of thing," he said.

"Ah well, brought up on the farm with brothers who were always talking about anything new they'd heard about in the way of machinery I couldn't help it. And anyway, I meant what I said at Daisy's, machines can be beautiful too."

"Yes, they can," said Stanley, "but it's true what Ed said, when you're struggling to put together just a part of one and there's lots of muck, like oil, involved (and in a workshop the noise is deafening most of the time) then it's hard to see the beauty at that moment!"

"Of course." Kate looked at Stanley reflectively. "Are you Sprinton born and bred, Stan?" Before he had time to answer they arrived at the park and Ed

bowed and waved them all through the gates, as might a lord admitting invited guests to his estate. It wasn't difficult to reach a consensus that the changes made to the park had improved it beyond recognition. What had before been a bleak expanse of grass on an incline was transformed into a flowered and wooded space of winding paths leading to a rocky pond where water trickled down from a fountain cunningly embedded in an uneven sculpted wall. Pressed by Kate, they had to agree that the improvements to the park were both 'engineering' and beautiful. Rosie added that the sound of the water trickling and splashing down the rough rock face was musical. Kate wanted to know how it had been done and Stanley explained how. "Could you do something like this in an ordinary town house garden?" Kate asked. "Like in Aunt Daisy's garden?" "Well, yes, but you'd have to install a pump somewhere," Stanley replied. The park had been extended to include a little copse of trees, once just unused scrubland, at the far end away from the gate and iron railings and, by the time they had explored this new addition to the park the sun had started to go down. It was time to go home. "I'll have to love you and leave you," Kate said as Ed was closing the park gates behind them. Ed looked slightly alarmed," Oh, we can't let you walk all alone across the town at this time," he said. Suddenly emboldened Stanley broke in,
"I think we're going in the same direction. I'd be happy to accompany you, Miss Atkinson, if you'll let me."
"Oh good," interjected Ed, before Kate had had time to reply, "then you'll be safe cousin Kate, and my duty is done!"

   Kate and Stanley parted company with Ed, Rosie and Peter and set off in the direction of the town centre.
"So," said Kate, "I never got an answer to my question. Have you always lived in Sprinton, Stan?"
"No," said Stanley, "but we moved here when I was nine, after my father died, so," he laughed, " it feels as if I've always lived here and I don't remember so much about the other place…" his voice trailed off and Kate detected something reluctant in his voice.
"Is Horner's a good place to work?" She asked changing the subject, "Ed doesn't seem so keen!" Stanley grinned,
"Oh, Ed moans a lot, but he's actually pretty good at the work. And anyway there's not a lot of choice in this town if you want skilled work and haven't got the schooling for something in an office, which in any case would never suit me. I like making things - even if it's mucky!" This exchange seemed

miraculously to break the ice, and for the rest of the walk through the town Stanley found himself opening up and speaking in a way he would never have thought possible, even just a few hours ago, to a girl whom he had only just met - and who, what's more, was surely the most beautiful being he'd ever encountered.

Kate's lodgings were in a house just a few streets away from Stanley's, but it was clearly a more affluent street than West Sidings. They paused outside the house and for a moment or two Stanley found himself tongue tied. But realising that he could not let this girl disappear from his life without at least making one attempt to see her again he searched his mind quickly for ideas. Suddenly inspiration struck and Stanley remembered a poster he had seen pasted up on the notice board outside the town hall.

"Do you like music?" He asked quickly, hoping against hope that he already knew the answer to that.

"Oh yes," replied Kate, "Why?"

"I see next Saturday afternoon one of the colliery bands is going to give a concert in Gravity Park. Would you like to walk over there and hear them?" Stanley held his breath while he momentarily waited for an answer: an answer that he obscurely felt would decide his fate.

"Yes, I'd like that!" Kate answered and when Stanley dared to turn and look at her he found she was smiling. He walked the rest of his way home in something of a daze.

CHAPTER 4

Kate and Stanley

The following week seemed to Stanley to creep by very slowly, even though everything apparently went on as normal. But the normal had suddenly become strange since Stanley felt that the world for him had been transformed since Sunday at Ed's house, though Ed hardly mentioned the day they had all spent there together. At home Stanley was cheerful, but cheerful in a more outgoing way than usual. Sarah noticed the change in him without knowing at all what had caused it. Since it was a change that had taken place since the previous Sunday she surmised that it was due to the fact that Stanley had enjoyed the company of other young people in what was clearly a happy home. Sarah cared very much that Stanley should be happy. They appreciated, each in their own way, the home that they now had together after the years spent apart in the aftermath of Charles' death. Sarah was careful not to pry but she couldn't resist trying out one or two leading questions when the opportunity arose.
"Does Mrs Williams have a cook?" she asked innocently. But Stanley was irritatingly vague about the question.
"I don't know," came the reply, "but she didn't have any help that I could see on Sunday." It was only when Stanley let out that a visiting female cousin had helped to bring the food to table that Sarah began to suspect that this might have something to do with her son's unusually high spirits. For the time being, however, nothing more was said and it wasn't until Saturday came around that the mystery of Stanley's high spirits appeared to be solved.
 On Saturdays Stanley finished work at lunchtime. He was always home by one o'clock and, if his mother had not been needed at The Bull that day, then they would have dinner together at home. This was such a Saturday and on such Saturdays Stanley often went to his allotment in the afternoon. Usually he would ask his mother if there was anything she particularly wanted him to bring back to have with their Sunday lunch, the next day. But today Stanley made no move to go out after lunch. Instead he seemed to want to busy himself in the kitchen, and then he put a pan of water on the fire to heat up as they always did

when they wanted warm water for washing. "I don't think you need to heat up water for that little bit of washing up," Sarah said slyly.

"Oh it's not for the pots, it's for me," said Stanley quickly. "Mother, there's a concert in Gravity Park this afternoon. It's the Doddington Colliery Band and," he hesitated, "some of us thought we'd go and hear it…" Sarah smiled at the "some of us" and decided not to ask Stanley to be more specific. Instead she said that sounded very nice and she was going to have a rest and to finish a piece of knitting that she was doing for her sister. Stanley was thus left free to take particular care over his washing, to discard his work clothes which he had had on all week, and to put on his best, in truth they were his only other clothes, usually kept for Sundays and special occasions.

If not with a song on his lips at least with one in his heart, Stanley stepped out of the house just after half past two. He had offered to come for Kate at her lodgings but Kate said she would prefer to meet him inside the park, beside the pond. She didn't want her landlady, nor any of the neighbours, speculating on "Miss Atkinson's gentleman friend" at this early stage of their acquaintance. Although she had a positive feeling about him she had to acknowledge that, in truth, they were still strangers to one another.

At first when he went through the gates to the park Stanley could see no one he knew, and certainly not the person he was waiting for. There were a lot of people milling about and numerous family groups near the pond where water trickled pleasantly down the sculpted rocks and small children had to be pulled back from leaning too far over the edge. He stood watching this activity for a while and then he felt that someone was touching his arm. He turned and found himself looking into the smiling face of Kate Atkinson.

Chairs had been put out to form a semicircle, three rows deep, on the grass around the bandstand. A few people had already sat down but more were moving towards the chairs and others simply chose to stand behind the seating area to listen. Stanley managed to get them seats at one end of the second row where they also had a good view of the musicians who were beginning to assemble and arrange their instruments.

The Doddington Colliery Band was famous across the whole of the north of the country and it lived up to its reputation on that sunny Saturday afternoon in Sprinton. Its success could be gauged by the fact that the audience, which perhaps encompassed sixty or seventy people at the beginning of the concert, eventually swelled to nearer two hundred before it was half way through. As the last glorious tones of the massed brass instruments died away, more than an hour later, the applause of the seated and standing audience was sufficient evidence that they had not disappointed. Stanley, anxious that his initiative in inviting Kate to attend the concert had not been misplaced, was relieved to see that she was applauding with enthusiasm.

"That was splendid! Didn't you think so?" Kate burst out. "Have you heard them before?" Stanley found himself momentarily embarrassed at the idea that he was a seasoned brass band follower, for in truth this was his very first concert. However, Kate didn't wait for his answer but went on to talk about music.

"Now that's a wonderful invention, the gramophone, isn't it?" she said. Stanley had to admit he had never heard one, and his knowledge of music in general had been curtailed when misfortune struck his family.

When he was very young, before things started to go wrong at home, Stanley had sung in the choir of the church to which his mother took him and his brothers every Sunday. The choirmaster told his mother that Stanley had a good voice and that he would have a chance of gaining a scholarship to the Melcaster cathedral school in a few years time. Any hope of that was extinguished with the death of his father and the move from Melcaster to Sprinton. For the rest of his childhood years there was no money to spare except for the necessities of life, and, in truth he had never felt the lack of any of the other things, until now when, his heart stirred, partly by the music but also by the beauty, and the spirit, of his companion, he began to experience feelings that were the harbingers of yearnings for which music suddenly seemed to be the natural expression.

"Ed says he has persuaded his father that they should get one," Kate continued, "and when he does we'll go to Aunt Daisy's and hear it." Stanley made a silent resolve to find out more about the gramophone and the kinds of music that could be heard on it. In the meantime, and only partly to cover up his ignorance on the subject, he proposed that they should take a cup of tea at the little summer cafe that had just opened its doors, or rather its kiosk, not far from the bandstand and the pond. When he put out his hand to help Kate rise from her chair, for she had brought a parasol as well as a beaded purse, Stanley felt a thrill of happiness which caused the more usual seriousness of his countenance to relax into a smile. Kate looked into his face and smiled back.

....

This first outing together was the beginning of the courtship of Kate Atkinson and Stanley Ruskin. In the first couple of months there were weeks when they could not meet. (Kate was still in the habit of going home to the farm at the weekend once or twice a month.) But the meetings between them then became more frequent, and regular. Ed was let into the secret early on - or rather he guessed, since Stanley could not conceal his admiration for Ed's cousin and there was a repeat of the Sunday lunch when they had first met. Stanley was also concerned not to be suspected of going behind Ed's back nor of damaging the reputation of his cousin. But Ed declared himself to be rather 'tickled' by the fact that his true, but, as he thought rather shy, friend had been able to take the initiative - he may have said 'taken the bull by the horns' - and invite Kate out already at the end of their first meeting. Of course he liked to take the credit for having brought them together. Only after their second walking out together did Stanley tell his mother about Kate.

Sarah received the news with equanimity. Stanley had always been very open with his mother about friends he had made and people he worked with and Sarah, with her own past life in mind, was slow to pass judgement, and preferred to listen rather than come too soon with questions and opinions. In the event she felt reassured by Stanley's account of Kate's background, and the fact that she regularly went home to visit them.

For a single young woman to live alone, away from her family, was not very common. But since she obviously still kept in close contact with her aunt and cousins in the town, and since she held a quite senior and responsible position at Binns, where she had now worked for a number of years, Sarah concluded that this was a girl, indeed a woman, who was reliable and steady. Not, it seemed, any flibbertigibbet who might be simply playing with her son's affections. In addition, there was the fact that Stanley was clearly truly smitten with her. His eyes shone when he talked about her, which he increasingly did when he saw that his mother's attitude was leaning towards the positive. Thus it was that in high summer, when he was three months into his acquaintance, indeed courtship of Kate, he proposed to Sarah that he should bring her home to meet her. "Bring her on Sunday afternoon," said Sarah, "then we can have a chat over a cup of tea and I might even bake some scones." Stanley's face lit up and, it being the middle of the week and no prospect of seeing Kate until the weekend, he went to his room to write a note to her which he posted that very evening.

....

Kate was not given to nervousness. From her childhood on the farm, with brothers always ready to tease and challenge her, and a father who talked to her, and argued with her, as if she was an adult, she had developed a confidence that was not easily shaken. Nevertheless, the impending visit to Stanley's home to meet his mother did cause Kate to take particular care over her appearance and to think about what she should say to Stanley's mother. Stanley had told her about his early life, about the death of his father and about the years when he was living in his uncle's house. She knew about the joy of their reunion, after four years living apart, when Sarah had found a new position and they were once again able to have a proper home together. From the way that Stanley spoke about his mother Kate concluded that as well as being an affectionate parent she must be a wise one too. The bond between mother and son was strong. Yes, she was after all a little bit nervous about meeting her.

Stanley had on several occasions come to Kate's lodgings to collect her to take her to some pre-arranged event or for their now regular Sunday afternoon walk. Of course he never went into her rooms but, having knocked on the door he simply waited for her to join him. This Sunday was no different except that the landlady's girl answered the door even quicker than usual and before Stanley could open his mouth she had informed him that "Miss Atkinson will be out in just one minute sir" and she shut the door again. Stanley was for a moment nonplussed by the unusual suddenness of this greeting but after less than a minute the door opened again and Kate emerged with, unusually for her, an ever so slightly nervous smile on her face. Kate's eyes said, "Will I do?" Stanley's lips answered, "You look grand!"

Sarah had set out the tea things on the little table she had in the sitting room of their house in West Sidings. When she was given the tenancy she had nothing in the way of furniture but she had managed to bring with her from her earlier more prosperous life half, which meant six, cups, saucers and tea plates, of a flower-patterned, China tea service. After the death of Mrs. Tanner when she had helped the cousin to clear and prepare the house to be sold, the cousin, grateful for Sarah's help and knowing of her plight, had given her the wardrobe and bed, both somewhat old but of good quality, from the room that she had occupied when living with Mrs Tanner; in addition, the cousin offered Sarah one white, lace edged linen tablecloth from Mrs Tanner's large collection. The table that she now set, with three pretty cups and saucers on the pristine white tablecloth, had come from her brother's hotel, as had the upright chairs, which had been cleverly repaired and restained by Bill Blackwood so that you could not detect at all that they had ever been broken. Thus, when she set out the tea things and arranged the room Sarah could look around her without shame at her poverty, indeed with a certain pride at what she had been able to create since the catastrophe following Charles' death.

When Sarah heard the front door opening she went into the hall to greet the girl who it seemed had captured Stanley's heart and, before they had been sitting at table half an hour, she found that she could begin to understand why. There was a natural dignity and openness in her manner which appealed to Sarah and, aware of the dark and troubled period in her own and Stanley's past, she was not about to interrogate Kate about her family or her circumstances. No, she would keep to topics of neutral and general interest. Kate, in any case, and spontaneously, broke the ice by praising Sarah's scones and relating that this was one thing she missed from home: she had no cooking facilities at her lodgings. In fact, before the visit was halfway through the only person who was still on tenterhooks was Stanley, who could not quite get over his double anxiety that his mother should like and approve of Kate and Kate should like and understand his mother. It was not until the visit was over and Stanley was walking Kate back to her lodgings that it truly dawned on him that his mother had taken to Kate and that the feeling was mutual. They had not gone many yards from the house when Kate took Stanley's arm and said,
"Your mother is a very fine person, Stan. I hope she liked me." Stanley squeezed Kate's arm in his and, "I know she did" he said.

Back in number three, West Sidings, Sarah cleared away the tea things and thought about the visit. As she stood at the kitchen sink washing out the cups and saucers she spoke to herself aloud: "I do believe that this is the one," she said. As far as she knew, and Sarah felt in her bones that she *did* know, Stanley had not walked out with any other girl. There were girl cousins in the family and even a few who worked at Horner's, in the office, whom Sarah knew that Stanley had mixed with on the few occasions when there had been social events sponsored by the company. But Stanley had never spoken about any of them in particular, other than a casual remark in passing, when identifying for his mother who exactly had been in the group on a particular occasion, at an event or on a picnic - sometimes, in the summer, with cousins. No, this was different, and after that afternoon visit Sarah was quite sure that she was witnessing the beginning of something serious.

....

Ed's comic pronouncement of economic doom for Sprinton and the wider world did not, at least immediately, materialise. Instead the town was experiencing a period of prosperity and expansion and Kate had risen in the ranks at Binns' to become chief buyer in the fabrics department. Her meeting with Stanley, at the point in her life where she was feeling restless and dissatisfied, had changed her. There was a depth to Stanley that answered to something in Kate's nature and from the very beginning they had lively conversations and he often made her laugh. It was the kind of talk such as she had had with her father and with younger brother, Colin and which she had missed since leaving home.

There had been few books in Stanley's childhood but in the move to Sprinton after their father's death Sarah had managed to salvage not only the half China tea service but also a handful of books: there was the Bible, some sheet music, an old copy of Lamb's Tales from Shakespeare and a rather large one volume Encyclopaedia. This latter had come from Charles' family home and Sarah had never seen Charles look in it but, nevertheless, something prompted her to save it from the wreckage of her husband's family fortunes and bring it with her when they moved back to Sprinton. The modest trunk containing all that she had managed to take from Melcaster, had been lodged in her brother's attic at the Blue Lion for the years when she was living-in at Mrs Tanner's, and when Stanley was lodging at the Blue Lion. When the day came for the move from Mrs Tanner's house and into the little house in West Sidings, Alec Benson brought his sister's trunk back to her. She unpacked the tea service and the bed linen which she had also brought from their old home, and put the tea service into the one kitchen cupboard, but the books she left in the trunk since there was nowhere just then to put them. The next day Stanley too moved out of the Blue Lion and came to join his mother in the new house. When he had put away his few things in the chest of drawers, he opened the trunk, which had been put in his room, and found the books. His attention, and curiosity, was aroused by the encyclopaedia, of which he had no memory from his former home. He placed the three on top of the chest of drawers. The Bible and Tales from Shakespeare lay one on top of the other; the encyclopaedia was big enough to stand up on its own. The room suddenly looked lived in, as if there was someone there. Curiosity prompted him to pick up the encyclopaedia; he sat himself down on the bed, a real bed with a proper mattress and linen sheets, crossed his legs and opened the encyclopaedia at random. It opened at P and the first entry was 'Pyramid'. Half an hour later he had not moved and his mind and imagination were in the deserts of Egypt and about to delve into the mystery surrounding Tutankhamun's tomb. He was hooked and, from that day forward Stanley took down the encyclopaedia, 'his' encyclopaedia - his mother said it should be his - opened it at random, and learnt something new. It was his treasure trove and became his most prized possession. What he could never have suspected then was that it would ever play a role in securing the affection of the beautiful girl with whom he would one day fall in love.

It was the occasion of Stanley's second 'walking out' with Kate. They met by the market cross in the middle of the town and walked once again towards Gravity Park, a walk which took them right past Binns' department store and a window display of dresses and fine fabrics of many colours. Kate stopped and pointed out to Stanley a roll of shimmering many coloured silk,
"Stanley, isn't that beautiful, and to think it comes from the work of a little silk worm that lives on mulberry leaves!"
"Yes, it is beautiful," replied Stanley, "And do you know how it got here, all the way from China, if it's Chinese silk at any rate?" And Stanley found himself talking of the Silk Road and how it wound its way from China, across deserts and mountain ranges until it reached Europe. He stopped, suddenly aware that his companion was regarding him with wide open eyes.
"How do you know all that?" Kate burst out.
"Oh I read it somewhere," he said, blushing, and afraid that he might have been boring her. But he wasn't, and the talk came around quite naturally to places to which they had never been but could dream of visiting. Kate's ultimate was Paris but Stanley, inspired by the letters they received from Jack, in Canada, combined with what he had found out about that country from his encyclopaedia, confessed that he would favour a journey across the vast prairies and through the Rocky Mountains to the Pacific coast of North America. Over tea and plum bread at the park's Pavilion, Stanley told Kate more about his family: about Jack who had now been many years working on Canadian railways and who wrote telling them of his experiences; the work was hard but for a qualified engineer or mechanic the money was good; you could save a lot - and sometimes it was dangerous work and sometimes it was exciting. In parts you had to watch out for wolves and bears and moose, and the climate was certainly hard in winter, but he really would recommend one of his brothers to try their luck and join him. Fred, who worked on the railways in Melcaster, had been tempted, and thought about it, but then he got married and the idea was shelved.

"Would you think about going?" Kate asked, her heart sinking a little as she realised that the answer could have significant consequences for her. There was a struggle in her mind between her own just dawning hopes and the part of her that knew it should want Stanley to fulfil his own dreams. Stanley smiled and shook his head. He did not at that point feel ready to explain his reluctance to embark on an adventure such as Jack's, but he knew that those childhood years away from a proper home had everything to do with it. Later, when they knew each other better he would tell her more. Just now a part explanation would have to do, and anyway it was the truth as far as it went,

"No," he said, "I'm not after that kind of adventure, and anyway my mother would then be left alone. Charlie has moved away and Aunt Annie has her hands full with Bert." The long term effects of Bert's accident, ten years before, had now rendered him almost immobile and the couple's small means had become even smaller. This fact Stanley kept to himself for the time being but it was something that he and Sarah had in mind, for Annie and Bert had effectively, if not formally, adopted Charlie and had given him a loving home since the day the three of them, Sarah, Charlie and Stanley, had arrived in Sprinton. Charlie had blossomed and gained in confidence under their kindly guidance and now for the last two years he had held a respectable and responsible position with one of the county's main retail suppliers in a town in the north. He truly had become the son that Annie and Bert could never have. Sarah in no way begrudged them her third son, for her situation when they arrived in Sprinton had been desperate and Annie and Bert had stepped in and welcomed Charlie with open arms. They had only been sorry that they were unable to take in Stanley too. So now neither Sarah nor Charlie nor Stanley would be willing to see the couple reduced to humiliating poverty without giving them what help they could. All of this lurked in the back of Stanley's mind when he answered Kate's question. One day he hoped he might be able to tell her all this, and more, but not today.

Innocent of what lay behind Stanley's answer Kate could only feel tremendous relief - and joy - at what she heard. Moreover, what Stanley told her confirmed that they had something else in common: Kate's oldest brother had also gone to Canada, and did not seem minded to return to the old country any time soon. To Stanley she said,

"Our Harry went ten years ago and he seems to have got his own land now, in the prairies, but he doesn't write very often. Father was very upset when it happened because it was very sudden. I wasn't much more than ten at the time so it all went rather over my head, but it seems Harry'd been planning it for some time and he just announced at the last minute that he was going. He and father never got on for some reason; I don't know why, just one of those things I suppose." She stopped, lost momentarily in sombre thoughts. Stanley, whose eyes had never left her face during this speech, suddenly noticed that there were tears in her eyes.

"Were you very fond of Harry?" He asked, concerned. Kate looked up thoughtfully at Stanley, "Yes, but you see he was twelve years older than me so, in a way more like an uncle than a brother. He carried me around on his shoulder when I was very little, and later he'd tease me. But what made me sad was more that father was so upset because even though they often didn't get on I know he was hoping that Harry would follow him and take over the farm, with Will, who's second in the family. There were nine of us you see. And it just seemed as if Harry had been making all these plans so secretively. Father felt very let down and as if he hadn't been given a chance to sort things out with Harry. I don't think it would have helped really because I think Harry just wanted to be free; he said to me he'd always felt as if all the decisions had been made for him already, and he wanted to escape. It wasn't that he hated the farm because in Canada he's stayed in farming; but now he's his own boss." She fell silent.

"What sort of farming does he do in Canada?" Stanley was genuinely curious, for Jack in his letters, and his own precious book, told him that the hundreds of miles and millions of acres of the Canadian prairies were principally waving seas of wheat and corn.

"I think it's all crops, no animals," she paused, "in fact he never was very keen on the animals. He was nearly gored by a short-horned bull we had when he was very young. He showed me the scar at his left shoulder once - when he was trying to scare me with angry bull stories!" She laughed, "I suppose that might also have been why he wasn't keen on that side of farming."

By the time they had finished their tea and left the park, after circling the band stand where they had listened to the music of the Colliery Band, and checking that the new waterfall and pond were still in working order, Kate knew that she was becoming seriously fond of Stanley Ruskin.

From this time on it not infrequently happened that Stanley would surprise Kate with some little piece of recondite knowledge, garnered from his encyclopaedia, that amused but also intrigued her. Not to be outdone she began to find little bits of 'uncommon' knowledge with which to test Stanley. It became a game between them, a teasing competition which often ended in laughter and, eventually, when they had known each other longer, with a kiss. Kate could never get Stanley to reveal the source of all his, what she termed 'odd facts', but anyway, on discovering that, despite his thirst for knowledge, he had never ventured into Sprinton's library, she persuaded him to join. Thus, quite soon the encyclopaedia on the top of his chest of drawers was joined by other books. And so, through what turned out to be a long hot summer, both love, and learning, bloomed.

CHAPTER 5

Meeting the families

In the six years that had passed since she moved from the farm into town, Kate had never gone more than a month without visiting the family back home. Occasionally it happened the other way round and Susan travelled to Sprinton, bringing Ivy, Kate's youngest sister, with her. They came to visit Kate, and Daisy, or on farming business, or simply "for fashion and frivolity" their father said, adding that he had no objection if they had the money; and he knew that Susan was a good manager and he could trust that if she said she had the money, then she had, and the expenditure she was planning would be justified. Over domestic expenditure George never questioned her judgement.

In the summer, when she had known Stanley for nearly three months, Kate was on a visit home and the whole family, those that still remained, were gathered round the kitchen table for Saturday's tea. William, as Kate had told Stanley, was the second son but, since Harry had gone to Canada, he had become the one who would take over the farm; and it was just as well because William had always loved the farming way of life and especially the animals. He still lived in the old house with George and Susan, and had shown no great interest in marrying. There had been one or two short-lived flirtings with girls from neighbouring farms and then William seemed to settle into being a bachelor-farmer. He was in any case still surrounded by family since he was joined in the running of the farm by Philip, his five years younger brother. Philip was different from William in one important respect, however, for he was not wedded to bachelorhood. Indeed, before his twenty third birthday had passed, he had courted and married Angela, the second daughter of a wool merchant whom he had met on one of the many occasions when he had to visit the sheep market of the county town and negotiate the sale of ewes and lambs. Now Philip had two young children of his own and the family had recently moved into a cottage, newly renovated, that belonged to the farm but which had been occupied for forty years by George's old shepherd until his death the previous year.

The only daughter still living at home was the youngest, Ivy. She hero-worshipped Kate and had declared early on that when she was sixteen she would do like Kate had done and would go and live in the town. In the

meantime she lived vicariously through her older sister, interrogating her every time she came home to give an account of what she had been doing, who she was seeing and, in particular whether she had a 'follower', in other words was she not yet courting? On this issue Ivy could not understand how her beautiful older sister could have been living in Sprinton for so long, and had never yet found a 'beau' (Ivy's word). Consequently she was seriously suspicious of Kate's constant denials of any emotional attachment, and fondly imagined that she really had a secret lover. This time, expecting the usual denial, which Ivy, as usual would not believe, they were all taken by surprise when Kate calmly replied to Ivy's regularly expected question,
"Well yes, sister Ivy," with mock formality, "I do believe I have a 'follower', as you so quaintly put it. His name is Stanley Ruskin and he works at Horner's in Sprinton where he served his apprenticeship and he is now a fully qualified engine fitter." Five pairs of eyes turned on Kate; the clatter of knives and forks ceased and suddenly there was silence.
"Is this true?" asked Susan.
"Mother, it is," replied Kate.
"Oh Kate, tell more," Ivy pleaded.
"But I have already told you everything," said Kate, cocking her head towards Ivy with a sly grin on her face.
"Oh no, no, you haven't. What does he look like and how did you meet?"
"I note your priorities, Ivy. Don't you think there might be more important qualities to consider than my friend's looks?"
"Does that mean he's ugly?" Ivy was shocked.
"Ivy, that's enough," from their mother. Susan turned to Kate,
"Is this serious then, Kate?" Kate almost blushed, conscious of all eyes upon her, and especially of the look of her father, slightly serious and intent on the other side of the table. She hesitated, just for a second, then,
"I think it is," she said.
"Is he a Sprinton lad? How long have you known him?" George spoke, a little gruffly, for the first time. Kate paused, considering for a moment how much she should tell them at this stage.
"Well he wasn't Sprinton born. The family moved here from Melcaster when Stan was nine, after his father died."
"So his mother's a widow…" this was part reflection, part question from Susan who immediately grasped the significance of the fact. "That can't have been easy. How many children…?" Susan considered the plight of the mother.

"No, it wasn't easy," said Kate. But Ivy was impatient with this tale of family history,
"But what is he like, Kate?" Kate smiled over at her little sister - though at fifteen and quite tall she was not really any longer in any way 'little'.
"Well, I'll have to bring him over to meet you all won't I?" She saw her father had a furrowed brow. "I've known him three months, father, and I do think you will like him. He's honest and serious and, Will, he can take any engine you like to show him, pull it apart and put it all back together again. He's a genius with engines." She knew this would appeal to her brothers and also to her father. George always had respect for anyone who had skills. If there was one person that she most wanted to get on Stanley's side then it was her father so, when she looked across the table and saw that her father's face had relaxed from its earlier stern look, she found herself smiling.
"He also has a sense of humour," she said, seeing that Ivy, now silenced, was also looking thoughtful. Ivy's face brightened.
"I first met Stanley at Aunt Daisy's house, mother. A Sunday when I went to lunch there. Ed works beside Stan at Horner's and they're good friends - so both Aunt Daisy and Ed can vouch for Stan," she laughed, "and they will."
"Horner's are a good company, at any rate," said William, who was always trying to convince their father that they should invest in the latest machinery, "the Wilton estate has a Horner's threshing machine that's driven by a steam engine. It can do the work of five men in half a day."
"Well Kate, it sounds as if William has already approved your young man, but you'd better bring him over so the rest of us can meet him anyway!" This from Susan who could sense the different anxieties of her daughter and her husband.
"Of course I want you to meet him and I'll bring him over very soon," Kate said. George patted her on the shoulder as he and William prepared to go out to the byre to see to the animals.

....

When Kate informed Stanley that she had told her family about him and that they wanted to meet him Stanley was both pleased and apprehensive. He had known in his own mind from almost the day that they had met that Kate was the girl he wanted 'to have and to hold, from that day forward and for evermore'; but he couldn't, at that time, be quite sure that the same was true of Kate. It wasn't in fact, until a few weeks later that he knew for certain how she felt. It happened thus: in the course of one of their, by now quite regular walks in the countryside, on a sunny Sunday afternoon, he helped Kate over a stream where she had to lift her dress so that it would not get wet, and on the other side, finding her hand still in his, he leant forward and impulsively kissed her on the cheek. Without hesitation Kate put her right hand on Stanley's cheek and returned his kiss, but on the lips. This was not only bold but it was a decisive moment for both of them and Stanley knew that Kate felt as he did. They continued their country walk, for a while in silence, but with Stanley's arm around Kate's waist. After a while they stopped, faced one another, and laughed in mutual delight.

Soon after that Kate asked Stanley to bring his mother over to her lodgings where she could return Sarah's courtesy visit. Kate had been in the same lodgings for more than five years. It was the home she had made for herself after leaving her Aunt Daisy's house where she had stayed first in Sprinton. Her landlady, then recently widowed, had let out as a sitting-bedroom what had previously been her quite large dining room. It had a smaller room leading off it, formerly a pantry, where Kate could prepare simple meals for herself and, a gas ring having been installed, where she could heat water for washing and to make tea. Mrs Roberts, a refined and genteel lady, had been left in straitened circumstances when her husband died and found it necessary not only to dismiss her cook and her personal maid but also to augment her income by letting out those now surplus rooms in order that she could remain in the house where she had spent the more than thirty years of her married life. Kate was lucky with her landlady, for Mrs Roberts was not at all interfering, but she was always concerned that everything in the house worked well. She had been used to a comfortable home with all the modern conveniences of the day: her husband had seen to that. But Mrs Roberts had no children and when she agreed to let her rooms to Kate, at that time just seventeen, she had been a little concerned that so young a girl, but recently come into the town from the countryside, should be without the protection of a parent, and so she, in ways that she could, 'kept an eye on her'.

Mrs Roberts had long had all her dairy wants delivered to the house by the Williams' dairy, and it was the housemaid - the only one of her servants whom Mrs Roberts could afford to keep on and whom she regarded as indispensable - who, taking the order to the dairy had let out that there were now rooms to let in her employer's house. Daisy had accompanied Kate when she came to see the rooms so Mrs Roberts knew that she had interested relatives in the town, and that they were responsible and respectable people; reassured by this she nevertheless kept an eye on Kate while she was living under her roof.

Now, five years on, there was a comfortable, without being intimate, relationship between Kate and her landlady so that when she told Mrs Roberts that she was expecting company on the following Sunday afternoon and who the company was, Mrs Roberts was only concerned to be helpful. She merely wondered if Miss Atkinson had sufficient China for her tea table since Kate had only ever had one visitor at a time to her rooms, and that always a girl friend, either Lucy Staines or one of the girls from work. But Kate assured her that she had; the only thing that she was missing was a vase in which to put the flowers that she had begged from her aunt's garden, to decorate the table. Mrs Roberts was happy to lend Kate a vase.

The visit served to further Sarah's good opinion of Kate and to convince her that this was the girl for her son. In some ways toughened by childhood experiences and in other ways made vulnerable, Sarah knew in her bones that Stanley, whose confidence had grown since he had started work, would always need a champion. Indeed, who didn't? Seeing Kate with Stanley she felt increasingly that she was likely to be a good champion. And what about Kate? Would Stanley be the one for her? Sarah hoped he would be. That Kate was warm-hearted she had already seen and it was obvious from the way she spoke about the business she was in that she could hold her own in any company. Still, she needed approval too, and in particular, Stanley's approval. Sarah saw that from the way in which Kate from time to time shot a glance in Stanley's direction that said, "Am I doing all right? Do you think your mother approves of me?" She did.

The visit went on for much longer than either side had anticipated and by the time Sarah, suddenly noticing the time said, "Oh goodness me Stanley, it really is time that we were going," Kate could reply, with sincerity, that for her part there was no need to hurry. Nevertheless, and with some laughter at a story that Stanley had just told, the party broke up.

………………………………………………………..

It had rained all morning and, in spite of himself, Stanley found that his spirits too were dampened a little in anticipation of travelling out to the farm to be introduced to Kate's family. He began to feel as he imagined a new recruit to a battalion might feel when about to be inspected by the whole troup. Kate tried to reassure him, "They are sure to like you, Stan, because they know I do, and they trust my judgement. Also, my father has great respect for anyone who knows things, and William," Kate chuckled, "was on your side as soon as I said the words 'knows all about engines'!" Stanley looked alarmed, "Heavens I hope you haven't given them the impression I'm some sort of mechanical genius."

"Well, no, not quite," Kate looked at Stanley teasingly, "but as near as I could! Anyway they're good people and they want most of all that I'm happy, and since they can see, and will see when they meet you, that you make me happy, why, they'll be eating out of your hand in no time." She smiled at Stanley, and pecked him on the cheek. It is doubtful whether Kate's words reassured him but the kiss and the look in her eyes somehow did.

The motorbus taking Kate and Stanley from Sprinton to Daneby, the nearest village to the Atkinson's farm, was a recent innovation in the district. It meant that the villagers and those living in outlying farms on the bus route no longer had to rely on carters carrying produce to and from the town, or on their own horse drawn vehicles, which had mostly been open to all weathers. The elements smiled on Kate and Stanley at all events for the rain had stopped by the time the bus let them off at a junction with a narrow lane which led to the farm. A short walk, Kate's brothers had closely calculated the distance to be three hundred and fifty five yards, led them to the gate.

Long before George, with a loan from the bank, had bought the farm, it had been named Willow Farm; and there was justification for the name since a little brook which ran across a meadow below the rise on which the farmhouse had been built, was bordered with sturdy willow trees. In her childhood it had been a favourite haunt of Kate's when, after school and her chores, she could take a book and run down the meadow to the willow trees by the brook and perch herself on the broad overhanging trunk of one of them. Here she was completely out of sight of the house or even of anyone in the meadow below it. In between her reading, and thinking about something she had just read, she would dangle her legs down towards the stream. Approaching the gate to Willow Farm, with Stanley beside her, Kate resolved that she would take him down to the willow trees before they left to return to Sprinton.

When they opened the gate into the house yard William was just emerging from the main barn where the milk heifers had just been relieved of their 'white gold,' as Philip, when a young boy had once fancifully dubbed the creamy milk that their prize dairy cows habitually produced. At the sight of Kate, William's face broke into a broad smile. "Well, bless me, you made good time eh?" He turned to Stanley, "You must be Stanley." William turned a muddy hand palm up to Stanley and pulled a face. "I won't shake yours," he said, "Goldie's just backed into me and landed me in the mud. We had a lot of rain yesterday," he said, turning to Kate, "and water in the crew yard ran mud into the milking barn." They reached the door of the house, which stood open, and Kate called out as they entered, "Mother! We're here."

As it turned out Stanley's fears about the visit were quite soon laid to rest. William set the tone when, as they sat down to the good Willow Farm Sunday dinner, he asked Stanley about a new threshing machine that he had seen advertised in The Farming Gazette. Did he know anything about it? Stanley did and, without going into detail that he knew would be boring for some members of the family, he was able to give William some useful information about it. George, also drawn into the discussion because he knew how much the future prosperity of the farm meant to his two present sons, found himself expanding, for Stanley's sake, on the situation in farming in general. He also gave Stanley some of the history of Willow Farm and Stanley, whose love of the countryside had begun in the years in which he had lived at the Blue Lion, found himself drawn into the story. He relaxed and told them about his experiences on his uncle's land just outside the town so that, when Kate interjected at one point to tell them that Stanley was a proven expert on edible fungi, well then the ice was well and truly broken. Philip offered to show Stanley over the land and barns and as they rose from the table Kate pressed Stanley to go with Philip while she was helping her mother and sister Ivy to clear away and wash up.

Philip was proud of what they were achieving on the farm, and he was the one who was master of the details and in particular of all that had to do with the crops. But Stanley did not need to feign interest in things like crop rotation or strains of different cereals since, from labouring on his uncle's piece of land outside Sprinton, he had learned enough to know the importance of choosing the right things to plant for the kind of soil and the position of the fields you had. Also, simply being outside in the open air, with a free view of sky and land always filled him with pleasure.

The afternoon passed quickly, Stanley was surprised to find; but before it was time to take the bus back into Sprinton Kate detached him from a conversation her father was having with Stanley and took him down the meadow to the willow trees where she had spent much of her happy free time as a child. The stream beneath the willow trees was flowing quickly and gurgling over rocks in the water.

"What a lovely spot," said Stanley, surveying the scene reflectively. The sun shot darts of sparkling reflection on the swift flowing water and a pair of warblers trilled and hopped about in the branches of another willow growing out of the opposite bank. "I loved it more than anything," replied Kate. "It was the only place I could read and not be disturbed too. My mother could never really accept that reading was an activity, so if I was found reading in the house, at least downstairs, she would immediately find me 'something to do', as she put it." Kate laughed, and pointed to a spot in the stream beneath the broad limb of the willow where she had told Stanley that she used to lie. "But I did fall in once when I was day-dreaming here. It was summer and the water was shallow so I just got a bit of a soaking. I told my mother I had slipped when I was trying to fish for tiddlers. If she knew the truth she would have thought I was just trying to sneak away to avoid a chore!" When they returned to the house there was just time to say goodbye to everybody before walking back along the lane to the Sprinton road where the bus would pick them up.

Waiting by the side of the road Stanley slipped his arm around Kate's waist and gave her a half-smile, "Well they didn't set the dogs on me," he said. Kate laughed, "Not only that," she replied, "but my father told me that you were, in his words, 'all right'. And, very important, he said 'and he doesn't look down on country folk like too many townees do.' No Stan, I'm afraid you're 'in', so now you'll have to put up with them like I do," with a smile. Stanley looked at her, "Well, I don't think that will be so difficult," he said. "I liked them all and I thought, 'what a great place to grow up in'!" Kate's expression, for a moment, became serious. "Yes, it was," she said, "but you know you're awfully dependant on the weather and they had, well we all had, some hard years too when the crops failed because there'd been too much rain, and wind, so the wheat and barley were flattened - and sometimes rotten." She paused, "I've seen my mother and father sitting at the kitchen table and my father saying, 'I don't know what we're going to do this winter'. "Her face brightened, "But they always managed somehow, and we never starved - like some did." The bus appeared round a bend in the narrow, country road, and slowed to a halt beside them.

CHAPTER 6

Binns and a Crisis

Binns Emporium had grown and expanded its business steadily in the six years since Kate left the farm to come and live and work in the town. Kate had grown with it; she knew the trade thoroughly and had still an enthusiastic interest in the textiles side of the business. Nevertheless in the year before she met Stanley she came to the realisation that she had advanced as far in the company as she was ever going to go, since she had no desire to move sideways and sit in one of the offices upstairs, away from the 'front stage shop', and become an administrator or book-keeper. Learning book-keeping had been useful but it also clarified her mind about what she definitely did not want to do.

At the same time something was missing in her personal life. It wasn't that there were no young men in her surroundings to take an interest in her - or she to them. None of the youths who worked for the company, whether on the retail side or in the offices, could have failed to notice her. She had even been dubbed by one of them as the 'queen' of the textiles department. There had been one or two mild flirtations with some of the young pretenders, but none had exerted more than a passing appeal to Kate. It was just at this time in her life when she had gone to her Aunt Daisy's for Sunday lunch - and met Stanley.

It was odd, she found herself reflecting quite early on in their acquaintance, Stanley had had no more schooling than she had and he had scarcely read anything until Kate induced him to join the library, and yet she realised very soon that he had thought about a lot of things and about some things deeply. And then the talking began. They talked about family and growing up; they talked about hopes and dreams, about ideas and of everything from 'death' to the meaning of life. Kate teased and provoked; Stanley countered and rebutted, sometimes clinching an argument with some item of fact that he remembered from his encyclopaedia - which became known between them as "the Bible"! With growing confidence Stanley teased her back or asserted there were flaws in Kate's arguments and begged to be allowed to point out what they were. Warm feelings and friendship grew.

....

It was nearly a year since that fateful Sunday dinner at Daisy's house when Kate fell ill. There had already been talk between Kate and Stanley about long-term plans and a future together. Stanley had finished his apprenticeship and was qualified. He was good at his job and was valued at the firm, but valued only to the degree that all competent labourers on the workshop floor were. In spite of there now being a fledgling trade union which was gaining support among the workforce, there was still an overriding feeling that the bosses had the whip hand. And they had, for, although the town's population had grown considerably in the previous decade, the expansion of industry had not quite kept pace and there were more looking for work than there were jobs to be filled. Stanley's wages were only just about enough to support a family and if a young couple married, then children were sure to arrive soon afterwards. By the standards of the day Kate's wages, for an unmarried female were good; but if Kate were to marry and become pregnant she would have to give up her job and they would be completely dependent on Stanley's wages for their living. They had come to an understanding that they must wait and save up before there could be any question of marriage.

Industry had not perhaps expanded significantly but nevertheless the population and retail trade had. In the spring Binns' employees were informed that extensive modernisation and renovation work would be carried out on the shop's premises and the work would begin in what was the textiles department. The work involved taking out old windows and putting in new, bigger ones. The main entrance to the store was also to be enlarged. Structural changes of this kind meant that for a period, and the management anticipated that this would mean days rather than weeks, there would be a measure of temporary enclosure of window and door sized gaps in walls. This would be some kind of sheeting which would surely keep out the worst of the cold and wind but employees were advised in any case to come to work dressed more warmly than they otherwise normally would. For the period of the work thus envisaged the company was prepared to modify its otherwise strict dress code.

The sincere expectations of the management, and hopes of the employees, were disappointed. For reasons that were never satisfactorily explained, and which probably never could have been, the building work, which in practice exposed the employees on the shop floor to considerable degrees of cold and discomfort, took almost three weeks instead of the ten days foretold.

When Kate met Stanley in the town square on the Saturday afternoon at the end of the first week of building work at Binns, she told him of the conditions they had been working under that week.

"I've never been so cold in my life," she said, "and I had on an extra jumper and Ivy's woolen scarf. Come on, Stan, let's walk really fast round the square a few times. I must get warm." Stanley looked at her unusually pinched, pale face and, "No," he said, "we'll walk fast just to Kennedy's and get the hottest pot of tea they can give us."

With the second pot and her hands clasped around the third cup of steaming tea, and a scone with jam inside her, Kate's face regained some of its colour and Stanley's apprehension that Kate might be unwell, lessened. When they parted at tea-time, having arranged to meet for their customary Sunday walk the next day, Kate seemed much like her old self again. Their walk the following day also passed off much as usual. Stanley had news to tell her about Jack, who had now been in Canada for almost a decade, and his most recent letter hinted that he might be coming home for a visit within the year. Kate's family news was that their father had just had a letter from Colin in which he too hinted that he might be about to depart on a voyage abroad with his regiment, but he couldn't at that moment divulge any detail. The family speculated that perhaps Colin was about to depart for India, but nobody knew anything for sure. As usual, when they parted on Sunday evening it was with the understanding that they would meet the following Saturday afternoon when both had finished work for the weekend.

The following week passed as most did: sometimes Kate would send Stanley a note mid week telling him that she had seen or heard something that might interest him; sometimes Stanley wrote to Kate telling her about something that had happened at work, or that he loved her and longed for Saturday to arrive. It was not especially unusual that no note should have been passed between them. Nevertheless Stanley had a niggling sense of unease that he hadn't received any word from Kate and after work on the Wednesday he decided that when he had finished his tea he would walk round to her lodgings if only just to see how she was. It was almost dark when he arrived, and the curtains in both parts of the house were already drawn across. Stanley scarcely had time to raise the knocker a second time when the door flew open and there was Polly, Mrs Robert's live-in maid, looking wide-eyed and anxious.

"Oh, it's you, Mr Ruskin, I thought maybe it was the doctor coming back!" Stanley's heart missed a beat, "What is it," he cried, "Is it Miss Atkinson? Is she ill?" It never occurred to him that it might be Polly's employer who was ill and not Kate at all.

"Oh, sir, she's got a terrible temperature and we called the doctor. It's Dr Frazer, you know, please come in. He's given her some medicine and left a bottle that she has to take every four hours. We was just deciding what to do. We think we should get a message to her mother to come but Miss Atkinson will insist she'll be much better in the morning…" her voice trailed away as Mrs Roberts appeared from another part of the house.

"Ah, it's you, Mr Ruskin," she said, "Yes, we're really quite concerned about your friend. She went off to work this morning just as usual, though I had met her yesterday evening when she came back from work and she was looking quite 'peaky' I thought, but she said she was fine. Anyway, just after lunchtime today we heard the door go and it was Miss Atkinson coming in looking not well at all. She said she would go and lie down and Polly took her in some hot herbal tea, which she took…" Stanley, feeling real anxiety now, broke in before Mrs Roberts had finished,

"Mrs Roberts, please, do you mind if I see her, just for a few minutes?" Mrs Roberts had seen the anguish in Stanley's face and she exchanged a glance with Polly.

"Well, under the circumstances, you may, but just a couple of minutes, mind. Polly go and see how she is, will you?" She meant, of course, that Polly should check that Kate was 'decent' since the proprieties would normally not allow a young man to see his young woman in bed, at least not unsupervised. Polly knocked and went through to Kate's rooms.

"You know," said Stanley, thinking aloud and turning to Mrs Roberts while they waited for Polly to return, "Miss Atkinson has her aunt and family in the town. I could let them know, and if she isn't any better in the morning the Williamses would certainly get a message to the farm. They fetch milk from them every day." Polly appeared from Kate's part of the house,

"That's all right," she said, "but she's really very poorly. Don't stay, sir, but come on through."

By means of a hinged screen Kate had been able to divide her large room into both sitting room and sleeping area. When Stanley came past the screen he was shocked to see how both pale and at the same time flushed her face looked. Kate lifted her head and smiled weakly at Stanley.

"Oh Stan, you shouldn't have come. I'll be better tomorrow," she managed to murmur, but her laboured breathing belied the words. Stanley bent over her and touched her cheek. "No Kate," he said, "you need somebody here. The Williamses will get a message to the farm tomorrow and Polly here will keep an eye on you tonight." Kate had closed her eyes and seemed to have drifted into sleep though her breathing remained harsh. Polly touched him on the arm and Stanley released the fevered hand he had been holding and followed Polly out of the room.

Mrs Roberts was waiting in the hall when Stanley emerged from Kate's room. "I don't suppose you have a telephone, Mrs Roberts, do you?" He asked. "I'm afraid not, but the Green Man in North Street does I believe," she replied, referring to a pub that was well known in that part of the town. Stanley had remembered that Ed Williams had told him not so long ago that his father had recently had a telephone installed for the sake of the business. If he could reach the Williamses then he felt sure that Daisy would come over. He explained to Mrs Roberts what he was going to do and she assured Stanley that they would keep an eye on Kate in the meantime.

"There's a bell just beside the bed, too," Mrs Roberts told him. "It rings in my kitchen and we're bound to hear it. Polly told Miss Atkinson that she should ring it if she needs anything." Stanley hurried round to the Green Man. There were a few men in the bar but it was midweek quiet. The publican agreed to let Stanley use his phone and led him into the little office room behind the bar. Stanley had only used a phone once before but the publican showed him what to do and he was relieved when, after just three rings at the other end, he heard Evan's voice.

Daisy was truly alarmed when Stanley described Kate's appearance and condition and told her that a doctor had been called. There was no way of contacting the farm that night, for the Atkinsons had no phone and no vehicles would be likely to travel in that direction so late at night but Evan would bring Daisy round to Mrs Roberts' within the hour. She would sleep on the sofa in the sitting room part of Kate's room and in the morning Evan would set out earlier than usual on his milk collecting round of the farms near the Atkinson's and would deliver the news of Kate's illness to her parents. There was nothing more that Stanley could do that night but the sight of Kate's flushed face and the rasping sound of her breathing haunted him through the night and sleep all but deserted him until the early hours of the morning.

When Stanley had arrived back home after returning from Mrs Roberts' house he found his mother waiting in her dressing gown in their little kitchen, though it was much past her usual bedtime. Stanley, in his anxiety, had lost track of the time and was surprised to find that it was almost eleven o'clock. Sarah saw at once that Stanley was beside himself with worry about Kate and, with the experience of losing her two daughters to an influenza that started with what had appeared to be only a cold, she knew what the dangers could be. Stanley was galvanized by the fear of losing her. Sarah also knew how distressing it could be when other people, in their well-intentioned but fumbling ignorance, tried to give more encouragement and hope than they had certain knowledge of. It was better to say little and to listen rather than speak. She got Stanley to tell her how he had found Kate and what he had done and then contented herself with telling him that he had done all he could for the time being and he had better go to bed himself and get what rest he could so that in the morning he was ready to do whatever he was called upon to do.

Stanley truly passed the worst night of his life; it was worse by far than the nights when the rats ran over his bed in his uncle's house. You could kill a rat with impunity and you had no emotional involvement with the object of your fear and dislike. This, in contrast, was a fear of something that you could do nothing about; it was the fear of losing the living being who meant the most to you in life. It was the feeling of powerlessness that was the torture. When sleep came to him, in the early hours of the morning, it was a troubled, fear filled sleep, and Stanley felt only relief when he woke; it was light and he would be able to go to the house where Kate lay and find out how she was.

When Polly opened the door in answer to Stanley's knock she saw by his white face and tense look around the eyes that he had had little sleep. She beckoned him into the hall. "Mrs Williams came soon after you left, Mr Ruskin," said Polly. "She has slept on the sofa in Miss Atkinson's room. I'll just see how they are." Polly made for Kate's rooms and a minute later Daisy came into the hall and approached Stanley.

"Stanley, it's a good thing you sent for me," she said. "Kate's not had a good night, but she's no worse, and now, thankfully she's fallen asleep. In fact her breathing sounds better than last night." Stanley could only nod dumbly, but felt a slight sensation of relief. "Are you on your way to work?" Another nod from Stanley who was experiencing a riot of conflicting emotions, anxiety tempered by a faint quiver of hope and then more anxiety, since he knew realistically there was a long road to travel yet before they could know what the outcome would be. Daisy touched Stanley's arm.

"The doctor will be here any minute," she said. "He'll come again later too. Come by after you finish work and we'll know better how she is then." What more could she say? Daisy looked at Stanley's face and saw the depth of his love for Kate. "Off you go," she said kindly, "or you'll be late for work."

....

The next week passed in a sort of haze, and the following two in a half haze. Susan arrived from the farm on the morning of the second day and Daisy returned to her own family but came by every day with groceries and anything else they needed. Stanley called in every morning on his way to work and every evening on his way home from work. The doctor came every day, confirmed on the third day that it was pneumonia Kate had and that it would take some weeks before she could be pronounced out of danger. Mrs Roberts made no fuss about having such a serious invalid in her house; she was kind-hearted and in the five years Kate had lived in her house she had not only got used to having her there, nearby, but she had begun to regard her, just a little, as the daughter that she had never been able to have. Nevertheless Kate's mother and aunt felt that it was likely to become an encumbrance after a time, and no one knew how long it would really take for Kate to be restored to health. When the situation was explained to Dr Frazer he conceded, after two more days that Kate might safely be moved to Willow Farm if she was very warmly dressed, padded round with blankets and there were no draughts in the vehicle. In an act of generosity, and not entirely within the rules, the good doctor finally requisitioned one of the, now three, hospital vehicles to carry out the transportation of Kate from her rooms in Mrs Roberts' house to Willow Farm. The move took place on a sunny April day. Stanley saw off the party which consisted of Kate, her mother, Susan, a nurse from the Cottage Hospital, and the driver.

Susan managed to send a message back to her sister, Daisy, and thence to Stanley, to say that Kate had arrived safely and without any harmful effects from the journey. Stanley's anxiety about Kate was not lessened by the move but merely changed its form. He felt much more the anxiety of distance. He could not go to the place where she lay every day and hear, first hand, how she was, nor feel that she was nearby. The distance suddenly felt enormous. He had no control at all over the situation, no opportunity to glimpse her face if she should suddenly be better - he could not bear to think of the other alternative, if she should become worse. And yet he knew that taking her home to the direct care of her family was undoubtedly the right thing to do. One thing at least, he could get news of her every day by going by Ed's house on his way home from work. Since Evan went daily by Willow Farm to collect their milk for the Williamses' dairy a report on Kate's condition was sent at the same time. Thus two weeks passed; to Stanley it seemed a surreal time of suspended animation. Nothing mattered except that one moment each day when he got news of Kate.

At first consumed by anxiety and a sensation of powerlessness in the face of Kate's illness Stanley one day, after a conversation with his friend Ed Williams, saw a way out of his immediate imprisoning situation. If he had to mortgage his soul, he would do it. He would get a bicycle. He could then cycle out to Willow Farm whenever he was free, even a weekday evening if he wanted, for the nights were getting lighter - it was May already, and ten miles would be nothing to him. Stanley had been saving as much as he could from his wages for several months, as had Kate from hers, since they had talked about marriage, though it seemed but a distant hope at the time. What was clear was that to effect his plan he would need to use some of what he had saved, for a bicycle would cost the equivalent of more than a month's wages. When he reckoned up the sums, however, he still had not got enough. Sarah had noticed Stanley scribbling down figures on a piece of paper and scratching his head in perplexity. At length she asked, "What are you doing, Stan? You haven't any debts have you?" A spectre from the past rose momentarily up before her, though she could not imagine, given their common experience of her husband's road to ruin, that Stanley would really have got himself into financial difficulties. "Oh no, mother," Stanley began, and then the whole of his bicycling plan came out. Almost before he had finished, Sarah interrupted him: she had some savings of her own. Her son could surely not imagine that after what had happened to them when Charles died, leaving his widow penniless, that she would not have made sure that she could never find herself in that humiliating position again. No, ever since they had come to Sprinton and Sarah was working for Mrs Tanner, she had been careful to save some of her wages, against any possible new catastrophe. She could give Stanley what he needed to complete the purchase of the bicycle. Stanley's face was transformed, "But no, it will be a loan," he cried, "of course I shall pay you back."
"Well, well, we shall see about that," countered Sarah. She knew the agony of mind that Stanley had been suffering since Kate fell ill; indeed she felt some of it herself for, over the course of the year since Stanley had met her, Kate had been drawn into their family circle and Sarah saw that she meant everything to her son. She had lost her own two daughters, when they were scarcely in their teens. She felt keenly for Stanley his fear of losing Kate. The bicycle must be bought. Within the week Stanley's resolution was realised. He collected his bicycle from Sprinton's main dealer after work on Friday. On Saturday, after work, he hurried home, collected from his mother the sandwiches which she had made and packed for him, and rolled out the bicycle which he had learnt to ride

just the evening before. He could not be persuaded to have lunch before he set out, "Mother, I'd rather start straight away. I can eat later," he had said. Stuffing the packet of sandwiches into the pocket of his jacket he mounted the bicycle and set off.

Reports from the farm in the last few days had been more hopeful at least. It was now more than three weeks since Kate had fallen ill and only two days since the message had come back that for the first time Kate had been able to leave her bed and sit in a chair. Susan hoped that soon she would be able to come downstairs.

With this thought in his head Stanley pedalled like a man possessed - as indeed he was - the ten miles to Willow Farm. He didn't know, he said much later to Kate, that ten miles could be so little, why, he hardly noticed them! He didn't even notice some of the bigger puddles and one or two potholes that he was obliged to ride through. Ed, who had been in possession of a bicycle for some time, would have had to admit that, for a novice, Stanley had surmounted the problems of an unmended road rather well. He arrived at the farm only slightly muddied. As he opened the gate, Philip was coming out of the milking shed and caught sight of him.

"Wow, Stanley, that was quick. Didn't think the news would have got to Sprinton yet." Stanley was nonplussed but, since Philip was smiling he guessed that the news could only be good. Before he could reply Philip nodded towards the now less than pristine bicycle,

"That's a great looking machine. Have you just got it?"

"Yes," replied Stanley, "but what's the news? How's Kate?"

"Oh, they've got her downstairs," said Philip, "Just this afternoon. Go on in and you'll see her. But," giving Stanley's muddy shoes the once over, "best leave those shoes and the cape in the porch." Stanley propped the bike up outside the porch and then called out, "Hello! Can I come in?" He stepped out of his shoes and threw aside the cape he had been wearing. Susan's voice answered from the furthest room, which was the sitting room. The sitting, or 'best' room as it was often referred to, was at the back of the house and looked out on the meadow that sloped down to the willow bordered stream. Here a fire was usually only lit on Sundays but today logs were burning brightly in the grate and sending out rays of heat to the nearest armchair and sofa that encircled the fireplace. In the armchair, propped at her back by cushions and wrapped around in a blanket, sat Kate. Her face, paler and thinner than before the illness, lit up when Stanley entered the room, "Oh Stan," she looked at her mother and then back to Stanley, "is it really you?" Stanley's grin was the answer she got.

"Mother, is this your doing?" Susan was smiling too but she shook her head, "Not at all," she said, "but" to Stanley, "you've come at just the right time, Stanley. You'll be the tonic she's been needing," nodding back at Kate. "And now, don't exhaust her, while I go and make a pot of tea, and you can try and persuade her to eat something, because it's been the devil's own job to get anything down her except soup!" Susan disappeared towards the kitchen and Stanley drew a chair over beside Kate. For some minutes no words were exchanged. At length,

"My God, Kate...I thought, I was afraid," his voice tailed off and all he could do was gaze, again. Kate managed a smile,

"Oh, I couldn't leave without plaguing you a little longer." She reached for his hand and they sat thus connected until Susan came in with a tray on which were not only the tea things but a plate of ham sandwiches.

"Our own ham from our own pig, Miss, so you'd better try and show your thanks to the animal by tasting him at least," Susan said, trying to tempt her daughter to extend her appetite beyond the soups that had been her main diet for the last two weeks. Kate gave a little laugh,

"Oh well, I'd better do homage to our brother pig then," she said and reached for the plate. Since they had carried Kate home from Sprinton none of them had heard her laugh. The sound which all the family connected with this, their most high-spirited daughter, had not been heard, and some of them had feared it might never be heard again.

One hour and three ham sandwiches later Kate confessed herself tired and Susan helped her back upstairs to her bed.

"Stay and have tea with us Stanley," she called over her shoulder as she led Kate out of the room. "Yes, do, Stan", Kate's weaker voice added.

Stanley needed no more urging for, although it would seem odd to be sitting round the big farmhouse table without Kate being there, yet still he knew she was close by. If she should need anything, or call for him, he could be beside her in seconds. No, it was not difficult to agree to stay for tea and indeed, he put off leaving until the last minute. Susan saw him hesitating as he was about to leave, "Go on up and tell her you're going," she said, reading his mind. Stanley nodded and ran up the stairs. He tapped on the door and put his head round. Kate appeared to be sleeping but just as he was about to withdraw she opened her eyes and, seeing Stanley, she smiled, "I'm so glad…" she murmured before her eyes closed once again. "I'll come again tomorrow," he said.

The ride home seemed no longer than the ride out, indeed his state of mind was almost euphoric compared to the apprehension that had accompanied him when he left Sprinton. "She's much better," were Stanley's first words when he opened the back door and found his mother in the kitchen. Sarah smiled and sat down at their little kitchen table to hear Stanley's full account of his visit to Willow Farm.

Over the next three weeks Stanley spent more time on his bike than in his bed! He didn't notice and indeed he gained more muscle power in his legs than he had ever had before. He didn't notice that either for, the greatest gain of all was Kate's steady improvement in health. At the end of the second month Dr Frazer proclaimed her free of all congestion and, after a final examination, he declared that he considered that no permanent damage had been done to her lungs. They were, he said, as healthy as they had been before she caught the pneumonia.

CHAPTER 7

Moves

When Kate went back to work at Binns things were not quite the same. The company had kept her position open for her to return to, which was a relief. That she had been a valued employee was not in doubt, but there was more to it than that. It emerged that Kate had not been the only one to fall ill during the time of rebuilding, but she had been more seriously ill than any of the others. Nevertheless it would have given the company very bad publicity if it came out that a number of its employees had fallen ill, and one very seriously, due to the bad working conditions while building work was being done. Binns, an old and respected company that had a reputation for treating its workers well, at a time when that could not be taken for granted, did not want its reputation to be tarnished. Hence all its employees who had fallen ill had their jobs to go back to, and Kate had been absent for two months, the longest time of all. The shop had been enlarged; there was now a ready-made clothes department for men as well as women. Kate's realm in textiles was much the same but, the company had plans to open two new branches in two other smaller towns and word soon got around that the company was looking to send some of its most tried and trusted staff to run and establish these new branches. Of course these were much smaller than the Sprinton shop, but the person sent would be in charge and would have a lot of freedom to organise the business as they thought fit.

    Kate heard these rumours as soon as she returned to work but, concerned with getting back into the swing of things she paid little attention. However, before she had been back a week, the managing director of the company, Mark Edwards, asked her to go to see him in his office. It was Friday afternoon. For a moment Kate felt a frisson of fear: were they going to terminate her employment because she had been away for so long? When she was shown into the director's office, a large and pleasant room at the top of the building, she was not a little surprised to see that three of the five directors were gathered there sitting behind a long mahogany table at which directors meetings were usually held. Kate's apprehension was somewhat allayed however when the managing director began by telling her that the company valued her as a most competent and diligent member of their staff. He went on to say that, from the beginning she had shown a genuine interest in what she was doing, and at crucial moments in the company's history, when something above the ordinary was demanded, she had demonstrated imagination and foresight. Now, he said, they were aiming to expand by opening two new branches, one in Laverton, thirty miles south of Sprinton, and the other in High Bridge, fifteen miles north of Sprinton. The company would like to offer her the position of manageress at the Laverton branch. The director, registering Kate's surprise, went quickly on to add that Laverton was considered to be beneficial, as far as health was concerned, for people who had had any problem with their lungs. It had a long history as a small spa town; its mineral waters and its air, fresher than that of Sprinton, which lay in a hollow between the fens to the east and the uplands of the midlands, was also healthier. Kate was genuinely completely taken by surprise and, uncharacteristically was momentarily speechless. The director, perhaps interpreting her silence as reflecting some doubt she might have about the proposal, added quickly that the salary they anticipated for the post would also be higher than she had been getting in her present position. She would, after all, be taking on, and expected to exercise, a considerable degree of personal responsibility. She would be in charge and the directors expected that she would, at times, have occasion to exercise her own judgement in making decisions independent of the parent company.

Since she was truly taken by surprise and could not immediately gather her thoughts together to make a considered response, Kate could only answer for the moment that she felt honoured by the confidence that they showed in her and that she really must have a little time to consider all the aspects of it before giving her answer. The directors suggested she take the weekend to think it over and they would expect to have her decision at the beginning of the following week.

Kate had never envisaged leaving Sprinton, but if she had thought about it earlier then that would have been when the situation was different. She surely could not move away from Stanley, who she hoped to marry, even though, at the moment, that was more a hope than an event she could see happening in the near future. These thoughts and more flashed through her head as she made her way down to her department on the ground floor. Fortunately it was near to closing time, so the fact that she felt her mind preoccupied was not obvious to the rest of the staff and soon the blinds were being pulled down and the caretaker was standing by the door waiting for the staff to leave so that he could lock up.

Kate was thoughtful on her way home and her thoughts led her to the conclusion that she must see and speak to Stanley that very evening. Only very rarely had they been able to meet any time during the working week so, when Kate knocked on the door of number six, West Sidings, and it was opened by Stanley who had himself only just arrived home from work, his face when he saw her showed first surprise followed almost at once by concern. Kate spoke before Stanley had had time to open his mouth. "Stan, I need to talk to you, something happened at work today," Stanley looked alarmed, "oh no it's not bad, but I need to talk to you. Is your mother at home?" Sarah hadn't yet, as it happened, arrived back from The Bull. A lot of guests were due that evening and she needed to be there to make sure everything was in order Stanley explained. He led Kate into the kitchen and pulled out a chair for her at the kitchen table. She took a deep breath and began, "Stan, the directors just called me up to see them and…". Somewhat hesitantly she repeated the proposal made to her less than an hour before. "Stan, this was a complete surprise to me. I'd no idea of any such thing. Thing is, my first thought was, of course, I couldn't think of taking it, of going away from Sprinton, and you. But then I started to wonder," she looked at him uncertainly, "you know, the money could make quite a big difference and we would save more quickly and maybe have enough to start with after, well…" A hand gesture finished the sentence and her eyes searched Stanley's face anxiously. He knew what she meant. The move could mean that they would be able to marry much sooner. They both longed for it. But then, where would they live? If Sprinton then Kate would have to give up her well-paid job. If Laverton then Stanley would have to find work in another, smaller, town that had, as far as he knew, no engineering workshops. Stanley put these thoughts into words and they found themselves discussing seriously the proposal that Kate, at first hearing, had been on the point of dismissing as impossible.

"It is a nice town," Stanley eventually said reflectively. He had once passed through Laverton. One of Horner's engines used to drive machines in the town of Boxley needed a new part, and Stanley had had to accompany the chief engineer to carry out the work. Boxley was ten miles south of Laverton and they had passed through Laverton on the way. "And the air is supposed to be good…" he hesitated, not wanting to suggest that Kate was anything other than perfectly recovered from her recent illness, so he finished, "you know, for health." Their talk petered out, but it felt somehow optimistic. For Kate, it seemed to confirm that first vague intimation, as she walked to Stanley's house, that there might in fact be something to be said for the move. In addition their talk had shown that Stanley was not appalled at the idea, as he might have been, and as she thought he would be. They agreed to think it over, each 'in his or her own castle' as someone had said, and to talk further on the subject when they met the next day, their own, free, Saturday afternoon. When Kate left Stanley's house to return to her rooms at Mrs Robert's she found her steps were lighter and even there was perhaps a tingle of something like excitement somewhere around her heart, and in her head.

When Kate went to work on the following Monday morning it was with the feeling that a momentous decision had been made and a momentous change was about to take place in her life - well, not only in hers but in Stanley's too. It was with some trepidation that she went up to the top floor and requested an appointment to speak to the managing director.

The weekend meetings with Stanley had been taken up with discussing the proposal that had been made to Kate by her employers. If she accepted the offer and moved to Laverton what were the implications for their future together. Kate's doubts had all been concerned with the effect on Stanley of her moving away. "Kate, I want us to be together, soon," Stanley said. "And this move could help that. I also think Laverton would be a healthier place to live than Sprinton." He looked at her face, just as beautiful as it ever was, and yet somewhat paler and somewhat thinner than before the illness. Stanley had been finding out more about Laverton, and what he had heard, and read - he too had become a regular at the town's library - had persuaded him that a move to Laverton might be the making of them both. Laverton was renowned for its mineral water springs and for the quality of its air. There were no industries relying on coal furnaces or heavy metal production and while that might seem to be a negative aspect in terms of employment opportunities for a mechanic, there were, it seemed, openings for other kinds of mechanical workshops. The only large business in the town in fact was a distillery which made oils and essences from the fields of lavenders, peppermints and other herbs which were grown nearby and in the surrounding countryside. It was said indeed that in the spring and summer the air was full of the scents of the flowers and herbs that were used in the production of those oils and perfumes. Who would not exchange the smells of the dirt and oils of heavy industry for the scents and oils of lavender and herbs? Yes, Laverton would be a good place for Kate to be and, although Dr Frazer had pronounced her fully recovered from the pneumonia, Stanley couldn't help noticing that she still seemed weaker than before, and sometimes she coughed in a way that made Stanley uneasy, even though Kate insisted that she simply felt a tickle in her throat and it really was nothing at all.

Kate was given an appointment to see Mark Edwards just after lunchtime. He had taken over as managing director just two years before Kate joined the company. Due to ill health his father had been forced to retire early. Mark Edwards was thus thrust into the position of highest authority and responsibility when he was still quite a young man. He came into the position with enthusiasm and proved to have ideas about the future of the company which were both forward looking and practical. The business had been started by Samuel Binns, his maternal grandfather, fifty years before, as a retailer of textiles made in the nearby midland industrial towns but, under the founder's son and now his grandson the firm had been expanding ever since.

Mark Edwards was also a good reader of people. He observed his staff closely and could see qualities in them which he judged to be of value to the present and future prosperity of the company. Kate he had noticed from the beginning because he saw that she was not just concerned to carry out her duties correctly but she was also genuinely interested in the materials in her department. She knew how they were produced, their qualities, and even their history. More than that she was good at dealing with customers of all sorts. Yes, he was convinced that she would be the right choice for the new shop in Laverton.

"Miss Atkinson," he said when Kate entered his office and told him that she would like to take up his offer of the position of manager of the new shop, "I feel sure that you will not regret your decision, and I am confident that you will maintain the reputation of the firm for quality and service. We, I speak of all the directors, not only myself, have seen that you are a good organizer and can get your staff to work well together and in a positive spirit. These are all important qualities in a manager." He paused and then continued, "Well now, let us discuss in more detail the arrangements and the plans that we have for the Laverton shop."

Kate was detained for another hour while the managing director explained their plan for the branch in Laverton and what her part in it would be. At the end of the discussion Mark Edwards suggested that Kate should go and visit the town, the company would pay her fare. She could look about, visit the premises that they were already negotiating to rent, and perhaps even start looking for lodgings for herself. Kate had made no mention of Stanley - she did not want to complicate the situation by raising doubts in the director's mind about how long she could be counted on to remain in her post, but she silently resolved that she would take Stanley with her on that exploratory visit. It was important that he should see everything too, and she wanted to hear what he thought of the place.

It was early summer and the Laverton shop was projected to open at the beginning of August. Laverton being something of a spa and holiday town there was a sizable increase in the population in the months of July and August and the company hoped that they would be able to attract a good clientele of both visitors and residents before the season had ended. That would surely help them to be able to account themselves properly established in the town. Kate began to feel quite excited at the prospect of the move and the new venture.

"We are to specialize in materials and accessories to begin with," she told Stanley when they met that evening - she wanted to tell him all that had transpired in her interview with Mark Edwards. Her face lit up and in her voice there was a spirit and enthusiasm that Stanley suddenly realised had been missing since Kate had been ill, and which was formerly such an integral part of her. He smiled back at her, "And you will be the best accessory of all!" She laughed. "You'll come with me to look at the place, won't you?"

Stanley pulled a comical face, "well, if I must….when do you want to go?"

The following Saturday was agreed upon. Laverton had no railway station but there was a train service from Sprinton to the town of Boxley from which to Laverton was a short bus-ride. Kate was given the day off to make the visit and Stanley, who had been working overtime for several weeks, got time off from Horner's too.

The visit to Laverton confirmed both Kate and Stanley in the conviction that the move was a good idea. The town had a permanent population of not quite ten thousand people which was swelled in the summer months by several thousand visitors. Those who came to benefit from the spa facilities, the mineral waters, warm baths and herbal infusions, usually stayed a week, lodging in the spa hotel, in one of the inns or, taking lodgings in private houses. A good number of the permanent residents of the town made a supplementary income from taking in lodgers who were visiting the baths or trying the waters, for a shorter or longer time. Laverton had become a spa town in the eighteenth century when the mineral and hot spring waters were first 'discovered' to have health benefits by a doctor Fenwick when he made a visit to friends who lived in the town. The good doctor decided to settle in Laverton himself, had built a fine stone house on land close to the head of the spring and advertised in London and other parts of the country, offering accommodation and treatment for asthmatic and respiratory disorders. Within less than a decade the spa town of Laverton had almost doubled in size; many more fine stone houses were built as well as a colonnaded bath house. Having become frustrated by the difficulty of obtaining good quality herbal medicines, which were a supplement to the bath and water treatments, the Doctor then decided that he would have to cultivate and process his own. He bought several hundred acres of land close to the town on which he grew his own herbs, lavenders and peppermints. Aided by his son, who had trained as an apothecary, he then designed and directed the building of a distillery where the herbs could be variously processed. Between hospitality for the spa clients and sowing, tending, harvesting and processing the herbs at the distillery, there was no shortage of employment for the inhabitants of Laverton. At the time when Kate moved from Sprinton to Laverton it was a bustling and thriving community, the potential for which Mark Edwards had seen when he first explored new locations for the expansion of his company.

On that first visit Kate and Stanley went first to the premises where the shop would be and met the landlord who was in the process of overseeing the cleaning and repainting of the interior after the departure of the previous tenant. The building was in the market place, on the corner where two main roads met. A market was held twice a week, on Wednesdays and Saturdays. On the Saturday of Kate and Stanley's visit the market was bustling with local and out-of-town shoppers. The interior of the proposed shop was a large area with a big display window and a door opening onto the street. Behind the shop were two more rooms, one obviously a store room and a smaller room which would serve as both office and staff room. There was an outside privy.

Looking around the shop space Kate could begin to imagine how she would like to set out and display her goods and the disposition of the counter and cabinets. "Oh Stan, you should be running this business with me," Kate exclaimed, after Stanley had suggested an improvement on one of her ideas. The landlord was a stocky, middle-aged man with long greying side whiskers. He was polite but taciturn and gave the impression of having a somewhat jaded view of human nature, which might well have been due to experiences he had had with some of his tenants. He was clearly relieved to have got rid of the previous one who had, it seemed, been less than conscientious about paying the rent and he was more than satisfied to be getting a branch of Binns Emporium as the new tenant. Binns of Sprinton was renowned in the district; it was the longest established and most reliable retail business in the area. To get Binns as a tenant was in truth the best any proprietor could hope for. Consequently, when Stanley noticed and pointed out that the heater, a paraffin stove, which would be essential during the winter half of the year, was grossly under-dimensioned for the space that it was supposed to heat, the landlord conceded the point straight away and promised that he would install a bigger and better heater before the autumn chills should begin to be felt.

After visiting the proposed shop they took a stroll around the rest of the town and it had to be said that they found that 'every prospect pleased'. As well as the Spa Hotel, which was close to the Bath House in The High Street, there were two more hotels and several inns which also had accommodation. The Victoria Hotel and one of the biggest inns were on the north side of the marketplace, beside the Town Hall, while the New Inn, beside the chemist and the police station were opposite, on the south side of the marketplace, and behind them ran the river Deane, where punts and rowing boats could be hired during the summer months.

The air too, they declared, seemed fresh and invigorating, although, since the day of their visit was rather warm and still, that judgement might have been more a comment on their mood than an accurate report on the quality of the air. All in all it was a happy and optimistic day and it is doubtful whether even a heavy shower of rain could have dampened their spirits. But no shower materialised and when they took the bus on the first leg of their return journey to Sprinton it was with a sense of happy expectation about Kate's move to Laverton.

On the Saturday following the visit to Laverton Kate took the afternoon bus out to Willow farm. It was the first visit home since her illness, and she had not said anything to the family about what had been happening since she went back to work. She found William driving the cows into the barn for milking. He called out to Kate as the last of the herd went in, "They're round the back at the henhouse," he said, "we've had foxes again. Lost half a dozen of the good layers. They'll be pleased to see you...that'll cheer them up" and he disappeared into the barn.

Kate found her parents at the henhouse. They had been burying the unusable remains of the ravaged chickens and blocking up all entry holes they could find to the henhouse. Susan greeted Kate, "This is the second time this month and we thought we'd blocked off all the ways in there were," she said. "Well, we've done all we can for now. George," calling to her husband who was in the meadow beyond the chicken run, "We'll go and make a cup of tea." Susan put her arm through Kate's and they made their way to the house. "This is infuriating, love," she said, giving Kate's arm a squeeze. "Well, you're looking better at least," she stepped away from Kate's side to get a good look at her face, "You've got the colour back in your cheeks and I do believe you've put on a little weight - good."

"So how has it been back at Binns'?" Susan asked as they were setting out the tea things in the kitchen. Kate sat down at the kitchen table and looked over at her mother. "Well, interesting!" She replied. Before Susan could respond she hurried on, "Mother, I'm offered promotion. The only thing is, it means moving." Susan now was looking puzzled.

"Moving? What do you mean?" And so Kate told her mother about the new Binns that was going to open in Laverton and that she had accepted the position of manageress in the new shop. "Well, and what does Stanley think about that?" was Susan's response.

"Well, we went together last Saturday to Laverton to see the shop - it's being painted and refurbished at the moment. We met the owner of the premises and he's pleased to be getting Binns as a tenant. And Stanley is all in favour of the move. We saw all over the town. It's very pleasant, with the spa and all."

"Where will you live?"

"Well, I'll probably have to find lodgings and we did ask around on Saturday but, the landlord, his name's Anderson, said that there's a flat above the shop (he owns the whole building) which is now vacant. It needs a bit of 'fixing up' before he lets it out again but that would be a possibility - depending on what he charges of course. I think what I'll do is I'll take lodgings for a month to start with and then see what happens about the flat." George came into the kitchen at that point and so of course Kate had to repeat all that she had just told her mother.

In the six years that it had now been since Kate left the farm to go and live and work in Sprinton George's sadness at the loss of his favourite daughter had been transmuted by time into acceptance of the inevitable. The children were now all grown up and, apart from the three still at home, dispersed out into the world. William and Philip were running the farm and Ivy did her bit too, as well as taking a good many of the heavier household chores off Susan's hands. Susan was still fiercely in command around the house - and henhouse - but she was troubled with rheumatism so that the assistance of Ivy in the washing and cleaning, and with the chickens, was become not just a help but a necessity.

"I don't know what I'd do now," Susan confided to George on more than one occasion, "if Ivy had decided to follow Kate and move into town. We would have to get a girl in from one of the other farms!" So they were content that Ivy had changed her mind and stayed on the farm after all. As for the other children well, closest was Rose, who had married her farmer, John Newton, and lived just six miles away at Newton Farm near the village of Selby. She was now the mother of three small children whose ages ranged from four to two and the baby just six months old, so there was rarely the time or opportunity for Rose to visit Willow Farm. It was usually Susan, together with Ivy, who managed to trot over to see Rose instead. They would harness up the pony and trap and, carefully depositing in a basket a gift of a couple of dozen eggs and a stone jar of almost a gallon of their creamy milk, they would trot the leafy lanes to visit Rose and see the babes at Newton Farm. Rose and Jack had no chickens, nor cattle, John having decided to concentrate his efforts on cereal crops, sugar beet and potatoes, so the gifts from Willow Farm were always very welcome.

Violet, who had gone into service, was almost always at the London house of her employers nowadays and only once or twice a year at their country house, Foxton Manor, from whence a visit home was possible. Kate was in Sprinton, at ten miles distant and, last and furthest away (apart from Harry who had now been in Canada for almost ten years) was Colin who was, well, sometimes they didn't know where he was, for the army moved his regiment, George said, 'in mysterious ways' and they often didn't know where Colin was until he was somewhere else!

Well, so now Kate would be moving a bit further away from home. From Willow Farm to Laverton must be at least forty miles and the journey there would involve both buses and a train journey. The so far regular visits of Kate home, once a fortnight in the first years in Sprinton, once a month in the last two years, would inevitably be less frequent. It could not be helped, that was, increasingly it seemed, how life was; but at least everyone knew that Laverton had a reputation as a healthy place to live - and they had all been seriously worried when Kate fell ill with pneumonia and had to be carried home to be nursed. George had never known such personal anxiety in his life before. The war, which had been raging for nearly a year now, meant less to him than Kate's illness. He really had had fears that he was going to lose his favourite daughter, so that, when the crisis came, the fever subsided and she started to improve George knew that whatever happened afterwards, and wherever she was, nothing mattered except that she was alive and could always be reached somehow. When Kate went for the bus back to Sprinton her parents waved her off, therefore, not with sorrow in their hearts but in the knowledge that she was very much alive, was happy and about to embark on a new venture. Forty miles distance, with the promise of meeting again really quite soon, was as nothing to what might have been the silence of eternity.

CHAPTER 8

Getting Ready

There was much that had to be arranged in the following few weeks. Word came that the premises in Laverton were now ready for the new tenant to move in and so the goods had to be chosen and ordered from manufacturers and wholesalers. The managing director proposed to visit the premises and check that everything had been done satisfactorily and to sign the contract for renting for an initial period of two years - all being well this would be extended for a further period as yet unspecified. Mark Edwards took Kate with him and it was the longest journey she had ever been in a motor car. She marvelled at how comfortable it was and that they could travel the forty miles so quickly.

The premises were deemed satisfactory and Mark Edwards approved the suggestions Kate made about the positioning of the counter and other furnishings that would be needed to accommodate the stock. The ideas that Kate had for the window dressing and for the accessories would necessitate customised stands and hangers. A list was made of all that was needed and, before they set out to return to Sprinton, Kate went to call on a Mrs Taylor in North Street who had a room to let. The house proved to be large and well kept so that she had no difficulty in deciding to take it; what was more, the house stood only a short distance from the site of the new Binns. It was in a spirit of optimism and even elation that both parties climbed back into the motor for the return journey to Sprinton.

The move to Laverton took place at the end of July. "You really need a donkey," Stanley, who was helping her, joked, "but donkeys aren't allowed on trains, so you'll have to make do with me!" Stanley's light-heartedness had the beneficial effect of dissipating some of the tension that Kate was feeling in the throes of packing and deciding what to leave behind and what to take. In the course of the six years in which she had lived under the roof of Mrs Robert's house she had accumulated some household goods and, since she hoped they would be needed in the not too distant future, she was anxious to keep them, but they would have to be stored somewhere for the time being. Her parents offered to take them back to the farm, and even Sarah said that they could be stored at West Sidings, but the dilemma was best solved when Mrs Roberts suggested leaving everything she didn't need immediately, with her. After all, she said, she had rooms to spare apart from the ones Kate had occupied for the last six years. In truth, Mrs Roberts was more than a little sad to say goodbye to Kate whom she had come to regard as 'almost' a daughter. "You will come back to see me, won't you?" she pleaded. Kate promised that she would.

It was an emotional farewell to Sprinton. Not including the family at Willow farm, everyone who meant anything to her was in that town: Stanley first and foremost, of course, but then there was Aunt Daisy and her cousins, Lucy Staines and the girls from Binns, and Sarah. Was she really doing the right thing in moving to another town where she knew no one? She looked back at Stanley as they boarded the train that would take them on the first part of the journey. Heaving her two cases into the carriage behind her Stanley looked up at Kate and read the anxiety in her face. "It'll be fine," he said, "don't worry." When they were settled in their seats Stanley took her hand. "It's not very far you know. I'll write every week and come down as often as I can."

The lodgings in Laverton were comfortable, and the two sisters whose house it was were welcoming and friendly, the elder being a widow and the younger engaged to a young man who was in the army and whose battalion had recently been sent to France. When Stanley left to return to Sprinton the two sisters invited Kate to join them for tea, so that it was only later when she retired to her own room that she felt the first pangs not exactly of loneliness but rather of 'aloneness' and an acute longing to be able to speak to Stanley. To stave off this feeling she set about unpacking her things. There was one large wardrobe, with a full length mirror on the inside of the door, and a chest of drawers: the two together provided room and to spare for the clothes, the toiletries and the few other things which she had brought with her. These last consisted of her little clock, the first present from her parents when she had left home and moved into the town to begin work; writing paper, pen and ink because, for the first time since leaving home she was going to have to keep in touch with family and friends by post; and two books, so that she would have something to read in the evenings after she came home from work and the evening meal was over. She had already ascertained that Laverton had a library and reckoned with joining it as soon as she could. There was a small drop-leaf table in her room too and one upright and one, also small, arm-chair. The elder sister, Mrs Taylor, whose house it was, had told Kate that while she assumed that she would eat her evening meal with her and her sister, nevertheless, if she wished on some occasions to eat in her own room, she could.

After the unpacking, and everything now in its place, she sat down at the little table to write to Stanley. "Dearest," she wrote, "I have unpacked all my things and am almost settled in, but oh, how I miss you already." She paused and lifted pen from paper. "I don't somehow think I'll send this," she said out loud to herself, "but it feels good to write it anyway." Then she began again on another sheet of paper,

'The sisters are being very kind. They invited me to have tea with them and I learnt something of their history. Mrs Taylor was the oldest in their family and her husband died two years ago of a consumption. There are twelve years and three brothers between her and Miss Emily, the younger one, whose young man, her fiancé, signed up nine months ago and whose battalion was recently sent over to France. She seems a rather sweet person and is understandably quite anxious about her fiancé. She is also a very skilled seamstress. She showed me a dress she has just finished, for a lady in the town, which is beautifully done. When I listened to her talk about her fiancé too I thought that I have no cause really to complain about our separation. We have a good roof over our heads and, all being well, a much smaller chance of being killed or maimed in the near future. But it has made me very aware of the dangers of being anywhere near weapons so - please, please take care..'

She lifted the pen from paper again and fell into a reverie with her head resting on her hand. Under orders from the government, Horner's, like so many engineering works all over the country, were in the process of moving their production from railway and agricultural engines to munitions. The war had not been over by Christmas as had at first, optimistically, been prophesied, and more and more young men seemed blithely to be joining the armed forces. Workplaces like Stanley's were not in the battlefield, but they were more dangerous than they had been. A shiver went down her spine when she thought about it, but writing to Stanley made her feel better anyway. It was as near to a conversation with him as she could get at the moment.

Back in Sprinton, after he had had something to eat and had told his mother about Laverton and Kate's lodgings, Stanley went up to his room and sat down to write a letter too.

Standing, as it did, on the market place and at the junction of two main roads the Laverton Binns was number one, Market Place. For a reason that she couldn't quite explain, Kate felt that this was somehow a good omen, and when she arrived at the shop early on Monday morning, put her key in the lock and opened the door her heart lifted as at the beginning of an adventure. With the directors of Binns in Sprinton it had been agreed that the Laverton shop should open for the first time on Tuesday since Kate would need one whole day at least to get everything unpacked and in place in the shop. Mark Edwards was going to come down on the Thursday to see how everything was going and to hear Kate's progress report. The landlord had let her into the premises and given her the keys the day before and, being more than pleased at acquiring such a prestigious tenant as Binns, he very willingly helped Kate with all the lifting, carrying and moving of heavy goods and shop furnishings that required more muscle strength than she had. After the earlier visit to Laverton with Mr. Edwards, Kate, having retained a clear image of the interior in her mind, made sketches of possible arrangements of glass cabinets, of stands and window displays. By the end of Monday afternoon, and with the help of the landlord, she had everything in place - she was particularly pleased with her window-dressing and hoped that it would attract potential customers to enter the shop - ; the till, a shining new black one with brass keys, sat on a piece of matting on a corner of the largest glass cabinet. It had been agreed with the directors that during the first week of opening customers would be offered one yard of narrow lace edging, white or beige, or four pearl buttons, free, to all who spent at least one guinea.

The Laverton Binns had been advertised in the local paper and a bold but elegant metal framed glass sign, with the name Binns in red enamel, had been in place above the shop window for a week before the opening. Nevertheless, when she went to open the door to admit 'the public' Kate was agreeably surprised to find that there was already quite a crowd of people waiting to come in. In fact, the whole of the day, except for the lunchtime closing hour, was busy beyond anything she could have imagined. By closing time at five thirty in the afternoon she could not count, off hand, the yards of white lace and number of pearl buttons, that she had wrapped and included with the purchases of those customers who had spent more than one guinea. It took her more than an hour after closing time to count up the takings, to estimate how many yards of lace and how many pearl buttons she had left, and how many yards of cotton, silk and woollen cloth, of trimming for hats, and pairs of cotton and crocheted gloves, among other things, that she had sold. She could imagine that one week of trading at the same rate might empty the shop. She had better get a message to Mr. Edwards, who was coming on Thursday, to tell him to bring some items with him from Sprinton, or else she stood a fair chance of being embarrassed before the week was out. It was also brought home to her that the installation of a telephone needed to be given top priority. And her next thought was that she would have given the world to be able at that moment to speak to Stanley.

When she got home to The Cedars (the rather grand name of the house, which, not quite accurately, referred to the single large and beautiful cedar of Lebanon that stood in the garden behind the house) the sisters were agog to hear how her first day of trading had gone.
"My dear Miss Atkinson," breathlessly from the younger sister, "we came by before lunchtime intending to come in but there appeared to be more ladies inside than could comfortably be accommodated so we decided we would wait until tomorrow. Are you very pleased with your opening day?" Kate confessed that she was very pleased indeed, "But, you know, the test only comes after two or three months. People are always intrigued by the new - I just hope we can establish a good steady business…" she paused, "but yes, it was a very good day and there were a lot of enquiries about all sorts of things." She stopped, suddenly overcome with tiredness, and accepted with gratitude the cup of tea which Mrs Taylor offered her adding, as Kate raised it to her lips, "I added something a little stronger Miss Atkinson. You must be really quite tired!"

The following day was much like the first and it became clear to her that Mark Edwards had been quite right in thinking that all those seasonal visitors to Laverton who came principally for the baths and the mineral waters, were in fact often in need of a break from their cures; and there was almost nothing by way of retail outlets in Laverton except for groceries and a dairy. The establishment of a Laverton Binns looked to be fulfilling a need that had been waiting to be satisfied.

The Cedars was one of the few private houses in the town which boasted a telephone so Kate, with Mrs Taylor's willing permission, had been able to contact Mark Edwards in Sprinton and request that he bring with him, on the morrow, certain additional items which she could see that she was soon going to run out of, if demand remained the same as it had been in the first few days.

The elation that the first two days of trading had given rise to did not fade and Kate could not help smiling when Mark Edwards arrived at the shop just before eleven the next morning. He soon saw that the report Kate had given him over the telephone was more than justified for, until she closed the shop at noon for lunch hour, he was not able to have more than a couple of minutes uninterrupted conversation with her. New customers were arriving all the time.

"Well, one thing is clear" was the first thing he said when Kate had closed and locked the shop door after the last remaining customer. "We must get you at least a part time assistant." They then fell to discussing all that had happened since the opening, what had been sold, what questions customers had asked and, finally, how they should proceed. Mark Edwards had no doubt that he, and his fellow directors of course, had made the right choice in getting Kate to manage the new shop. As he waited between each burst of customers for Kate to be free to talk to him he observed her in her work. There was a graciousness, a charm even in the way she spoke and greeted each one. At the same time she was clearly in command and she had the ability to reassure customers even when she was unable to answer a question she had been asked.

As he watched her a new thought struck him. How was it that a young woman with her looks was not already married? Well, thank goodness for that, of course, but there must surely be someone. Perhaps she had a fiancé who was fighting in France - and so many of them never came back. How little he knew about the personal life of even a most, was the word 'cherished', employee? When Kate turned to him with a smile after seeing out the last customer, Mark Edwards, with a conscious effort, recalled his mind to the business in hand.

By the time he left to drive back to Sprinton in mid afternoon a number of things had been decided, chief among which was that a female sales assistant should be taken on, initially part time, and a telephone should be installed as soon as possible. Furthermore Kate was empowered to order stock direct from the wholesalers and manufacturers and, lastly, Mark Edwards would pay a visit at least once a month, to give her support, he hastened to add, as well as getting her business report and checking up on the premises (they might have to increase, somehow, the storage capacity - and Mark Edwards feared there might be a problem with damp along the outside wall of the store room.) Altogether it had been a successful day, Kate reflected, and, by Saturday lunchtime when she closed, she could say it had been a successful first week. Of course it was true, as she had said to the sisters, that you couldn't really tell how the business was going until you had weathered at least the first three months but, nevertheless, there were strong indications that the Laverton Binns was likely to flourish. There was no other shop like it in the town, nowhere at all where you could buy textiles or clothing accessories and the questions she had been asked most often during that first week were: could they get their materials made up into dresses, blouses or skirts in Laverton and was the Laverton Binns going to have ready made ladies outfits?

The following Monday morning Kate put a notice in her window advertising the position of sales assistant, part time. Before the morning was over she had had six young women come into the shop wishing to be considered for the position. Two were very young, much like Kate had been when she moved into Sprinton from the farm at seventeen. They were working as maids in two of the town's hotels and wanted to do something different. The oldest applicant was a single woman of twenty nine. Her face wore a somewhat serious expression and her dress was likewise, dark and severe. She had been the companion to a wealthy widow of a local corn merchant. The widow had now also died and Miss Lewis, for such was her name, had decided that she too would try something different. She had no experience of retail or fashion but, she assured Kate, she knew good cloth when she saw it and, what was more she had 'sharp eyes'. Slightly mystified by this Kate looked a question mark at Miss Lewis, who returned a meaningful look at her and tapped the side of her nose, "I can pick out a thief before she's picked up the goods," she said, "and I know you'll need to have sharp eyes in a shop like this one." Miss Lewis, Kate decided was the least suited for the job but, as with the others, she made a note of her name and address and said she would let her know.

One of the remaining three applicants was a young woman of twenty three - she volunteered her age when starting to explain why she wanted the position and why she thought she would be suitable. She wore a wedding ring, the only one of the six who had, and, until very recently it would have been rare to find a married woman seeking work outside her home. But times were changing, and since the war had begun they were changing dramatically. Although the dress and jacket the young Lily James was wearing looked as though they were far from new yet there was a neatness and cut about them that showed taste and a sense of style. She had never worked in a shop before, she explained, but she had sewn and made her own and her family's clothes since she was very young. After leaving school though, at thirteen, Lily had had to go and be, as she put it, 'maid of all work' to a farming family just outside the town, since her father became crippled and they were a large family. At eighteen she was married to the boy 'who followed the plough' on the Dugdale's farm. He had joined up in the first months of the war. "He said he thought he could provide better for us in the army than on the farm," Lily said, almost angrily, "and then he got himself killed," it was almost a whisper. "I'm living back at home and my mam takes care of Will" (her two year old son) " so there wouldn't be any problem if the hours were irregular, nor the days of the week. I've been doing some sewing and alterations, like, for some of the town folks, but it doesn't bring in enough." She looked down, as if ashamed to admit the poverty in which her family were living. But when she looked up there was a glint of defiance in her eyes and she went on, "I still follows the fashions though. Some of the misses give me the magazines and I've made some of they dresses in there. These cloths are lovely. I know I could learn all about them - and sew them up," she added with a wistful glance at the rolls of cloth displayed around the shop. It wasn't just the girl's sadness or her plight that touched Kate's heart though. It was her yearnings and aspiration that she recognised. Something told her that Lily could develop, that there was potential within her despite the buffetings of misfortune and tragedy. Her will was not broken. Kate knew that she would give Lily James the job.

CHAPTER 9

Beginnings, War and a Wedding

Setting out early on Sunday morning, at the end of the second week of August, Stanley cycled the thirty miles from Sprinton to visit Kate. Since he had first acquired the bike when she was ill Stanley had discovered the joys of bicycling. The activity of peddling, in itself he had found was therapeutic; it exercised the body while freeing up the mind. A thirty mile ride was good thinking time.

When he arrived he wheeled the bicycle round to the back of the house, as Kate had instructed, and she came out to greet him. Stanley held her close, overwhelmed by a tangle of emotions, of love mixed with relief that all had gone so well for her in the new venture; for, if truth be told, he had been not a little plagued by guilt, imagining that perhaps he had pushed her too much into accepting the position, and that his motives, at least the financial one, were somehow not honourable. If she had been unhappy in Laverton he knew he would feel that he was partly responsible; but his fear had proved unfounded and those first two weeks had been little short of a triumph for her.

She wanted Stanley to see what the shop looked like fully furnished and with all her goods displayed and so she took him first of all to see it. He was full of praise and couldn't help but be impressed.

Afterwards they went to the Victoria Hotel for lunch. Kate had been told that the Victoria served a good traditional Sunday lunch for a very reasonable price. The report was true, it was just that they had so much to talk about that the Victoria's good roast beef got rather little attention. When they left the Victoria they wandered in the fields which bordered the river Deane and sat in the shade of a willow tree on the river bank. The sun shone, the meadow flowers were in full bloom and the trees in summer leaf. Sometimes they sat silent but entwined. It was a day they wished would never end. Returning to the Cedars in the late afternoon the sisters offered to serve them tea and some of Mrs Taylor's renowned fruitcake on the lawn beside the cedar tree.

It was with a much lighter heart at any rate, that Stanley prepared to leave Kate and return to Sprinton. The two hours ride, sometimes uphill, seemed somehow nothing at all. He knew that Kate was happy, that the shop looked like being a success, and she was in high spirits. He had seen too that the bloom had returned to her cheeks and the climate agreed with her. It agreed with Stanley too. There was a scent of lavender in the air, and something else, just a faint perfume that came and went. Yes, it was a good place for Kate to be, he thought. In fact it would be a good place for them both to live.

The following year saw the Laverton Binns go from strength to strength. Under Kate's guidance and instruction her part-time assistant, Lily James, learnt how to deal with customers, of all kinds, and not to be intimidated, to be mannerly and to remain calm. Lily also learnt all that Kate could teach her about materials, whether wool or cotton or silk and linen. They extended their range of accessories to hats and bags and were considering having some readymade ladies garments since they were always being asked if they could recommend any local dressmakers. One result of this was that, beginning in a small way, Kate commissioned a more than willing Lily to take on alterations to gowns, sometimes it was gussets, sometimes hems or waistlines; and when she had satisfied herself that Lily's work was good, they agreed that she might make bespoke garments. Branching out into selling ready made garments would have to wait though, since the war meant that the supply of materials did not stretch much further than to military or very plain day wear.

Lily alone, however, even in wartime, could not satisfy local demand and so, in the next few months, through new contacts, Kate managed to acquire a band of willing, local seamstresses, to whom she could refer her customers. Emily Dickens, the younger of Kate's landladies, was one of them. From time to time, indeed increasingly often, she became willing to put her talents to work and, skilled with the needle and with an artist's eye for style, she was able to create garments of beauty even in those difficult times. This work became important to Emily for a number of reasons. The money it earned her gave her a degree of independence and the means to contribute to the expenses of the household which she shared with her sister. But at the beginning it was chiefly important as a distraction and channel for grief when the news reached them that her fiancé, not many months at the Front, in France, had been killed in battle at a place called Loos.

Kate came back to the house at lunchtime one day to find all the curtains at the front drawn and when she stepped into the hall the sound of sobbing stopped her in her tracks. Mrs Taylor came out of the back parlour, white faced and with the unmistakable signs of recent tears on her cheeks. "Oh, Miss Atkinson, terrible news. My sister's young man has been killed." Together they went back into the parlour and Kate put her arm round the stricken girl.

It was just a few weeks after this that Kate, pretending that one of the other dressmakers had more commissions to fulfil than she could manage, asked Emily if she could possibly step into the breach, and help her out. Thrown out to her as a lifeline at a time of crisis, this activity became a way of life for Emily Dickens and eventually it was not only a busy one but she also found it fulfilling since she began to make her own patterns and design garments for which, after the war was over, there was an ever increasing demand.

Mark Edwards, as agreed, came once a month from Sprinton to see how the Laverton shop, and Kate, were getting on and to oversee the premises. It became his custom to take Kate for lunch at The Victoria on those occasions so that they could discuss the business away from the shop and in a more relaxed atmosphere. It allowed him to get to know his key staff better and there might sometimes be things, he thought, that needed to be discussed just between the two of them.

Six months after opening it became clear that they did need more storage space and there was a problem with damp. Behind the shop and adjoining the back store room was a stone built outhouse which had once been a one horse stable and carriage house when the former owner of the building drove her pony and trap to visit friends and relatives around the neighbourhood. It had stood empty for a number of years but, unlike the former storeroom, it was dry and mainly just in need of some plaster and paint on the inside, before it could become usable again. Mark Edwards persuaded the landlord that it could be worth his while to have the outhouse renovated since Binns would then be prepared to rent it from him in addition to the other premises. In this way the business was able to expand and, as it turned out, in all directions. The former coach house and stable gave more inside storage space than the store room behind the shop had; consequently that store room could be added to the shop - part of the wall between them was knocked down so that the original store room became simply an extension of the shop area - and by the middle of the second year they were able to begin selling some readymade ladies garments and their turnover was soon more than doubled. One part-time sales assistant was not enough and another had to be taken on. Lily had become excellent as sales woman but she was also doing dressmaking and alterations so that in effect she worked more than a full week. When the shop area was extended Kate had persuaded Mr Edwards to invest in one of the latest sewing machines and a curtained-off cubicle in the shop extension became Lily's sewing domain. Yes, the Laverton Binns was doing very well indeed and so was Kate, as manager. The only fly in the ointment, but it became a bigger one as time went on, was the separation from Stanley. Kate's longing for them to be together was becoming ever more intense.

....

By the end of the second year of war Horners had converted almost entirely to manufacturing munitions, and there seemed to be no end to the demand, as bloody battle succeeded ever bloodier battle in a conflict that had been meant to be over within a few months, but wasn't. Of course it was understood that the priority must be to produce as many of the most effective weapons as possible so that the Enemy could be defeated and the war ended. But Stanley was finding the work more and more repugnant. He began to hate the fact that day after day he was spending his working hours making machines the function of which was solely and specifically for the killing of human beings. It was depressing. The news coming out of Europe was depressing too, and the sight of more and more trainloads of wounded and crippled soldiers returning from France and Flanders was darkening everyone's mood. The first close death, so far, had been that of the younger brother of one of Stanley's oldest workmates, Jim Corbett. Jim came in to work late one morning. It had never happened before and indeed he was usually the first to arrive in the assembly workshop. When he came in, an hour late, his ashen face put an end to all speculation. Wilf had been killed when he was scarcely out of his trench. Their mother was distraught and another brother had joined up just a fortnight before. The mood in the workshop that morning was sombre, for there was scarcely a man there who had not a family member who was also at the front. Stanley felt a frisson of fear too. Jack was in Canada and Fred's work on the railways was essential to the continued running of them but, Charlie was in danger, and their mother was wracked with anxiety because of something that had happened a few weeks before.

Although it was true that Charlie had blossomed from the time when he went to live with his aunt and uncle after Sarah had brought her two younger sons to Sprinton in the aftermath of their father's death, yet physically Charlie remained delicate. Throughout his childhood he easily fell prey to infections and his sight in one eye was poor. He had struggled with his disabilities and overcome them to the extent that he had been able to leave school, at fourteen, with good reports, in spite of sometimes being absent, for weeks, because of illness. What

Charlie lacked in strength he made up for in determination, however, and he soon found himself a job with an old and respected firm of grain and cereal wholesalers. He had been with the firm for eight years now; he knew the business inside out and was well regarded by the firm and his workmates. His competence and dedication had brought him promotion and a move to the firm's main branch in High Bridge, fifteen miles north of Sprinton, where he had now been living and working for the past three years. One lunchtime Charlie had been walking through the town centre when two girls approached him and suddenly he found a white feather had been thrust at him. One of the girls made a mocking remark about the fact that he was not in uniform, before they made off in the direction of the market. Charlie stopped in his tracks, stunned, the white feather clinging to the front of his woollen jacket. The next day he went to the recruiting office and filled in the forms for the army. He went home to Sprinton the following weekend and in the course of a walk with Stanley told him what had happened and what he had done.

"I felt so ashamed," he said to his brother. "I couldn't bear it. I'm not a coward, Stan. I'm not - I just didn't think they'd ever accept me."

"I know you're not Charlie and you didn't need to go joining up. Whatever they say, this war is terrible; I hate what I'm doing. All these guns we make, you know they think up new and better ways to kill every day. Have you told Aunt Annie and Bert? They'll be heartbroken if you go."

"I know," Charlie's face was pinched and grey. "But I've got to, don't you see? After that I've got to go. I can't even walk down the street now without feeling that I'm being watched and despised."

Charlie wouldn't tell his mother what he had done so it was up to Stanley to tell her when Charlie had left them and gone back north. Sarah couldn't believe it and was beside herself with anguish. "Oh Stan, why did he have to do that? He's not fit. If they take him he'll die. I know he'll die - he could die before he's even been in any fighting..." Sarah had been toughened by her own tragedies and experiences, but this was a blow too much. She sank down at the kitchen table pale-faced. It was all that Stanley could do to calm her and control his own fear and horror at what could soon befall them. Stanley had never felt the absence of Kate as acutely as at that moment.

In the event their state of seemingly unbearable suspense lasted no more than two weeks, though it was the longest two weeks either Stanley or Sarah could remember; and they tried not to burden each other with the intensity of their anxiety. What those two weeks must have been like for Charlie was hard to imagine for his worry was more complex. If he was accepted then the likelihood was that he would be killed in battle or, due to his fragile constitution, would succumb to disease since the climate in northern France in autumn and winter, combined with the wet and rat infested conditions in the trenches, could easily prove fatal. If he was rejected then he would be stuck in the place where he had been already, unjustly and from ignorance, assaulted and humiliated.

Charlie *was* rejected by the military, not because of his weak chest but because of his eye. The army medical officer who had tested him wrote, with underlinings, that he would never be able to aim any weapon accurately and he could be a danger to their own side, as well as unable practically to inflict any directed harm on the enemy. Although he could realistically have expected this result Charlie was crushed by it. He could not face continuing to live and work as before and he found some excuse for giving up his job in High Bridge and moved back to Sprinton where he effectively went into hiding with his aunt and uncle. For a time he hardly went out of the house and scarcely spoke. The unspoken fear of Annie and Bert, of Sarah and Stanley, was that Charlie might take his own life. For Sarah and Stanley's family these were the most harrowing months of all.

Then the war entered a new phase, its third year and, ironically, this might be said to have saved Charlie's life. So many men had left Horner's to go and fight, that the factory was now critically short-handed. Under normal circumstances Charlie would never have been taken on by them for the work was physically too demanding and heavy; but so acute was the labour shortage that normal restrictions were being waived, or the company turned a blind eye to them and Charlie, even with his one defective eye and weak chest, was taken on. Stanley had a hand in it too, for he sensed that desperate measures were needed to get Charlie out of the deep hole of despair in which he had found himself, and which his family found they were powerless to help him out of. Consequently, for the first time in their adult lives the two brothers were now working for the same firm but, while Stanley grew to detesting more and more the end product of the work, Charlie was comforted by the feeling that he was now contributing to the war effort and could not be accused of cowardice or of trying, by any means, to avoid the conflict. It took time for Charlie to come out of his depression but, with the routine of the work, even the sometimes deafening noise and the smell of grease and metal, it was clear that they were in the midst of hard and warlike machinery; and Charlie finally regained, if not exactly his former cheerfulness, at least a degree of composure. Unbeknown to

Charlie, his brother had managed to get him a position supervising a machine that mass produced smaller components of one of their tanks. In this way he was saved from the heavier tasks of hauling, lathing and fitting together parts of bigger weapons, tasks for which he had in any case never been trained. Supervision of 'his' machine was also important work since, deprived of anyone to supervise it, after the previous man had gone into the army, it had been malfunctioning and holding up production much too often; consequently Charlie's work really was essential and he felt that it was.

It was not long after this, and in what turned out to be the last months of the war, that the Atkinsons too suffered the loss of a son. William and Philip had been running the farm, almost single-handedly, as their labourers had either volunteered or been called up into the army. They were left in place since, whatever happened the population had somehow to continue to be fed. In this respect they were fortunate, and William in any case was now in his forties. But the youngest son of the family, the formerly wayward and maverick Colin, who seemed to have found his niche when he went off and joined the Limeshire Yeomanry, had been drafted with his battalion into the war from the very beginning. In a world that was fast moving into machines that could travel faster than any horse, it had been Colin's happy fate to find one sphere where the horse was not yet outmoded - the Yeomanry regiments. In the first years of the conflict his battalion had been on active service in a part of the world he would otherwise probably never have seen, as he sailed through the Mediterranean with his fellows, horses and baggage. Colin's thirst for activity and excitement was amply satisfied in the initial period of what became a World War, and in the deserts of North Africa he fought but suffered no injury. Then modernity caught up with Colin and his companions-in-arms, and the horse was taken out of warfare. Some among them, in sorrow and a kind of protest, buried their saddles in the desert sands. Posted, redirected back to Europe, surrounded finally by cold and deadly machines, and men still feeling the loss of their warm-blooded, four-legged friends, Colin was killed under grey northern skies just a few months before the war ended.

News of Colin's death reached the farm on a weekend when Kate happened to be visiting. They were blessed at least, Susan said, in being able to grieve together. Among all the siblings it was undoubtedly Kate who had been closest to Colin. She and their mother had been able to see past the changeability, the restlessness of this youngest son and brother, had been able perhaps to perceive that Colin was afflicted with more imagination than the others, that, in different circumstances he might have gone far - in a different world. Kate had had some of her best conversations, some of her wildest fits of laughter with that five year younger brother. Susan too had perceived that there was something different about her youngest, and had worried about him not fitting in. She had been more protective of Colin than of any of the others. They had heard only occasionally from him in the two years before his death, often not knowing which country he was in, and never imagining that he might be on a different continent; and now he would be away for always, buried too, in a foreign land. However appropriate that might seem to be, for a prodigal son, for the family it remained a lasting sorrow that Colin had never come home.

When Kate returned to Laverton, after the week that she had spent with her family, she was in a serious frame of mind, although there had been a second important consolation in that week on the farm, and that was that she had been able to see a lot of Stanley. He came out to Willow farm the day after she arrived, just twelve hours after news of Colin's death had reached them, and his presence, close, but not immediate family, was comforting in the way that a friend not directly affected by a tragedy can be. Stanley fulfilled the role of a listening ear, a confessor even, for thoughts and feelings that different members of the family had about Colin and his death. Prompted too by what had happened Kate and Stanley had some serious discussions about their own futures together. They agreed that they could no longer bear being apart. In Colin's death, far away, they discovered an urgency to their being together.

It was decided that Stanley would look for work in Laverton, for he was becoming deeply unhappy making weapons of war at Horner's, and as soon as he had secured employment they would marry and settle together in that town. The major unknown was: how long would it take for Stanley to find work away from Sprinton. The hope was that it could help that Kate was now on the spot and well established in the town. She was known and respected as the manager of the Laverton Binns and, through the people that she knew, and her local knowledge, they hoped that she would have a good chance of hearing about any jobs for which Stanley's mechanical training would be appropriate. There was one other complicating factor: would Stanley be released by Horner's if he did get the offer of work in Laverton? The number of men who had left or been drafted into the armed forces in the previous year had so depleted the work-force that the production of weapons had gone down instead of up and munitions factories like Horner's were empowered to compulsorily retain any workers considered essential to output. They could certainly argue that Stanley was essential to the maintenance of their production levels. Well, they would cross that bridge when they came to it.

Mercifully it proved to be a bridge they did not need to cross, for the war ended and, two months after the end of hostilities, Stanley secured employment in Laverton. The job he was offered came about, fortuitously, more or less as a result of the war ending. The distillery of essential oils and essences, which had been in a period of expansion before the war began, had suffered a drastic decline while it lasted and, had the war continued, the existence of the distillery might well have been in question. Most of the fields of lavender and herbs had been replaced by acres of cereals. But with the Armistice, there began a return to civilian life and all that that entailed. A depleted, but hungry and suffering population began to rediscover a need for the things of peace and of beauty, things such as perfumed oils and scented soaps. The distillery began to revive, fields could be planted once again with peppermints and lavenders. Although on a smaller scale than before the war, nevertheless the plant could continue - if competent mechanics could be found who would be able to learn the processes and run the machines. The contrast in the end product of the work could not have been greater - from metals fashioned by fiery furnaces into deadly weapons of war to sweet-smelling oils and essences, fashioned from the flowers of the field. For Stanley it was a transformation 'devoutly to be wished'. The wages were lower and the processes simpler than when he was turning out weapons in Sprinton, but to Stanley the nature of the work was infinitely preferable. In addition and at long last they could set a date for their wedding. It was to be in the second month of the new year.

In the immediate aftermath of war, when everything to do with civil life was in short supply, weddings, of necessity, had to be modest and simple affairs. Kate's parents, some of her siblings and their families would be easily the biggest contingent of guests at Kate and Stanley's wedding; Stanley's mother, Sarah, his brothers Fred and Charlie, with Fred's wife and Charlie's adoptive 'parents', Aunt Annie and Uncle Bert, composed the total on Stanley's side. Kate's youngest sister, Ivy, clad in a new and stylish blue woolen dress, which Kate had assisted in the making of, acted proudly as her maid of honour. Stanley's oldest friend in Sprinton, Kate's cousin Ed, the very one who had been unwittingly responsible for their first meeting, was Stanley's Best Man. Ed needed no prompting to take credit for what he claimed was his matchmaker role!

The ceremony took place on a bright and crisp winter's day, at the little country church of St. Michael's, in the village where Kate and all her brothers and sisters had gone to school. Afterwards the party returned to Willow Farm, where Kate's parents, with the help of two of the village women, had prepared a wedding breakfast, the like of which had not been seen since before the war. With foresight, and a conviction that sometime soon life must take a turn for the better, Susan had been saving the two well cured hams that were the centrepiece of the wedding feast, and apples stored since the autumn before furnished four large apple tarts to follow the hams and roast potatoes. A cake, made with Willow Farm's own eggs and flour ground from their own wheat, sweetened with local honey and the Williamses' butter, and crowned with slivers of glacéed cherries, preserved and saved by Susan in a sealed jar since the beginning of the war, was the centrepiece of the table. There was locally brewed beer for the men, Susan's homemade elderberry wine for the women and an elderflower cordial for the children (the elder of whom delighted of course in pretending that they too were drinking wine.) Kate was radiant in a peach coloured dress trimmed with lace collar and cuffs, and with a curly lambswool jacket, and Stanley, in a new suit and buttonhole, could not stop smiling the whole day long.

In late afternoon, as the sun was getting lower in the sky, a charabanc hired for the purpose, came to fetch the Sprinton guests and the bridal couple back to the town. Sarah had arranged for Stanley and Kate to spend their wedding night in the best room that The Bull had to offer. When applied to, her employer, and landlord of the hotel, Mr Grimes, said that this should be regarded as his wedding present to the pair. Bernard Grimes regarded Sarah as the best Housekeeper he had ever had, quite apart from the fact that she had appeared as if by magic and stepped into the breach the day after the sudden death of her predecessor, Mrs Chalmers. Since that day, now more than ten years past, he had met Stanley on a number of occasions, and, knowing by then Sarah's history, had also been able to form a just opinion of Stanley's merits as her son. He was pleased to let the young couple spend their wedding night in the best room his hotel had to offer, in what in any case, the last week of February, was the low season of the year.

The following day, Sunday, was going to be a busy one for they were to carry out the move to Laverton. The Williamses, with Ed driving, had put their lorry at the young couple's disposal - that same vehicle which normally collected churns of milk from the farms in the district. A few pieces of furniture donated by the Atkinsons had been brought into town the day before; now they had to collect from Mrs Roberts the things that Kate had left with her when she first moved to Laverton, and the box of Stanley's stuff and his bicycle from West Sidings. This last was the most emotional event of all for it recalled the drama and trauma of those first years in Sprinton and the joy when Sarah secured the tenancy of the little house in West Sidings. Stanley remembered with emotion the day that he had moved from the Blue Lion, where he had slept in his uncle's attic room for five childhood years, and into a house with his mother once again. The years in West Sidings had been the happiest years of Stanley's youth.

Stanley was also very conscious of the fact that now, with his move away from Sprinton, his mother would be living alone. This fact was the one that had caused Stanley the most soul searching when he and Kate had begun their serious discussions about their future together. But when he first broached the subject with his mother, Sarah immediately cut off his regrets: "You needn't worry about me, son," she said. "There can only be one queen in any house, and it has to be your wife. Of course I'll miss you being here. I won't deny it, but Stan, above all, I want you to be happy and I know you've found the right girl. Kate and I get on fine and if ever there should be, which God forbid, any disagreement between us I'm sure we'd be able to sort it out. You have to have your own life, and your own household - it's only right.

"You know," she said, "I've never said this to you before but, I do think if old Mrs Ruskin hadn't been so interfering in our household when we were young, your father might not have taken to the drink like he did. The thing was, not only was I wrong for Charles, in her eyes, but he could do no right either. Always being compared to HIS father and found wanting.... no, no, young couples need their own freedom to breathe. You're a good son, Stanley and I'm sure Kate won't make you less of one. In any case I'll still have family all around. Charlie is back in town and Annie and Bert are nearby, and Alec who's a good brother, as you know. He's past seventy now but he fusses over me as if I was still his little sister.....I suppose to him I still am!" She smiled at the sudden image of her six foot two inch brother, even though now a little shrunken and bent, trying still to protect her.

West Sidings was the last port of call when the 'milk' lorry, all loaded up, was ready to set off for the thirty mile drive south, to Laverton. There were tears on both sides, for Sarah, despite her recent brave words to her son, couldn't help but feel bereft; his room was now empty of all that was him - except for one book left on the chest of drawers. His most precious book, the Encyclopaedia, so important in the early days 'of Kate', Stanley could never have left behind. At this moment of parting Stanley suddenly felt the wrench at going away, for good, from the mother who had suffered much herself but who had yet given him so much love and support. Their home in West Sidings, which had materialised just when Stanley was about to leave school, had ushered in the happiest period of his youth. Kate stood back as they made their farewells, but at last, as they were about to climb into the cab, with Ed already at the wheel, she came forward and folded Sarah into her arms, saying, "You must come and visit us very soon. You shall be our first guest."

Then they were off, and on the road to their own, new, married life.

END OF PART ONE

PART TWO: The Beginning of a New

CHAPTER 10

Married Life: Above the Shop

The first married home of Stanley and Kate was the rooms above the Laverton Binns which had been renovated when the shop was about to open. The flat had been modernised and a bathroom with toilet had been incorporated into what was now a fully independent, self-contained flat with a staircase down to ground level where there was a porch and outside door opening onto the street. For almost two years the landlord's older, widowed sister had lived there. Now she had gone to live with a daughter in Suffolk and, since the new year the flat had been empty. It was not difficult to negotiate with Dan Anderson for the tenancy. If there was one thing better than having Binns as the occupant of the shop it was to have the manager of the shop as the tenant of the living quarters above it. The rooms still had the brightness and feel of a place newly decorated, for Nancy, the widowed sister, had been meticulous and house proud and she had had a hand in directing the refurbishment of the property from the moment it became clear that it would be she who would be living there.

    Directly above the shop was a large sitting room with two good sized windows that looked out over the Market Place. The room was light and airy; the woodwork eggshell white and the wallpaper patterned simply with a cream and pale rose stripe. When Kate viewed the room, emptied of all furniture except for a sofa covered in flowered chintz, which had been left behind by Nancy, she felt immediately that this could be her home.

The day after their wedding when Stanley and Kate arrived in Laverton, they had very little by way of furniture, but they had used some of the money they had been saving to buy and install a bed, wardrobe and dressing table ordered from a furniture shop in nearby Boxley. On the back of the lorry driven by Ed from Sprinton, was a table and four upright chairs (all given by the Atkinsons) that would furnish the kitchen; there was an Indian rug for the bedroom and Kate's household goods, which included a small armchair, a bookcase, and books that had been stored with Mrs Roberts for the past two years. Stanley's stuff consisted mainly of his bicycle, the gardening tools he had equipped himself with for his allotment, a few books, including two in particular, and some general workshop tools that could come in handy if anything needed doing about the house. Ed helped them unload, admired the situation and the size and sunniness of the sitting room, and shared with them the first cup of tea made in their first married home, before he set off to drive the lorry, now empty, back to Sprinton. This was the second emotional moment of the day. It signalled the final, complete break with Stanley's life in Sprinton, the last nine years of which had been his first years of work and of friendship with Ed and his family. For Kate it marked the end of her single life and the beginning of a life with Stanley. She had always been fond of her cousins and aunt Daisy and her feelings for them had only been made stronger since they had been instrumental in bringing her and Stanley together. They waved goodbye to Ed and went indoors to begin their married life.

Stanley had visited the Laverton distillery twice in the weeks before their marriage. On both occasions the retiring engineer had shown him over the works and instructed him in all the phases of the steam extraction and refining processes, together with on the spot demonstrations of the same. On the later occasion the second in command, the foreman, had also been there and had been able to show Stanley how they should work together and coordinate the different aspects of the work. Stanley drew to the man who was the foreman. He clearly knew the business inside out and had worked at the distillery for almost ten years, excluding the two last years of the war, but there was a modesty coupled with a quiet pride in what he was doing that appealed to Stanley. Michael Chivers seemed to handle both the machines that they were using and supervising, and the plants that went into them, with respect; his attitude conveyed to Stanley a sense that what they were doing was worthwhile and he knew that, although the work was less well paid than that at Horner's, yet he was going to like what he was doing much more.

The first week was demanding, since it was a case of learning a completely different set of routines for the order in which things had to be done, as well as *what* was to be done. But at the end of it there was the satisfying feeling that something agreeable and beneficial to human beings had been made rather than something that would be life shattering and deadly. He entertained Kate daily with an account of what he had learned: she entertained him with accounts of incidents that had happened 'downstairs', in Kate's arena of competence which was, literally, beneath their feet in the shop below.

Then there was the 'learning to live together' bit, and it was hard to say which of them had the most to teach or the most to learn. Stanley knew a lot about the domestic arts, especially about food and cooking, due to his childhood years spent in the kitchen of The Blue Lion; and Kate knew things about repairs and plumbing which she had learnt and been privy to, growing up on the farm, with brothers and a very practical mother to inform her. When the chores, which in their newly-wed euphoric state never seemed like *chores*, had been done - or before they were done - why then it was time to go to bed. And in passion they were equals. Teasing her, and pretending to be shocked by a suggestion she made, Stanley would ask her where she could possibly have come by one of her ideas. "Well, m'lud," she countered, "it's becos' I was brung up on the farm - don't yer know", before both of them collapsed in laughter - and a joyful lust took over. After a wait of years, of illness, then of separation with Kate in Laverton and Stanley in Sprinton, of family worries and of wartime, their first period of married life, together, was perfect bliss.

The promise that Kate had made Sarah when they left Sprinton, was kept. She was their first visitor to the flat in Laverton. It was a Saturday in April; the daffodils were in bloom and trees were in bud. Stanley had gone to Boxley to meet his mother off the train. While he was away Kate was about to exercise a new domestic skill: she was baking scones. It was only the second time she had done it in the flat, but she thought they looked right when she lifted them out of the oven and tested them with the pressure of a finger.

The table was set. There was even a vase of narcisi on it (the vase was a wedding present from one of her cousins). It reminded Kate momentarily of the time when she had invited Sarah to her rooms at Mrs Roberts, when she had only known Stanley a few months, and of how nervous she had been. There was no nervousness now, for she had known Sarah for more than two years, and there was a mutual respect and liking, between them. Sarah was to stay the night, so Kate, with Stanley's help, had spent much of the morning trying to make the small room which was entered from one end of the sitting room, into a passable spare bedroom. Through Kate's connections in the town they had acquired a single, second-hand bed which fitted into the little corner room, allowing just enough space at the side for a bedside table and room at the end of the bed for a chair.

Sarah's response when she entered the sitting room were gratifying to Kate. "Oh my dear, what a lovely sunny room," she cried, "and here was me wondering if it wouldn't be dark living up those stairs above the shop." Sarah was a little out of breath but she resisted Stanley's attempt to get her to sit down on the sofa. "No, let me look around first," she said and moved over to one of the windows to look out over the Market Place. Turning back her eyes swept approvingly around the room. Apart from the sofa there was only a small low table, Kate's bookcase, full of books, along the short wall facing the sofa, one of the upright chairs that had come from Willow Farm and the armchair that Mrs Roberts had gifted from Kate's room in her house. Kate had been busy since they moved in and enlisted the help of Lily James to make two sets of light and leaf patterned curtains to match the chintz of the sofa, for the two windows. On the wall above the bookcase were two watercolour landscapes which had been painted by an aunt of Susan's, and which had always hung on the wall of an upstairs landing at the farm. As a little girl Kate had admired them and often asked her mother about the painter. Susan had promised that when she got a home of her own, the water colours should be hers. Sarah's eyes went from Stanley to Kate beside him. "You've made this just lovely," she said, smiling. And the scones too met with her approval.

When Sarah left on Sunday afternoon to return to Sprinton by the evening train, Kate felt that her visit had somehow conferred on the flat the title of home. Over the course of the summer months there were more visits, including from Kate's parents who came one weekend. George had frequently confided to his wife that he could never contemplate living in a town, far less in an upstairs flat, but after the visit he was compelled to admit that, as these things went, their living quarters were not bad at all. He could even see that a certain amount of interest could be had from simply watching the life that went on in the market place from a comfortable chair at the sitting room window - where Kate had ensconced him for an hour while she took her mother on a courtesy visit to see Mrs Taylor and her sister at the Cedars.

In July her oldest friend, Lucy Staines, came for several days and there was much catching up to do of news and confidences - chief among which was that Lucy had had a proposal of marriage from the young man with whom she had been 'walking out' for the last year, but she was undecided about whether to accept him, for he had begun to speak about the opportunities there were for young people in 'the colonies', and Lucy did not want to move away from her family. Discussing the pros and cons of this dilemma were the main topic of conversation between the two women, to which they returned time and again in the course of the stay.

The visit signalled the welcome continuation of a friendship which had begun in early childhood and both would have been loath to see it ended. Lucy's dilemma did prove the truth of an old adage that Susan had often impressed on Kate, as a talkative child, "It is sometimes more important to be a good listener than an eager talker." So Kate discussed Lucy's dilemma a little with Stanley, but she tried, with Lucy, to listen more than speak and avoided giving determined advice. It was in any case an enjoyable visit. Stanley took to Lucy and they had some lively conversations around the dinner table and in the course of walks in the countryside around the town. On a warm Sunday afternoon, they had an excursion on the river Deane, with Stanley rowing.

Thus the first year of their marriage passed. The Laverton Binns continued to do well under Kate's direction and Stanley settled into his new work at the distillery which he found infinitely preferable to the munitions factory. It was a good thing that his first instinctive response to Michael Chivers had been a positive one since it soon became clear that they needed to work closely together as a team. Though cautious at the beginning of a new work relationship, Stanley was soon won over by the friendly but businesslike manner of his workmate, and his positive commitment to what they were doing.

Michael Chivers was one of the lucky ones who had survived active service in the war. Perhaps that was why he was happy and contented in what he was doing - he knew how bad life might have been and he knew how lucky he was simply to be still alive with all his limbs intact. At any rate he and Stanley became friends before many months had passed.

Michael had a wife and son, a boy of seven, who was the apple of his father's eye, and when Stanley had been working with him for a while he and Kate were invited to his house for tea on a Sunday afternoon. The Chivers lived in a little, old, stone-built cottage about a quarter of a mile from the centre of Laverton. It was at the side of one of the biggest fields of lavender belonging to the distillery and the scent of the lavender was palpable as you approached the cottage along Gypsey Lane. Half a century before, it had been a farm labourer's cottage belonging to a well-known farming family, the Gibsons, on whose land it stood. Now it belonged to the distillery and Michael and his wife had lived there for almost ten years. Agnes was in many ways the polar opposite of her husband: where Michael was above middle height and spare in build, his wife was a whole head shorter and buxom; where Michael was, not exactly taciturn, but careful and considered in his speech, talk and laughter were life-blood to Agnes.

The walk from the Ruskins' flat on the Market Place to the lavender fields on Gypsey Lane, on a summer's afternoon, was a delight in itself. Laverton was still a small town and the countryside pressed in close. The Chivers' house stood end on to the lane so that the 'front' door was at the side and opened onto a garden at the side and back of the house. On this warm Sunday afternoon it stood wide open and a tap on the door brought Agnes to it.

"Oh, my dear Mrs Ruskin, do do come in," and she grasped Kate's hand, drawing her inside.

At the back of the house, tucked in a sheltered spot, Michael had made an arbour from which you could look down the whole length of the garden to a low fence at the bottom. This formed the boundary between the Chivers' garden and the field of lavender. In the arbour, on a table made by Michael, Agnes had set out her best china. And in the course of that afternoon the foundations of a friendship between Agnes and Kate were laid. Stanley, who already had respect for Michael's integrity and trustworthiness, found that they had other things in common too. The garden, though no more than the width of the house, was long and more than half of its length was given to growing an amazing variety of fruits and vegetables. One of the things that Stanley had been sorry to leave in Sprinton, was his allotment and, although he did not want to say it to Kate, it did irk him, living in the flat, that he had not the possibility of stepping out into the open air, and into a piece of land that he could cultivate for himself.

The time spent with Michael in his garden that summer afternoon was pleasure of the deepest kind. Some people, mistakenly in Stanley's view, thought that the flat fenland landscape was uninteresting and dull, but the wide sweep of skies in this part of the world presented an ever-changing kaleidoscope of scudding cloud, against a background of varying blues. Today the sky was an unblemished arc of the bluest blue, a sea of air inviting to immense liberation from the shackles of earth. As his eyes scanned the carpet of lavender fields in full bloom and scent, as far as the eye could see, to the blue horizon where earth met sky, Stanley experienced a sensation that he imagined birds must feel rising into the air and seeming to glimpse beyond the horizon. For a long moment the two men stood, both silent, gazing eastwards and skywards, as if waiting for something, awestruck. It was like that moment, in childhood, when you could lie on your back in a grassy field and have the queerest sensation that you were going to fall into the sky.

Michael's son, Thomas, had been following his father and Stanley as they walked around talking. Puzzled by the unaccustomed silence of the adults he pulled at his father's arm, "Aren't you going to dig?" he asked. Michael laughed and patted his son's head.

"He's a great help to me in the garden," he said to Stanley. "He's a champion digger and he knows how to plant too. No, we're not going to dig today, Thomas. But I think your mother might need a little help with the cake. Will you go and see?"

In the arbour Kate and Agnes had been getting to know one another. Raised in a family of eight (Agnes was the fifth) and with her father a farm labourer, it was always going to be a struggle for survival in such a household. Kate knew immediately what the circumstances of Agnes's life as a child would have been; although better off than the labourer's family, hers had had those struggles too, and the number of children to bring up was not the least of them. But Agnes had clearly always been a fighter and, more than that, she had the capacity to believe that things would work out if you were always prepared to work and had a little faith. And as far as she was concerned, they had.

As a girl, soon after finishing school, Agnes had been working for Dr Murray, mainly looking after his young children, and Michael (who she had just known as 'one of the boys' at school) had started working at the distillery. Doctor Murray had a financial, as well as a professional interest in the distillery and often had occasion to visit it. Sometimes Agnes was sent to fetch some herbal distillations that he was needing for some of his patients and on one of these occasions she happened to bump into Michael. Thus was their school time acquaintance renewed and now they had been together for ten years. They would never be rich, said Agnes, but they had enough, and a little more, and Michael - she clearly admired the talents of her husband - could grow nearly all the food they needed (barring meat), and he could mend anything that was broken and make anything that required carpentry. There was only one thing that bothered her, and it was not about her husband, but her son.

"I never like to boast, Mrs Ruskin, and I won't, but it seems to me that our Thomas has got a good head on him too. He can add up and work things out in his head as well as any child I've ever seen and yet he's having such a hard time with his reading. That really bothers me because I've a feeling he could go far, get a real education if you know what I mean. But his teacher says he just won't, or can't, get his letters right. I don't understand it and he gets so upset when I try to make him practice." For the first time that afternoon the sunny smile left her face and she was silent. Kate's heart went out to her, caught in the worst dilemma of any loving mother: her son needed something that she could not give. Kate remembered how the same things had been said of her own younger brother, but she had been able to help him. Now Colin was dead, buried in some field of northern France. A thought came to her: perhaps she could help Agnes's Thomas. Perhaps *he* could have the brighter future that Colin and thousands like him, all young men, had been denied.

"Has he any books at home?" she asked hesitantly. Agnes looked up,

"Oh yes, we've the books - a bit ragged some of them for they've come through a good many hands. He likes looking at them all right, well some of them, but when he tries to make out the words he gets so frustrated and he just flings them away. There've been some tears I can tell you, but he'll run up the stairs so we can't see." She fell silent again,

" Mrs Chivers, Agnes," Kate broke in, "one of my brothers was like that and I helped him with his reading. Would you let me try with Thomas? I have some of my brother's books still and I might be able to help him." Agnes's look was a mixture of awe and disbelief,

"Could you really, Mrs Ruskin? But when would you have time - with the shop, and all?" Kate considered this a moment,

"Wednesday is our half-closing day," she said. "When does Thomas finish school, - three o'clock, three thirty?"

"Three o'clock on a Wednesday."

"Well then, could you bring him to me at the flat, leave him with me for an hour and I'll see if I can help. That is," she added, "if he can be persuaded that he will be coming for something that is enjoyable - and not as a punishment!"

They discussed how this could be done and, just as they were finishing, Thomas appeared, sent by his father to help his mother with the cake.

CHAPTER 11

New Life and Old Love

Agnes arrived with Thomas very punctually at a quarter past three on the following Wednesday afternoon. Kate made a cup of tea for herself and Agnes but offered Thomas a glass of apple juice. Willow Farm had a small orchard of apple trees and, as children, Kate and her siblings had always helped their mother to make the apple juice. Susan still made it, albeit in smaller quantities now, and Kate had some at home in Laverton. It proved to be popular with Thomas too and he liked even more the gingerbread men that she had made specially the evening before.

"Are you sure you really want to do this?" Stanley had asked, observing the amount of work that she was putting into the preparation of the next day's visit. "Oh yes," Kate replied. "You know it really can make a difference. It did with Colin," she hesitated, "and he seems such a bright boy. I'd like to give it a try. You don't mind, do you?" Stanley didn't and nothing more was said .

Kate knew that for it to work Thomas had to feel that there was something tangible that he would like about being in Kate's company, and in the house, for the afternoon. An hour is nothing to an adult but it could seem like an eternity to a child if he was being asked to do something that he anyway had always found difficult.

When Susan was clearing out some of Colin's things, after his death, she asked Kate if there was anything in particular that she would like. Kate took the books that she had helped her brother to read with, also a catapult that he had always carried about with him, and a little set of toy soldiers and horses which Colin had prized above everything, and which had been given to him by his fifteen year older brother William, when Colin was eight. Kate now took these things out of the box she had kept them in, for she saw that she might be able to use them with Thomas.

Colin had responded to rhyme and the music of language in verse, and so Kate had begun with the nursery rhymes and Stephenson's 'A Child's Garden of Verses' and her brother had made fast progress when there were things and creatures in the verses that he was interested in. For Colin that had meant animals and soldiers. So Kate had the books, the soldiers and horses ready for when Thomas should arrive. She had also written some individual words on pieces of paper and she had crayons and paper to hand. When Stanley saw what she had accumulated he said, "Goodness, Kate, you should have been a teacher!" Kate laughed, "Well, you know, I wouldn't have minded that".

When they had had their cup of tea and Thomas had finished his apple juice and his second gingerbread man, Agnes went away to do some errands in the town and to visit a sister who was sick. It was agreed that she would come back to fetch Thomas at five o'clock. When Kate opened the box of toys Thomas immediately took a liking to the painted toy soldiers. Kate explained to him about the origins of the colours and their weapons (all things that she had learnt from Colin). His interest caught, it was not difficult then to get him onto, first, "The Grand Old Duke of York" marching his soldiers up and down, and later, using his interest in numbers, getting him onto "One, two buckle my shoe…" into which Kate introduced some of her own variations which she guessed would appeal more than the story of 'maids a courting'.

At the end of their first session Thomas had read aloud "The Grand old Duke of York" without error, and he knew it off by heart; he had learnt the spelling of a number of words, had written them out and sounded the individual letters. He was rewarded with one more gingerbread man and was happily marching the soldiers up and down, when his mother returned.

The Wednesday afternoons became a regular and after this first meeting Thomas came with his mother quite willingly. The sessions with Kate had a number of other good effects, not least was the fact that Thomas became much happier about going to school. Agnes was happy too, especially after one occasion when, waiting for Thomas outside the school, his teacher came out to tell her how much his reading had improved. The Wednesday meetings also cemented the friendship between Kate and Agnes, and over the following months the two women got to know one another well.

The Laverton Binns had become a byword among all the women, not only of the town but of the surrounding countryside too. To get more choice in ladies' fashions, accessories or materials it was necessary to travel to Boxley, a full ten miles away. A motorbus route had recently been established but there were only two buses a day, in each direction, and women coming in from the surrounding countryside, which usually meant from outlying farms, or from smaller villages, always had to rely on pony and trap or farm wagons, and there was little chance of matching their journeys with the times of the motor buses.

Kate had a good hand with her staff and with the company's suppliers. She was now well known in the district as the manager of the Laverton Binns. Her reputation naturally enhanced the reputation of Binns too, and director Mark Edwards who came once a month to visit from Sprinton was quite sure that they had never done a better day's work than the day they appointed Kate, then Miss Atkinson, and now Mrs Ruskin, to open and manage the new Binns. The shop was so well patronized that it had become necessary early on to take on more staff. Kate's first appointee, the young widow, Lily James, had proved the soundness of her judgement. Lily learned quickly, not only the business but all sorts of other necessary qualities for anyone in the retail trade, and in particular the trade in women's clothes and accessories. In addition she had proved gifted, like Emily Dickens, as a seamstress. Kate now felt confident that if the occasion arose, any kind of major or minor crisis, then Lily James could be put in charge at least temporarily.

And such an occasion could, quite suddenly, arise. She had been married just over a year when, one fine morning, Kate felt quite sick. The following mornings were the same and then, one day, she really was sick. The sickness passed, thankfully before it was time to go downstairs and open the shop, but the signs were clear to Kate. After a few more days she made a pretext for asking Lily if she could come early and open up for a while. Then she told Stanley, innocent of this kind of knowledge, what she suspected, and she went to visit Dr. Murray; and the doctor confirmed her suspicions.

The rejoicing at home, and there was rejoicing, was not however, 'unconfined'. Most married women after all, did not continue to work, once married. A few did and Kate was one of them; but almost none could continue to work after the birth of their first child. It was 'when' not 'if' Kate stopped working, that their income would be cut by half, just at the point when their expenses would have increased. Not only that but there were clouds on the horizon at the distillery too. The problem was not trivial and it was the one that most filled their conversations in the weeks ahead.

Kate put off telling Mark Edwards about her condition for as long as she could. She suspected, even though he must know that this was likely to happen sometime, that it would be a blow, as much to him personally, as to the company. During the three years since the opening of the Laverton Binns, Mark Edwards had increasingly come to rely on Kate. Professionally, as co-workers in the company, they were in accord. But more than that, and without a word being said, nor any gesture being made, Kate sensed that had circumstances been different then Mr Edwards might very possibly have declared that he had warmer feelings for her than the merely professional. Kate's personal feelings, since their second meeting, had been all for Stanley, and she never doubted them. But she was sensitive to others' feelings and she would not knowingly administer a hurt, however inevitable or unintentional. Telling Mark Edwards that she would have to leave his employ in a few months time was therefore not an entirely simple matter.

The cloud hanging over the distillery was even more significant. In the first two years after the end of the war the fortunes of the distillery appeared to revive. Some fields returned to their pre-war crops of lavenders and mints - but only some of them. The first two harvests were good, but not as good as they needed to be for the quality of their end products to match the pre-war quality. In addition, and after one season of optimism and post-war euphoria, it was becoming clear that the economy of the whole country was entering recession. Unemployment was rising and, apart from the medical application of some of their products, fewer people seemed to be willing, or to have the means, to spend anything on essential oils and essences. The continued existence of the distillery was seriously in question.

The first hint of trouble had come when Stanley was nearing the end of his first year with the company. Dr. Murray came regularly, both to oversee some of the processes, and to collect quantities of some of the essences which he needed for some of his patients. On one visit, otherwise routine, he came into the distilling room to speak to Michael, who was attending to one of the boilers, and it appeared to Stanley, who was working at the other side of the building, as if the doctor was agitated about something. The noise of the machinery prevented Stanley from hearing anything that was said, but when he went over to Michael after the doctor had left he saw that his friend was staring at the ground and looking unusually serious. Was something wrong, he wanted to know? Michael looked up, "I think there is," he said, "Oh it's not the boilers, but, Murray says demand is down and we have to reduce production by a third for a few weeks. The distillery has debts. I don't like the sound of this, Stan."

Business went on anyway, and seemed for a while even to pick up again, but, towards the end of the winter, and just before Kate discovered she was pregnant, another downturn struck and there was no sign of improvement. Michael took Stanley aside:
"I think we're in real trouble," he said. "If things don't improve in the next few weeks this place will shut down." Stanley found it hard to believe.

"But our things are known worldwide, Michael. Haven't sales abroad been going up this last year?"

"They were, but there's been a dive since the beginning of this winter, apparently. I was talking to Reg in 'sales' yesterday and he said orders have almost halved since last winter."

Stanley took the news home to Kate; however, thinking that perhaps Michael was being unduly pessimistic, he tried not to dramatise the situation. After all nothing official had been said and it was possible that Michael's fears were exaggerated.

The following week it was confirmed that Kate was pregnant. About the pregnancy Stanley was happy, but he couldn't help feeling a real unease about their finances and his job. Since they hadn't been told anything definitive at the distillery Stanley didn't want to alarm Kate unduly at this time. She was still feeling sick in the mornings and she was trying to decide when would be the right moment to break the news of her leaving, to Mark Edwards.

At work though, Stanley and Michael had started to discuss what now seemed increasingly likely to happen, and what they each should do when the evil day came. Michael was clear that he was going to start looking now for a new job, and that the best place for men with their mechanical skills was Boxley. It was ten miles away but there were several big engineering works in that town and, since so many young men, skilled or not so skilled, had been killed in the war, it was one of the towns which had suffered from a scarcity of labour, when hostilities ceased. Michael thought that both he and Stanley would have a good chance of finding suitable work in Boxley. The thought of working, or, even more unwelcome, of living, in a big town, filled Stanley with dismay however. Sprinton had been big enough, Laverton was perfect, in size and atmosphere - he had seen Kate restored to health there and was not prepared to sacrifice that. But working and *not* living in Boxley would likely entail a ten mile cycle ride to and from work each day, with only the occasional relief of the motorbus journey instead - since most of the engineering in Boxley involved shift work for much of the workforce.

While Stanley wrestled with his problem, and said as little as possible to Kate until things that were uncertain should become certain, Kate's mind was exercised by an even more concrete dilemma. She wondered how they would manage in their upstairs flat, with a baby whose crying would be very audible in the shop below, with narrow stairs down to the ground and very limited space outdoors for hanging out the washing; the yard at the back hardly got any sun since it was enclosed on three sides by buildings. It was just feasible when there was only the two of them, though sheets and towels had often to be properly dried on clothes horses ranged around the sitting room fire, or hung on the pulley up above their heads in the kitchen. But, as the middle child in a large family Kate knew the washing that babies entailed and, in particular, the nappies. More than half a dozen, each more than two feet square, could, under certain circumstances, be got through in one day! Her mother, Susan, had been lucky - on the farm there was plenty of room, outside, for multiple washing lines getting both sun and breeze. At the back of their flat on the Market Place in Laverton there was room for at most two lines, of no more than fifteen yards each and almost entirely in the shade. The little wash-house in the yard only had room for the boiler and a mangle.

Kate had come to the conclusion that not only would she be giving up work before the baby was born, but, that they would be compelled to move house too. Then Stanley came home with news that overshadowed all the rest: the distillery would be closing in two months time.

When Mark Edwards drove into Laverton on the following Thursday, he little knew what was in store for him. He had reckoned with the fact that since Kate had got married, more than a year before, then it was likely that he would lose her 'to motherhood' before long. This was not a matter of indifference to him for, not only had she proved to be a manager 'par excellence', but also his meetings with her once a month had been the most precious times to him personally for some time. As the months went by, however, and Kate made no announcement to him and, at the same time, gave as much care and attention to the business as she had always done, he began to wonder if perhaps her marriage, like his, was going to be childless.

Mark Edwards was not a sentimental man but he was a man of feeling. His marriage, though, had proved a cold one. Perhaps it was his one sentimental lapse, when young, which had brought him to personal shipwreck. He had married a pretty girl, who flattered him by responding to his advances, and only after a hasty marriage, and the decline of the first period of passion - or was it only lust - did he discover that they had little in common. Perhaps they could have come to some kind of workable accord if children had come along, (Dorothy suffered a miscarriage two months after the wedding) but none did, and Dorothy's, at bottom conventional, nature settled into the only constant interests she had, the house, its contents and the social status she enjoyed as the wife of the senior Director of Binns. Mark Edwards had tried, in the early years of their marriage, to get her to extend her interests, but to no avail. His distraction from that loveless marriage hereafter was in another love, a love that he, in common with the rest of his family, had had since early childhood, it was the love of horses and riding.

Mark Edwards' mother was the daughter of the founder of Sprinton's very successful department store, and in her childhood and youth she had mixed with the 'cream' of Sprinton society; before she was twenty she had met and was being courted by the son of her father's friend. Philip Edwards was joint heir to the well-known stud farm of Longtoft near High Bridge, and the marriage between Philip Edwards and Rachel Binns was considered to be both perfectly natural and mutually advantageous. As it turned out, however, Philip Edwards was drawn more and more into his father-in-law's business as it expanded in Sprinton, while his twenty-minute-younger, twin brother, Peter, gradually took over the stud farm from their father.

Two sons and one daughter were born to Rachel and Philip Edwards and from early childhood all three were frequent visitors to their grandfather's stud farm and all had ponies which they learned to ride almost as soon as they could walk. Mark was the oldest of the siblings and was destined early on to follow his father and mother into the Binns department store business. But his love of horses, riding and breeding, never diminished; in fact it sustained him through periods good and bad throughout his life. He had tried to get Dorothy to learn to ride when they were first married, but she was too nervous and after one fall from a docile pony, from which she suffered no injury but only fright, she could not be persuaded to get back into any kind of saddle at all. Later Mark Edwards ruefully reflected that that had been just as well since, after realising how little they had in common, it meant that his time at the stud farm and riding over the countryside, which he loved, would at least never be encroached upon.

Curiously, or perhaps not so curiously, Mark's love of horses had led him to another interest which became in time almost as compelling. His grandfather Edwards, after whom he was named, possessed two paintings of thoroughbred race horses. Their shining coats and muscled bodies were so beautifully and meticulously depicted that Mark, when just a child, and visiting his grandfather on a rainy Sunday in winter, stood transfixed before them. His grandfather came upon him staring at one of the pictures and, perceiving the child's admiration, began to tell him about the painter, Stubbs. He had studied the anatomy of the horse intently, his grandfather told him, so that he could get it right when he put the paint on canvas. Grandfather Edwards not only knew about horses it seemed, but he also knew about painting. What other animals did Mark especially like, he asked his grandson. When Mark said, 'tigers', his grandfather, chuckling, beckoned to the little boy to follow him into his study. This was a room into which no one was allowed except by invitation of Old Mark Edwards himself. Two walls of the room were lined with bookshelves and there appeared to be no spaces on any of them; against the third wall stood a tall oakwood cupboard and from it his grandfather took out what appeared to be a large board. When he turned it round Mark was amazed, and even for a moment alarmed, so vivid were the colours and so fierce was the expression on the face of the tiger, half hidden in exotic undergrowth, that it seemed as if the animal might leap out of the picture at any minute. There had not yet been time to get it framed, his grandfather explained. He had only recently bought it, quite cheaply, in Paris. Did Mark think the artist had captured the character of the beast? The child nodded, speechless. That day began Mark Edwards admiration for the skill of artists and a love of the art. He began drawing at home and soon went on to painting. He loved colour with a passion and although his tastes and style changed as he got older, he never forgot that first meeting with the tiger in the vivid jungle, painted by a Frenchman. In his last years at school an astute teacher told Mark that he had a talent and that he ought to develop it.

Mark Edwards' future was already staked out for him, however, and he was not, in fact, unwilling to follow his parents into the family firm. It had been started by grandfather Binns; it was the family project and was still a 'work in progress'. He felt it was incumbent on him to carry it on, but he also enjoyed the business. It was complex, and there was always something happening. When his father, in middle age, began to withdraw from the firm, as disease crippled him, Mark was given his head in making suggestions for future development and the idea of opening two new branches of the firm in other towns was his. No, he had not been reluctant to join the family business and, for the time being his outside interests had to take second place, except for one: he could not give up riding. He still kept a horse, or rather his horse was kept for him, at the stables at Longtoft, and he tried to ride at least once a week, usually on a Saturday afternoon. This was his one outlet from the frustrations of his married life and it was the one he adhered to, come rain or shine.

His interest in art, begun with Stubbs and the tigers of Henri Rousseau, and extended under that one insightful teacher at school, had resulted in him becoming a competent artist both in water colours and oils and he attended exhibitions whenever he could. But in the first busy years of his working life there was no time for art exhibitions, and subsequently, after the first few years of marriage, the atmosphere of his home was such that he could not think of picking up a brush to paint. That interest, and that side of his nature was, in a sense, anaesthetised; it lay dormant.

It was some three years after Mark Edwards had taken over the running of the company, when Kate Atkinson, just seventeen and recently moved into the town from the countryside, came to work at Binns. Mark Edwards made a point of walking right through the store, through every department every day of the week except Saturdays. He liked to get to know all the staff and as he came to the textiles department he saw that, behind the counter, there was a tall dark-haired girl whom he had not met before, though he had signed the papers approving her appointment. It was Mr Widdicombe and the buyer, Miss Wilson, who had interviewed her and recommended taking her on. Now he paused at the counter where Kate Atkinson was looking intently at the display of newly arrived silks which had been arranged in a waterfall effect on a stand behind. Mark Edwards leaned forward and inclined his head as Kate turned towards him.
"Good morning," he said putting out his hand. "You must be Miss Atkinson." Kate nodded and took the proffered hand. It didn't often happen but, on this occasion, on only her second day at work, she was taken by surprise and was just a little over-awed. She knew who was speaking to her, of course: the de facto boss of the firm had been spoken about by everyone she had met in the building so far, and in such a manner that she had the impression that in the kingdom of Binns this gentleman was King. Regaining her composure she returned the greeting, just managing to resist the impulse to curtsey - she had also been told that, despite the fact that 'the young Mr Edwards' liked things to be done his way and was a stickler for appearances, yet he did not like a lot of formality.
"How are you getting on?" he asked her, and, noticing properly for the first time the display of the silks behind her, his face registered a moment of surprise followed shortly by approval. "Did you make that display?" he asked.
"Oh, Miss Wilson just asked me to," Kate rejoined, afraid for a moment that she was suspected of exceeding her authority. One of the first things she had learnt was that the 'way' the goods were arranged for the eye of the customer was very

important. Mark Edwards nodded, "I like that," he said, "carry on." And with that he continued his walk through the store.

For the whole of her first year at Binns Kate remained the most junior employee of the firm and there were few occasions when 'young Mr Edwards' had any reason to speak to her beyond the barest formalities; nevertheless he had noticed her and he observed how she got on with both customers and co-workers. In particular he observed that her displays of their textiles were always eye-catching; indeed, with his own painterly experienced eye he thought them artistic.

When, five years later, Miss Wilson retired from the firm Miss Atkinson, though only in her early twenties, was the obvious choice to replace her. Mark Edwards had no doubt about the matter, but he thought that they should have a chat, so that it was clear to the rest of the staff, as well as to Kate herself, that she was being officially promoted. He came by the textiles and sewing department one quiet Tuesday afternoon when there was customarily a lull in business and he found Kate in the process of making a list of materials that she wanted to order.

"Ah, Miss Atkinson," he began, "I trust Miss Wilson has left everything with you in good order." Kate replied that she had and, she continued, she had been looking through a collection of samples from the manufacturers, left behind by Miss Wilson, and she had found among them some silks which she had never seen before and which she thought had been forgotten.

"The thing is," carried away by enthusiasm, she continued, "several of them are rather beautiful, but not terribly expensive and, I am sure they would make up, especially, into the kind of loose blouse that is very fashionable this year," she paused, suddenly self-conscious of the fact that she had momentarily forgotten who she was speaking to. This was a *man*, her employer, who was quite possibly not really interested in ladies' silk blouses except insofar as it was possible to estimate how many yards of the material they could hope to sell. His response took her by surprise:

"Let me see," he said, reaching for the book of samples that she was holding. He studied them for a few minutes in silence and Kate saw that his face had a serious, appraising look. "I agree with you," he said, handing the book back to her. "Order some and we'll see how they go." He looked at her again. "Silk is an amazing material isn't it, so flexible too - a lot of people don't realise how warm it is. Did you know that the Chinese have been writing and painting on silk, for thousands of years?"

"Yes, I believe so. I saw some pictures in a book recently and there were silk paintings of horses, more than a thousand years old." Noticing the look of surprise on her employer's face she added, as if she needed to explain herself, "It's a big book in the library. I was showing a friend…" the friend was, of course, Stanley, with whom she had also had a conversation about silk, not so long ago. Mark Edwards looked at her, intrigued, by this new, to him, aspect of Miss Atkinson's character. Then, suddenly,

"Do you ride?" he found himself asking. Kate laughed,

"Well, only bare-back, when I was younger. On Florrie," she said, naming the cart-horse, beloved by the whole family, which for more than fifteen years had been their only means of transporting the loads of crops and vegetables from the fields into their barn and from the barn to market in Sprinton. Seeing the puzzled look on Mark Edwards' face she smiled and added,

"I was brought up on a farm, you see. We only had one horse for riding and she was the property of my brothers, and my father. But Florrie had a good broad back and I used to sit on her and ride up and down the fields while they were loading the hay-cart behind her." She stopped, momentarily arrested by the only painful image associated with Florrie: the time when, pulling the heavily-laden cart up the only sloping field on the farm, Florrie stumbled and ten year old Lionel, following too closely behind her, received a fatal kick to the head.

The image that flashed across Mark Edwards' mind in the silence that followed was of a dark-haired, bright-eyed little girl, the younger Kate Atkinson, on the broad back of a sturdy horse, crossing a sun-drenched summer meadow, laughing.

CHAPTER 12

Change...All Around

Something was different in Binns that morning. The blind to the window which looked out on the yard at the back was usually down so that nobody could see the bleak outdoor space behind the building where the dustbins were. It was only raised when, for a few minutes, they opened that window to let in fresh air before opening the shop. This morning the blind was, unusually, half up; more daylight came into the shop but the amount didn't compensate for the ugliness of the view. As Mark Edwards opened the shop door Kate emerged from the back extension where she had been talking to Lily James. For the moment the shop was empty of customers.
"Oh, Mr Edwards, good morning," she began, "the cord to the back window blind broke when it was pulled up this morning." She didn't want to apportion blame to anyone in particular since they all knew that the cord had been looking worn for a long time. Nevertheless, it seemed to Mark Edwards that Kate was unusually discomposed over what was, although irritating, a triviality.
"I'm sure we can get it sorted," he said, and noting that she still looked tense and distracted, found himself asking, "Is there something else the matter?"
Without directly answering his question, she replied,
"May I speak to you, privately?" With a sinking heart Mark Edwards followed Kate into the little office behind the shop.

Well, of course, it had been bound to happen, he reflected as he drove back to Sprinton later that afternoon. He had been trying to pretend to himself that perhaps it wouldn't. Or rather he had been trying not to think about it at all. It wasn't that he resented the fact that she would become a mother, or that he resented the idea of the child. It was the fact that he would lose her, pure and simple. It hit him that the loss of those once a month Thursdays (often, over the last two years, once a fortnight) had become a kind of personal lifeline. His horses and riding, suddenly seemed less important, compared to this loss.

    His wife had a theory that for each day of the week her husband's face bore a different expression when he returned home from work. It was a fancy that Mark Edwards had often found irritating; it was like a very tired joke that would bear no more repeating and yet it was repeated several times a week. According to Dorothy his Thursday face was usually his most benign. She had met, or at any rate seen, Kate Atkinson on a few occasions before the move to Laverton, but Dorothy was not greatly gifted with imagination and she was, unashamedly, a snob; consequently, despite Kate Atkinson's striking good looks, and from all accounts competence at her work, Dorothy was still able to dismiss her as a humble employee of her husband's who, moreover, came of 'simple' - she had actually used that word, of Kate, to her husband - country people. As the daughter of one of the town's two solicitors, Dorothy had early on imbibed the idea from her mother that all 'country folk' were socially quite beneath her and the idea that her husband might have been seriously 'smitten' by one of his employees would never have entered her head. In any case, in addition to Kate's, in Dorothy's eyes, humble background, she was more than ten years younger than her husband - a mere slip of a girl.

When Mark Edwards entered his house with a face unusually sombre, therefore, on a Thursday, Dorothy was not greatly concerned when he told her that Mrs Ruskin was expecting a baby and would have to give up her job in three or four months time. Dorothy could never take very seriously, or concern herself, with Binns related problems that her husband mentioned, and would like to have shared, or merely 'aired' with her. She really believed that her husband was 'king' in his emporium and that he only had to say the word and his wishes would be carried out. So what, really, was there to talk about? Mark Edwards had long since given up the idea that he might discuss, or even sometimes just mention business related matters, to his wife, but on this occasion he felt compelled to - today it felt as if it was a matter of life and death. Of course he would get no consolation from her, nor even understanding about finding a replacement who would be as good at the job. But he needed to talk about Kate, and it was the only neutral way he could find to do it.

"Well, it was bound to happen, wasn't it?" Dorothy put into words the reflection that her husband had been bitterly repeating to himself all the way home on his drive back from Laverton. "Can't one of the other girls take over when she goes? Isn't that other girl, the seamstress, what's her name, Lily something...can't she take over? I must say she made a nice job of that silk blouse she ran up for me." Realising that he had reached the limits of his wife's interest in the matter he went through to the kitchen where Mrs Harrison, the cook, was tidying up before going to her own home. In his misery he scarcely noticed that Mrs Harrison was annoyed at having to get out the bread and butter again to make him the ham sandwich that he absent-mindedly asked for. On Thursdays she was supposed to finish by six, and it was already half-past.

....

Whittle's 'Sweet Shop and Tobacconist' had been in business on the market place in Laverton for more than fifty years. In fact it was Henry Whittle, the same who was now white-haired and somewhat stooped, who had opened up his shop in optimism and youth fifty three years before. An inheritance from a bachelor uncle who died suddenly when Henry was just twenty had allowed him to buy the leasehold of this property on the market place and to stock it with various tobaccos, pipes and sweets, and as time went on, with chocolates too. Henry's shop had flourished. He had married when young and after some years his wife had borne him two sons but tragically she died, with the second child, shortly after childbirth. Henry, with the occasional help of a housekeeper, had brought up the older boy on his own.

When he came of age, and had left school, William went into the business with his father and his face became as familiar behind the counter as that of Henry Whittle himself. But the congenital heart condition that had carried off Henry's uncle in middle age also fatally afflicted William before he was forty and, since William had never married, Henry once again found himself in sole charge of the little kingdom which he had founded in his youth. "Time like an ever rolling stream bears all its sons away". Henry had heard that hymn sung in church too many times - an uncle, not old, a wife still young, an infant son, an adult son, well now there was no one left to be borne away, save he himself. He had decided that the time had come to sell and to move in, as invited, with his widowed sister who lived just outside the town. Anything that was left, when he died, was to go to his nephew and nieces, and it would be simpler all round if it was 'just money'. None of them were interested in the business in any case. He made out his own sign: 'For Sale, business and property' and put it in the window behind a display of pipes.

....

Kate believed that hard work should be acknowledged and be seen to be appreciated. Lily James had amply rewarded her judgement in taking her on just days after the Laverton Binns had opened. In addition her skill as a seamstress and her sense of style became known among the female population of the town and brought more customers in. The part-time assistant, Maureen, was also hard-working and reliable. She had been taken on towards the end of the first year of trading when the increasing success of the store was even stretching the capacities of two full-time staff. Kate couldn't do all the backroom and paper work as well as, together with Lily, deal with all the customers. Someone was needed who could check the store-room, evaluate and put in orders to manufacturers and warehouses, and see that all bills and wages were paid. Maureen was one of the two young girls, then working as hotel maids, who had answered Kate's advertisement at the beginning. Failing to get that first job but wishing to finish with hotel work, Maureen signed up for a course in typing and bookkeeping, on Saturdays, at a college in Boxley. One year later she was working three and a half days a week, at Binns in Laverton. Most of her time was spent at her typewriter and desk in the office behind the shop, but since she had discovered in herself a flair for figures and that she liked keeping track of stock and keeping things in order, she found the work congenial.

Kate's method for showing that the work that Lily and Maureen were doing was appreciated, was to go to Henry Whittle's shop once a fortnight on a Friday and buy, out of her own pocket, a little selection of good chocolates or crystallised fruits which she gave them at the close of business that day. Lily and Maureen already regarded themselves as the most fortunate of all the working girls in Laverton in their posts at Binns. This gesture of Mrs Ruskin's just proved to them that they had the best employer in the town. Lily James in particular was conscious of a debt of gratitude to Kate for giving her the job when she was at a low point in her adult life.

On the same day that Henry Whittle put the 'For Sale' notice in his window, Kate came in in the afternoon to buy the treats for her staff. The notice came as something of a surprise since she had been one of Henry's regular customers ever since her move to Laverton, a move in which Henry Whittle had taken a constant and friendly interest. They had begun by exchanging pleasantries and views on the weather and trade in Laverton but, as time went on, their conversations had touched on all kinds of topics, views of life - even on one occasion, death. But Henry had never said a word that hinted at any plans for retirement.

"Mr Whittle, good day," Kate said, as she entered the shop to the ringing of the bell on a coiled spring above her head. "But this is a surprise, are you retiring?" Henry gave a rueful little smile, raised his hands in a gesture of acceptance and then, with guarded relief, told Kate the story of how he had come to that decision. "So, that's the way it is," he concluded, "I'm beginning to feel my age, you see. I didn't want to carry on until I'm so decrepit that I don't know what

I'm doing...or till they have to carry me out in a box. Better to go while you've still got your wits about you. Now, Mrs Ruskin, what can I get you today?"
It was only when she was crossing the market place to go back to Binns that a little germ of an idea entered Kate's head. Might it be possible?

The question of what Stanley was going to do after the distillery closed in less than two months time, was still the most pressing and serious that they had to face. Sunday was normally their day of freedom and relaxation but Kate had decided this time to save until Sunday the idea she had had after her last visit to Henry Whittle's sweet shop.
"Stan," Kate began as Stanley came into the room after Sunday lunch, "when I went to the sweet shop on Friday there was a For Sale sign in the window and Mr Whittle told me he's retiring, as soon as he can sell up. He wants to sell the whole property but, it got me to thinking - we've talked about being our own boss instead of working for someone else - what about if we had a shop together?" Stanley's brow furrowed a little so she hurried on. "There is still something that Laverton lacks, you see, and I know it because we get asked all the time by visitors if there's somewhere where they can get a cup of tea in the town, and there really isn't. The Victoria only serves lunches and the New Inn only breakfasts for residents. Otherwise it's mainly a pub." She paused, watching Stanley's face for a response. The fate of his own family's fortunes flashed through his mind. He was about to say what a risky business such ventures often were, if you had no money 'behind you'. The look of hopeful expectation on Kate's face suddenly checked him. Why be so negative?
"You know," he said finally, and choosing his words carefully, "that's not a bad idea, except," and he looked her in the eye and continued, levelly, "you need more money to get started, than we've got." They both fell silent.
"I could ask him if he would be willing to let us rent the business from him," Kate's eyes pleaded. Stanley looked at her,
"Well, you can ask," he said, thinking 'I don't know how we could pay more than one month's rent in advance to begin with, but...'

Since he was going to have to find a replacement for Kate pretty soon and consequently consider various changes at the Laverton shop, Mark Edwards decided he would go down to Laverton again the following Thursday. When he arrived in the town, however, he did not immediately go to the shop, but decided to carry out another commission first.

Mark Edwards was not a big or regular smoker but he did enjoy a certain good cigar from time to time. The usual time was at home, after Sunday's lunch when, if they had no guests, he would withdraw to the book-lined room he called his work-room (it was really his retreat), smoke his cigar, drink a venerable brandy and contemplate some beautiful paintings - he had a collection of large art books which he never tired of looking at, especially since he had given up painting himself.

Shortly after the opening of the Laverton Binns, wandering around the market place to do a survey of the other business premises in the town, he had come upon Henry Whittle's shop. The first time he saw it he registered it in his mind as mainly a sweetshop. It was only on a later investigation that his eye was caught by an array of pipes in the window and then, going into the shop, he discovered that Henry Whittle also carried some good cigars and, in particular, one make that he was especially fond of but could not always find in Sprinton. It was, for a cigar, quite a mild tobacco but left behind a pleasant almost perfumed after-taste. Since that day he always took back with him to Sprinton two or three of those cigars.

When he approached the shop now he was surprised to see the For Sale notice in the window.

"Well Mr Whittle," he began, "I had better lay in a store of my favourites if you are leaving the business, in case your successor decides to go into some other kind of trade." Henry Whittle chuckled,

"Ah Mr Edwards, and there was me thinking you had an interest in the business yourself!" Mark Edwards looked surprised, which prompted the tobacconist to reply, "Why, don't tell me it wasn't you who sent Mrs Ruskin to find out what I was up to and whether I might be interested in renting out the shop?"

Mark Edwards was nonplussed by this, not having spoken to Kate since the previous Thursday. He made some noncommittal response to Henry Whittle's remark which was not quite a denial but might have been, and concluded his purchase somewhat more quickly than he was in the habit of doing.

Henry Whittle's remark had baffled him and he didn't welcome being baffled. Kate was in the process of arranging a display of new materials in the window when he passed in front and entered the shop. To Kate's "Good morning, Mr Edwards," he, more brusquely than was his custom, responded with a, "Mrs Ruskin, may I have a word?" Mystified, Kate followed him into the office at the back. Maureen didn't work on Thursdays so the office was empty.

"Mrs Ruskin, Kate - if I may - I have just visited Mr Whittle's shop and, I fear he should not have told me, but I suppose it was due to a misunderstanding, he said that you were making enquiries about renting his business. Of course I have no right to pry but I was just a little mystified, since last week - "

"Oh no, it is not what you think," Kate broke in, realising that she had been suspected of a dishonesty. "Yes, I *was* asking Mr Whittle if he could consider renting out his business." She rushed on, "You see, the distillery will be closing down in six weeks time and Stanley will be without a job." She had not yet got round to telling her employer of this other aspect of her near future. Now it seemed she would have to. Suddenly she felt unhappy and, unusually for her, quite close to tears. She controlled herself, with an effort, and went on,

"He might be able to get work in Boxley; very probably he could but, he doesn't want that, and neither of us wants to move there. We want to stay in Laverton." She paused, "The thing is, we've talked before about having a business, a shop of our own." She hesitated, not quite wanting to let everything about their situation be exposed to the view of her employer. But Mr Edwards had always been very decent and fair with her. Perhaps she would just have to admit the truth.

"It's a dream at least," she said. "It will have to remain a dream I'm afraid because we haven't the means to…. well, understandably Mr Whittle would want three months rent in advance and then there's the house.." Mark Edwards looked relieved but also puzzled. Kate went on,

"The flat here is going to be difficult with a baby - there's too little room outside to hang washing and it doesn't get any sun. And then there's the noise - from a baby I mean… so we would have wanted to rent the house as well as the business." She fell silent again. "It's just not possible I'm afraid, so we'll have to think of something else. If the worst comes to the worst we'll just have to move to Boxley…." She felt a compulsion now to get everything said. She did not want there to be any misunderstanding. Mr Edwards had been good to her and she had loved her work. There must be no cloud over her leaving it. She lifted her face to look at the man.

"I'll lend you the money." The words dropped into the silence between them. In his head he had said 'give' but he knew that would never be accepted. Of course it was not simply altruistic, but what did that matter? She need never know that, no one need know. And whether it was to be a blessing or a curse would only be known to him too. What was clear was that, if they accepted his offer then they would stay in Laverton. They would still be nearby. He could still see her, drop in at the shop. He would be justified. He had known her for ten years, and loved....? But, would she accept the loan - or rather, would Stanley?

At least in this they were of one mind, and the one was a question. How could she persuade Stanley that they should accept the loan offered by Mr. Edwards? It was just to get them started he had said; he knew how it was at the very beginning of a new venture, before you had had time to make a profit; his grandfather had told him many times he said, what a struggle the first two years had been when he opened the first Binns - and how small it was to begin with. He understood the fear that Stanley had of beginning with a debt (she had explained to him, just briefly, the origin of that fear) and it was very natural, but also honourable, in that it showed that he would be concerned about repaying it. If it would make Stanley happier about accepting the loan he, the lender, could make it a part of the agreement that they should begin repaying it from the very outset, but by a small sum initially, since they must have some capacity at the beginning to make some investments whether in stock or in furnishings. (Kate had told him about her idea of being able to serve teas at small tables in the shop because there was nowhere in the town which did.)

When Kate broached the subject, that evening, with Stanley, it was just as she had predicted. Stanley was against taking any kinds of loan when he couldn't see immediately that he had the means of paying them back. Kate bit her tongue to stop herself from pointing out that if you could see you had the means of paying back a loan from the moment you took it, then it implied that you didn't really need the loan to start with. Without directly attributing any views to Mr Edwards, she was careful to repeat all the points he had made about starting a business and the way in which repayment of a loan could be arranged. Mark Edwards had also become very thoughtful when Kate outlined her idea about serving teas at little tables in the shop. "That's a very good idea," he said. "I hadn't thought much about that before, but you are quite right, and in the summer particularly when a lot of visitors come here... that's a very good idea."
"I really think we could make a business out of that, Stanley" she said, without mentioning Mark Edwards name at all.

    Kate understood Stanley well enough to know when not to push an argument too hard. She decided to say no more for the time being - at least that evening! She was quite sure that he would be thinking over all that she had said anyway.

Mark Edwards had urged her to talk it all over with Stanley, soberly and carefully - it took a real effort on his part not to sound as if *he* was the supplicant, who was begging to be allowed to make the loan. He hoped that he had managed, to some degree at least, to sound dispassionate in urging them to accept his munificence as a business agreement between, how should he put it, 'old and trusted - he hesitated - colleagues.'

Mark Edwards mood, as he drove back to Sprinton that evening, was lighter, by much, than the Thursday before. Nothing was decided, of course, in fact it was all still an open question but, nevertheless, he felt hopeful. One big thing in his favour, he knew, was that Kate very much wanted to grasp this opportunity. He thought of her shining eyes and the enthusiasm in her voice, when she talked about her idea. She longed to have her tea shop - and she saw that his promised loan could make it possible.

When he walked into his house Dorothy came into the hall just as he opened the front door. "Ah now, you have your Thursday face back on," she remarked. "Have you found someone to replace that Mrs Ruskin?" He should have been irritated, he knew, by almost every word in that greeting, but he just couldn't summon up the energy. In fact, he found his face giving way to something that might be interpreted as a somewhat wry smile.

....

"Kate," Stanley began, when he came into the kitchen next morning, "Do you know how to make ice cream?" She didn't, but Stanley had watched it being made by his uncle at the Blue Lion in Sprinton and he had helped Bill Blackwood pack ice with straw in the hotel's ice cellar.
"We could serve ice cream as well as teas!" he said.
"Stanley, are you telling me you're agreeable to accepting the loan from Mr Edwards? Are you sure?"
"Well," said Stanley, "it seems to me that this is like a kind of cross-roads, and it may be a unique opportunity to do something we both know we'd like to do. And in addition, I don't like the idea of looking back years later and thinking 'we missed a great opportunity there'. You know it seems almost criminal to say no when....well, we're alive and - what was it that *your* Shakespeare said about a 'tide in the affairs of men which taken at the flood...etc.' "
"Goodness Stanley," she came over and put her arms up around his neck, "you are full of surprises - and when did you get time to read *your* Shakespeare?"

"Ah well," he grinned and kissed her," actually it was a quotation I saw somewhere. But I really like ice cream!"

That evening and Saturday they discussed again the matter of the loan and all the ins and outs of it. Kate wanted to be really sure that Stanley's heart was in it too and that he wasn't just going along with it because he knew how much she wanted her tearoom. And Stanley wanted to be sure that, apart from the financial aspect, Kate wasn't going to be taking on too much work when they were just about to start their family. When they had exhausted all the arguments and came to the mutual conclusion that they should grasp this opportunity and take the risk, then Kate was anxious to let Mark Edwards know that they wanted to accept his offer. She had her employer's home telephone number, given to her by him 'in case of any emergency or problem arising out of business hours' he had said - he hoped she might ring him some time, for some reason, or any, but she never had.

She told Stanley she would telephone Mr Edwards on Sunday morning. "I think it is better than waiting to Monday," she said, "because as soon as he gets into work he'll be inundated with business. Tomorrow he won't be bothered with lots of other things." So she waited until Sunday morning.

Dorothy had been expecting a call from one of her female friends and she was surprised, and a little irritated when the voice at the other end of the line was not the familiar one that she wanted. She held out the receiver and Kate heard her calling to her husband, "Mark, it's for you. It's that woman at the Laverton shop, Mrs Ruskin." She put her hand over the mouthpiece and added, as he was about to take it from her. "Don't be long. I'm expecting a call from Elizabeth about our Charity do next week. What is she doing, ringing you on a Sunday anyway." Mark Edwards glared at her and frowned as he took the receiver from her.
"Hello, Kate -er Mrs Ruskin, what can I do for you?" he managed, watching with displeasure as his wife turned her back and went into the sitting room.
"Mr Edwards, I'm sorry to have disturbed you on a Sunday," he brushed aside her apology, angry at his wife's behaviour and the way that she had referred to Kate, which he realised she would have heard.
"I just wanted to tell you that we would like to accept your offer of the loan - if it," she hesitated, for one moment gripped with the fear that he might have thought better of it, especially if he had discussed what he proposed to do, with the woman who had answered the phone, "if it still stands" she ended.

"Of course it does," he replied, still irritated by the impression that he knew his wife had given. "Have you ever known me to go back on my word?" He spoke softly, imagining her, uncharacteristically nervous, at the other end of the line. Then, summoning up a businesslike tone, he went on,
"Is Stanley in agreement? Have you discussed it all with him?" His wife passed back through the hall, frowning, and made for the kitchen. This house was far too big for just two people he had said often, but for once he was glad.
"Oh yes," he heard Kate say, "We've talked about it all."
"All right then. The first thing to do is for you to talk to Mr Whittle, as soon as possible," a horrible possibility crossed his mind, "in case he's had any offers in the meantime. I don't think it's likely, but you never know. Then discuss the terms for a tenancy that would be acceptable to both parties." He lowered his voice. He had no intention of telling his wife anything about the content of this conversation, for a number of very different reasons. He made a decision.
"I think it would be a good idea if I came down to Laverton sooner than usual," he said. "We need to make some arrangements," he lowered his voice again, "and there may be some things that I can advise you about. I will come on Tuesday, in the afternoon, and we can discuss everything then."

When he had put down the phone he was filled with feelings of both joy and elation. Quite apart from the feelings that he harboured, in his heart, for Kate personally, there was nothing that he enjoyed more than planning a new venture. This was not *his* affair, but he knew that he would be able to be of use to the two of them in a number of ways relating to running a business. It was not just about the money, though that was important of course.
"What was that about then?" Dorothy emerged from the kitchen with decanter in hand. They always had a sherry before lunch on Sunday and she had seen that the decanter was almost empty.
"Oh, just some Laverton business," her husband replied. "I shall have to go down on Tuesday this week." Dorothy's interest had already been satisfied and at that moment the telephone rang again. Mark Edwards took the decanter from her and made for the sitting room. Dorothy was already speaking to Elizabeth and explaining with some annoyance why her friend had not been able to get through to her ten minutes before. Really, their telephone was not usually so busy on a Sunday morning.

CHAPTER 13

Moving

At a slack period on Monday morning Kate put Lily in charge and went across the marketplace to Mr Whittle's shop. She was reassured at least to see that the For Sale notice was still in the window; and Henry Whittle confirmed that no, he hadn't had any interested buyers as yet. He reckoned that it could take some time, anyway. There wasn't much money about at the moment and there was a lot of unemployment. " 'A home for heroes' my eye," he said, quoting a slogan that had appeared on some posters just after the war ended. "Many of those poor young men have scarcely got a roof over their heads." Then Kate explained why she had come to his shop on a Monday morning which was not her usual time at all. Henry Whittle looked pensive. In spite of what he had just said, he was hoping to sell the place "get it all off my hands" he said, "although it is quite a wrench, seeing your life's work disappear, just like that." He looked at Kate, now visibly in the 'expectant' state. "I suppose your husband would be looking to run the business to start with," he said, nodding at her as yet modest 'bump' "seeing as you're going to have your hands full soon". He smiled, and Kate, guessing that this might indicate a softening of his determination to sell, and only to sell, launched her full battery of arguments, and not a little charm, against him.

When she returned to Binns after a discussion lasting a good half hour - only two customers had come into the shop in that time - she had not got an absolute definitive answer from Henry Whittle but he would give her one the next morning. Henry had a soft spot for Mrs Ruskin, whose period as manageress of the new store in Laverton he had followed with interest. He was also the first of all the shopkeepers on the marketplace to whom she had spoken and where she had become a regular customer. Not only that but she had felt from the beginning that Henry Whittle was both an honest and a shrewd man. She had learnt a lot from him about the local economy, about other businesses and even local history.

Before that morning, he had reached a determination to get rid of everything. After all he had no family that was interested in carrying on the business as it was. Now, after the conversation with Kate he found himself perversely tempted to stay around and see what this young couple would make of the whole thing. It was clear from Mrs Ruskin's demeanour that she had energy, and a good head on her. Her reputation as manager of the famous store was a byword for excellence in the town. Well well, he had been wondering exactly what he would do in his retirement. In spite of what he had said to Mrs Ruskin when she came in the Friday before, he did not feel the least bit 'gaga' even though he was past seventy. It certainly would be an interest, to follow what was happening with the shop; he might even be able to help them with bits from his fund of local knowledge. He didn't need the money immediately from the sale, and renting the whole thing out would give him a little income to be going on with. He got on well with his sister, who had invited him to move in and share her big house with her; but it would nevertheless be nice to have an excuse to regularly go into the town, to have something 'to keep an eye on' - without having to *do* any of the work himself. Moreover, what finally tipped the balance perhaps, was the fact that he had had the notice in his window for one whole week; he had mentioned his intention to sell for some time before that to a number of other, potentially interested people, but he had not had a single serious enquiry - until Mrs Ruskin came along. The state of being 'in suspense' about anything really did upset him, more and more the older he got. When he went upstairs to bed that night, above the shop, he had made up his mind about what to do.

When Kate entered Whittle's Sweetshop and Tobacconist's the next morning she was met by a serious-faced Henry Whittle behind the counter who looked at her searchingly under his eyebrows. Her heart missed a beat. She had felt so sure the day before that she had managed to persuade him to let her and Stanley rent the business from him, instead of selling it. But it looked as if -
"All right Mrs Ruskin," and his face relaxed a little though it was still serious. "Well, we'd better thrash out the details and then we can draw up a contract. I think two years to start with; that should give you time to see if you can make a go of it - which means a profit and a living wage for you and your husband. Then we can make an assessment after that. I may need to sell, you know - or I might be dead!" But Henry's throaty laugh as he spoke suggested that he did not really think his health was in immediate danger.

Mark Edwards was not quite sure what the situation would be when he arrived in Laverton in the early afternoon of Tuesday. As well as the business of the loan to "the Ruskins" - he was trying to train himself to think of it under that heading and not just as a loan to Kate - it was also sinking in that he must start seriously to consider who could take over from her as manager when she left. He knew that Lily James was proving to be very capable and that Kate thought highly of her; but his fear was that she was still very young. Her only experience had been in the Laverton shop and she had no experience in hiring or being in charge of other staff. It was a bit of a conundrum. There was no one suitable he could think of in the Sprinton store who would be interested in moving to Laverton either. It really had been a piece of great good fortune, he thought ruefully, that when they were planning the opening of the Laverton store, now more than four years back, they had thought of Kate Atkinson, and that she had been willing to take it on and move. The only other possibility was to advertise the position both around Laverton and in Boxley - The Boxley Advertiser was the obvious place - and hope that someone with experience perhaps from one of the bigger stores, of which there were several in Boxley, would apply. Well, he would discuss this with Kate too, but not today.

There were five directors of Binns. Apart from Mark Edwards himself, who was now the managing director, there were his parents, a very old family friend who was also the firm's lawyer, and, finally, the chief accountant of the firm. This last, Nigel Pitt, as a very young man had been taken on by his shrewd grandfather who thought he showed promise in the accounting department. His grandfather's judgement, as in so many other things, had turned out to be sound and Nigel Pitt became invaluable to the firm as financial advisor as well as chief book-keeper. The only one that Mark Edwards had consulted concerning the loan that he was about to make to the Ruskins, was the lawyer who was his personal friend, Graham Linley. There was in fact no reason to bring the firm into it at all since it was a personal loan. The money had nothing to do with either the business or his wife, but he wanted to be able to present the young couple, for their own peace of mind much more than his - he wouldn't have cared if he never saw a penny of it again - with a contract that set out clearly the terms that they had agreed informally. For that he needed the advice of a legal friend and so he had turned to Graham. Thus he had a preliminary paper with him when he went to meet Kate in Laverton on Tuesday afternoon.

....

At the distillery, the mood was sombre. The closure, now only a few weeks away, meant the end of employment for fifteen people. A few of them, already too old to serve in the war, had worked at the distillery continuously for more than twenty years. For them, now in their fifties, it was going to be difficult to find other work. Michael had good hopes of a job in one of the engineering companies in Boxley. He had already written and been to visit and had a verbal offer from one. Stanley had remained vague and non-committal about his plans, not wanting to say anything about the idea that he and Kate had until there was something definite to report, whether negative or positive. His vagueness, which his concerned friend thought was due to a strange indecisiveness on Stanley's part, made Michael anxious about his friend's future, "And with a baby on the way," he said to Agnes, "I don't understand it. It's not like Stan."

Stanley was about to put Michael's mind at rest, however. He had finished work early the day before and had gone home to meet Kate and Mr Edwards. (This was not so difficult to arrange now that the boilers were more often running at half capacity, and they ceased distilling earlier in the afternoon). It was the first time Mark Edwards had had a real conversation with Stanley and this one was anyway rather a special one. Stanley, for example, had little knowledge of the law or of contracts; nevertheless he asked intelligent questions about the agreement that he and Kate were entering into, and Mark Edwards couldn't help but be impressed by his manner. He also saw that Stanley was devoted to Kate. This showed in the way that he sometimes glanced at her and the concern that he expressed for her well-being.

The agreement was drawn up; the three of them went over to see Henry Whittle, who pulled down the blind, and turned the Closed sign to the outside. It didn't take long before everything was signed and sealed. In six weeks time Henry would move out of the house and in with his sister; the Ruskins would take over his remaining stock and order in some new.

Stanley told all this to Michael who greeted the news with both surprise and approval, "Why you sly devil. I never thought when you told me you wouldn't mind having a shop and being your own boss, that you were in the process of doing it! Good for you, Stan, and your missus is an expert at that already. Hey!" a thought occurred to him, "You do know you'll be exchanging one boss for another, don't you!" He laughed and slapped Stanley on the back. "And you won't be able to escape when you finish work.... Ha!" he teased, "but I wouldn't mind working for Mrs Ruskin. If you ever decide to quit, just give me the nod, will you?" Stanley smiled; he knew that Michael admired Kate, "Not likely," he answered. "*That* boss is taken and, I can promise you," he wagged a finger at his friend, "that this is going to be a close *partnership* - no bosses or else two!" They returned to their work, Michael still shaking his head in wonderment at what had been going on, under his very nose as it were, and he hadn't suspected a thing.

The drive from Laverton back to Sprinton had become Mark Edwards' "thinking time". There was often a lot to think about on this particular journey. This time no less than others but....he felt tranquil, content, as if - and he had no way of knowing if this was a just comparison, since he had no children, but - he thought it might have been something like the feeling a man would get after just hearing that he had become a father! No, that was ridiculous... but anyway he felt happier in a contented way than he had felt for a long time. He thought back to the meeting he had had with Kate and Stanley, upstairs in their flat sitting around the kitchen table. It felt like a home, in a way that his own house never did. Kate and Stanley, both serious, but Kate with a light in her eyes (her lovely eyes), Stanley pensive, serious, a more watchful look in his. His heart had been touched by how vulnerable they seemed, and young. Suddenly he felt that somehow in bringing about this contract, this agreement between them, he had become the guardian of their happiness. Yes, that was it. Her lover he could never be, but couldn't he be their guardian, a kind of guardian at any rate?

A motorbus loomed up in front of him. It was the one that passed near the Atkinson's farm. It was an omen - all the omens were good omens today. That meant he was only a few miles from the stables. If he took a slightly different road he could be there in twenty minutes. He could call in and say hello to Beatrix, or Trixy, as he and all the stable hands called her. Trixy had been his horse since she was two years old, and now she was nearly ten. When she was born to one of their best broodmares, his niece, aged seven, was allowed to name the foal. She chose Beatrix. "Why Beatrix?" She was asked, "That's quite a long name if you want to call a horse to you."

"It wasn't too long for Beatrix," the child replied with her child's precise logic. "Beatrix who?" Mark had interposed, curious about the workings of the child mind. "Beatrix Potter", came the reply. "She wrote the Tale of Squirrel Nutkin and Peter Rabbit. They're my favourite stories." So Beatrix it was, on paper and on her stall - but it soon became shortened to Trixy when it turned out that she was an unusually lively, not to say frisky little " B…" according to all the stable hands who had to see to her and look after her in the everyday. Eventually Mark, whose horse she was destined to be, called her Trixy too. He had ridden her regularly for almost eight years. She turned out to be a good jumper and they had competed together for a few seasons, until she sprained one of her forelegs. After that, not wishing her to suffer any more hurt, he simply rode her over the open countryside or through the woods that came to within a mile of the stables. He had missed last Saturday's ride, having been obliged to go up to High Bridge to sort out a problem the shop there had had with one of its key suppliers. It was always a blot on the week if he had to miss a ride. Yes, he would call in on Beatrix.

The head stable lad, Vince Talbot, who was now rather older than the word 'lad' implied, was just finishing bedding down and feeding the stabled horses when he arrived.

"Oh afternoon, Mr Mark," he greeted him. "You weren't aiming to take her out were you?"

"No, no," came the reply. "I was just passing by and thought I'd look in; I missed last Saturday you know."

"Ay, ay so you did. Well, I'm just on my way. See you this Saturday?"

"You certainly will. Goodnight Vince." Hearing the familiar voice of her master Trixy came to the front of her stall and put her head out. Mark Edwards stroked her neck and ran his hand down her nose. Except for the occasional whinnying from one of the other stalls and the sound of shuffling straw it was quiet. All the men had gone home. Mark Edwards patted and stroked the mare's neck, murmuring into her ear. Her ear twitched and she turned towards him, listening, as she always did, to the story he had to tell her, the story of his love.

The advertisement in the Boxley Advertiser for the position of manager of the Laverton Binns brought in four applications, three from Boxley of which one was male, the other two female, and one from High Bridge (the post was advertised within the company too). All had a background in the retail trade, three in ladies garments or accessories; the male applicant seemed to have had a more supervisory position in charge of men's and women's outdoor and footwear at Boxley's biggest department store. Something in his letter of application suggested that he saw the Laverton position as a kind of winding down towards his eventual retirement - the man was the oldest applicant and expressed a desire to move to a smaller town than Boxley "where the pace of life was slower".

"I'm afraid that disqualifies him straight away," Mark Edwards said as he went through the letters of application with Kate. "What does he think we are - a little village shop where everyone falls asleep in the afternoon!" They decided to interview the two women from Boxley and Mark Edwards himself would go to High Bridge and talk to the woman who had applied from there.

In the event none of the applicants seemed to be suitable. Kate knew exactly what was wanted and her questions, though not unkindly asked, were to the point. Mark Edwards mainly listened and was again impressed by her professionalism and grieved anew by the fact that, professionally, Binns was losing her. His subsequent conversation with the woman who had applied in High Bridge brought no better result. There was now only one month left before Kate was due to leave.

On his next Thursday visit he took her to lunch at the Victoria so that they could discuss what was to be done. The balance of their professional relationship seemed to have shifted in the weeks since Kate had told him of her pregnancy and, on the issue of finding someone to replace her, they seemed to have become equals; the realisation came to Mark Edwards that he had come to rely on her judgement almost implicitly.

Having just decided that none of the outside applicants that they had had 'cut the mustard', they were sitting for the moment in silence, each with their own thoughts, as they waited to be served. Kate was the first to break the silence, "I know you think that Lily is a bit young for the responsibility," she said, "but I really do think that she would grow into it, at least if she got the chance to take over things gradually. If she knew there was someone she could turn to for help when there's something she didn't know quite how to deal with…." Her companion looked over at her and frowned slightly as he took in what she had just said,

"You mean that I should act - temporarily," he paused, emphasizing the last word, "as manager of the Laverton Binns?"

"Yes, couldn't you?" She looked at him and, emboldened by his tone, reserved perhaps but thoughtful, ventured, "Lily knows all the routines; she knows our customers. She knows a lot about our suppliers and manufacturers. You wouldn't need to be here all the time." She smiled at him, adding, "No more probably than over this last month, maybe less, once a fortnight…." she paused, "You could have regular telephone contact, once or twice a week. A lot of things can be sorted out over the phone and Lily is quite used to answering the telephone now." She added, "I've trained her, you know. She used to be quite frightened of it but not any more." Mark Edwards regarded her under his brows, from across the table. It seemed to him that the fourteen years difference between them were diminishing by the hour. He shook his head and turned back to the matter in hand.

"Well," he said, for indecisiveness was not one of his faults.

"All right, Mrs Ruskin," emphasizing the name that, in the course of the last month he had almost given over in favour of 'Kate'. Pause. "We'll give it a try." Kate blushed. She didn't quite know why. Was it due to his use of "We". Had she acquired some kind of power over this man who, until recently she had regarded as her respected, and decent, but somewhat distant, boss?

Later that afternoon Kate had a long talk with Lily. She could tell that, although she expressed some nervousness at the prospect of 'partly' stepping into Kate's shoes when she left, yet there was at the same time excitement in her face at the challenge; even, at the end of their talk, eagerness - like a horse in the starting box just before a race began. Kate carefully explained that Mr Edwards would be the manager to whom she could turn for advice but she, Lily, would be assistant manager responsible for the day to day running of the shop. They would of course have to take on one more assistant, probably part-time to begin with, since Lily would have less time to serve customers and more 'backroom' responsibilities. Kate would spend a good amount of her time in this, her last, month, training Lily for her new position.

When Lily and Maureen had gone home and the shop was closed, she rang Mark Edwards, who she rightly guessed would still be at Binns in Sprinton, and told him about her conversation with Lily. Sitting in his spacious office on the top floor of the store, with the early evening sun flooding the room, Mark Edwards smiled into the telephone. Of course he took in all that the woman on the other end of the line was saying but in his mind's eye he was seeing her face and reflecting that within a week he would be seeing her again, in the flesh, her soon to be maternal flesh, and they would talk 'of many things,' and not just the staffing of Binns.

At home that evening Dorothy showed an unusual amount of interest in his affairs by asking him how the appointment of a manager to replace 'that Mrs Ruskin', was going. To avoid there being any misunderstandings or complaints in the future about the more frequent visits he was making to Laverton, and coming home late, he thought it best to give her a summary of what was happening. Her only comment, which succeeded in irritating him as so many of her comments on the business did, was to wonder aloud how it could be so difficult to find someone who could run a shop "in a little place like Laverton. It can't be that complicated surely?" In order to prevent himself from making a useless and angry retort to this he said he had some paperwork to do and retreated to his workroom. His wife's voice followed him. "You shouldn't need to do all this paperwork, Mark. You're the Managing Director. You should delegate more."

In the flat above Binns in Laverton Kate and Stanley were having their tea and Kate had just finished telling Stanley about the conversation with Mr Edwards over lunch at the Victoria and the subsequent talk she had had with Lily.
"I think she'll do all right," Kate said, "she learns fast and the responsibility - it could be the making of her. And since Mr Edwards will be the official manager she knows she's got someone who knows all about the business to fall back on. He's a good boss, you know, Stan. Not like some… he cares about the staff. We saw that in Sprinton." As she came round to Stanley's side of the table he caught hold of her and pulled her onto his knee.
"But Mr Edwards has been really lucky to have you, sweetheart, and I hope you haven't taken too much on," he patted her swelling front lightly, "the 'two' of you - coaching Lily, and Thomas still coming every week. Shouldn't you be using your afternoon off to rest?" He looked up at her. "I do wonder if this isn't the worst time to be moving *and* arranging and opening up the shop!" But Kate would have none of it. She felt fine, really well,
"We're a tough breed, you know, Stanley. My mother did her farm work up to the last day, literally, of nine out of ten pregnancies."
"And which was the exception?" Stanley looked at her quizzically, perched on his knee as she grinned down at him.
"Well, me," she laughed, "Mother said I'd made her sicker than all the others put together - and she claimed I was a most troublesome baby who never wanted to sleep and give her a break!"
"Well, I'm glad she decided to keep you and not give you *back* to the gypsies!" Kate reached for a cushion to hit him with as she got up off his knee.

There was indeed a lot to be seen to before the move. Henry Whittle had invited them to visit the house which was both above and behind the shop. On the ground floor beside the shop was a living room and behind that was a kitchen and a scullery with a toilet leading off it. Outside there was a wash and coal-house and, beyond, a long walled garden to the river at the end. The back of the house and garden was south-facing and got whatever sun there was. The row of trees on the other side of the river cast shade only onto the very end of the garden. Upstairs was a sitting room and a bedroom looking onto the Market Place, and behind, one more bedroom and a bathroom that Henry Whittle had had made from a third small bedroom, when he got married. There was also another stair up to a top floor which contained two more bedrooms looking out onto the market place. These rooms were totally empty and hadn't been used for years. Henry couldn't remember the last time he'd even been up there.

After William had died, now eight years ago, he had done practically nothing to the house and lived more and more solely on the ground floor, only going upstairs to sleep. The life, his neighbours said, had gone out of him, and who could wonder at it. He wasn't prepared to spend much on renovation he told the Ruskins, since he would be selling eventually, but if they wanted to redecorate any of the rooms they were welcome to do it; but that would have to be at their own expense. The cooking range in the kitchen was still good, he said, though he hardly used it nowadays. He would have the upstairs toilet seen to - something needed replacing - but otherwise the bathroom was in good condition. His son had had the bathroom modernised just a year before he died.

Stanley devoted the month before they were due to move to painting, wallpapering and repairing. Two weekends Michael came and helped him with wallpapering, "All those hours your wife has given to helping our Thomas, I should think I can spare these few to do a bit of wallpapering," he had said when Stanley protested that he was taking his friend from precious time at home. And Agnes wouldn't hear of anything else. She said she knew that otherwise Kate would insist on doing more than she ought at this stage of her pregnancy and, she confided to Michael, "she's been looking a bit peaky these last few weeks but she *will* go on doing as much."

At last it was time for the move. Kate had six weeks to go before her 'due' date - although these could never be *very* accurately predicted Dr Murray had told her. Henry Whittle had moved in with his sister the month before but he had offered to continue coming to the shop every day until Stanley had the house ready. Stanley gratefully accepted the offer; he also realised that for Henry it made for a gentler withdrawal from the scene of his more than fifty year life in his shop. And it gave Stanley a chance to make his and Kate's preparations for the reopening, 'Under new management' as the sign they were making out, said. They had decided that, from the day they moved into the house, the shop would be closed for one week while they repainted, rearranged and furnished the interior.

There was a wood merchant's yard on the outskirts of the town and Stanley, who had made the requisite measurements on the chosen wall, went in search of wood for the task he had in mind. The wood merchant cut and Stanley bevelled, stained and polished the wood, which was pine. He planned to have three, semi-circular, fold-down tables fixed to one wall of the shop, where two people could sit and share a pot of tea, ("or ice cream!" Stanley added when he showed Kate his plan). Michael came again to help him fix the tables to the wall.

Doing the rounds of junkyards within a five mile radius of Laverton - his bicycle really had earned its keep - Stanley had managed to bring home six cane chairs which needed just a little repair, and staining, before they could be used quite neatly and, Kate said, prettily, at the fold-down tables. When they moved the counter and put up more shelves on another wall, for the ceiling in the shop was high, they found that there really was quite a lot of empty space where they could have a number of free-standing small tables too.

Kate was in the habit of visiting Mrs Taylor, at the Cedars, where she had lived for the first two years of her time in Laverton; on one such visit, happening to mention the preparations they were making for the imminent re-opening of Whittle's shop, and the space they found they had for a few more tables, Mrs Taylor threw up her hands and cried "Oh my dear, if it's tables you need why we have an outhouse full of them which I should be delighted to get rid of. You know, in my poor dear father-in-law's time they had a quite extensive croquet lawn at the back here. My husband told me that it was a regular feature of his childhood, in the summer, to have friends of his parents and relatives for croquet parties and tea on the back lawn. When that ceased and his parents died - shortly before we got married - the tables and chairs were all piled up and stored, in the outhouse you see beyond the cedar tree. You are welcome to look and see if they would be suitable for your teashop. You may take as many as you like - I fear they would need to be repainted but, do take a look." Kate went and looked. Certainly they needed a coat of paint, and while the table tops were slatted wood, the supports, for they folded flat, were all of metal. But, to start with she thought they would do very well. Could they take four tables, and the chairs that went with them? "My dear, as many as you like. Perhaps you could use one yourselves in your garden - take five or six!"

Stanley managed to borrow a handcart and came to fetch the tables and chairs from the Cedars. Mrs Taylor had had a soft spot for Stanley ever since that very first visit when he cycled down from Sprinton to visit Kate just two weeks after the opening of the Laverton Binns. Mrs Taylor remembered how she and her sister had looked at them sitting out on the same back lawn, where they had served them tea and fruit-cake; they had looked at one another and said, "That really is love!" A lump came to her throat now, watching from the same window as Stanley fetched and loaded the little tables and chairs on the cart, refusing to let his heavily pregnant wife help him and persuading her to just hold the door of the outhouse open while he dealt with the tables and chairs. It was a ploy to keep her occupied and out of harm's way Mrs Taylor could see. Tears came to her eyes as she thought of her sister whose fiancé had been killed in the war. Emily, she knew, would never be able to have the experience that she was just then witnessing from her window.

For the removal from the flat to Mr Whittle's house, a distance of something less than two hundred yards, a cart and horse was in any case needed, and once again Michael Chivers came up trumps - or rather Agnes did. Among her several brothers was James who was a tenant farmer. It was his horse, Lupin, pulling his cart, that Agnes had procured from her brother to enable the Ruskins to move, one Saturday, from one end of the marketplace to the other. Michael and James both helped Stanley with the big and heavy stuff, while Agnes tried to keep Kate from doing more than she should, either in the old place or the new. Thomas, now eight and a half, and deeply attached to "Auntie Ruskin" as he called Kate, ran between the two, sometimes 'helping' his father and Stanley and sometimes running to see what the women were doing. It was all very exciting. He had never been involved in a house moving before.

When James departed with Lupin and an empty cart there was a sense of satisfaction, as well as the tiredness, which comes at the completion of a house move. Michael and Agnes, and Thomas of course, stayed on to help with any final bits of moving heavy stuff from one part of a room into another, in case the first option turned out not to have been quite right. The front bedroom, directly over the shop, was to be Kate and Stanley's bedroom and the sitting room next to it Kate wanted to be their usual sitting room. It had a similar 'feel' to it as the one above Binns, due to it being up above street level, looking down over the marketplace though from a different side. Kate knew that would be her favourite room.

In the week that followed Stanley did all that was needed to get the shop ready to open. Under direction from Kate, he painted the tables and chairs that had come from the Cedars, and Lily was enlisted, and paid - although she protested at that - to make ten little cushion covers for ten small cushions for the metal chairs, which otherwise, Kate reasoned, would feel too cold and unyielding. The re-stained and plaited cane chairs didn't need cushions. The atmosphere and appearance of the shop had changed completely. What had for a decade been dark and not a little musty, with vestiges of old tobacco smells in the air, was now light, bright and airy. Against the white of the metal chairs and the table supports, the little cushions were a warm red. The tablecloths, also made by Lily, were a pale grey heavy cotton material that also happened to be popular that summer for ladies' dresses. Such a thing - light grey tablecloths - had never been seen before; and the grey was reflected in the colour of the new shelves on the wall behind the counter full of big jars of multi-coloured sweets.

The space given to pipes, tobacco and cigars was much reduced, the cigars and tobacco being kept in a closed glass cabinet on the short wall at one end of the counter away from the door. That way there was scarcely any presence of tobacco detectable by the average human "olfactory" system, said Kate to Stanley, teasingly. (He did indeed have to resort to a dictionary for a definition of "olfactory".) Kate wanted the shop to have a scent of pure good chocolate in it, and not tobacco. All was now ready.

Henry Whittle stayed away from the market place during the Ruskins first week of opening. He knew that it would look quite different from 'his' shop and although he had listened to Stanley's account of what he and Kate wanted to do, and he was not unsympathetic, but indeed quite intrigued and interested to see how it would go, yet he was not quite certain what his feelings would be when he saw it and went inside. Both Kate and Stanley had been very welcoming and insisted that he must come. Kate even said that she hoped she could ask his advice if she needed it. Nevertheless Henry felt, on several counts, that it would be better if he kept his nose out of it, at least for the first week or so.

They had decided not to advertise the fact that they would be serving teas if requested. They would leave that to people to discover when they came in to buy sweets and chocolate, or tobacco - but they were not going to allow smoking in the shop. "That would very likely discourage the ladies who I envisage as being our most frequent patrons for tea," Kate said. They agreed that they would let news of what they had to offer be spread by word of mouth, "the quickest growing grapevine to be found in any small town or village," Kate said. Not least of course in this case was the fact that Kate personally already had a reputation in the town among the entire female population, as the respected and well liked manager of Binns. Many of them were likely to come into the 'new' Whittle's out of pure curiosity.

And they did - and they stayed to buy chocolate and to order a pot of tea - and sponge cake. Stanley's knowledge of the domestic arts, in particular baking, were about to bear fruit! He had watched, indeed helped, the cook and her assistant at the Blue Lion in Sprinton, so many times over the more than four years he spent there, that he really could, he said, make sponge cakes and simnel cake (the Blue Lion Easter speciality) blindfolded, if need be! The chocolates that Kate had also added to their sweet assortments, also found popularity as did glasses of hot chocolate. Stanley proved to be their mainstay in the kitchen, not only as chief baker, which he was, but also because, having an aptitude for dealing with all things mechanical, he had read up all he could find on everything from ovens to hot chocolate and ice cream machines.

The sweet and tea shop looked like being a success, if the first week was anything to go by. It was unique in what it offered and, Stanley maintained, it could even be seen as a companion piece to Binns. Mark Edwards paid them a visit at the end of their first week of trading. He came in when Kate was just about to serve two ladies with the scones they had ordered with their tea. She had her back to him.

"I wonder, Mrs Ruskin, if you have any of those cigars that I am particularly fond of?" She turned to face him, smiling.

"Why, Mr Edwards, I think that you might just be in luck," she nodded towards the two ladies who were chatting as one poured out the tea. "Just one moment and I will be with you." He watched as she moved over to serve the customers with their scones.

"Well," he said, when she returned and slipped behind the counter, "I can see you are going to be a great success here, just as you were at Binns. In fact, aren't you starting to steal away our customers? Please tell them that they have to come to us after they have finished here!" Kate laughed,

"But my dear sir, the ladies only come here *after* they have exhausted themselves, and their purses, at your excellent emporium just across the way!" He looked around appreciatively, then, lowering his voice slightly, "Seriously, my dear Kate, this is beautiful," he said, and looked her directly in the face. He went on, "I won't stay for tea - today, but another time certainly." He nodded towards the pipe and cigar cabinet. "I hope you will not give up that side of the business entirely. I would miss," he leant towards her and paused, a rueful look on his face, "I would miss terribly not being able to get my favourite smokes from you."

"I wouldn't think," she returned, "of not having them."

In the course of the first two weeks of opening it was brought home to them, how many friends and well-wishers they had in Laverton. There seemed to be a steady stream of people they knew visiting the shop every day - as well as many they didn't. Mrs Taylor from the Cedars came the second day with a friend; she bought chocolates and shared a pot of tea and cherry cake with her friend, and declared herself to be tickled by the fact that they were sitting on chairs, at one of the tables, that years before had been part of the croquet teas at the Cedars. She thought the Ruskins had made a really lovely job of refurbishing them. "Really artistic," she declared quite loudly to the friend who was deaf.

Agnes came in the first week too, with a sister, and Thomas, who had been promised a glass of 'real lemonade' and a big piece of chocolate cake as consolation for the fact that, as Kate explained to him, his Wednesday fun days would have to be discontinued for a while as she was needed by Stanley to get the teashop established *and,* his mother told him, she was going to have a baby very soon. This last upset Thomas the most because, not knowing the details about how people came by babies, he got it into his head that he was being replaced by a baby because he was somehow unsatisfactory. This hurt him very much for he had become very attached to Auntie Ruskin, and it was clear to him that babies were very boring. It had taken Kate a long time to persuade him that he was mistaken, but he was mollified at last.

Henry Whittle finally came at the beginning of the second week. He had heard so much about the new shop from other people that he could no longer resist; when he arrived he was greeted warmly by Kate, who came round from behind the counter and shook his hand. He was so disarmed by her greeting that he felt quite overcome and found himself, as he recounted to his sister when he got home, 'babbling' to Kate about what a lovely job they had made of 'the old place'. He would not have recognised it he said, if he'd been led in there blindfold. No, in the end, all the reservations that he imagined he might have, melted away, and he could only wish them every success. To his sister he added, "You know it could be a little goldmine. I hope for their sake it is - they're a nice young couple."

CHAPTER 14

End of a Marriage

As the acting manager of the Laverton Binns Mark Edwards had decided to keep to Thursdays for his visits; but he also decided that he would come every Thursday if possible. This was a temporary arrangement he told his wife. Possibly only for a year until the young woman who he had made assistant manager, "you know, the one who made you that dress you were so pleased with, Lily James."

"It was a blouse," his wife replied coldly. "I thought you said she was too young?"

"Yes, well, she seems to be very competent, better than any who answered the advertisement, and Kay - Mrs Ruskin, had a high opinion of her. We decided to give her a chance...." It could not have been predicted that this exchange with his wife, although tediously familiar in its underlying tone of hostility, would change the whole course of their lives.

"I wouldn't have thought it was very wise to let your staff tell you what to do -" Dorothy said in that slightly disparaging tone that she had adopted of late whenever the Laverton shop, and in particular its manager was mentioned.

"Mrs Ruskin", her husband said angrily, "has been with the company for ten years. She's the best head of a department and manager we've ever had or are likely to have. She has more intelligence in her little finger than yo - "He was shouting now and he was shaking. Dorothy went white and appeared to be rooted to the spot. Dimly aware of what he had revealed in this outburst, and fearing that he might physically assault his wife if he stayed in the room, he strode out and slammed the door. He must get out of this wretched prison and breathe some fresh untainted air. He flew out of the house and down the garden path trying to calm himself. He continued through the spinney at the bottom to the gate into the field beyond. It was all his own land: the field a meadow, the grass knee high and dotted with wild flowers. He leaned on the five barred gate and gazed over it unseeing. He came to a realisation. He could not go on with this 'sham' - no, not 'sham' - 'dead' marriage. Why had he stayed so long - no, why had *they* stayed so long? He leant on the gate, his head bowed.

Dorothy had remained on the spot where he had shouted at her and stormed out of the room, and out of the house. Then she collapsed onto the nearest sofa, in tears, her hands over her face. For the first time she faced her misery. It had been coming a long time. Why? "Oh, mummy," she cried, appealing to the one person who had steered her life, who had been the measure of all things, right up until her death five years before. Why had it gone wrong? She had done all the right things...she was sure.

Back at the beginning, she was one of Sprinton's 'society' crowd of young people. At twenty she was one of the prettier girls, light brown hair, curly, and sky-blue eyes, medium height, slim. She had met Mark Edwards at the tennis club, was partnered with him for a friendly match against High Bridge, a much smaller club, and they were tipped to win. Her friend, Eunice, drew up the tables and put her with him. She had only met him once before. She had been away, in France, for six months. Her mother said, to rise in society you needed a little 'continental polish' and some French. But Dorothy was miserable. The family she was sent to *were* polished, were cultivated: she couldn't keep up and she hated foreign languages, she decided. The private girls' school that her father had paid fees for had emphasized etiquette and deportment but neglected culture - and French. She came back with entrenched views about all continentals, but the French in particular, and a conviction, that her mother endorsed, that the English middle and upper classes were the epitome of everything. When Mark Edwards was kind to her after they lost their match to the High Bridge pair she was ready to follow him to the world's end - but her mother had taught her, and emphasised that, as far as young men were concerned, she must 'always keep them guessing'.

Mark Edwards, at twenty five, and just settling into the family business, after three years at Cambridge, was the handsomest in their 'set', six foot one, brown hair, serious hazel eyes. She fell in love that afternoon - no, it was infatuation. She was infatuated for two years - until the miscarriage.

When Dorothy told her mother that she had fallen in love with her tennis partner of the afternoon, and that his name was Mark Edwards, Edith Pridmore was ecstatic. Her daughter had met and fallen for the most eligible, and rumoured to be, richest of the cream of Sprinton's society, and he was apparently smitten too. Whatever she did she must not let him go - Mark Edwards was the best catch in town. Dorothy was to hear that phrase almost every day from now on. Her friends Eunice and Mary Turner confirmed it, if in slightly different words.

"Darling, he's a dish," they said, and, after only three months, "when are you going to announce the engagement?"

Their conversations when they met - and the meetings became ever more frequent - was largely light and flirtatious and, when they became steadily and seriously entangled, it was largely wordless. She had known Mark Edwards for almost six months when Dorothy discovered she was pregnant. He turned pale and fell silent when she told him. According to the ethics and practice of his class, if he was a decent and honourable man he must marry her. He was, and he did. The strong physical appeal that she still exerted over him, he decided must be love - yes, this would work out. It could be a good marriage.

Despite the wedding being arranged at fairly short notice, it went off in style and the couple travelled to Eastbourne for a week's honeymoon at the resort's best hotel. When they returned to Sprinton they moved into the house called The Four Winds where they had stayed ever since. There were ten acres of land belonging to the house, including the spinney and the meadow. In the early, hopeful days of the marriage, Mark planned to build a stable on the meadow big enough for two horses, or one horse and a pony. He hoped to teach his wife to ride, and there would be children later he guessed. Little could either of them have known that only two months into the marriage its death knell would be sounded.

At just over half way through the pregnancy, Dorothy miscarried. She was taken to a private clinic where she rested and recovered. When she returned home she excused herself for a time from physical intimacy. She was not ready, she said, she needed more time to heal. Mark understood; he would never press her, he said: he was not a brute. Two more weeks turned into two months and Dorothy flinched from intimacy. When it resumed, less and less often, it became clear that this aspect of marriage had become for Dorothy an unwelcome and joyless duty. At the same time, and with every week that passed it also became clear that they had little in common. They were a mismatched pair.

After the failed attempt to get Dorothy to learn to ride, and then to take up other interests, which also failed, Mark was compelled to desist. He threw himself more and more into the business, which absorbed most of his waking hours, and he maintained a small share in the stud farm; his chief relaxation was riding. Frustration and an aching lack of human physical contact of any kind led him into a few short-lived affairs, but none of them had enough depth of feeling or anything approaching 'the marriage of true minds' for which he profoundly yearned. Until, that was, his attention was drawn to Miss Kate Atkinson and he had the good sense to appoint her manager of the new Binns store in Laverton.

Dorothy's trajectory in the marriage had been different. She concentrated most of her efforts on looking after, embellishing and maintaining the house. Her tastes and favoured style of interior design were entirely conventional. She knew what was reputedly good and acceptable from her reading of the magazines, from her friends and their houses, and from her mother. She recognised quality in furniture, in china and objets d'art (a phrase in French that she did not forget). And she took up charity work, because that was acceptable in the milieu in which she now moved, in fact it was really 'de rigueur' (another French expression which she grudgingly accepted it was necessary to know 'in her circles'). All her friends were involved too, in charity work, and she would scarcely have known what to do with herself if she didn't have it. Since she had lost all taste or desire for physical intimacy she never drifted into having affairs - she knew what she would be forced into if she had. It was possibly some deep-seated compensatory need that drove her then into having always two or three siamese or Burmese cats about the house, even though she was inordinately house-proud. She never could take an active interest in her husband's business. It was simply 'there', the bedrock on which her comfortable, nay, expensive way of life was based. It was the machine, immaculately maintained and well oiled whose owner and director, her husband, she had justly won in the arranged lottery that her mother had closely supervised her in winning. "Oh, mother, what did I do wrong?" She moaned miserably into the unresponsive air. She really had no idea.

Mark raised his eyes and looked over the meadow. In earlier times he would have delighted in painting the scene. Why had he given it up? He made a decision; no, the decision had been made. He went back to the house. Dorothy was moving about in the kitchen, taking things out of a cupboard and putting them back again. Her face was blank; there were signs of dried tears on her cheeks. Her husband came in behind her. He steeled himself and said,
"I'm leaving. You can file for divorce if you like, for desertion. You can keep the house - I know" his tone had a bitter edge to it, "it means more to you than anything." Then, more softly, her shoulders shook but she stayed with her back to him, "or if you prefer just separation. I don't mind." He paused, she made no move. "Dorothy," she looked up, half turned towards him, "this marriage has been dead for years. You know it has," she tried to shake her head, but he stopped her with a gesture, and said more softly, "You must have been unhappy too. It can't just have been me." He sighed, put his hands out in front of him.

"I'm sorry. We should have done this years ago." She turned towards him, a look, a mixture of resentment and despair came over her face.

"I suppose you'll be going to your sainted 'Mrs Ruskin' now, will you". The sneer that she managed to get into saying Kate's name took all the pity he had been feeling for his wife, away.

"Mrs Ruskin", he said coldly, "is a happily married woman. And her husband is a fine and decent man. Leave her out of this." She looked daggers at him but said nothing.

"I'm going now," he said, no longer looking at her. "I shall come and fetch the things I want tomorrow afternoon. I believe you have your Ladies' Guild meeting then. We need not meet." He turned and walked out of the room. She stood still for a long time. She heard him moving about upstairs, collecting some things into a suitcase, presumably. He came down and went into his 'workroom'. When he came out into the hall he was carrying the suitcase and a portfolio in the other hand. Dorothy stood in the hall, the kitchen door closed behind her. She said nothing. He glanced briefly in her direction before leaving; she heard his footsteps going down the steps and across the gravel to his car. The car started and crunched slowly over the driveway to the gate. And then he was gone.

When he drove away he actually had no idea where he would go. At a pinch he could sleep in the car: the back seat was big and roomy, but then he would have to find somewhere to park where it wouldn't attract unwanted attention - not so easy. He couldn't bed down in the straw beside Trixy - that mad idea *had* flitted across his mind. He had to smile at it. He certainly couldn't go to his parents' house: apart from the fact that his father was now quite badly crippled with arthritis and needed help from both the nurse who came to him in the evening, as well as his mother, going there would also mean immediate, long and difficult explanations, and he simply wasn't up to it at the moment. Two other possibilities, a friend and a cousin, were dismissed for various reasons. No, the only real option was his closest and long time friend, Graham Linley. He tried to think about whether there would be any problem in the future about having gone to Graham, since he was also the company's chief lawyer and a senior director of Binns. His mind was too exhausted by the upheaval of the evening to come to any rational conclusion about that so he finally had to say to himself, 'Let it be.' He drove into Sprinton and parked behind the store in the space that was marked with his name. He would have to go to his office and telephone

Graham to see if he could put him up for the night. Graham lived in a tall, Regency, terraced town house not far from Binns. He was a bachelor, a few years older than Mark, who was known among his colleagues to have 'a good friend' Bernard, also a lawyer, to whom he was very close, but they did not live together. He got through quickly - the operator was not very busy - and Graham, immediately concerned when he heard the voice on the other end of the line, told him to come round at once.

He left the car where it was and walked round to Graham's house, less than five minutes away: the walk did him good. Graham led him up to his sitting room, on the first floor,
"Let me have those, old chap," he said, taking from him the case and portfolio, "I was just sitting here with a brandy and my notes on the Bulmer's case. And you look as if you could do with the same -" allowing himself a slight smile, "but without the notes of course. Take a seat." Mark suddenly realised how exhausted he was. He sank gratefully into the winged chair offered him, opposite his friend's. He closed his eyes briefly and opened them to find Graham handing him a glass. The liquid winked and glowed. He thought what a rich deep golden colour it had. Graham, seated opposite, observed him with a slightly furrowed brow. "Don't feel you have to tell all just now," he said. "You look whacked. We can take the full story tomorrow." Nevertheless he had to give Graham the gist of what had passed between him and his wife an hour before.

....

Lily was getting into her stride as the new assistant manager of the Laverton Binns. Kate had given her a good run-in before she left, and afterwards, until the baby was born, she came back a couple of times a week to see how Lily was getting on and to let her ask for advice if she needed it. A new part-time girl, Phyllis, had been taken on and Lily gained in confidence from training her. Kate saw that she was doing well, and when Mark Edwards visited, almost every Thursday, he seemed to be satisfied too. It did seem as if he was a bit abstracted for a couple of weeks. Perhaps there had been a problem in Sprinton. They had heard nothing in Laverton, but then why would they if something happened that didn't concern the Laverton shop.

He made a point of calling in at the Ruskins' tea shop whenever he came - well, all except once - and Kate always made sure that she had in the cigars that he liked. Just once it was odd - he was in, made a few disjointed remarks, had his usual hot chocolate and obviously wanted to engage her in conversation. She wondered if he might be ill; he looked paler than usual but he said nothing and when he left, he had forgotten his cigars. She went after him. She called out, "Mr Edwards!...Mark!" He turned at the sound of his name, saw that she could not hurry to reach him, and ran back, anxiety for her written on his face. "Oh, my dear, of course, I'm sorry". He took the box from her and grasped her hand, holding it for a long time. "You must not run like that," he said, anguish in his face. She smiled, trying to reassure him,

"It's quite all right," she said, "I wasn't running. I can't!" She returned the grasp of his hand and looked into his face. Suddenly she saw what was in his heart. She glanced down, then, "You don't need to worry, I'm fine," looking back up at him. He nodded, released her hand and turned to go.

Stanley emerged from the kitchen as Kate came back in the door.
"Oh, there you are," he said, "I called but got no reply, I was worried!"
"Is everyone worrying about me this morning - "she protested, brow wrinkling.
"Who's 'everyone'?" said Stanley looking around, for the shop was empty. So she told him about Mark Edwards visit, and how, uncharacteristically, he had left his cigars behind. "I wondered if he might be ill?" She said. "I went after him with them and he told me not to run....". She didn't mention the look she had seen in his eyes.

"Now *you* look worried," said Stanley. "Was there something else?"
"No," she replied, "but he just wasn't himself." She left it at that. After all, what else could she say? A look in the eyes. You could be mistaken. His mind might just have been on some other problem. Without words you couldn't be sure. She was though. But what to do about it? There wasn't anything to be done. She liked the man. He had been good to her - professionally speaking. He was being good to them, her and Stanley....personally. She didn't want the relationship to change. Stanley got on well with Mr Ed.. no 'Mark' too. They had conversations about other things than the business nowadays. Mark Edwards was interested in mechanical things, modern inventions. He went into the finer points of motor car engines, of which he had some experience, and Stanley followed him with as much interest, and could tell him about engines he had worked on. No, she didn't want anything to change. She would just behave as before. She didn't work for him now. *He* came into *their* shop. They talked about all sorts of things, like equals. Why, they had almost become friends the three of them. It would be all right.

....,

Dorothy wanted a legal separation and not a divorce. Her father, an uncle and a cousin were all solicitors. She didn't lack for legal advice. They all recommended she file for divorce. She would get more material goods and money if it was a clear divorce, and her husband had even invited her to enter desertion as the plea. But Dorothy could not contemplate what she felt would be the ultimate in humiliation and loss of face, with divorce. A divorce was made public. *She* would be seen to have been the one who had failed. She, who had won, to the puzzlement of some of her contemporaries, the richest, most handsome, in short the most eligible, of the elite youth of their town - had at last been deserted, cast aside by the 'prince'. And while he was still a handsome, fine-looking man, she had lost a lot of the prettiness of her youth. She stopped playing tennis before she was thirty and replaced the exercise by nothing more demanding than attending charity functions or driving around several counties to quality and antique auctions. In short, she had put on more weight than was 'becoming' for someone of her height and bone structure. No, she could not face the 'fate worse than death', which for her would be divorce. And the final consideration against it was that she felt sure that if Mark was freed from her by a divorce there would be several of her old acquaintances, if not friends, who would have no compunction in setting their, not so maidenly, caps at him.

A legal separation was painful enough but it had none of the finality that the word 'divorce' connoted. It could even suggest that at some time a reconciliation might take place. That idea was of course for public consumption. Dorothy knew that no reconciliation would ever take place - it was a face saving ploy for herself alone. At this stage, that was enough.

Graham was prepared to give his friend all the advice and help he could but, he suggested that to avoid any possible doubts, or loopholes that his wife's lawyers might search out to question Graham's legal impartiality, it would be better for Mark to be officially represented by someone else. He took this advice and Bernard was chosen to publicly represent him. Thereafter, he entrusted the details to Bernard for, although as Managing Director of Binns he did pay attention to detail, in affairs of the heart, of personal conduct, he was magnanimous not petty. The settlement was fair, generous in fact. Dorothy was guaranteed the house and garden and enough of a monthly allowance for its upkeep and for her personal expenditure. The rest of the adjoining land, the copse and the meadow remained Mark's. To do her justice Dorothy had never been interested in what lay beyond the garden and made no claim to it. Mark couldn't remember her even walking through the copse, far less the meadow - which he had always loved. The house Mark had long regarded as too big even for the two of them, but it was literally Dorothy's 'pride and joy' (as much at least as she was capable of joy he had reflected glumly). Perhaps it had become the substitute for the lost child. He did not want to think about that. Certainly it did represent for her her standing in society, and her social position was to Dorothy the most important thing in her life.

This being settled, Mark turned his attention to other things. The thing he had to decide for himself was: where was he going to live now? He had moved back in with his parents for the time being. Their house was itself big enough for a family with several children even though they had moved there after Mark and his siblings had left their childhood home, which was even bigger; but to begin with his parents had a cook and a live-in maid. They still had a live-in maid but the cook now came in only to make lunches and leave things ready for his parents' tea. Staying there was absolutely a temporary measure.

His parents had been less upset and disapproving of his separation from Dorothy than he expected. No one in their family before had been divorced or even separated, but that didn't mean that all the marriages had been happy. His mother had often said that her own parents were not well suited to one another. More to the point they always thought that Dorothy had tricked their son into marriage by deliberately becoming pregnant. Mark himself quarrelled with them over this, for he didn't believe it, but they never warmed to Dorothy. They sympathised when she suffered the miscarriage and assumed, as happened in most cases, that there would be other pregnancies and eventually children. But none came along and they understood before long that there was a fundamental incompatibility between their son and his wife, and then, that there were not likely to be any children from that marriage.

"Crabbéd age and youth cannot live together," went the old saying. Well, his parents weren't 'crabbed', at least not mentally, and he himself wasn't in his first youth, but the saying was true anyhow. He must think about the options. The most obvious thing was to buy or rent a house in Sprinton where the company was based. He found himself for some reason totally against doing that. The whole town, seeing it, moving about in it, reminded him of the personal failure of his last thirteen years, the years of his sterile, in every sense, marriage. It was, for him now, like a ghost town from which all life had fled.

His parents were still there and the original store with all his colleagues, but they were all part of that life of the failed marriage which he had now ended. Ah well, he would take a little time to think about it. In the meantime the business was demanding his attention. One of their chief woollen suppliers had gone out of business and they needed to find a new one. He seemed to remember that some time before, Kate had mentioned a new manufacturer, whose textiles, including woollen cloth, she had seen samples of and liked. His next visit to Laverton was due. He would ask her about that when he went for his cigars.

CHAPTER 15

New Beginnings

Lily was getting into her stride now managing the shop and as she gained experience she naturally assumed more authority. Mark came once a week, but a lot could happen, 'on her patch' in between times. For her own self respect and pride in her work, she didn't want to be phoning him for advice every other day; and the same went for her other source of assistance and inspiration, Mrs Ruskin. She knew she could call on her at any time; Kate had emphasized that she should feel free to do so. But Lily knew that she had her hands full with their new venture, The Teashop (they had officially named it now and put a sign up over the window.) The time was also approaching for her confinement and the last couple of times when she called in to ask Lily how she was getting on, Lily thought she looked quite pale and tired. She wasn't going to trouble her if she could possibly avoid it.

Mark still enjoyed the drive to Laverton; his heart lifted as the miles rolled by. It seemed to him that very often the clouds literally broke up and the sun came out as he approached the lowland town. The countryside to the west and north was gently rolling upland; Laverton was the first settlement down on the plain, at the cusp of the two landscapes. He never failed to be reminded of the time when he and Kate, then Miss Atkinson, had driven down to survey the shop and make arrangements for the opening. Kate had only been in a car once before she confessed to him, and that had been for a short journey near Sprinton. Her delight in their journey was tangible. He found himself infected by her innocent pleasure in each new view of the countryside and even the furnishing of the interior of the car. Also that day he had learnt more about her, her growing up on the farm and her family, than he had known before. When he learned what they had to contend with in the sowing and harvesting of crops, against the vicissitudes of disease and weather it filled him with respect for their tenacity and fortitude. There had been nothing superficial in Kate Atkinson's conversation. When he looked back to that drive he came to the conclusion that that had been the day when he started to fall in love with her.

He parked the car in the usual place and walked round, as he always liked to do, to come in by the shop door, on the market place. This was one of the things that slightly dulled his pleasure when he came nowadays, however. When he got into the shop, the bell jingled above his head - and *she* was not there. He missed that first sight of her always cheerful and responsive face, and her greeting, "Good morning, Mr Edwards!" But anyway he would go over to The Teashop later and find out about that manufacturer. First, there were things to be seen to here and he went to find Lily, who, in a lull before many customers arrived was trying to get on with an autumn dress that was promised to a regular customer. He appeared through the curtain that separated off Lily's sewing room and she looked up, startled; she had been so engrossed in what she was doing that she hadn't heard the bell when Mark Edwards entered the shop. He didn't often go into "the sewing den", as Phyllis dubbed it, and now he looked around it with interest but a degree of concern.
"Hello Lily, you haven't got much room here, have you?" Lily was a little discomforted by not having heard her boss come in and the fear that he might think she was not paying attention to the main part of the job.
"I'm sorry, Mr Edwards," she began,"I was trying to get something finished for Mrs Bradshaw and ….." she didn't have time to finish her apology.
"Lily, do you really have time now to do the dress-making as well as all the other things in the shop?" She blushed, reading criticism into his remark rather than the quite genuine concern that he felt when he found her working in such a tiny space. She found it difficult to formulate an answer to this,
"Well, I only do it when everything else is done," she stammered, "and there are no customers in the shop. Mostly I do the dressmaking after the shop is closed." She not infrequently, in fact, stayed until eight or nine o'clock at night to get something finished, and her mother complained, not that she was left with the little boy for most of the time, but because she thought Lily should not be bicycling home - it was a mile outside the town - often in the dark. Mark Edwards looked around the sewing den again, and back at her. Kate had, right at the beginning, told him Lily's story, about her husband being killed, quite early in the war, leaving her with a small child and part responsibility for supporting her family since her father, a farm worker, had been invalided.
"I suppose you don't want to give up the dressmaking…" he was thoughtful.
"Well no, sir," she replied, "I do like doing it and," she paused, "it does help with, you know the costs at home."
"Have you got a sewing machine at home?"

"Yes, but it's a very old one and very slow. I prefer to stay here after hours and use this one. It's much, much quicker...." she stopped. He looked at her, "If you had a better machine at home would you have the space and peace to work in?" Slightly puzzled by this interrogation she hesitated, "Well yes, once Will is in bed... there's an alcove where I have my sewing machine." She laughed, "I often sew on summer evenings when the others have gone to bed. It's more difficult in winter for the gaslighting is not so good. My eyes get tired and we try not to use too many of the candles. That's why I like staying here to work, with the electricity and that..."
"Ah, so you haven't electricity...yet?"
"No, not yet," she replied softly. It had been a hot topic at home and they had concluded that they couldn't afford to have electricity installed...'yet'. But with Lily's promotion, and higher wages now at Binns, they might manage it 'in a year or two'.
"Well, as long as you feel you can manage it all, but don't make yourself ill. We can't afford to lose you and I don't want you working yourself to death." Then, changing the subject,
"Shall we look at the books now?"

Another thing that Mark missed now that Kate had gone was, their lunches together at the Victoria. He had started making a habit of taking her there when he came on Thursdays. The excuse initially had been that the lunch was a kind of acknowledgement that she was doing excellent work for the company and that she was a senior employee. Sometimes there were also work related issues that could profitably be discussed over lunch. But more and more he had come to look forward to their lunches for the pleasure of her company and the talks that they had which had nothing to do with work. Those occasions were over and he missed them acutely. The visits to the teashop, which also were an excuse for a chat, were not the same because they were constantly being 'interrupted' by her customers. In all conscience he couldn't stay around and prevent her from doing her job, which was moreover the fulfilment of a dream. He could at least comfort himself with the fact that he had helped her materially to fulfil that dream. But lunches at the Victoria were not the same without her and he nowadays often skipped them and merely went for a pint of something, and a sandwich at the New Inn instead.

 This was such a day and, he had just emerged from the New Inn and was making his way across the marketplace intending to go for his cigars and ask

Kate about the woollen manufacturer. He might as well do that now, while he was out. Then he saw her, a woman, perhaps twenty yards ahead, with her back to him but in obvious distress, leaning on the stone edge of the fountain in the centre of the marketplace. As he hurried towards her, she turned, and he saw that it was Kate.

"Heavens, what's the matter? Are you ill?" He caught hold of her. "Come on, I'll get you home." She lifted her head,

"I suddenly felt dizzy," she said. As he half carried her the few yards to her door he noticed how flushed her face was and, even through her clothes she felt hot. Stanley came from behind the counter as they entered the teashop.

"Stanley, you had better get Kate to bed, and get the doctor. She nearly fainted out there. I think she's got a temperature too. She feels very hot." Stanley, for a moment paralysed with shock, moved quickly then to take Kate into his arms. It was no time to stand on ceremony. There was clearly something wrong.

Kate had told him that Sarah was coming to help them when the baby arrived. Had she arrived yet? She had not. She was due the next day. They needed a woman to help Kate, Mark said. He would go directly to fetch the doctor. If there was no one else he could send Phyllis over to help him. She was very capable.

He never quite understood how it was that he had taken command of the situation. It was instinctive. He just knew it was critical. Stanley was in shock and the sight of his wife, flushed and half fainting in his arms, had robbed him of the power of rational action and of speech. But Mark was mercifully not afflicted in the same way. He was instead consumed by a terrible fear, the fear that Kate was about to give birth and that she had a fever that could be fatal to her in the process. He knew about puerperal fever. It had been a possibility when Dorothy miscarried all those years ago, but she had escaped. The thought that Kate might succumb, filled him with horror.

Leaving Stanley getting his wife to the stairs, he ran to the doctor's house, a few yards up the High Street. The doctor was at home, just preparing to begin his afternoon surgery. He took up his black bag and allowed himself to be hurried by Mark past his waiting room of patients to the bedside of Mrs Ruskin.

Mark could scarcely remember what happened next. He had ushered the doctor through the shop into the house behind. The closed sign had been put up and the two customers who'd been there when Mark brought in the sick Kate, had left. Stanley appeared at the top of the stairs, white-faced. The doctor went up and Mark withdrew into the teashop and sat down at one of the tables. He

stayed there unmoving for a long time. At some point Dr Murray came down and into the shop. "I need to telephone," he said looking around, "for the midwife." Mark indicated the shelf where he knew the telephone was kept. After the doctor had gone back up the stairs to Kate, he sat on numb, unable to think. He wouldn't move until he knew how she was, what was happening. He got up and paced the floor. He went into the hall behind, looked up the stairs. He heard the low voices of the doctor and Stanley. He went back into the shop. The wait was unbearable. Finally, footsteps down the stairs. "She's all right for the moment." It was Stanley, gasping, looking distraught. He waited. "The doctor's given her something to bring down her temperature and the midwife is coming. Thank you for your help...." He pressed Mark's hand. "I must go and make cold compresses...".
"You'll let me know, won't you...." he touched Stanley's shoulder.
"Of course".
"And if there's anything..." he paused, "anything, you know."
"Yes." He looked at the other man. "Thank God you saw her. Thank God you were there."

He had lost all sense of time. When he passed their own shop window he saw two anxious faces looking out. Lily and Phyllis hurried towards him as he entered. "Oh, Mr Edwards we were getting worried. What happened? We couldn't think what could be keeping you." He looked at them in some bewilderment before realisation dawned on him. He took out his pocket watch. It said ten minutes past four.
"Good heavens!" Gathering his thoughts, which were still anxiously taken up with what was happening in the house on the other side of the marketplace, he told them, still somewhat disjointedly, and in brief, what had happened.

The atmosphere was sombre for the rest of the afternoon. Customers came and went. Lily and Phyllis attended to them as they always did, although without, some of their clients noted, the usual smiles. Phyllis was less affected; she had met Kate just a few times, the first being when Kate had interviewed her for the job, days before she left. But Lily was deeply affected. Kate had taken her on, taken a chance with her, as she knew, had become her mentor and chief supporter; she was kind and then she had persuaded Mr Edwards, the head of the whole company, to let her try out her managerial skills - which she, Kate, had taught her.

They sat in the office going over some accounts; Phyllis had gone home. Mark asked a question. He got no answer. He looked up from the account book. Lily was sitting, her face blank, stricken.

"Oh, Mr Edwards, she will be all right won't she?" And so he found himself trying to comfort and give hope to Lily, who was showing all the anguish that he was feeling too, on the inside.

He sent her home then, earlier than usual, but he wanted to be alone and, well, of course he would lock and tidy up. It would give him something to do. He needed to speak to Dan Anderson anyway and he would not be back at the property until after six. He busied himself with inessentials until he heard Dan Anderson arrive in the backyard. He went out to him.

"Ah, Mr Anderson. Is the flat still empty?" The landlord was unhitching the drayhorse from the cart she had been pulling. He looked up,

"Yes, do you want to keep it on?"

"No, no, it's not that but, I have work to do here tomorrow - "he made it up as he went along, "and I thought I would just stay the night, instead of going back to Sprinton and coming again early."

"Well there's nothing left there except the sofa and the mattress from the old bed in the little room. I haven't had time to get rid of that yet. They didn't want it, the Ruskins. You'd be more comfortable in the New Inn."

"No, I want to be on the spot," Mark said. Well, "folk were queer," Dan Anderson thought. Could Binns be in trouble?

"You're welcome to stay there," was what he said. "But it ain't exactly comfortable."

"Doesn't matter. I have things to do in the office anyway," he lied. The landlord looked at his tenant. Perhaps the man was ill. But all he said was, "Wait a minute. I'll get the key."

It was true the flat was almost empty. The only furniture in the sitting room was the sofa which had previously belonged to Anderson's sister; in the kitchen was one wooden chair and an upturned crate beside it and, in the tiny bedroom they had made for guests at the end of the sitting room was a mattress. To Mark, however there was more than a breath of Kate in the place still. It was the curtains, those light, thistledown curtains that moved softly in the breeze when he opened one window to let in some air. The flat had been shut up since they had moved out six weeks before. The curtains, which Kate had got Lily to make for them, and which were somehow so like her! How could curtains be like a person....Anyway they were left, for the time being, because the windows in Henry Whittle's house were much bigger, on the first upstairs floor, and much smaller on the top floor.

The way the curtains swayed and danced in the draught of air from the window now - it seemed as if she spoke to him. He shook himself, went into the kitchen, deserted except for the one wooden chair. He couldn't remember it from the day when they had sat round the table there - there was no table now - and worked out the details of the agreement for his loan to them. He saw Stanley's serious face bending over the paper, and Kate's happy one as she moved back and forth making them a cup of tea before they went over to Henry Whittle at his shop. The house was more or less bare and yet her spirit was still in it. He felt himself smiling at the memory, in the empty kitchen.

Then, as suddenly, he was overcome with tiredness and hunger. He had eaten nothing since the sandwich at the New Inn - wasn't that in another life? But what was happening with Kate? The happiness of a minute ago evaporated and was replaced by a twist of fear and anxiety. He couldn't stay inside; he must get out. It was twilight when he emerged into the marketplace. The lamplighter was making his rounds with ladder and lantern. He walked into the centre of the marketplace, to the fountain where he had found Kate, dizzy, in the afternoon. From there he could look up to the windows of their house to see if there was light, or the curtains open. The curtains of what must be hers, hers and Stanley's, bedroom, were partly drawn across, but not completely. There was light inside. He could tell nothing. No sound came from the house, no cries, no voices, no indication of life - or death. He wandered around for a while and then went into the New Inn. The landlord agreed to serve him with a plate of ham and cold potatoes accompanied by a pint of their local brew. He discovered that he was hungry.

When he got back he met Dan Anderson coming out of his house next door with a bundle in his arms.

"Ah, I was just coming over to you. Can't have you sleeping on a bare mattress," he said, and thrust the bundle at him. "These should make you a bit more comfortable." Touched by the man's unexpected thoughtfulness, he could only nod his thanks.

"Just leave them in the house, when you go," he said. "I'll pick it up later," and he turned back into his own house.

Mark unlocked the back door and climbed the stairs to the flat. He carried the bundle through to the bedroom and dumped it on the mattress. There was nothing to do but go to bed. It was dark now outside. His pocket watch told him it was ten minutes past ten. Just six hours since he had come back from the other house, and he knew nothing. Labour could last a lot longer than that but, for a woman who was ill besides, that must be dangerous mustn't it? So many horrors and fears engulfed him. He was exhausted but knew he would never sleep, and if she was still in labour there would be no respite for her either this night. He must escape these thoughts somehow. He got up from the bed, took the shop keys and went back down the stairs. There was yesterday's newspaper and a few old copies of fashion and design magazines that had belonged either to Kate or Lily in the office. He had seen them there. Anything rather than only the terrible and agonizing thoughts in his own head to distract him. The shop was dark and silent. He realised that he had never been there at that time before. Even in winter on his monthly Thursday visits he usually left to drive back to Sprinton before three in the afternoon. The light in the office was sufficient, but not bright. He found the paper and magazines and then his eye alighted on the pile of sample books which Kate had always been looking in to see if there was something new that she liked and thought would sell well. He sat down in 'Maureen's' chair, which was adjusted to the height suited to her at the typewriter, and took up one of the sample books. It was an older one, with last year's date on it, and he saw that someone had scribbled notes and slipped them in beside some of the materials. Just a few words each time or only a question mark, occasionally even an exclamation mark. 'This one - definite' or 'might go for day blouses' even 'heavenly' once or twice and once only, 'no, cancel'. It was all Kate's handwriting. He knew it well. He read each one, searched greedily for more, took up another sample book and turned the pages as if searching for a map or a message. Finally he sat still, holding one of the sample books open at a section on winter tweeds. The sample was of an olive greeny mixture, a fine wool. She had put in a note 'lovely for a riding jacket, ladies (or mens, Mark E?)' He stared at the note, ran his finger over it, buried his face in his hand leaning on the open book.

 Back in the flat upstairs he dragged the mattress out of the tiny bedroom and into the living room. The tiny bedroom felt claustrophobic, like a prison cell. He positioned the mattress on the floor in front of the sofa. On the short wall opposite the sofa the bookcase, 'her' bookcase, had been. There was a faint mark on the wall left by the end of it. Dan Anderson's bundle contained a sheet, a pillow, a blanket and a towel. He half undressed and put his clothes on the chair which he had fetched from the kitchen, then lay down on the bed he had

163

made on the floor and looked into the darkness. If he closed his eyes he saw only images of pain. There was nothing he could do to influence the outcome of what was happening in that room so close by yet out of bounds. He could only keep watch and 'will her' to live. He had extracted that note from the sample book in the office. He put out his hand to check that it was still in the pocket of his jacket. He passed a wretched night, tossing and turning, and plagued by nightmares when he at last fell asleep in the early hours of the morning.

He was awakened by a banging on a door somewhere and then a voice shouting his name outside in the street. He leapt up from the mattress and peered out of the window. Stanley was in the street below looking up. Wide eyed but in a state of excitement he called up,
"Mr Edwards! I didn't know you were here. I rang you in Sprinton, your parents' house. We have a little girl, just two hours ago. Kate is tired, but Murray says she'll be all right....."
"Get round to the back," Mark called. "I'm coming down."

Opening the back door at the bottom of the stairs Stanley almost fell into his arms. "She's all right, she'll be all right," he repeated over and over; and then, the strain of the last eighteen hours suddenly spent, Stanley wept.

A little while later he walked with Stanley back to his house. They parted at the Teashop door, "Tell her…," he said. Tell her what - thank God, a hundred thousand times, that you are still alive. His hand on Stanley's shoulder, "Yes, I will," Stanley said, going in to sleep, almost asleep already.

Mark went into the New Inn and had breakfast. He asked for two eggs, had everything, and drank three cups of hot strong tea. Revived, he walked twice round the marketplace for the exercise, glanced up at Kate's window as he passed. There was nothing to be seen, but how different it felt from the night before.

When Lily and Phyllis arrived, more or less together, at nine o'clock, Mark came from the back office, and told them the good news. "Oh my," cried Lily, "oh thank goodness. I could hardly sleep last night," she said, "for thinking about her. And a little girl…." she hesitated, "all, all right, Mr Edwards?" He smiled,
"I believe so." They were all smiling.

None of the customers had anything to complain about that morning. The serious faces of the day before had gone. Later Lily came to the office where Mark was dictating a letter to Maureen.

"Excuse me sir," she said. "Could we send flowers to Mrs Ruskin, from all of us? I can do it in my lunch hour." Mark Edwards looked up,
"Yes, of course. What a good idea. Here," he went to get a pound note out of his pocket. Lily protested, laughing,
"That's too much, sir. And we all want to contribute…" looking a question at Maureen who nodded agreement.
"No, it isn't too much. Make it the best bouquet ever…and," looking around, "what's the nicest pink ribbon we have, or a rosette… Now, ladies, this is your department. Take what you think is the best and give it with the flowers."
"We'll deliver them together," Lily said, "at lunchtime, and a card."
"Yes, do that," he said. The letter was finished and just before lunchtime the three of them went off on their errand armed with the satin pink ribbon they had chosen and a rosette of white and pink lace that Lily, in less than half an hour, had gathered and sewn into an exotic flower which she sewed on to the ribbon. He locked the door after them and watched as they crossed the road to the flower shop on the other side.

He had told Stanley that he would be going back to Sprinton that afternoon. He wouldn't be back in Laverton until the following week. Did Stanley mind if he rang at the weekend to find out how they were, Kate and the baby. Of course he didn't mind. Although he said nothing at that moment Stanley did believe that Mark Edwards actions the day before had quite possibly saved Kate's life. He felt an immense debt of gratitude to the man.

While the girls were out for lunch, Mark Edwards sat in the office and wrote a letter. It was to Dan Anderson and when he had finished it he put it in an envelope addressed to Anderson and then in a second envelope addressed to Lily, with a note attached. Maureen was the first to come back to the shop. She reported that they had bought the flowers, a beautiful bouquet she said, of red and white roses, and fern, and Stanley had answered the door when they rang the bell. He told them that Kate and the baby were well, both sleeping just then but that she would love the flowers when she saw them.

Mark was anxious now to get back to Sprinton. He was overcome with tiredness. He needed to sleep and he didn't want to fall asleep at the wheel. He gave the letter to Maureen to give to Lily, her instructions were inside.

…………………………………………………………………

Rachel Edwards put down the phone in the hall, and went into the sitting room where her husband was ensconced in an armchair with a rug over his legs. His wheelchair sat just inside the door. It had only recently become necessary, after a second fall in the house confirmed that he was no longer able to move about safely on his own legs. Philip Edwards in his youth, like the rest of his family, had spent much of his free time on horseback. The sense of freedom it gave and of being at one with a living creature, was more exhilarating than anything he knew. The onset of his disease in middle age had robbed him, therefore, of one of the major activities which for him made life worth living. Twenty years of the disease had brought him to a degree of acceptance, but angry acceptance, as his wife could testify. He looked up from the book that he was reading as his wife came in.

"That was Mark," she said. "He'll be back early. I had better tell Irene to put out three cups." She turned to go. He called after her,

"I wish he could find someone decent to settle down with. Have children. He's not too old." She turned back and leaned over his chair from behind. He twisted his head to look up at her. "We've been lucky," he said, then, "No, I've been lucky Rache… not many I know would have put up with," he indicated his legs. She put a hand on his shoulder,

"I've been lucky too," she said, leaning her cheek on his head.

"Ah no, my dear, you've drawn the short straw I'm afraid." His wife paused, patted his shoulder and straightened up saying,

"No, Philip - Audrey and Don Rivers, three sons, all lost in the war. They drew the short straw, and many like them. I, we *have* been lucky."

As he turned into the drive of his parents' house Mark was still working out what he would say to them about his future, well now *immediate* future, plans. As he crunched over the gravel to the steps up, one of the dogs, the black labrador, lolloped over to greet him. At thirteen Jet was the oldest of the dogs and Mark's particular favourite, but he could see, as he came towards him, that even to feebly wag his tail was an effort. He fondled the dog's head, "Hello old pal - 'never died a winter yet eh?'" Jet ambled in front of him to the side door. He wanted in.

His mother had heard the car driving in and came across the hall to meet him. "Hello darling, how was the ride?" He pecked her on the cheek,

"It was fine, very quiet. Where is he?"

"In the sitting room. I'll tell Irene to bring in the tea. But you look tired, were you working late?"

"No, not really but…" he made towards the sitting room, "I'll tell you later.." He said hello to his father and then went upstairs to freshen up. When he came down again the tea and some biscuits were set out on the little table beside his mother. He sat down on the sofa opposite his parents and, while his mother poured the tea, he told them an edited version of the events of the past two days. His father looked serious, his mother concerned,

"Goodness me, poor Mr Ruskin. But how fortunate that you happened to be there. It must have been a very anxious day - for everybody. But it ended well? And they have a little girl. Is the mother out of danger?" Rachel remembered Kate very clearly. When she was in charge of the textiles department at the Sprinton Binns, she had consulted Kate, "Miss Atkinson", on a number of occasions over choice of materials for various garments. "She always had such lovely displays of cloth, Mark. And she knew style. You know, I was really sorry to see her go to Laverton but she was obviously the right choice for the new shop." There was quiet for a few minutes, while the tale that their son had told them, sank in." Well, that must have been very upsetting, for her husband too. I do hope Mrs Ruskin makes a full recovery. I shall write her a note and send a card." She paused, "Of course when her husband rang us this morning I didn't really understand what it was all about and the poor young man sounded both excited and a little confused. I'm afraid I didn't help him much - all I could say was that you weren't here, that you had stayed in Laverton."

"And how is it going, Mark?" his father asked. Although he could no longer be in charge, Philip Edwards was as interested in the business as he had ever been. It was in truth the main sorrow of his life that, when the disease progressed, he had been compelled, in his fifties, to abdicate from running the company. Alert in mind and with everything about it in his head he found himself defeated once more, by his body: the riding had gone first, then, running the company a decade later. His interest in it though had not diminished and his detailed knowledge remained. Mark still consulted him over various business matters or when he himself had an idea about which he wanted a second opinion. His father was a rich repository of knowledge, especially historical, about the company; and he had had the good sense, after he handed over command to his son, not to constantly interfere or criticise what he was doing.

"How is the new girl making out in Laverton?" he wanted to know.

"She's doing well," Mark said, and, seeing that this topic offered a way in to what he wanted to tell them, he went on, "of course she has a lot to learn yet but we'll get there. Actually, about that there's something I ought to tell you..."

Trixy was as anxious as Mark to get out into open countryside and the ride they had together that Saturday was the most exhilarating and the longest for many weeks. He had started the day by telephoning Laverton to find out how Kate and the baby were, and when Stanley's report was good - Kate was stronger that day and rested, and the baby was lusty - he felt rejuvenated himself. Stanley's mother, Sarah, had arrived and she was obviously taking over the domestic side of life, so that Stanley could re-open the shop and take care of the business. A woman was to come in to clean and do the washing three times a week.

That Saturday Mark and Trixy ventured further than they usually did. After the open countryside when they left the stables, they cantered through the woods, nearly a full mile and came out onto a lane that led to the village of Upperton. Upperton boasted a pub that brewed its own beer and was well-known around the whole district for its lunches of Upperton bread and chutney, and local cheese and home-cured ham. Mark decided to make a break there. He tied up Trixy in the corner of the adjoining field where there was a tethering post and a horse trough and made his way into the oak-beamed bar of the Hare and Hounds. It was quiet, two men only, from their attire obviously farmers, chatting country matters at the bar. Mark ordered his beer and lunch and went and sat in an alcove. He was content to sit, and look, and think. His parents, especially his father, had been dubious about his plan and somewhat perplexed. His mother less so but still... Nevertheless they had to admit that nowadays with the telephone and the motor car a lot of things could be managed even at a distance, and well, it was only half the week when he would be away from Sprinton.
"As long as you don't lose touch with what's going on here," his father had said. "This is Head Office, Mark. You always need to know what your staff are thinking. Don't lose control, that's all." He assured them he wouldn't. He would only be three nights a week in Laverton, which meant only two whole days - just one more than at present. The thing that convinced his father that it was an idea at least to follow up, was when Mark showed him evidence that the Laverton shop was doing very well indeed - better, for example, than the one in High Bridge which was a town of comparable size to Laverton. And, they might

seriously want to look for bigger premises so that they could expand the business there.

Before lunch on Sunday he telephoned Laverton again and Stanley's report was encouraging. Kate had regained her appetite and had been out of bed for a couple of hours. The baby had started nursing and was doing well. Mark was learning a lot about new motherhood and babies from his telephone calls to Stanley. He relayed all Stanley's news to his mother who, touched by Mark's account of what had happened, was taking considerable interest in the progress of Mrs Ruskin and her baby. She had had only good experiences in her contacts with Kate at Binns in Sprinton and had come to rely quite heavily on Kate's judgement in matters of textile choices and styles. She had found that she could always be sure of getting an honest opinion from her and, the girl didn't flatter.

Mark's sister Isabel and her family arrived for Sunday lunch and before the visit was over it seemed that the whole family knew about what had happened in Laverton, involving Kate Atkinson (as they still thought of her) and Mark. And Mark was tasked with telling Mrs Ruskin, when he was able to see her, that his whole family in Sprinton and beyond sent their best wishes for her health and that of the baby.

After lunch on Tuesday Mark set off for Laverton. He needed to meet with Dan Anderson, he said, and make arrangements to take over the tenancy of the flat. Jet wandered out across the drive as Mark was about to leave. His mother ran out to pull the dog clear and waved him off.

"It looked as if he was trying to stop him from leaving," she remarked to her husband later.

"That's nonsense," he said. "I believe the poor old thing is going blind." Rachel looked out of the window to the gate at the end of the drive.

"I do hope Mrs Ruskin will be all right," she said. "I must write that note and get it in the post." Then, turning back to her husband, "what a pity Mark hadn't met someone like her ten years ago…"

That momentous Friday it had come to him in a flash, when he went to give back the key to Dan Anderson. Why not take the flat himself and divide his time between Sprinton and Laverton? He could stay in his parents house when he needed to be in Sprinton - he knew they would be pleased to have him there: there was plenty of room. The part of the house where their live-in cook had stayed, when they first moved in, was effectively a separate apartment. He could be as independent as he wanted to be and yet join them when he wanted to.

He had taken a liking to the flat above Binns in Laverton on that very first occasion he was in it, with Kate and Stanley discussing their agreement. It had felt like a home then and it still felt like that, or at least all the reminders of Kate made it seem homelike even without most of the furniture - there were still the curtains!

There was something else as well. Leaning on the gate into the meadow the day he left the marriage, he suddenly realised that it had been a long time since he had noticed beauty. He had loved that meadow before, for its grasses, its wild flowers, the hedgerows, the way the sun shone on it at different times of the day and seasons of the year. Sometimes there were horses there. The beauty and his urge to paint had gone hand in hand, for years, from school time until...when? A few years, three maybe, into the marriage. And then, when he realised that he could no longer paint, in that joyless house, he stopped seeing beauty. He had almost extinguished his own spirit - perhaps it was only the feelings that he had discovered later for Kate Atkinson that were keeping his spirit alive. They were the candle in an otherwise dark room. At that moment, at the gate, he felt the urge to start painting again. But he could only do it where there was light and warmth. He could not do it there. He could not do it in Sprinton.

The flat above the shop in Laverton, was basically L - shaped. The sitting-room, the biggest room, was the foot of the 'L'; the kitchen, the bathroom and the big bedroom were the long side of the 'L', with a landing running from the sitting room to the other rooms, and the stairs down halfway along. The big bedroom at the end was the width of the house and it had two windows, one onto the backyard, thus north facing, and the other in the opposite wall. It was a good big room for a bedroom and, bare of all furniture - there was just one floor to ceiling cupboard built into the end wall - it crossed his mind that it would make an excellent studio; the deciding factor was the north facing window. The light in that room would be perfect, especially if a blind was fitted over the other one.

He signed a one year contract for the flat that same afternoon. He wanted to be able to use it as soon as possible so he would have to get at least the bare minimum of furniture. He drove into Boxley, chose a kitchen table and a couple of chairs, a low bookcase that he would put where Kate's had been, a low coffee table to have in front of the sofa - which Dan Anderson was quite happy for him to keep - and a wardrobe with drawers, for clothes, to have at the other end of the sitting room, near the door into the tiny bedroom, where he intended to sleep. He also bought a number of lamps. All of these things could be delivered at the end of the week.

When he got back to Laverton, which was busy, for it was still the holiday season, he managed to book a room at the Victoria, the only one available - the New Inn was full - . This time he wanted to be comfortable and get a decent night's sleep and he was exhausted after all he had managed to pack into the half day since leaving his parents' house. He had an intense desire too to see Kate before going back to Sprinton the next day. He wanted to see that she really was on the way to recovery; he had not seen her, nor spoken to her, since the dramatic events of the previous Thursday when he found her ill by the fountain. He rang and spoke to Stanley early evening and asked if he might call in, if Kate was up to seeing anybody, just for a few minutes, he didn't want to tire her. That would be all right, Stanley said. Kate had been out of bed and sitting in a chair all that afternoon and she wanted to thank Mark for what he had done for 'them' - Stanley said 'them' - on that critical day. Late morning would probably be best.

He slept better that night than he had done for several weeks. He woke refreshed, had breakfast in his room and washed and dressed with particular care. He had some things to attend to at the shop first thing and then, just before eleven, he went to the flower shop and chose some flowers to take to Kate.

A girl he had not seen before, though she looked vaguely familiar, was serving a customer when he entered the teashop, but she smiled when she saw him and called out for Stanley. As the customer was leaving she said, "It's Mr Edwards isn't it?" And she put out her hand to shake his, "I'm Ivy," she said, "I've come to help them out for a while until Kate is back on her feet."
"Oh, you're Kate's sister..." he said, shaking her hand. Yes, there was a family resemblance.
"That's right....straight off the farm to the big city," she rolled her eyes and laughed. Mark smiled,
"Well I don't think you need to be too overwhelmed by this 'big city'," he said, "and the natives are quite friendly." Stanley appeared through the curtain that separated the shop from the house behind,
"Ah, you've met my sister-in-law, have you?" he said. "We're very grateful she could come at short notice like this," nodding with a smile at Ivy," and she's getting the hang of everything, no trouble at all." Ivy chuckled,
"Well I can tell you, gentlemen, serving a pot of tea and sponge cake to well brought up young ladies is a mite easier than trying to get a litter of ten piglets

171

to their milk machine!" They laughed, the ice broken. Stanley steered Mark through to the house, and up the stairs
"How is she?" Mark asked. Stanley's face broke into a smile,
"Much better today," he said. "You'll see." They did. Kate was sitting in an armchair with one hand rocking a cradle on her right hand side. She stretched out her other hand to Mark.,
"Oh, I knew I heard your voices," she said. Mark took the stretched out hand but bent over and kissed her cheek. He knew he was 'grinning like an idiot' but it couldn't be helped; he also knew he had never kissed her before, but that had been instinctive too. Seeing her looking like her old self, if perhaps a little paler, but with the same dark, now shining eyes, looking at him, filled him with joy. For a minute he could do nothing but look. At length his gaze shifted over to the cradle. He took a step nearer to see the tiny creature sleeping soundly there, "So this is she who caused all that trouble…". He glanced back at Kate who was looking with tenderness at her daughter. Turning to Stanley who had much the same expression on his face, Mark felt unaccountably a lump rising in his throat. So this was parental love - as it should be. "Sit down," said Stanley bringing forward a chair between the cradle and the bed. A voice called from downstairs. It was Ivy, who needed Stanley's help.
"Excuse me," he said and disappeared.
"I am so, so glad – " Mark said, unable to get any further.
"Mark," her voice was gentle, "I do, truly believe that you saved my life." The look she gave him was as near a look of love as he could ever expect to get from her he knew. He returned her look and they sat in silence.
"What are you going to call her?"
"Stella, she was born with the morning star…just before dawn."
They heard Stanley coming back up the stairs.
"Kate, have you asked him?"
"No, I was waiting for you," she replied. Stanley hesitated a fraction of a second,
"Mark, we'd like you to be godfather, will you?"
"I would be honoured," he said.

    Before he left he told them that he had taken their old flat for a year. He felt Lily needed more experience before he could make her manager, he said, and the one day a week he had been giving Laverton wasn't enough to allow him to supervise the shop properly - there might even be an argument for expanding the business there. He said nothing about his plan to make the bedroom into a studio, not wanting to announce in advance things that were still only possibilities in his head. Moreover, as far as he knew, nobody in the company had any idea that he painted - *had* painted, he corrected himself, for it was more than ten years since he had picked up a brush.

He ate a quick pub lunch at the New Inn before setting off for Sprinton. There would be quite a lot to see to in the next twenty four hours. He wanted to fetch, or arrange to fetch, some personal things that were still in the house he had shared with Dorothy. In the separation agreement it was stipulated that the contents of one room in the house, his 'workroom' or den, were not to be touched and that he would arrange for their removal within six months of the separation. Several other items in the house were also his and would be removed at the same time: the most important to Mark personally were the Stubbs painting and Henri Rousseau's tiger, both of which had been left to him by his grandfather. The Stubbs had always, since, hung on a wall of the dining room. Dorothy considered that it gave an appropriate dignity to the room; the Rousseau tiger on the other hand she could not bear; and she could not understand how Mark could ever have liked such a painting, far less have it on the wall of a house where it would have to be seen every day. So Mark had kept it in his den.

Otherwise the things that he would be removing were: his books, his easels and all his painting gear, the wing chair where he sat with cigar and brandy on Sunday afternoons and the, to him, beautiful old oak desk and the studded chair that went with it, which he had inherited from grandfather Binns. Yes, there were a few things to arrange and, to avoid any confrontations with Dorothy, perhaps it would be best to do it through his lawyer.

His mother came out of the house as he was parking the car and came to meet him. When she got up to him he saw that there were tears in her eyes.
"Oh heavens mother what is it? Is it father?" he asked. No, she answered him, it was not his father, it was Jet. When she came down that morning and went into the scullery where his basket was, she found him lying dead on the floor beside his basket. He must have had a heart attack, and not long before since his body was still warm. Stunned, he put his arm around his mother's shoulders. For a while nothing was said.
"Well," he managed at last, " he can't have suffered at any rate. That's a blessing at least. He was very tired, you know. Last weekend when I came he

hardly had the strength to lift his tail." Rachel looked up at her son and nodded, drying away her tears.

"You know," she said, "he tried to stop you leaving. He wandered out in front of your car when you were about to drive off. I had to run out and pull him back. Your father said that was nonsense but I'm sure that's what he was doing."

His arm around her shoulder, hers around his waist, they went towards the house together.

In the event the removal was arranged more easily than Mark had anticipated. Dorothy raised no difficulty about when it should happen; on the contrary, Bernard said, when reporting back to Mark on the conversation he had had with her, she seemed rather anxious to have it done and, in her own words, "see the back of it all". How it was to be done was all arranged. The company had recently invested in a motor lorry. This was one of Mark's initiatives. It would have the dual function of being contracted to carry out smaller house removals, using the Binns driver and man, and, to fetch and carry goods from warehouses and suppliers to any of the three Binns shops, or between shops. It was not booked for any particular job on the following Tuesday, and Dorothy had no objection to it being done then. Relieved that that matter was settled Mark could then turn his attention to business in Sprinton. After the conversation with his father he wanted to make sure that no employee in the store or the office could get the idea, because he would be spending more time in Laverton from now on, that he was less interested or committed to the business. He had a long conversation with Nigel Pitt during which he mentioned to him the possibility of expanding the Laverton business if it continued to increase in volume. He also did his usual tour of the whole store, and talked at length to all the department heads. He was determined to show that he knew what was happening in every department, both 'front of house' serving customers and also in the offices upstairs. At the end of Thursday he felt confident that he had done that. He timetabled the monthly meeting that he always had with heads of departments and Nigel Pitt, for the following Monday afternoon.

There was only one duty in that day at Sprinton that he found he wasn't equal to - the burying of Jet. He got his mother to contact Dawkins their gardener, who agreed to do the necessary. He did a tour of the garden with his mother to find a suitable place, and they settled on a spot near a pear tree where Jet always liked to lie in the summer half of the year. He had often gone to lie there after he had been following Dawkins around as he did the gardening. Dawkins was affected by the death of Jet too, although, as he said to Mrs Edwards, he had seen it coming for a while now. At any rate he would do the burying and he offered to make a plaque to mark the spot with Jet's name and dates on it. When they worked out the dates Mark realised with a jolt that Jet's life almost exactly coincided with the duration of his marriage to Dorothy. The realisation of that made the burying of Jet seem doubly significant. Symbolically he was burying his marriage too.

That evening he loaded the car with things that he would take with him to Laverton the next day. His mother, with the help of Gladys the cook, had sorted out and packed in a cardboard box some china and kitchen utensils that they agreed Mark would need in the Laverton flat, even if he was not going to do very much cooking himself. Also his mother supplied him with bed linen and towels from her own ample store. He set off the next morning just as Dawkins was arriving to carry out the obsequies on Jet.

"Will you be all right?" he asked his mother, seeing Dawkins going to the toolshed to fetch a spade.

"Yes, yes, of course. I shall go inside and sit with your father until it is done," she assured him. "Don't worry. Now off you go and ring us this evening when everything is in place. And don't forget to remember us to Mrs Ruskin when you see her."

Dawkins sank the spade into the earth near the pear tree as Mark drove out through the gates and onto the road to Laverton.

He had just had time to carry everything from the car into the flat in Laverton when the furniture he had bought in Boxley arrived. The wardrobe with drawers gave a bit of trouble on the stairs but otherwise everything was brought in and put into place quite quickly, and when the men left to return to Boxley and Mark walked through all the rooms it felt quite homely and almost furnished. In addition to some china and bed linen his mother had also given him two Indian rugs, a square one to go in the sitting room in the area behind the sofa, where his desk would also sit, and a smaller one for the space between the coffee table, just delivered, and the bookcase on the end wall, also just delivered but, at the moment, empty of books. The box containing the china and kitchen utensils sat in the kitchen waiting to be unpacked and housed. That could wait a bit longer he decided. Time to go down to the shop and see how business was doing and then to get some lunch. He was suddenly very hungry and he thought he might go to the Victoria for once and get a proper meal instead of the beer and a sandwich that he had had rather too many of recently.

A proper lunch at the Victoria, as well as calling to mind all the lunches he had had there with Kate, also, or because of that, helped him to relax. It had been a pretty hectic week since the Friday before. He seemed to have been going 'like a yo-yo', as his nanny used to say, between Laverton and Sprinton and from one emotional turmoil to another. As he sat over his coffee, it came to him what he needed to do next to achieve peace of mind. When he left the Victoria he made straight for the teashop.

Ivy was in charge. She had obviously learnt a lot in the two days that Mark had been away. So much so indeed that he felt constrained to compliment her on her competence and her manner. He was then about to ask her about Kate and the baby when an older woman came through the curtain from the house behind and he was introduced to Stanley's mother. Sarah had heard all about Mark's part in the dramatic events of the week before and she added her thanks and gratitude, to those of the rest of the family, for what he had done. Embarrassed by so much attention for what he had felt to be 'simply' instinctive behaviour, Mark was relieved when Stanley appeared, told him that Kate was now up and about, and took him through to the garden where she was to be found with the baby sleeping in a pram nearby.

Kate was bending over the pram adjusting the hood to keep the sun from shining directly on the baby's face.
"How's my goddaughter doing?" he asked. Turning, Kate smiled,
"She's doing well. How is her godfather? Have you just arrived?" Mark told them that he had possession of the flat and that the furniture he had ordered had arrived from Boxley and was in place and then, the reason he had called in was because he wanted to ask Kate about - the curtains! Did she want the curtains from the flat? No, she assured him, they didn't want them because the windows of this house were completely different.
"Can I buy them off you then?"
"No, you cannot," said Kate, looking severe, "they are a present!" She laughed. "The curtains can be regarded as a housewarming gift," and to Stanley, "Don't you agree, Stan?" He did, then added, grinning,
"Perhaps we can find something more exciting to add to it." There was an expectant air about him, an impatience to say something.

"Do you like ice cream, Mark?" It turned out that between everything else that there was to see to Stanley had been creating an ice box in a shed at the back of the house and, he had just made his first batch of ice cream.

"Have you really? Well, I do like ice cream, and I'm prepared to be the guinea pig!" Mark said. Stanley fetched another chair and then vanished inside. He reappeared with a tray on which were two glass bowls and three spoons. Each one tasted, without speaking. Then, looking over at Stanley, Mark shook his head in wonder and, "Stanley, this is going to be a great success. It's delicious!" he said. Kate smiled at this accolade for Stanley, and Stanley nodded and looked gratified. They finished the two bowls between them and then there was a conversation about the technicalities of ice cream making and keeping and the question of how much could and should be made at one go.

When he left the Ruskins to go back to Binns and 'his place' above it Mark felt happier than he had been for a long, long time.

He reckoned on staying in Laverton until Sunday, then returning to Sprinton, having the monthly meeting with senior Binns staff on Monday afternoon and on Tuesday morning he would employ the new Binns motor lorry to fetch his stuff from The Four Winds and take it to his flat in Laverton. He would remain in Laverton until Friday morning, then return to Sprinton and, after that weekend hope to establish a regular division of his time between the two towns. The main complicating factor, curiously enough, was neither the business nor human attachments but - his horse! His weekly ride with Trixy was important to him and he could anticipate that it might turn out not to be so convenient to have to be in Sprinton on Saturdays. But that was a conundrum that he would have to think about and sort out later.

Back at the shop he told the girls that they would soon be able to enjoy superlative ice cream at the Teashop as well as tea and cake. In fact he would treat them all to some of the Ruskins' ice cream at their lunchtime next day - if they had any! He hadn't felt so light-hearted for ages and his mood affected Lily and Phyllis and even Maureen in the office, so that there was laughter between them and with customers, for the rest of the afternoon. He told Lily that he would pull down the blind and lock up for once and they could all go home as soon as the last customer had left.

When he climbed the stairs to his flat he was suddenly hit by tiredness and a desire to sleep, though it was still broad daylight outside. Well anyway the bed had to be made up sometime so, he might as well do it now. He found the box

with the bed linen and towels and had just lifted everything out and had put some of it on the sofa when there was a loud knock at the outside door downstairs. He thought it might be Dan Anderson come to see that everything was all right with his new tenant. But it wasn't the landlord, it was Ivy.
"My sister sent me," she said when Mark, with a towel in one hand, opened the door and found her there. "I was to see if you need help with anything," she added, and pleaded, "Please say yes or I'll get into trouble with Kate. I'm good at finding places to put things, and making up beds!" Recovering from his surprise, he motioned Ivy inside,
"Your sister was right," he said with a weary smile, "and you *can* help me," and she followed him up the stairs.
"You know," said Ivy, "I was never in this house when Kate and Stanley lived here. When Mother and Father visited I had to hold the fort at home and then somehow it just never happened." Then, as they entered the sitting room, "Oh my, but this is a nice room - in fact it's nicer than the one they've got now."
"Yes, it is a nice room," he agreed, and moving to the window he added, "you see I have a good view of the whole of the marketplace, so I can observe how well the competition is doing and," he said slyly, "see if the staff at that new tea shop are doing a good job!" She pulled a face at him,
"You needn't worry about that. I've now got three people telling me what to do! So," she looked around, "what can I do first?"

Within a short time Ivy had made up the bed, found the best place to put the spare bed linen, and had unpacked and put away the china and kitchen utensils. "That's the lot, then" she said. "Well, that didn't take long."
"No, but it was a great help," he said. "And next week my books and some other stuff will be coming. Could you give me a hand then do you think?" A pause and a quizzical look. "If your sister will let you go of course." Ivy giggled, "Oh I think I can handle her," she said.

When Ivy had gone he did a tour of his domain once more and he went along to the big bedroom at the end of the landing. He had evaded Ivy's query about that room. There was nothing in it he told her and he didn't need it at the moment. There was indeed no furniture in the room but from the built-in cupboard on the far wall he now took out the portfolio that he had brought from The Four Winds. He fetched the old wooden chair from the kitchen and sat down in the empty room to examine the contents of the portfolio. There weren't many. Several were life-size pencil and charcoal sketches of the same subject. He had tried, from memory, to draw the head and shoulders of Kate Atkinson.

One of them, the fourth attempt, wasn't bad: he had captured the expression of the face, the eyes especially, and the proportions were right. The first three he would discard. He looked at the last one for a long time. It was the face that he knew he would have to paint before long. The only thing remaining in the portfolio was a large water colour that he had done more than a decade before. He had meant to have it framed and up on the wall of his den, for he was pleased with it. It made him smile because he had captured the beauty of the scene. It was a picture of the meadow that he loved, the meadow beyond the spinney, over which he had gazed, unseeing, leaning on the gate, just a few months before. The sun shone, in his painting, and the meadow was long grassed and flowery: it was high summer. It was time to put it up on his wall. He put the portfolio back in the cupboard and went back to the sitting-room. Yes, he was feeling more at home in this house with every hour that passed. All it needed now was that bookcase to be filled with his books and his desk and armchair in place behind the sofa and it would be truly a home. He decided to change his weekend plan. He would drive back to Sprinton on Saturday afternoon so that he could set out early on Sunday for his ride with Trixy. He had told Talbot at the stables that he would be coming on Sunday this week anyway. It was the end of a warm late summer's day. He opened the sitting room window to let in some air and the curtains moved gently in greeting. He thought about Kate.

CHAPTER 16

Christenings

He arrived at The Four Winds just minutes before the Binns lorry. Dorothy had informed Bernard that she would not be at the house but that someone would be there to let them in to remove what had been agreed should be removed. Mark was relieved that he would not have to see or speak to his wife - whom, he now realised, he had long since ceased to think of as 'wife' at all. However, he was somewhat surprised when he saw the person to whom Dorothy had given the keys and charged with overseeing the removal. Elisabeth Bailey, although perhaps Dorothy's closest friend now, had been one of her acquaintances who were most surprised when Dorothy 'captured' Mark Edwards all those years ago. Elisabeth herself had always had a soft spot for Mark and had been inclined, in her heart, to take his part when Dorothy made complaints about her husband in the early years of their rupture. Looking at her now, tall, good-looking, and with a face that was animated in a way quite unlike Dorothy's, the thought crossed his mind that a different choice fourteen years ago could have had a very different outcome.

"I'm sorry about this, Mark. Dorothy asked me to do it for her." She looked at him with a wry expression on her face, more apologetic than anything. She put the key in the lock. "I'll let you in and then I have an errand to do in the village. How long do you think you'll need? Well anyway, I'll come back in an hour and if you haven't finished I'll make myself a cup of tea and you'll find me in the kitchen...." He nodded and thanked her and pushed open the door.

It was strange, a weird, uncomfortable feeling even to be back in this house. He had lived there for thirteen years until very recently, and yet it felt as if he was revisiting his very distant past. He shivered slightly: the day was warm but the house, to him, had the atmosphere of a museum, and it was cold. No, he didn't want to stay any longer than necessary. Alf Gilbert, the driver, and the lad, Rooney, were waiting outside. They had been looking, with curiosity, at the outside of the house. "A big place, ain't it?" The lad looked up at the castellated stonework above the upper floor, "And just the two of them!"
"Only one now," said Alf. Mark showed in the doorway. They went in and began the removal.

On the drive to Laverton, later, Mark had time to think over the events of the day. Strangest of all in a strange, strange day, had been the conversation with Elisabeth Bailey in the kitchen of The Four Winds, just before they left. When she came back to the house from her errand in the village, they had not yet finished the packing. The last thing to be taken down and which needed to be wrapped most carefully was the painting by Stubbs. It was also the only thing that caused Mark any emotion in removing it. Usually he understood very well why he was feeling what he was feeling; but this time he found himself confused. The Stubbs had sat on the wall above the dining room fireplace for more than ten years and one thing he was forced to agree with Dorothy about was that it looked right there. The result was that he actually felt uncomfortable when he took it down. Its placing, on that wall, in that room, represented almost the only occasion when they had come anywhere near to having the same feeling about a painting; and even then they had come to liking it for different reasons and from quite different perspectives. When it was lifted down it left a patch of wall that was darker than the rest, since the sun, streaming in through the window opposite, had over the years faded the colour of the walls except where pictures were hanging. He knew that when Dorothy came into the room and saw the space and the patch where it had been, that it would be a blow. "The cruellest blow of all", the quotation brought him back to earth with a thump - for in this case there was a sad irony in it. The irony cleared his mind at least. There was no question of leaving the painting behind anyway for, among other things, it always reminded him of the day when his grandfather found him gazing at the picture and took him into his study to show him a painting of a tiger. It was the day from which he dated his fascination and love of making pictures; and it was the day that had cemented the affection between Mark and his grandfather.

It was at that moment that Elisabeth came into the room. "Sorry to interrupt you," she said, "I just wondered if you'd like a cup of tea before you go. Oh!" She stopped, catching sight of the picture which was on the floor leaning against the mantelpiece, "the Stubbs! Of course, I'd forgotten it was yours. Isn't it magnificent? And Dorothy worried that it was somehow indecent! I don't think she's ever paid attention to classical statuary…." she laughed. "Would you like a cup?" The two men came in to wrap up the painting.

"No tea, thanks, but I'll get a drink of water before we go. I'll come through to the kitchen when we're ready."

The painting was first wrapped in muslin, then brown paper, and tied securely with string. When they had finished the men carried it out to the lorry and Mark walked across the familiar, yet alien, hall to the kitchen. Elisabeth was sitting at the kitchen table cradling a cup of tea in her hands. She looked up as Mark came in and made as if to get up.

"No, stay where you are," he said, taking a glass out of a cupboard and turning on the tap. "Well, that's done." He turned and leaned against the sink, facing her. "And how is your family, Elisabeth? You have two boys I believe." He had to say something that had nothing to do with what he was there for. She didn't answer him but looked up at him and said, "It's a funny thing, marriage, isn't it? You think you know exactly what you're doing when you go into it and then you find out that you didn't...." she looked away, somewhere into the past. 'Whatever this is about, I don't want it,' Mark thought. What he said was, "Well, I can't say I have that excuse - the ignorance of youth. I have to take the blame for the first fault, it was mine." He stopped, not wishing to pursue this line of conversation, at least not with Elisabeth. If he could have had it with an unmarried, unattached Kate a couple of years before he would have poured out his heart, warts and all, in sheer desperate hope: but that day had passed.

"Oh Mark, it was obvious to everyone that Dorothy was wrong for you!" She looked shocked at what she had let out and put her hand up to her mouth as if anxious to stop herself saying more.

"Really?" his tone was cold. She observed him, then said evenly,

"Yes. Dorothy's an old friend now; she's a good egg in many ways. She runs our charities like a general. She's raised hundreds of pounds for the war wounded, you know. But she's not up to you, Mark, in brains. And she can't laugh." She stopped. Silence between them. She looked sideways at him, "We'd have made a good couple, we two," she said. "I know what you're like. We'd have had fun together - and be friends." She sighed, looked down at her cup. He was cornered, baffled. 'But you have a husband and sons' he wanted to say, no that was wrong - it was all too much and much too late. What to say? "You have children," he said. "And that is......"

"Enough?" She said looking up. "Were you going to say...or 'a consolation'?" He was silent.

"But children have to be raised and at the end of it they leave, and there you are again, the two of you."

"I'm hardly the one to give any advice about choosing a mate," he said. "I made a disastrous mistake....". She looked at him.

"Has there never been anyone since, that you might have been happy with?" He didn't answer. Had Dorothy put her up to this interrogation?
"Dorothy thought there was someone, who used to work in the store here, a young girl from the country....?" She had got up from the table to put her cup in the sink. As she turned towards him he gripped her by the shoulders and looked her in the face, "Yes," he said through gritted teeth, "Kate Atkinson, and she is, unfortunately for me, happily married...." he paused, suddenly tired of all the dissimulation and suppression. "That's right, I loved..love her.... and she is happily married, so nothing will come of that." Elisabeth had turned pale and stepped back as he released his grip on her. His anger evaporated. Suddenly he felt pity for the woman in front of him.
"There is nothing to be done," he said, looking past her, then more softly, "Hearts can be broken you know.....can't be made as good as new again but - they can be patched up. I have to go. The men are waiting..." then, turning back, "I'm sorry." He leant forward and kissed her on the cheek. She remained mute, watched him go. He made a vow, even before he had started the car. He was never going to step inside that house again.

He in his car and the men in the lorry, made a short stop at his parents' house in Sprinton. They offloaded some boxes of books there, and the Stubbs. His father, once a great horseman, before the disease struck, loved that painting too and Mark knew it would not look right in the Laverton flat. As for the books, well, there were far too many and anyway it would be good to have things to read when he was in Sprinton. His mother took him to look briefly at where Jet was buried. Dawkins had not yet completed the plaque to mark the spot. Then he continued his journey south.

   He arrived ahead of the lorry, opened up the flat and made sure there were no obstacles in the way of the men when manoeuvring the desk up to the sitting room. That was the heaviest and most awkward thing they had to get up the stairs but if they took the drawers separately then it shouldn't be too bad. He then looked in on the shop, told the girls what was about to happen and found that Ivy, as requested, had been in and left a box of groceries for him. As usual nowadays there was a steady stream of customers but, in a brief lull Phyllis managed to tell him that they had all had a bowl of Mr Ruskin's ice cream on Saturday afternoon, which was delicious, and they wanted to thank him most warmly for the treat. "We got the last serving, sir," Phyllis informed him,"for two ladies came in after us wanting some and Mr Ruskin came out and said he was sorry but there was none left. They were very disappointed."

A few minutes later the arrival of the brand-new Binns lorry created a minor sensation among them, for it had not been in Laverton before. Phyllis saw it go past the window and then turn the corner in order to drive into the yard at the back of the shop. Maureen was in the office and watched it park at the back. "Oh my, it really is smart, Mr Edwards, sir!" she called, as she craned her head to see out of the window into the yard. Mark went out to see to the unloading.

It took less than an hour to get everything up into the flat and in place. When they had finished he gave the men some money and told them to go and slake their thirst before setting off on the journey back to Sprinton. Now he really felt that the flat had become a home. The desk, positioned behind the sofa, with its polished light oak top and the soft-red leather studded chair made from the same oak, set the seal on the transformation. Indeed they gave the whole room a sumptuous feeling; and the Indian rugs, which had some of the same red in their oriental designs, added to the effect. He had said that he would only be spending three nights a week there but he felt already, looking around the sitting room, that he would much rather be there than in Sprinton.

The boxes of books, rather a lot of them, were what remained to be unpacked and Ivy had committed to coming to do it for him as soon as the tea shop closed. In the meantime he went along the landing to the room at the end to see how he would organise his studio. His easels and all his painting gear had been dumped in the middle of the room. The cupboard built into the stonework across the end wall had shelves in it from halfway up to the ceiling and a bigger unshelved bottom half. This he had noticed when he inspected the flat the first time and it struck him then that quite a few canvases could be accommodated there. There were also narrow shelves along the wall beside the 'south' window where both jars of brushes and tubes of paint could be kept. The gear that had been brought from Sprinton that day included a collapsible table commonly used by decorators when pasting strips of wallpaper. Mark had acquired it when in an intense painting period in his teens - the period when he had rebelled, temporarily, at the idea that he should study at Cambridge after the years at his Public School where art was not highly rated. A disused stable in the grounds of his childhood home had been given to him to use as studio and during one of the periods when his mother was having redecorations carried out in the house Mark managed to buy the pasting table off one of the decorators. He recalled that time as he erected the table in his new studio. Setting out all his stuff made his fingers itch to get started. Yes, without, he hoped, neglecting the business there were changes he wanted to make in his life. He knew what he wanted to start with.....

There was a knock at the door downstairs and then Ivy's voice called up, "Mr Edwards, can I come in?" He closed the door of his studio and leaned over the bannisters. Ivy looked up and, just for a moment his heart missed a beat, for from that angle of the upturned face Ivy's resemblance to her older sister was striking.

"Yes, come on up," he managed to reply, just as the illusion faded. But Ivy was of a cheerful and buoyant disposition and, apart from her usefulness in practical matters, Mark was finding that her presence always made him feel optimistic. "Wow, you have got a lot of books!" She exclaimed when she saw the boxes in the sitting room. "How do you want them ordered…" she paused and, putting a finger against her cheek as if considering the question seriously, said, "oh, let me guess - by size or colour!" Mark shook his head at her, and smiled, "No….now pay attention miss - I want the leather bound sets all together, on that side; all poetry, novels and short stories…there. You know what poetry looks like?" Ivy, indignant at the aspersion cast on her education, protested, "Of course I do!" Then, indicating the bigger, bottom shelf he continued, "all the big, that's mainly art, books there, and everything else on those shelves between the two windows. Do you think you can manage that?" He looked at her with mock severity. "I'll try sir," she said meekly.

"I have some things to do downstairs," he said, meaning the shop. "It'll take me about half an hour. If there are some volumes you can't decide where they should go put them in a pile and I'll sort them when I come back, OK? And then I want you to show me how to boil an egg and make an omelette!" Ivy opened her eyes wide. Were there people who didn't know how to boil an egg or make an omelette?

"Wow!" She said again.

"And please stop saying 'wow!'" he said and left her to get on with unpacking the books.

When he came back up the stairs to the flat there was silence in the house which puzzled him a little until he opened the door to the sitting room and found Ivy sitting cross legged on the floor and silently turning over the pages of a book. She looked up when he came in, indicated the bookcase now full and ordered as he had instructed her, likewise the shelves between the two windows,

and no pile at all of 'undecideds'. She got up off the floor, the book that she had been looking at still in her hand,
"I read this a few years ago," she said, "Kate got it for me from the library in Sprinton. You have two of the others, but they're girls' books, aren't they?"
"Why, what is it?" He took the book out of her hand. "Louisa M. Alcott, *Little Women*...?" He looked puzzled, then enlightenment dawned, "Oh, I know, they are my sister's. I didn't realise they were on my shelves...That's right, she came to stay, with her daughter, Milly, some years ago...ah yes, she left them behind." He fell silent, remembering with reluctance the circumstances of the visit of Isabel and Milly, then a child of ten. It had been the last attempt he had made to get through Dorothy's resistance to intimacy and any talk of having children. He asked his sister, who had a happy home and family life, if she would come and stay, bringing Milly, who was talkative and affectionate. If any child could melt an unmaternal heart it was Milly. Mark was very fond of this niece. He had also hoped that Isabel might be able to broach the delicate issue of Dorothy's dislike of physical intimacy. He had never been able to understand it since in the first months of their acquaintance she had seemed keen - right up until the miscarriage in fact. Anyway, it had not worked. On the contrary it seemed as if Dorothy could not or would not respond to the child's spontaneous warmth. Eventually, Milly withdrew to Mark's side of the room and regarded Dorothy warily from there. Isabel too tried to speak to Dorothy as 'sister' or woman to woman but she would not be drawn.

Mark handed the book back to Ivy. "You are welcome to take it home with you if you want," he said, "or one of the others that you haven't read." Ivy's face lit up, "oh, could I really? Thank you."
"And now you have to show me how to boil an egg and make an omelette. And if I can do both of those things before you leave you may take two of Louisa M. Alcott's books and keep them."

He had decided that when he was in Laverton he would look after himself as much as possible. In his childhood home there had always been a cook and two servants in the house to do all the domestic work. Outside there was a gardener and a groom to look after the horses. In his years at Cambridge there were also college servants and he had learnt only to make tea and toast bread. Likewise in his married home, that there should be cook, maid and gardener - handyman was taken for granted. Now it was going to be different - a real break from his old life and habits. When he had finished his work in Laverton he wanted to be

free, with nobody else in the flat or likely to disturb him, so he could get on with his painting and break off only when he wanted to. The only exception to this was if he should happen at any time to be invited to take tea or supper with the Ruskins. And the reason he had made that exception was that - he had just been given such an invitation for the following day! Ivy had left it until she was about to leave, with the two Louisa Alcott's wrapped up in her hand, and then she said,
"Oh, my sister asked me to say you are invited to join us for supper tomorrow if you are free and have nothing else planned?"
"That's very kind," replied Mark, his heart lifting at the thought. "I would like that very much." Her task completed and invitation delivered, Ivy went home.

"You will have to excuse the informality of our supper table this evening, Mr Edwards", Sarah said as she ushered him into the dining room the next evening. "I'm afraid newborn infants do disrupt things!" She had told him that Kate was detained with the baby upstairs who was suffering a bout of colic.

For the first part of the meal Kate was missing from the table, but nevertheless it was an enjoyable occasion, and Mark felt that he was being welcomed and included in a family gathering. The conversation ranged from food and farming to technical advances, ice cream - and even Louisa M. Alcott, of whom Ivy had become even more of a fan than she was twenty four hours earlier. Eventually Kate came downstairs and could announce that little Stella was sleeping. She looked tired but she smiled warmly at Mark and asked him about the shop, Lily, and how the move had gone.

When he got back to the flat, just before dark - for Stanley had detained him after the breakup of the supper party, by taking him to see how he had arranged and improved his ice house - Mark had the feeling that he had somehow acquired and been accepted into a new family. He went to bed in a contented state of mind for the second night in the tiny bedroom and it didn't feel claustrophobic at all. Since the night was warm he had left a window open in the living room and the door from his narrow bedroom open into it. If he twisted his head slightly on his pillow he could see the curtains at the living room windows moving slightly in the current of air coming in the open window.

Over the following three months he established a new routine of work and living between Sprinton and Laverton. Mostly it worked so that he could ride Trixy either on Saturday or Sunday and it was clear to everyone that he was just as much in command of the firm as ever. There was even an expansion in the business, though not in retail trade. The first motor lorry had been so successful in its use for house removals that Mark decided, with the agreement of the other directors, that they should acquire a second lorry whose sole function would be in furniture removal.

Another change, which eventually resulted in Mark being able to spend more time in Laverton, was that his sister's son, Christopher, had joined the firm; a bright young man, with drive and ambition, Mark liked this nephew and had taken an interest in him as he was growing up. Nevertheless, he was firm in his insistence that when he joined the company he must spend a year at least working 'on the frontline' serving the public, their customers, in all the different departments of the business. Christopher had been with the company a year now and Mark had recently given him his last 'apprenticeship' test. He was to spend a month as removal man, together with the driver of the new lorry. At least once a month when Mark came back to Sprinton from his days in Laverton he had made a point of having Christopher up to his office for a chat. He wanted to know what he had been doing and what were his impressions of the part of the company he'd been working in. Mark knew that if the boy was serious about wanting to work in the company then he would take something positive from his experience in each of the departments, even if some of what he had to do was uncongenial. If he hadn't really been serious then that too would show in his response to the work.

Thus far Mark was pleased with Christopher's progress. He had made discreet enquiries among the people his nephew had been working with and the overwhelming impression had been positive. The young man had taken the work seriously and he had treated the staff he had been working with with respect. He asked for help if he needed it, they said, and he bowed to their experience. Further proof that Christopher had become seriously involved in the company and with the workforce, was that he ventured to make suggestions for changes and innovations. In fact he seemed enthusiastic about the company and about being involved in running it. It might be too early to say that Christopher could one day be put in charge of Binns, but at least the signs were good. There was no indication that Mark need be uneasy about the business when he was away in Laverton at any rate.

In Laverton, without anything specific being said, it just seemed to happen that he was invited to the Ruskins, one evening a week, for supper. He became a confidant of all the family and he found himself included in discussions of all kinds. He was particularly pleased when Stanley and Kate sought his advice or opinion about business matters, for he felt that, in that sphere at least he really could help them. He knew what not to do in order to avoid the pitfalls that lay in wait for inexperienced people just starting out.

One other member of the family appealed to him for support too. In Ivy's case it was not uncommonly because she wanted Mark to back her up in some dispute that she had with her sister. Here, of course, she was not always successful since Mark seemed often, unaccountably to Ivy, to be predisposed to side with Kate on most issues.

Sarah regarded Mark as the benevolent supporter of her son and his wife, that is to say of Stanley and Kate - she knew about the loan and the conditions attached to it - ; and she knew that he had performed a probably life-saving service for them all. What she also liked about him was that he never mentioned those things or suggested that they had anything to thank him for. Sarah had had a lot of experience, some of it bitter, of different sorts of people in her nearly seventy years 'in this vale of tears', as she had, years before, been wont to say, and Mr Edwards she ranked as one of the better among humankind.

And then there was Stella. When, at the age of two months, Kate suddenly presented him with the baby to hold on his knee, he was so taken by surprise and fearful of dropping her - that he almost dropped her. Laughing, Kate took her from him and then showed him how he should hold her safely but with no danger of dropping her nor of squeezing the life out of her. Stella, who had but recently started to smile, turned her head up to look at the strange man who was holding her, and won his heart with the biggest smile and gurgles of delight that she had yet been capable of. Mark readily admitted to Kate, much, much later that that was the moment at which he began to fall in love with a second member of the Ruskin family.

At supper at the Ruskins the following week they announced that they were planning to have the christening in three weeks' time. They hoped it would be convenient for the godparents. (Ivy was being honoured as godmother, about which she was very proud for it was the first time she had ever been asked). Mark said of course it was convenient. He considered it a great honour too and as long as they didn't ask him to give any speeches but merely to propose a toast, he would be quite happy. He had in fact been thinking much about 'guardianship' and care, but these thoughts he kept to himself. In his heart he knew that he would do all that lay in his power to prevent harm from coming to the child of the woman he loved.

The christening took place amid family rejoicing, as christenings should. In church the baby cried when the vicar splashed water on her forehead. The tea shop was decorated with ribbons and flowers and the members of the two, no three, families mingled and talked. "Well", said a jubilant Ivy, when the tea shop family and Mark were the only ones remaining, "now we've all been christened", and she cuddled the sleeping baby in her arms. "What do you mean 'all' ?" asked a smiling Kate.
"Well, Stella Maria Ruskin has got her name, Mark is godfather, and I'm godmother….we've all been christened," and she held the baby out to Mark, "a kiss for your goddaughter, Mark." He leant forward smiling and sealed the promise he had made both aloud and in his heart, with a kiss. Stella opened her eyes, saw a face that was not her mother's, very close to, and howled. It was a happy day.

PART THREE: Life is.........

CHAPTER 17

Compromise and Accommodations

Diana Stanton, after her divorce, had settled in Hampstead. The settlement she got from Donald had allowed her to keep the small, terraced house, quite close to the Heath, where she now lived on her own. Her property owning husband had a long established love nest with his latest mistress in another part of London, near Regent's Park. Diana also got a money settlement which made her financially independent. A lot of things had had to be agreed with Donald and kept under wraps in order for the divorce to be granted, but at last it was. Fortunately there were no children to be considered. Diana was a 'modern' woman; she was happy to regard herself as, and be called, 'a flapper'. What she had discovered in the very first years of the marriage was that - it was not a state that suited her. After the ladies' college she had attended in London and then 'coming out' just at the time of the new king's coronation, she found herself caught up in the suffragette movement, though she wanted more than just the vote: she wanted freedom and independence. Initially against the wishes of her family, she struck out for a working life of her own. Her circle of friends tended towards the bohemian: they included a couple of artists, a dancer and a female editor of a fashion magazine. Diana got work as a graphic artist designing advertisements for companies that produced household appliances. It was through this work that she met and married Donald Stanton; it was through this circle of friends that she met Mark Edwards.

Binns was renowned, first of all, for the variety and quality of the textiles it traded in. Mark's great-grandfather, Isaiah Binns, had come from a cloth weaving family in the West Country. Isaiah took over a mill in Manchester and his son Jacob moved to Sprinton and opened the first retail outlet for Binns fabrics. Textiles remained at the centre of the business and periodically new products or designs were exhibited or launched and Jacob's grandson, Mark, by himself or with Binns chief buyer, would go down to London to see if there was

anything new which was likely to appeal to Binns' customers. On one such visit, after business was concluded, Mark visited an old university friend who took him along to the opening of another friend's art exhibition. A number of fellow artists, designers and assorted bohemians - Paul, the friend, called them 'free spirits' - were there. Mark, after having been introduced to a few of them at the opening reception, took time to look at the paintings, for sale, on the walls. Stopping in front of one of the more intriguing works he became suddenly aware of a young woman by his side who was staring fixedly, with puckered brow at the same painting. She turned and looked straight at him. The first thing he noticed was that she had some of the bluest eyes he had ever seen. Taking the cigarette that she was smoking through a long holder out of her mouth, she said, "Don't you find that altogether too many of our contemporary artists are simply imitating what was being done in France forty years ago?" And she looked steadily into his face. Returning her gaze, he replied,
"That is sometimes true but I like the use of the blues in this one and the sense of the mysterious with the figure retreating into the distance. The artist has always achieved something if he, or she, causes the viewer to stop and wonder what is really going on in a picture....don't you think?" He looked at her quizzically.
"Hmn," she looked at the painting again and then back at Mark. "I don't think I've seen you at any of these do's before, have I?"
"No, you haven't. I'm just visiting," he said, "my friend Paul," nodding in his direction, "brought me here."
"Ah, you know Paul. Are you in the art business?"
"No, not at all, but I'm interested," he said.
"What do you do?" She asked bluntly..
"I sell textiles, among other things." She considered him, head on one side.
"You're a shopkeeper?" she said provocatively. He nodded assent, ignoring the provocation,
"Indeed."
"Here in London?" He was beginning to find her interrogation irritating, though there was definitely something attractive about her.
"No, not in London" he said briefly. She looked at him without speaking for a few seconds. He noted the oval face, the fair skin and serious but not unfriendly eyes.

"Shall we go and have a drink somewhere else - it's very hot here," she said suddenly. His look of surprise caused her to smile and, glancing across the crowded room, she added,
"Oh don't worry about Paul. He knows me and I'll deliver you back," she laughed, "in one piece! I'm Diana Stanton, by the way."

He hadn't known where this was leading and it was the first time ever that he had been openly, no *boldly* invited out by a woman. At first taken aback, astonished even, he then realised he was actually excited by the boldness of the gesture - or was he excited by her? It had been a long time since…..the last time.

Diana went away to say something to Paul; he didn't know what but Paul looked over towards him and Mark raised an eyebrow in response. Almost before he knew it they were outside, and Diana was guiding them to a nearby cocktail bar in a side street. She was obviously familiar with the place. She proposed a drink to him and ordered for them both. She looked at him,
"I suppose that seemed very forward of me," she said. "I saw the way you were looking at the paintings - like someone who knew what they were about….Are you married?" she asked suddenly. He was getting used to her bold directness. He decided he quite liked it. His answer was a quizzical raised eyebrow. She laughed and then the conversation took a different turn.

She *was* one of those 'free spirits' that Paul had mentioned. She had been married. She wasn't any longer and she wasn't intending to be. She had lovers. She enjoyed the physical….side of life. She made no promises about fidelity; it wasn't in her nature, though sometimes she had been faithful to one lover for a time. What about Mark? Mark had never had a conversation like this in his life before, with either man or woman. It was both exciting and a bit unnerving. He wondered if it was real. Was she real? He was trying to work out if she was genuine, or a fantasist. But there was something, an energy……a sexual energy? He decided to tell the truth about himself. It seemed the only thing to do with a woman like this…..and it seemed that he wanted her.

Yes, he too had been married but he wasn't any longer. And he didn't think he ever would be again. Not for the reason that Diana had given but because the only woman he would ever want to marry could not be his.

"Ha!" Diana laughed, "So you're a romantic - and a 'nester'." He had never heard the expression before. She went on, "So, you would, if you could, with *one* particular woman?" There was silence. He looked at her...ruefully perhaps. Her face was serious.

"Ah," she said, "sad but noble." He protested,
"Not so sad," but she broke in,
"Don't you ever think '- but there really are so many more fish in the sea'?"
"Well, we're all different," he retorted.

Shortly after that she took him back to the flat that she sometimes borrowed from a friend so she could spend the night in town.

Visits to London on Binns business had averaged about twice a year. After the meeting with Diana this was no longer enough. Pleading the wish to visit art exhibitions - the National Gallery, the Tate, the Royal Academy - Mark began to travel up to London about once every two months. He had begun to draw and paint again soon after he took the flat in Laverton so that his parents, and his sister, thought it quite natural that he should be 'keeping up' with the exhibitions and contemporary movements in the art world. His mother, Rachel, had always in fact been a warm supporter of her son's interest in art. It was she who had seen to it that Mark, in his teens, could take over the disused stable building as a studio. She believed in his talent and blamed Dorothy, once again, for the fact that he had stopped exercising that talent soon after they got married. She was particularly pleased that he had taken it up again and remarked on more than one occasion to her husband that that had been one of the most positive things to come out of Mark's 'move' to Laverton. His sister also was pleased at this development in her brother's life. When Isabel was scarcely more than a child she had often been the subject of his drawings and even, just before her 'coming out', of one full length oil painting, his most ambitious work to date - of which she was very fond and had on the wall in the sitting room of her house. Her husband also admired it.

It was when he returned from one of his visits to London, and Diana, that Mark learned that Kate had had a miscarriage. Ivy had hinted to him, some weeks before, that there might be another child expected in the family and, since Kate's first pregnancy, until the very end, had gone well, he had not given the information very much thought. Now he found himself cast into turmoil and anxiety. Almost he felt remorse that he had been away when it happened. It revived the trauma of Dorothy's miscarriage shortly after they were married. He had to go to the house and find out how she was. Ivy came to the door, saw his face and pulled him inside.

"It's all right," she said, "she's fine but she has to stay lying down for a couple more days. It happened two days ago - she hadn't gone more than two months so that was a good thing." Mark didn't understand much of this. He registered that Kate was not in any danger and could only murmur, "Oh, thank God, thank God." Ivy looked in his face, now registering relief. She thought, 'My goodness but he loves her!' A child started crying upstairs. Ivy looked over her shoulder but said, "It's all right, Stanley is with her. She's been a bit upset with all this going on around her and not understanding it. Of course we've just said that Mummy is ill and has to stay in bed for a few days."

"I have to go to Sprinton tomorrow," Mark said, "but I'll be back on Sunday. You'll let me know if anything changes, won't you?"

"Of course," she said gently.

"Is Stanley all right?"

"He is now," she said.

When he got back to the flat he went straight to the studio. On the easel was a half finished portrait, a smallish canvas for a small person. It was Stella and she was pouting. He had made some preliminary sketches, mostly when he was visiting them and they were sitting in the garden, the child playing nearby. You couldn't get a three year old to sit still and pose for more than a few minutes, even if you offered a bribe. You had to catch them on the hop as it were. He looked at the face. It was a child's face, no longer a baby, but the features not yet determined. Nevertheless he could see the mother in the child's eyes and in the forehead.

For a long time Stella could not say her full name. She started to speak at a little over a year but the 'St' of her name defeated her. If asked she would say that she was 'Ella' and for a long time it made her cross when anyone called her 'Stella' or corrected her when she pronounced herself to be 'Ella'. She was only persuaded to accept her full name when Mark pointed out to her that Stella meant star, like those that twinkled in the sky at night. She was a star, he said. But 'Ella' was not a star. She listened when he explained that to her and showed her pictures of some stars in a big book. She adored her father, Stanley, and she adored her 'nuncle Mark'. Why were they not stars, she asked. Ah well, Mark explained, to be a star you had to twinkle. Stella twinkled but Stanley and Mark were too big to twinkle. She considered this for a moment. Was Mummy a star then, she wanted to know. Did Mummy twinkle? Oh yes, said Mark, Mummy was definitely a star. Looking at the figure on the canvas he recalled that exchange with Stella and it made him smile. He took off jacket and waistcoat, rolled up his sleeves and mixed some colours on his palette. He wanted to get that cream and pastel green shade right for the smock that the child was wearing. He hadn't got it yet. He must get it before the light faded.

Sarah had returned to Sprinton four months after Stella's birth, but Ivy had stayed on and formed part of the Ruskins permanent household. "How ya gonna keep 'em down on the farm, After they've seen Paree…" the song said. For Ivy it didn't take Paris but simply Laverton, the tea shop, her sister's family and the friends she had made through the shop. Her parents, particularly her mother, Susan, had been sorry that she had not come back to the farm. Susan had come to rely on Ivy for a lot of the chores about the house and the animals, for she was getting older and quite stiff with rheumatism. Nevertheless they were conscious of the fact that, for their youngest, unattached daughter, staying at home on the farm meant very little contact with anyone of her own age. When she was very young Ivy had declared that she wasn't going to marry or leave home but, when she reached young adulthood she had begun to feel a certain restlessness. That feeling was intensified when Kate moved from Sprinton to Laverton. Kate, more than six years older than Ivy, had always been her favourite sister and idol. When Kate was in Sprinton she went home to the farm at least once a month and Ivy hung on her every word about life in the town, which always sounded exciting. When Kate moved to Laverton Ivy missed her visits intensely. Coming to stay and help out when Stella was born and Kate incapacitated for a time, was supposed to be just a temporary arrangement but Ivy felt more and more of a reluctance to return home. She made excuses for staying on several times, and Kate and Stanley were happy for her to stay since she was truly needed. Kate, however, was beginning to worry that their mother's need was greater.

The problem was resolved on the occasion of Stella's christening. George and Susan Atkinson arrived in Laverton the night before and the opportunity arose quite naturally to discuss the situation. It turned out, which the family in Laverton had not realised, that the Atkinsons had already taken on a local girl to help Susan with domestic chores and the chickens.
"She's one of Les Wilson's daughters," explained Susan, naming one of their former labourers. "She's a good worker and very helpful. She'll do whatever I ask her to do. A nice girl, and that family hasn't had it easy since the oldest boy

was killed in the war." Susan admitted that she had suspected that Ivy wanted to stay in Laverton with her sister, and she could understand it. They, she and George, didn't want to force her to come back to the country. And they could see that she was performing a real service in the Ruskin's household and that she was enjoying working in the tea shop. No, it was agreeable to everyone that Ivy should stay on in Laverton with Kate and Stanley, and with those spare bedrooms on the top floor there was room for her. Thus it was that Ivy became a valued and integral part of the Ruskin's household.

Three years on and The Teashop was now well established in Laverton and much frequented. Stanley's ice cream was locally famous, as were his cakes and Kate's varieties of quality chocolates and hot chocolate drinks. They still sold some tobaccos and cigars (Mark's favourites always of course); but the scent that accosted the visitor to the shop when she crossed the threshold was, of good quality chocolate. After the expiry of their two year tenancy of the property, Henry Whittle extended it for another three years. He was still very much alive, had become somewhat bored with the role of retired shopkeeper become mower of his sister's lawns, and had found another role for himself as assiduous frequenter and handyman when needed, of the tea shop, and overseer of the businesses on Laverton's market place. A fine wrought iron and beechwood seat which had been gifted to the town by the relatives of a notable citizen, was positioned on the central island not far from the fountain: here Henry Whittle was often to be found, surveying the life and businesses around him, and willing to offer his wisdom or advice to any other occupant of the bench. He had to admit that the Ruskins had built up a good business and if any visitor ever happened to ask him what was a good place to get afternoon, or just a pot, of tea, then his answer was given; in addition he would add that the same place offered the most delicious ice cream that you were ever likely to taste.

 By the time the tea shop had been open for three years Stanley was able to pay back the loan from Mark Edwards which had enabled them to open the shop in the first place. Mark seemed peculiarly reluctant to take back the money but Stanley was absolutely insistent and indeed wished to add on a sum as interest on the loan. This, Mark was at first determined to refuse, but when he saw that it was a matter of importance to Stanley's pride, he decided to accept it. Privately he had already been putting all of the Ruskins repayments into a fund that he intended to use, when she was older, for something that would benefit Stella.

Stanley was still under the influence of the fear engendered by the miscarriage; it was the third time, he confessed to Mark, when he really feared that they might lose Kate. He would not take that risk again. She was not strong. Mark understood that he meant that there would be no more children. He said nothing but he couldn't help feeling a sense of relief; and he knew Stanley well enough to be sure that he would do all in his power to prevent any more harm coming to the woman that they both, though unbeknown to Stanley, loved more than anyone else.

....

Diana Stanton had learned a lot about her 'lover from the North Countree', as she liked to dub him, slightly to Mark's annoyance. She had been his lover for two years now, but never exclusively, as she made clear. She had others and, the ground rules having been set out at the beginning, Mark never questioned her about the other men in her life. Their 'trysts' which lasted for a few days, several times a year, were enjoyable for both parties, but Mark was never in any danger of being 'in love' with Diana. The physical, which was the main part, was good, and Diana had a sense of humour, but she was always dispassionate about the relationship, never committing her inner self to it. That circumstance suited Mark; he would not have wanted it to be any different. It was not that he never gave any thought to Diana's character; indeed he did, for he could not help analysing the reasons that prevented him from being in danger of falling in love with her. Many would have said that physically she was quite lovely in a 'gamin' kind of way, and Mark would have agreed with them. Their sexual congress was entirely satisfactory. Nevertheless, beyond that there was a holding back that Mark sensed as something essential to Diana's personality. His marriage to Dorothy had shown him beyond any doubt that he could never *be* in love with someone whom he felt was ultimately aloof.

About some things, therefore, there was an element of mutual incomprehension. Diana could never understand Mark's continuing fidelity, in the deepest sense, to a woman who could never be his. She could never comprehend how such a love could endure. Mark, on his part, could not understand how Diana could be satisfied, over a long time, with having multiple liaisons, often running concurrently, none of which seemed to be more important to her than any other. He was no hypocrite so he could not be sorry about that fact, since it was what made his connection with Diana possible. It made him think, however, about the complexity of the human psyche and about why people were as they were. While not a philosopher, in spite of having read a considerable amount of philosophy at Cambridge, he did consider himself a student of humankind as it manifested itself in the real, everyday world. The world was a mysterious place, he had to conclude. People were mysterious - himself among them!

....

Eventually Mark was satisfied with the portrait of three year old Stella. It was the only portrait of a child that he had ever done and, later, when he gave them the painting, he admitted to Kate and Stanley that it had been a challenge. The smock that she was wearing in the painting had been a different kind of Christening present from the three female employees of Binns. One of the nicest of the materials for summer dresses that year had been a brushed cotton material in white with pastel green swirls in it and tiny silverish stars dotted here and there. It was one of the most expensive cotton materials they carried that year and only a few yards of it were left by late autumn when the christening was to take place. Lily James had the idea of making up a dress for Mrs. Ruskin's little girl in some of the remaining material, the stars on it were for Stella of course. Lily was an expert in the art of smocking as well as dressmaking. Phyllis and Maureen were happy to contribute towards it.

Lily came by to deliver the present before the christening. When the parcel was opened at the house, after they all came back from the church, everyone was amazed by the beauty of the dress, and Lily's smocking not least of all. What a good idea, they said too, to give something that would come into its own at a later date.

When Kate brought out the dress just before Stella's third birthday and explained that it was a present from 'the ladies at Binns' the little girl fell in love with it straight away, and after her birthday it was hard to persuade her that she could not have it on every day. Only after Mark told her that he was going to make a picture of her in her favourite dress could she be convinced that it was necessary to keep the dress clean for the painting. Mark managed to borrow it for a few days too, so that he could study it and reproduce the material, as it really was, in the picture. When at last the picture was finished and framed Mark decided he would invite the Ruskins, and Ivy, up to the flat for tea on a Sunday afternoon, and present the portrait to them. He was satisfied with it at last.

It was a long time since Kate and Stanley had been back in the flat where they had started their married life. When they came up the stairs and into the sitting room Kate, especially, looked around with approval.

"It's lovely, Mark," she said. "Especially your desk there and," she stopped, suddenly noticing a painting on the wall, "Oh, you've got it up at last. I love that scene." It was the painting of the flowery meadow. Stella had no memory of the house at all so she ran about exploring and then stopped, when her mother drew attention to it, in front of the meadow picture. She looked at it, and then at Mark. "Show me," she pleaded, holding up her arms. Mark picked her up and carried her close up to the painting. The child looked, examining as if with a practised eye. "Nice," she said smiling and leaning her face into Mark's, with one arm round his neck. Then, lifting her head and pointing at the picture, "Where's the tiger?" Everyone laughed, but Stella looked puzzled. Mark had told before the story of his grandfather taking the painting of the tiger in the jungle out of a cupboard to show him. He explained that the tiger was in another painting, not this one and that the tiger painting was at Mark's parents' house in Sprinton. One day, he promised, when she was bigger he would take her to see the tiger painting. In the meantime, he had got a picture for them that he hoped they would like.

He brought it into the room with a cloth covering it. They all looked expectant. Stella looked apprehensive. He lifted the cloth away. There was a gratifying, collective gasp of admiration. Stella's face was wreathed in smiles, "Is me," she called out and, pointing at the picture " my frock." Kate was the first to recover, "Mark, it's beautiful," she said, "I'm speechless." She looked at the others for help. Ivy put in, "You've got her to a 't'. That pout....and the dress."

Stanley could only smile and shake his head. He looked over at Mark. "I don't know what to say," he said, and laughed. "You should be 'court painter' if there was such a post. Well, well..." and he came closer to look. Mark put the painting up on top of the bookcase so they could view it at shoulder height.

"Well, it was quite a challenge," he said, "but yes, I'm satisfied now." He knew it was the best thing he had done so far. The child.....what was that line in Wordsworth's poem, "The child is father of the man...." and the daughter...what was she? The mother....perhaps he would be able to do a portrait of her one day....He had fathered the painting of the child at least.

CHAPTER 18

Death and Life Choices

There was a dream of horses. Two young thoroughbreds, with shining chestnut coats and flying manes galloping side by side across open countryside. He was riding one of them, the other had no rider and no saddle. He was thinking, "that horse is wild; she's going to win. I can't compete, but this is glorious. What air! What a sky...Rachel, jump into it!" He opened his eyes, and called, "Rachel!" His wife woke and turned towards him,
"Philip!" But he was gone.

The parish church of St. Barnabas, Sprinton's biggest, was full for the funeral. As well as the entire staff of the Sprinton Binns, other local business acquaintances, family and friends, there were the stud farm people and riders of the local hunt. Philip Edwards was laid to rest beside his father-in-law, Jacob Binns and his wife, in the Binns family plot. It had been agreed between them that it should be so. Philip had said to his wife, "I don't really care where you put me when I'm gone, but I want us to be together." And so they would be.

The biggest immediate change brought about in the company after Philip's death was that a new director was appointed. The choice, a fairly obvious one, fell on a cousin of Mark's who had already been working for the company for almost ten years. For the previous two years he had been active manager of the High Bridge shop, which had opened at the same time as the Laverton one, but it had not been doing very well - until Andrew Edwards took it over. He was put in for the specific purpose of 'building up the business', that meant, making it much more profitable than it had been. Andrew, taking some advice from Mark, succeeded in doing that. He showed himself to be loyal, and a good leader. Mark, having been rethinking his own life and career over the last couple of years, had been watching the progress of Andrew since he joined Binns and, based on what he observed, he began to form an idea for what his future in the company could be. The other family member who was showing promise in Binns was Christopher, Isabel's son, but he was still very young.

Whatever changes might take place in the future Philip Edwards had never had any reason to be dissatisfied with the way Mark ran the company. On the contrary Mark knew that his father had been proud of the way in which he had directed and overseen its expansion while maintaining the values that the business was founded on. If he should make changes in his own life now, and in particular with regard to his own position in the company, it would be in the knowledge that there were capable people of the right kind to carry on. He had not let his father down and he would not let his mother down either.

Rachel, the direct descendant of the founder, was also proud of what her forebears had achieved, but she was of a different bent. Her education and interests leant towards the cultural rather than the commercial; and it was she who had been eager to foster Mark's artistic talent. It was she who saw to it that the disused stable became a studio for him. She would not have objected if he had in fact rejected Cambridge and studied art seriously instead; but the male consensus in the family was against that and, to be fair, Mark at that time was keen to go into the family business anyway, and was not against the idea of a few years at university first. What all this meant now, however, was that Mark's plans for a change of occupation and position in the company would be met with more sympathy than would have been the case if his father had still been alive.

"Hasten slowly" he still regarded as a good motto, however. Consequently, for the time being he kept his own counsel about his future plans. It was never a good idea to create turbulence in the world of trade. His father's passing was a big enough event to be going on with. The rest could wait.

His time for both clearing his mind and for thinking things over was when riding Trixy across the open countryside around High Bridge. He felt most intensely alive then. There was a slight breeze but it wasn't cold. Trixy was on form too. She tossed her head and snorted as she jumped over a rivulet, not yet a stream and cantered up Thurlton Wold. They were both having a good time. The thing he wanted to think about was, for once, nothing to do with his own personal life. He felt, for the moment anyway, at peace about that. He had reached an accommodation with himself. No, what he was thinking about was Stella, his god daughter. She was seven now, an active and a bright child. She ran, jumped, did cartwheels, and generally showed great agility. Kate claimed that that was just as she had been as a child, on the farm. Sometimes she regretted that there was not the same outdoor space for all kinds of physical activity, for her daughter, such as she had had. That conversation, sometime back, had recalled to Mark the time, years before, when he had asked her if she rode, she behind the counter in Binns, and she told him no, only as a little girl riding bareback on Florrie while her brothers piled the cart with hay.

He had taken them all to visit the Atkinson's farm once, when Stella was five. Kate mentioned one day that she had had a letter from her mother. Her father had had a fall and had broken a leg. She said that they were planning a visit home to the farm. It was a year since the last time. She wanted her parents to see Stella and Stella to see her grandparents and the farm. They would have a little holiday. Mark immediately said that he was going to Sprinton the following weekend and could take them all in his car if they liked. Willow Farm was just a few miles further than Sprinton. Stella jumped up and down when she heard this. Kate and Ivy accepted the offer, with gratitude, and it was decided. Stanley too was pleased, for he had wanted them to have a break and see the family, but he could not go away himself. He had to stay at home and 'mind the shop'.

The Atkinsons had welcomed Mark warmly and he had a long conversation with William about farming matters. Later Kate took him to the stream and the willows after which the farm was named and after that to visit the two young cart horses that had replaced Florrie, who had died not long before. After a minute of shyness when they first arrived Stella then ran about exploring and was not content until her uncle William had lifted her up onto the back of Polly, the most docile of the two young horses, and held her there while walking Polly several times around the crew yard. Stella was thrilled into silence by this experience. Mark had left them to drive to Sprinton. He picked them up again on Monday afternoon and they returned to Laverton.

Looking back on that visit as he trotted with Trixy across the countryside Mark thought about persuading Stanley and Kate to let him teach Stella to ride. He had found stables and a riding school just a few miles from Laverton and he had engineered a visit to it one afternoon. He said to the Ruskins that he was considering moving Trixy there and was going to speak to the owner about it. (He had in truth been wondering whether it mightn't be a good idea to have Trixy near to Laverton, for he was spending more and more of his time there, and less in Sprinton). Would Kate and Stella like to accompany him and see the horses? Mark was quite sure, from the way that the child conducted herself around animals, that Stella would make a good rider.

That proved to be the right approach. The Fengate Stables had a number of small ponies that younger children could ride under supervision, either for a treat or as part of being given riding instruction. Stella was entranced by the ponies and wanted to ride one straightaway. She got her wish, closely monitored by Mark. They made several repeat visits. Mark wanted to be sure her interest was likely to last before he proposed teaching her to ride properly and on different animals. Kate also became infected by her daughter's enthusiasm, and, it had to be admitted, by Mark's encouragement.

Having satisfied himself that the Fengate Stables and riding school was well run, with dedicated, well-trained people, Mark had Trixy moved down from Longtoft and started to ride her regularly around the countryside near Laverton. One week, soon after he had moved Trixy to Fengate he proposed to Kate that they should visit the stables one afternoon when Stanley could come too and see how well his daughter was doing on the ponies.

They left it to a Sunday afternoon, in the spring, and the sun shining. Stella unknowingly helped to advance Mark's ulterior motive for she was excited at the prospect of showing her father all around the stable grounds and, especially, the horses and the ponies. Her eagerness to show off her skills on horseback were likely to make it increasingly difficult for Stanley to withstand the pleas of Stella, now backed up by Kate, to let her learn to ride properly and take care of her pony.

Given his own background and past circumstances, Mark knew that Stanley's main worry - which he would not want to embarrass himself by openly confessing to, would be the expense. Mark therefore had engaged in a degree of subterfuge which he hoped would obviate any such problem. He had got to know the manager and owner of Fengate stables quite well in the six months since he had been visiting and now housing Trixy with them. Not only did Ben Wilcox realise early on that Mark Edwards knew as much about horses and riding as he did, but the reputation of the Edwards family studfarm was renowned in the whole district and beyond. He had a great deal of respect for his views on anything equine and he also had respect and increasing regard for the man himself. The upshot was that Mark managed to negotiate special terms for six months of weekly riding lessons and pony care.

Stella learnt quickly and revelled in everything that had to do with 'her' pony. She only had one slight mishap when, in a few unsupervised moments she tried to do acrobatics on the broad back of one of them. She had been taken to a travelling circus that annually visited Laverton and was entranced by the acrobatics that one of the spangle-clad girls performed on the back of a white horse as she cantered round the circus ring. Some time after that visit Stella thought she would try to do the same. After managing to stand for a short while on the back of her pony she took a tumble, but fortunately no hurt. She got up quickly and brushed herself down, hoping that no one had noticed, but of course they had. She received a sharp reprimand from Mark, and promised not to do anything like that again. The incident had given Mark a fright. If anything should happen to Stella while she was riding or doing anything around horses he would never forgive himself and, more to the point, nor would her parents. It was he who had persuaded them to let Stella learn to ride. He did have one more weapon in his arsenal of threats to make sure she would not do anything similarly foolish or rash: he had started a painting of her favourite pony and she was anxious to know how it was progressing. She had better be good or that picture would never be finished. She was suitably chastened by this additional threat.

Mark had never intended to paint animals. He enjoyed portrait painting, and landscapes - the latter having recently, under his brush, become more impressionistic. However, one day he took Stella and Kate to Sprinton - they were going to visit the Williamses, Kate's Aunt Daisy - and they made a little detour to Mark's parents' house so that Mark could at last show Stella the tiger painting and coincidentally the Stubbs' horse. Stella was not frightened by the tiger but rather fascinated by it, and likewise when they looked at the Stubbs. She at once wanted Mark to make a picture of her pony. He made no promises though he said he might do a drawing of the pony sometime. It was the first time, in his father's case the only time, when the senior Edwards met their son's god daughter and her mother, as Mrs Ruskin.

When they left, Rachel waved them off and then went back into the house to her husband. "That's a very bright little girl," she said to him, "and the image of her mother. Mark seems very fond of her...and you know....if I didn't know any better I'd say he's half in love with the mother. I hope not but..." Her husband looked round at her and frowned.

"Well I hope you're wrong about that," he said, "for I never could abide a home-breaker and I would hate to see a son of mine engage in anything like that...."

His wife interrupted him, "Oh I don't think for a minute that anything is going on. She spoke fondly of her husband...and, well I could be wrong, I hope I am because it would be hopeless. She's too straight for anything underhand. It's just a pity for Mark if I am right....." the rest was left unfinished.

Soon after that visit Mark took his sketch pad and pencils with him when he went to the Fengate stables one day and he made some sketches. One was of Trixy whom he had been meaning to make a study of for some time. She would soon be approaching old age and Mark had had her and been riding her for more than fifteen years. In some ways she was his oldest confidente; she was the only creature to whom he had confessed all his feelings for Kate Atkinson and his agony at the hopelessness of it. Now the feelings he described to her were calmer and less urgent. But he wanted an image of Trixy while she was still, relatively, in her prime. He wanted an image that he would be able to look at and recognise as his friend of many years standing.

He also made some sketches, several, of Stella's pony Marigold. But then...it wasn't enough. Sketches, drawings were never enough for him. He had realised, subconsciously, a long, long time ago and then, consciously when he was of an age to analyse, that he was driven always by the urge to recreate the world as he saw it, in paint, in glowing colours, on canvas. It was the desire to freeze moments in time and make them accessible for all time, at least for all of *his* time; and it was the colours and the textures of those moments that he wanted above all to preserve. Of course you couldn't step into a canvas, as if into a time machine that would transport you back *into* that moment; you couldn't go back into that meadow of waist high grasses and wild flowers; you couldn't suddenly find yourself beside that shining chestnut coat and noble head of horse flesh and muscle; but if you had captured the vivid colours and the textures of that moment on canvas, then it felt as if you could. *That* was what he wanted to do. Consequently the sketches of Stella's pony, Marigold, did become a painting and after that so did those of Trixy. The portrait he most wanted to paint though was still to come.

When Mark dropped in one early summer Saturday afternoon, Stanley directed him to the garden at the back. The tea shop was busy. Ivy was running backwards and forwards with pots of tea, iced drinks and bowls of Stanley's fruit flavoured ice creams. Stanley was bringing up more of his ice cream from the ice house and both of them were keeping an eye on the oven where scones were being baked. Mark went through the house to the garden and found Kate and Stella sitting together reading aloud. Kate had been reading to and with Stella since she was a baby and the child knew off by heart not only nursery rhymes and fairy tales but even more, as she called them, 'grown-up' poetry. Her current love in stories was The Jungle Book. He came upon them from behind. They hadn't heard him coming. They were reading aloud in unison and he stopped and listened to their voices, Kate's low and melodious, Stella's the pure treble of a child. Their heads were together, Stella's hair a long dark shining curtain halfway down her back, Kate's supposedly gathered up with a comb on the top of her head, but one thick coil had escaped and hung down shielding the right side of her face; the colour of mother and daughter's hair was identical, a rich chestnut brown with flashes of coppery auburn in the sunlight. Mark's painterly eye was arrested by the beauty of the two heads together. He observed the scene and almost held his breath, then, a window catch grated behind him, two heads turned simultaneously, one face smiled and the child's voice called out his name.

He had wanted to paint Kate's portrait for a long time but he hadn't been able to make up his mind if it should be a studio portrait or not. Now he knew, it must be outdoors, in this garden. But how to arrange it he hadn't quite worked out. He must broach the subject with Kate, and Stanley too, though he had a fair idea that Stanley would be more than pleased that Mark should put Kate's image on canvas.

In the event he induced them to sit for two paintings. The two female heads of lustrous hair had captivated him, indeed moved him: he must paint them like that. Three quarters, no, even more, turned from the painter, one head, on the left, a little lower than the woman's, the bottom half of the picture the wrought iron back of the bench they were sitting on. The second was the portrait of Kate, full length, from the front, sitting in the garden, a book on her lap with her hand on it, but looking at the artist, head tilted a little and a quizzical, slightly teasing smile on her face. It was her second most characteristic expression. There was sun on the stone wall behind her, and a clematis climbing out of the picture. Both paintings were started in the garden and completed in the studio. He spent the whole summer on them. When they were finished and he could show them to the sitters he knew that they were the best things he had ever done.

He experienced a feeling of contentment after the paintings were finished and then a need to celebrate. He got an idea. Neither Ivy nor Stella had ever seen the sea. It was coming to the end of the holiday season but it was still warm. It had been one of those rare, memorable, long hot summers. Mark proposed to the Ruskin household that they should have a day at the sea. He would take them there. Nearest were the east coast resorts, one of which, as well as having miles of sandy beaches, also had a long and famous pier.

It would be hard to say who was the most excited at the prospect of the outing, the grown up Ivy or the child Stella. There was a large picnic basket that went with the car and could be strapped on the back. It contained a setting of six plates, mugs, knives, forks and spoons. There would be five of them on the outing. Kate and Ivy, with Stella's help, made pies and sandwiches and biscuits to take with them and there was fruit, a bottle of lemonade and flasks of tea. Apart from horse riding it was the most exciting thing Stella had yet experienced.

They set off early on a Sunday morning at the end of August. Stanley sat up front beside the driver, Mark; Kate and Ivy in the back seat with Stella between them. The picnic basket was strapped on the back of the car. Stanley took pleasure in observing the technique involved in driving and in thinking about what was going on under the bonnet; he and Mark had a companionable conversation about that and other matters which absorbed them for most of the journey. The back seat passengers enjoyed seeing the countryside they were passing through and commenting on it. Then there was a competition as to who would be first to catch a glimpse of the sea. Mark told them "any time now" and Stella climbed onto her mother's knee and craned her neck so she could be first. It appeared as a faint line on the horizon when there was suddenly no more land in the distance.

The town, an old seaside resort, was not large, the houses and shops mainly strung along a seashore road. To right and left the town petered out into sand dunes. Since it was coming to the end of the season there was plenty of room to park on an expanse of compacted sand beside the road. Mark and Stanley carried the picnic basket between them, the women carried blankets to sit on and towels for drying. They crossed the sand dunes and reached the beach beyond. The tide was in. Stella stood, awestruck, staring at the immense stretch of water before them which reached to the horizon, even into the sky it seemed. Ivy too let out a little gasp, an "Oh!" of wonder and discovery. They all gazed seawards.

Stella never forgot this, her first encounter with the primeval element of water from which we all are said to come. When in later life she became an artist herself and illustrator, it was seascapes and sailing ships that flowed most freely from her brush and her imagination.

It was a day to remember. Stella was so impatient that she forgot her parents and ran into the sea and got wet through. Ivy and Kate took off their stockings and shoes and paddled and laughed. Stanley took off his jacket, rolled up his trouser legs and paddled too and splashed his daughter. Then he swung her round and round just above the surface of the water and she squealed with delight. They saw some small crabs in the shallows and Ivy was afraid they might nip her toes. Mark said, "Ladies, if you'll forgive me, I must bathe." He disappeared back to the car to change and then waded out into deeper water and swam, to the admiration, especially, of Stella who declared, when he came out again, "Uncle Mark, you are like a fish. I want to do that too." When they were all dry they spread out the blankets and the contents of the picnic basket.

    Later Stanley helped Stella build sand castles with a complex system of moats and battlements. Ivy sat and watched and suggested improvements. Mark and Kate took a walk along the beach; it stretched for miles but they didn't go far. The sand was firm and warm, ridged with the pattern of waves from the recent high tide; the tide was going out. They wandered in silence a while. Kate was looking down to see what sea shells had been left behind by the retreating tide. She found some scallop shells and some long shards that shone on the inside like mother of pearl. "Aren't they beautiful?" She said holding them out in her hand towards Mark. He took one out of her hand and turned it over. "Yes, they are," he replied.

"How do you think they got such colours?" she said. "They shine, don't they?"

"They do. Like some people!" Kate laughed.

"You're the one who shines," she said with feeling, "what a good friend you are to us."

"I'll always be your friend," he said, looking at her. She glanced at him briefly, "I know."

    They set off on the journey home just after five. Stella fell asleep with her mother's arm around her. Stanley and Mark held a subdued conversation in the front, for a while. The women in the back were quiet except for when Ivy said, "I love the sea." And later, "I must go and live by the sea." Kate smiled at her and said nothing. And then, "What a lovely day," from Ivy again. "Mark!" She called out to the back of his head, "Thank you for this lovely day." Mark half turned his head, then looked at her in the rear view mirror, "You're welcome," he said, "but later comes the reckoning!" Ivy looked alarmed but he was grinning at her in the mirror, "Now you'll have to come and sit for your portrait, that means sitting still for several hours...." something that Ivy was notoriously unable to do. Kate said she was worse than Stella for not being able to sit still. "I don't believe you," she called out. "You don't need a portrait of me. You've done Kate."

"Oh but I do," he replied. "An artist always needs more practice. You're my next practice....". Ivy growled at him and the rest of the journey slipped by in a contented silence.

Shortly afterwards Mark's oldest friend, Graham Linley, came to visit him in Laverton. They had been at school together for a few years (Graham was the older) and he was one of the few people who knew about Mark's artistic talent and one of those who lamented the fact that he stopped painting after he got married. Mark told Graham that with the move to Laverton he had started painting again. Graham didn't paint himself but, together with his friend, Bernard, he collected modern art. He wanted to see Mark's studio and something of what he had been doing recently.

When he had checked in at the Victoria they had dinner in the dining room there and caught up on personal news. The Victoria had a back terrace looking onto a formal garden where you could smoke and have a brandy with your coffee - a combined pleasure that Mark could only enjoy in good company. Graham was some of the best company. Although his profession was the law, and he was a good lawyer, his leisure was not. He liked to say that 'the plastic arts' were his playground. His own father had been a not very successful sculptor and a ditto painter. He was insistent that Graham should get himself a solid profession so that if he, which God forbid, should have any artistic pretensions then he would always have a profession to fall back on. Graham never had any active artistic pretensions but he grew up surrounded by books about art, by works of art in the making and by practitioners of the arts - his father's friends and rivals - having endless discussions, sometimes heated, about the arts in the past, present and future. Instead of having artistic pretensions of his own, Graham had developed a keen sense for which trends in contemporary art were the most promising and would be worth investing in. He already possessed two paintings by Mark. One had been given to him by his friend many years before, as a present, because Graham had admired it. The second he had bought from Mark soon after the latter was married.

When Mark took him into his studio in the flat above Binns, and showed him what he had been doing over the last few years, Graham let out a low whistle. "My God, Mark," he said, "you've got more than enough for an exhibition." His eyes roved around the studio; Mark had taken out and propped some canvases against the walls. "You've got some good stuff here." He walked over to where a number of portraits or landscapes with a figure in them, were leaning. He

stopped in front of the one that Mark had finished most recently, of Kate sitting in the garden. "And this," glancing along at the other canvases there, "is the lady you told me about, I imagine....This, in particular, is very fine, Mark. And not for sale, I suppose, at the moment." Mark nodded. "I like these seascapes, especially this with figures in it, paddling. And this with sand dunes. Is it finished?" Mark shook his head.
"No, not quite," he said.
"Seriously, isn't it time you had an exhibition?"
"Well, I've been thinking about it," he answered. "But that takes time to organise, and I haven't had the time."
"That's what baffles me," looking around. "You're still running the company. How have you had time to do all this?" Mark laughed,
"Well, there have been some all night sessions in here," he said. "And I am doing a bit less in the company. I'm glad you hadn't noticed that, though! That's something I wanted to talk to you about...." Graham looked at him.
"All right," he said, "but can we finish here first? I'd really like to buy something."

Later, in the living room of the flat and over another brandy and one of the cigars that Mark was still getting from the Ruskins' tea shop, Mark outlined his idea for what he would like his function, a reduced function, to be in the company in the future. What did Graham think, from a business and legal point of view? Graham confessed that he was divided about it because he thought Mark had been so successful at running the company; he couldn't think anybody else would make such a good job of it as he had, and he would miss working closely with him as they had done now for more than twenty years. On the other hand, and seeing what he had produced, artistically, these last few years he had to admit that...well, he had a gift he should follow. In addition, something Mark omitted to mention when asking the question - he, Graham, had never known him happier than over the last five years. He fell silent. Then, "Mark, I'm going to say something you probably never before, nor ever again are likely to hear from a lawyer; but I've known you almost from the year dot and I've seen you up - and I've seen you down, and the down was awful and it was for too many years. I couldn't really say anything then, for any number of reasons, but I'd never like to see you like that again and the transformation to now is so good to see. Mark, I think you should follow your heart - or your instincts, whichever it is." He paused, raised his hands in mock horror, "My

God, if my legal colleagues could hear me now they'd want me debarred!" He smiled, and peered at his glass, "You know, I think this glass is empty, and," waving his cigar, "this has gone out! Dear me, how you mistreat your guests!"

The next morning Mark went over to the Victoria to join Graham for breakfast. He had promised him that before he went back to Sprinton he would take him to see the subject of his best portrait to date, where he could also, if he wished, taste some of the best ice cream he would ever have outside of Italy, and, if there were any to spare, he could buy a few of those cigars that he had been enjoying courtesy of himself. They did all of those things and then, over a glass of the landlord's local brew, at the New Inn, just before leaving, Graham delivered his final judgement on the visit and on what had been said. "The lady is all that you claimed for her, my dear Mark," he said. And, lowering his voice, "As you know my proclivities are in another direction, but, that doesn't mean I can't, with impartiality, see female beauty when it's in front of me. Your Kate is beautiful and, I would say, her spirit likewise. I can't help adding," he raised a teasing eyebrow at his friend, "that her husband is a fine looking man too! What a pity, eh, that the world weren't differently constituted..." He observed Mark across the table. "You know, I've often envied my 'straight' friends: their loves so easy, unencumbered, no need for subterfuge, no need to hide them; yet, here you are, in my position, almost. Having said that I think you've come to a workable accommodation with the situation. The world's not perfect, my friend. You know that. I know that. Every lawyer who ever lived knows that. You know what the impulse of every 'decent' lawyer is? Don't smirk, there are a few, decent ones I mean. The impulse of every decent lawyer is to shut off as many loopholes to imperfection as they can. And you know what the depressing thing is? Occasionally you manage to shut off one loophole and, as soon as you have, another one pops up in a different direction - something, somewhere, you couldn't have anticipated." Graham stared glumly into his glass, then roused himself. "Be glad at any rate that you didn't go into law. You can't be half a lawyer, in the way that you *can* keep a finger in your company pie. You're following your star. I envy you that. Doesn't matter what age you are. Just do it. Here's to you, friend." He raised his half-full glass, and Mark raised his. "I wish you all the luck in the world. You're doing the right thing," he said.

CHAPTER 19

Diana and Rita

Since he quite often arrived in the middle of the afternoon when Diana was out, she had given him a key. She said she didn't trust all her men friends and had once been let down badly, but she knew early on, she said, that Mark could be trusted.

He was sensitive to atmospheres, and this day there was something not quite as usual in the atmosphere. Later he realised what it was. On the kitchen table, propped up against the sugar bowl, he found a note in an envelope addressed to him, and dated three days before. Diana had been gone and the house shut up for seventy two hours.

Dear Mark, (she wrote)
I'm sorry about this. I know it's cowardly of me but I couldn't tell you to your face 'cos I'm sure you'll despise me after all I've said before about never wanting to get tied up with one person again. Well, I've got, I'm not sure - tired of not being tied I suppose, and, since you're not available 'for forever and a day' (that wouldn't do for me anyway) I've decided to give it a go with Reginald. I've been seeing him regularly, like you, for over a year and he's been on at me for a while to go away with him. I think he's 'my type', at any rate he's a decent chap so....Don't think too badly of me. Some of my best times have been with you but, there you are....I hope we'll meet again.
    Love (honest)
    Diana

It had come entirely out of the blue. There'd been no warning. Mark was surprised, looking back, at how stunned he was. She had been a regular feature of his life for more than three years. It was a shock to realise that he had come to depend on her always being there. That was his fault, of course, because she had never concealed the fact that he was one of several and she hadn't any intention of 'committing' to only one. Well, that was what she had been saying at least, but apparently she hadn't fooled only him, she had fooled herself too...until now.

Just as he sat down and was about to read the note over again, the telephone rang. He didn't know why he reached to answer it. Perhaps it flashed through his head that it could be Diana ringing to see if he might be there. Whatever the reason he found himself picking it up and giving Diana's number. A female voice broke in, but it wasn't Diana's.

"Hello, can I speak to Diana?" the voice said. "It's Rita."

"Uh, oh I'm sorry, she's not here. I don't know when she'll be back," he managed to stammer out. There was a pause at the other end, then,

"Is it Mark?" the voice said.

"Yes, er, have I met you?" The voice grunted,

"Yes, once, a long time ago. Oh, this is a nuisance. Has she gone away then?" Mark found himself waving the note at the phone,

"Apparently, yes. I just arrived. I found a note."

"Heavens! You didn't know? She didn't warn you?"

"She didn't, no."

"Oh God...this is awkward. She's left me in the lurch too!"

"Oh, I'm sorry. How?" He managed to get out.

"It's a buckaroo," she said, "she told me a week ago she would be going away and she asked me if I'd keep an eye on the house and look in and pick up the post. Since then, nothing, and she never gave me a key, so I was ringing to remind her I need one...Oh, bloody Diana. Who's she gone with, do you know?"

"Er, yes, the note says someone called Reginald..."

"Holy Moses, he's an accountant who can't be relied on, would you believe...that will never last. She really knows how to pick 'em!"

"She said in the note, I quote, 'he's a decent chap'." Rita snorted and they both fell silent. An idea struck him,

"Where do you live, Rita?"

"Ten minutes walk away, why?" she replied. She sounded suspicious and was careful not to give the address.

"Well, it strikes me, I'm not likely to be needing the key I've got any more, so, if you want it, you could come round now and get it?"

"Well, that's an idea. All right, thanks. Hold on, I'll be there in fifteen."

While he waited Mark walked through the whole of the house, upstairs and down. He wasn't sure why, and he never opened a cupboard or a drawer in any of the rooms - he never had. He imagined this was probably the last time he would be in that house and he wanted to know what he felt about it. He felt surprisingly little. What he realised was that the rooms felt singularly impersonal. It was almost difficult to recall the scenes of intense physical lust that had been enacted there over the course of the past three years. Everything

was in order, all Diana's knick-knacks in place, one or two nondescript prints on the walls, a few books shut away in a, possibly locked, cabinet, some magazines arranged on a coffee table. No, the house felt empty, as furnished as it was. He was in the kitchen, just having unlocked and opened the back door to let in some fresh air, when the front door-bell rang. He opened it to find a rather petite, dark-haired girl with big brown eyes, on the doorstep. "Hello, I'm Rita," she said and walked in past him down the hall to the kitchen.
"Oh good you've let in some fresh air," she said. "You know Diana never seems to open any windows," then she giggled, "oops, I guess you know more about that than I do". She put out a hand for shaking, "we'll have to do our own introductions I suppose," she said. "Rita Castelli, I actually work for your friend, Paul, in the office, scheduling exhibitions, correspondence with dealers and artists, that sort of thing. Paul doesn't gossip but he told me you're an artist to watch," she looked at him thoughtfully, "though a late starter….. It's Diana who's told me about you, mainly." She paused, and looked around the kitchen, "Yes, she always chooses the wrong one…."
"Well, here's the key," Mark broke in, not wanting to prolong either the conversation or the visit to the house. Rita took the key, looked a bit sheepish, as if she might have embarrassed both of them.
"Will you stay in London or are you going straight back up north?" Without waiting for an answer she went on, "Paul's out of town this week, I expect you know," he shook his head. "Actually, he's out of the country. He's in Paris seeing a retrospective and doing the rounds of some of the studios." She stopped, sensing she was speaking too much. She blushed. Mark looked at her. She had quite a sweet face, he decided; he liked the big eyes which were looking at that moment rather uncertain, not unlike the look that Stella had when she was literally caught with her fingers in a sweet jar, behind her mother's back, in the tea shop. To Rita, Mark looked intensely weary.
"Oh, I think I shall just go straight back 'up north' - this was going to be a short stay in any case. I have a meeting in Sprinton tomorrow afternoon so…" he suddenly felt very tired, thinking, 'I'm getting too old for this.' Rita moved to close the back door, and locked it.
"I've got a casserole in the oven at home," she said. "There's enough to feed me all week. That's what I do so I don't have to start from scratch every night when I get home from work. Come and have something to eat with me before you set out on that long drive." She looked at him almost shyly, "If you don't mind me saying so, you look as if you need it." She bit her lip, thinking maybe she'd

gone too far. But Mark gave a tired smile, "Thank you," he said, "that's a kind offer and..". She broke in, "...you'll accept? I've no ulterior motive, that's a promise. I don't share Diana's philosophy." He nodded, "All right, then I accept."

Rita lived in a flat in a building called Nightingale Mansions. "Guess why," said Rita. "I've never heard a nightingale anywhere near but Keats lived not far away." There were high black iron gates into a large forecourt.

"You can park in the forecourt," she said, "I don't think there's more than one other resident has a car."

Rita's flat was on the second floor. It had one bedroom, a large living room, small kitchen and bathroom. A truly wonderful aroma, a mixture of herbs, meat and vegetables greeted them as soon as Rita opened the door. Mark's eyes, which had been narrowed in tiredness, suddenly widened. Rita laughed, "I learned two skills at home," she said, "the most important was to cook, and aren't I glad! My nanny was also our cook. I adored her and part of her nannying was to show me how to make good food. I followed her about everywhere which meant many hours in the kitchen. She had me slicing things when I could hardly reach the counter let alone wield a knife. But, hey presto," she directed Mark to the sofa, "just make yourself comfortable while I get everything ready. If you want to use the bathroom it's through there..."

There was a homeliness about Rita's flat that Mark couldn't help comparing with Diana's immaculate house. There were things lying about that showed someone lived there. There was a colourful embroidery framed on one wall and a painting of what looked like an olive grove, with an old man in it, on another. The sofa was comfortable to a fault and had a colourful rug flung over it; it was old. He thought about Diana's very first judgement of him and concluded, not for the first time, that it must have been correct - he was by nature 'a nester'. Rita's 'nest', appealed to him much more than Diana's 'residence'.

At the meal, which fulfilled the expectations raised by the aroma, Mark learned more about Rita. Her father was Italian. A picture restorer, he had come to England just after the old queen died, appointed by someone at court to restore some of the Renaissance paintings in the royal collection. He had met Rita's mother, a maid in a grand Park Lane house, married her and never went back to Italy, except for a family visit a few years later. From that visit he brought back with him to England a young woman, from a poor family, who became the Castelli's cook and Rita's nanny. Cincia, was her name, but Rita always called her Ginny. So, the cooking she had taught Rita was largely Italian.

"Did Cincia go back to Italy?" asked Mark. Rita's face clouded over, "She was planning to go when the war ended. She had family in Liguria, a brother and sisters, nephews and nieces, and she had saved up most of her earnings with us for nearly twenty years. She wanted to buy a little house, she had enough she said, and to help her family; the war had ruined them. She had bought her train ticket. She was so excited." But then, Rita said, she got the Spanish flu'. She died the day before she should have gone back home. Rita's father had written to Cincia's family and told them what had happened. He said he would take 'all that she left behind' to them the following year. He did, said Rita, and that was an adventure if ever there was one. But he got to the village, handed over the few things she had left behind, and all the money, which turned out to be worth much less than Cincia had thought - because of the inflation. "So I'm glad she didn't live to see that," said Rita, "it would have broken her heart. That was her greatest worry, that her family should get the money she had saved for them. My father promised her, he kept saying, 'Cincia I'll take everything to them, every penny. You have my word.' And he did."

The second skill Rita had acquired at home was her father's language. She was fluent in Italian. After they had eaten Rita directed him to the sofa. She said she would make him a cup of real Italian coffee so he could keep awake for the journey home. But when she came with it fifteen minutes later Mark was fast asleep.

After only mild attempts at protest he ended up spending the night on Rita's sofa. She gave him his Italian coffee for breakfast instead, and a pastry she had made the day before. Then he set off to drive back to Laverton. He had a piece of paper in his pocket with Rita's telephone number on it, "in case you ever feel like calling in for another of my Italian dinners, when you're in London - just the dinner, mind, unless you have a taste for sleeping on old sofas." He anyway gave her a fatherly kiss, on the cheek, to say thank you just before he left.

is......an Adventure

"You think that I've got big feet?" Mark was reading what Stella had written about him. It was a homework assignment, 'Write fifty words' the teacher had said 'about a person who means a lot to you, but not a parent'. Stella's class had recently learnt how to do 'joined up writing' and Stella was in the advanced group that had been given the writing homework. It was called 'A Special Person' and Stella had chosen Mark as her special person.

"Yes," said Stella, "and nice eyes. I thought I shouldn't make it all too good."
"But I've only got big feet because I am big. If you were my size but had feet your size you'd fall over, you know." Stella giggled; she was used to Mark's teasing and she often had an answer for him, like now, "Yes," she said, "and if you were my size but had your feet you wouldn't be able to walk because you'd fall over *them*!" Mark caught hold of her and threatened to turn her upside down. A lot of words had to do with horses and riding (Mark told her how to spell 'stirrup'); but she did say, among other things, that Mark was kind. Kate looked up from the magazine she'd been reading while Stella's interview with Mark was going on. "Have you finished now?" she asked. "Have you counted your words?"
"It doesn't have to be exactly fifty. It can be sixty but not less than forty," Stella replied.
"Can you count that far?" Mark pretended surprise. She gave him a withering look, "Of course I can. But there are two extra questions. One is," and she peered at the paper where she had written them down, "Complete this sentence," she looked up. "What is it?" from Kate. Stella continued,
"Life is…. and then you have to add something."
"That seems rather advanced for eight year olds," Kate said, turning to Mark.
"What will you say?" he asked.
"Oh, I've already written it," she answered.
"And….?"
"Life is… an adventure." she said.
"Well, well" her mother murmured glancing at Mark, " 'Out of the mouths of babes and sucklings…' And what is the other question?"
"Oh, that's a question the special person has to answer," Stella said. She turned to Mark, "The question is: What makes you happiest?" Stella looked at him, her

pencil poised over the paper. Kate looked at him too. Mark regarded both of them and replied, "oh, that's easy: A day at the seaside."

....,..

After the second year at Cambridge, in the summer vacation, Mark had travelled with Paul on the continent. Paul lived in the rooms under him, on the same stair in college. Although he'd been 'directed', he said, into classics, alternatively theology - his father was canon of a cathedral, his grandfather had been a bishop - Paul was most interested in the art of the Renaissance. They spent six weeks of that summer vacation travelling around France and Italy. Paul had planned the itinerary and they began in Paris. When not at Cambridge Mark was still spending a lot of his time painting in his stable studio at his parents' home. What he wanted most to see was the new painting that had been coming out of France over the previous twenty years. The Paris visit was a revelation to him and it settled his own artistic inclinations for the foreseeable future. They had stayed two weeks in Paris and subsequently with an uncle of Paul's who had a house near a village called Biot in the South of France. After that they took train to Italy and Florence. Needless to say seeing all the works of the renaissance masters was a breathtaking and transforming experience. However, it was also brought home to Mark that, while he could, and did, admire the incredible skill of the renaissance artists, he had no taste for religious subjects. What he mainly took back, what entered his soul, from that visit to the south, both France and Italy, was the almost overwhelming experience of dazzling light and brilliant colour.

 He had only been back once since that first time, and that visit had been another event that hammered a nail in the coffin of his marriage. Thinking to rouse Dorothy from the lethargy that seemed to have settled on her after the miscarriage, he took her to the south of France. She went unwillingly, but he thought that would change when once he got her into the new milieu and the light of the south. However, she began to complain of the heat before the train had reached Marseilles; then she became ill, of something ill-defined, and the manners of all the people they met she found disgusting. She would not be mollified, in fact, until they were on the train back to Paris and then home to England. Because of her complaints and continued low spirits Mark too was unable to enjoy the three days that they spent in Paris before returning to England. He had wanted to renew acquaintance with the galleries that had entranced him on the first visit with Paul. But all seemed 'ashes in the mouth' and he returned to England in a state of high frustration and unhappiness.

All that was twenty years in the past and now his life was completely different. The strange occurrence following the aborted visit to Diana, when he found himself eating a dish 'fit for the gods' in a strange woman's flat in Hampstead, had had an effect on him. Thinking, for the first time for many years, about Italy and the magic of the south, he began to conceive a new plan in his head. He had always loved the language; couldn't he get Rita to teach him it? And wasn't it time he visited Paris and all those galleries again, and some new ones….and wasn't it time too that he took that train to the south once more, and showed that other sea to his Laverton family, and those colours, and that light?

He went to the shelves between the two windows where Ivy had neatly put all the books that didn't fit into any categories he had specified. Looking along one row he came to the book he was looking for. As he plucked it from the shelf he noticed that a little subsection of books, all sitting together, on all sorts of different topics were in fact yellow. He gave a little chuckle, "The minx!" he said out loud, recalling Ivy when she came to help him organise his library.

The book he had fetched out was an old, slightly battered but quite serviceable Italian grammar which also included some simple but useful dialogues. And inside the front cover was a song, 'O sole mio…' He read the words and then went over to the gramophone that he had sitting on its own table near the bookcase. In the cupboard underneath he had a pile of records. Ivy had labelled and catalogued them for him as well. He found the one he was looking for and took it out of its sleeve. He wound up the gramophone and put on the record. The warm tenor voice of Caruso singing 'O sole mio', filled the room. He thought then of the evening some months before when he had invited them, Kate and Stanley, over to hear a very recent recording he had bought which included some of the arias from The Pearl Fishers. Stanley sat on the floor with his knees drawn up, Kate was on the sofa and he had moved his wing chair near to the gramophone so that he would be nearby to wind it up again when needed. There was something about that evening that was unforgettable - harmony and transfiguration, he thought, and the music brought it about. Stanley had a fine tenor voice himself - he had heard it one Christmas when, with Ivy accompanying on the piano, Stanley sang some pieces from Handel. Goodness, he was almost middle aged and yet he felt that life was still full of possibilities. 'Out of the mouths of babes..' Kate had quoted; truly he, and they, he hoped, were going to embark on some new adventures. But, before they did he must get that blue right for the seascape he was thinking about. He picked up an overall that he had left on a chair on the landing and went along to his studio at the end. The new canvas was waiting expectantly on his easel.

The End